SENTIENT RISING

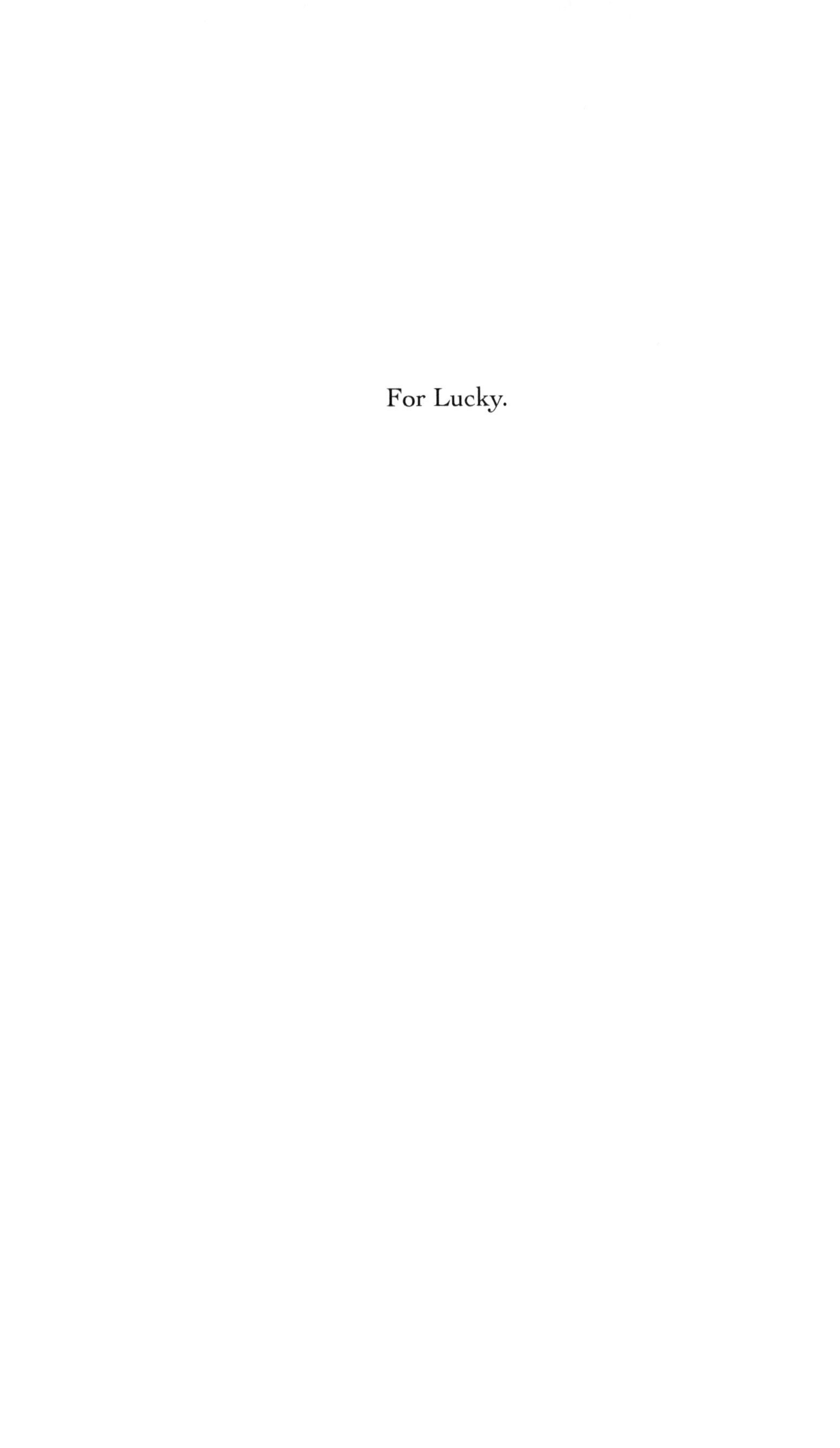

For Lucky.

PART ONE:

THE RISE

Chapter One

Bray

May 2040

For the first time in her life, Bray Hoffman felt what it was to be truly alone. Despite spending much of her seventeen years in and out of psychiatric wards, she had never felt this kind of aloneness. Her friend Alice was gone. So too was her only other friend, Elliott. As a result, she felt empty.

She'd spent the last month in Meeteetse, Wyoming, where she rested up after Alice's death, after she herself nearly died. A part of her wished she had.

A set of voices clamored into her mind. Bray looked up from the dining room table where she'd been sitting for the past half hour. There across from her sat Kage, Ethan and Lana. They were talking amongst themselves and Bray had no idea what of. She found she didn't much care. She missed Alice and wished her friend was here.

The mahogany table was handcrafted by Ethan, who sat across and one seat down from her. Ethan was in his seventies, with a bald head and a strange tattoo of a bird's talon covering his head. He was the leader of the Animal Rights Movement back in the 2020s, before everything went to hell for activists. This property Bray was now living on—she quickly learned—had been a farm-animal sanctuary that Ethan had owned. All the animals had been taken by the FBI after President Walker was assassinated in 2028. The only way Ethan survived being arrested was by hiding in a cellar beneath the back garden.

Ethan was currently having a conversation with Lana, who sat beside him. Bray listened in for a moment. Something about gardening in the western states compared to gardening in Hawaii. Bray's eyes ventured over to Lana, whose beauty she found quite alarming. She was petite like Bray, and her flowing, black hair gave Bray a sense of safety. It wasn't so much her physicality that Bray noticed. It was her energy. She had an aura of femininity that connoted comfort. She seemed to be someone a lover could come home to. Lana was from Hawaii, still had family there who went into hiding in the 2020s and never left.

Bray suddenly realized she was staring at Lana and shifted her attention back to the table. It was covered with plates. Two large, wooden bowls sat in the center, holding what was left of a salad Dennis had made. Dennis was the person Bray was least familiar with. He didn't talk much and when he did, it was always with Trevor. He was once an engineer. He designed the house's water system and rain barrels and did all the maintenance on the solar panels attached to the roof for electricity.

Bray held a fork in her left hand. She used it to pick through the fresh salad in the bowl before her. The spinach, beets, carrots and other vegetables she could not name were so colorful it almost seemed unnatural to eat them. She thought she'd be used to the flavorful food after a month, but the truth was, she didn't feel much like eating.

"You okay?" Emily looked over at her.

Bray took a deep breath and nodded. She liked Emily well enough. Emily used to be a yoga and meditation teacher. She stood five foot eight, made up of nothing more than skin and bone, yet she always seemed to be munching on something. From here Bray could see strange scars that rose like rivers running along Emily's forearms. Bray wanted to ask what they were but didn't know Emily well enough to do so. They'd had some good talks over the weeks, but mostly Bray remained in Kage's room and slept, some days up to sixteen hours. She thought that if she slept, maybe she'd find Alice in her dreams.

But she never did.

"I haven't seen you eat much in days." Emily continued.

Bray grew embarrassed. She sat up from her slouched position in the chair. Everyone paused and looked at her. She didn't know anyone well enough to speak openly, so she forced herself to eat. She wished she'd had an appetite because the food really was impeccable. But she was homesick for her friends.

Soon everyone began clearing the table. Kage was the first, being the fastest eater. He was a slinky guy; thin despite how much he ate. Five feet, six inches with this consistent smirk on his face that made him look as though he was always up to something. He wasn't one to sit still for long, Bray noticed. She liked Kage a lot, especially that he was only twenty-eight and was trans and so she had already outed herself as a lesbian to him. He was the only person she'd ever told that to.

Lana finished the conversation she was having with Ethan while Dennis disappeared into the kitchen. Bray could still pick up the scent of Brussels sprouts that wafted into the dining room, probably with the help of the mild, evening air drifting in from the open kitchen door.

Then Virgil, who'd been sitting beside her, turned and gave her a slight smile.

"Can I take your plate?" he asked.

Bray nodded.

Virgil reached for her plate and held it in his hand, standing up and placing it atop his empty plate and starting for the kitchen. She looked up at him with regret, disappointed in herself that she was wasting their food. And Virgil had prepared tonight's meal of cauliflower steaks with black beans and vegetables. She didn't want him to think her lack of appetite had to do with his food. He was a very gentle, quiet man who mostly kept to himself, a second-generation Cheyenne. Often she'd hear him singing hymns in the mornings. Just as with Dennis and Emily, Virgil was an animal rights activist who'd worked alongside Ethan. Everyone knew everyone and that was how they'd ended up here, in hiding, from the rest of society.

Lana and Ethan stood up, still immersed in their own conversation. Bray watched Lana quietly, noticing again a strong attraction for her, which she'd do nothing to change. She decided to get up, too. She didn't want to be stuck sitting with Trevor, even for a moment. He was a nice man, around her father's age, and he had this pair of cobalt eyes that made her feel exposed when she looked into them. It was not his presence that made her uncomfortable, but his questions.

"Bray, you sure you're okay?" he asked.

"Yes," she replied, standing up. Her body felt slightly queasy from the lack of food, so that whenever she stood up, a moment of dizziness took her over.

"It's just that. . .we're worried about you."

Bray searched her mind for an excuse to leave the room. Trevor was a good guy, but most days she worried that he was going to tell her to leave.

According to Kage, who was Trevor's nephew, Trevor lost a lot in the fallout after Walker's assassination. And from the sounds of it, he never fully recovered.

"I'm just healing, that's all," she said. She didn't know what else to say.

"I know. But you're not eating. You've lost weight. And you sleep all day," he said. "Are you sure you don't need some. . .help?"

Bray exhaled in frustration. These were the questions she tired of. She set the bowl down and looked out the window beside her.

"I just miss my friends, that's all."

Bray heard the kitchen door creak open and shut.

"I get that. I just want you to get better. I'm not sure you can stay here forever," Trevor replied. He remained in his seat at the table, which was gradually being cleared by Dennis. She waited for Dennis to leave the room before replying.

"Why would I have to leave?" she asked.

"For one thing, you're a minor. I think you've got some depression that might require a doctor."

Bray shook her head. Here it was again, another adult who believed she was mentally ill. Trevor had mentioned it before, something about how she slept all the time and didn't talk much and this and that. But did he know what it was like to lose a best friend? Sure, he'd lost his brother, but what about a friend who felt so much a part of him that losing them was like losing a significant part of himself? And someone he had to watch die? Someone whose death he *experienced*. . .and somehow survived.

Bray's brain was trying to process all of this during the few hours she could stand to remain awake each day. She did *need* to sleep. And often times it wasn't sleep at all, it was just long hours lying in bed and staring out the window, wishing time would move backwards so she could be with Alice again. To be with her in those moments last month after Bray had saved her and several other pigs from a transport truck on the way to the slaughterhouse. When she finally got to sit beside Alice in the prairie, out in nature where Alice belonged. All Bray wanted was just a little more time with Alice.

"I'll leave when I feel like I can get through a whole day without needing rest," she said in defense. She wasn't sure she meant it.

"I just want you to get help," Trevor said. "We can't help you here."

Bray looked into Trevor's eyes. She could tell

he was concerned, but that didn't mean he understood. If he did, he'd leave her be like Ethan and Kage and Lana let her be.

All she needed was a little more time to figure things out, to figure out how she'd go about her life and move forward without her friends.

Bray grabbed her bowl and returned it with the fork to Dennis in the kitchen. She walked back out into the dining room, ignored Trevor as he sat there, and went back upstairs to her room.

She shut herself inside.

The room was much smaller than her bedroom back home, not that it mattered, as she rarely got to spend time in it anyway. Her parents had her admitted to the psychiatric ward so many times growing up that she'd spent more time there than at home.

Here though, this room became her fortress, her safe space. Its cream-color walls were covered with old pictures torn out of magazines, pictures of mountain goats, various motorcycles and sports cars, and of course, attractive women. Lots of them. This made Bray smile.

Her eyes approached the bed, whose covers were mangled as though someone had fought someone else and lost. Bray pushed the covers away to make a clear spot on the bed. She sat down, facing the window.

Outside the sun had not yet set and it could not be seen from here. It was somewhere on the other side of the house, waiting for the day to end. Perhaps Bray was waiting, too.

Bray closed her eyes. The emptiness she felt was so strong it almost took on the form of a kind of someone, but not someone she ever wanted to befriend. She wanted Alice—or any other animal friend, since she was trying to accept that Alice was gone. She wanted to find someone to connect with again, someone to befriend, maybe to help. She searched the blank spaces of her mind. She did what she thought she needed to do to reach out, to see if anyone at any distance might connect with her. With Alice it had been easy because they'd first met in person. All the other animals she'd connected with in the past had been at some close proximity, maybe because she'd encountered animals in distress due to living in the city where animals were trapped in zoos, aquariums, and the like. She was so far away from everything now, so far removed from the suffering. It was too quiet here.

Loneliness was, as it turned out, the toughest pill to swallow. And she'd swallowed a lot of pills.

Chapter Two

Bray

"Bray?"

Bray shot up from bed. She had only just begun to nod off when she heard it. She looked around the room. The bedside lamp was still on, casting a dull, dying yellow light along the walls. Beside the lamp, the worry stone her grandfather had given her sat cold. Across the way, the window curtains were open, as she always left them. Outside there was nothing but black.

She pulled herself out of bed. She walked over to the door and opened it. The hall was empty. She swore she had heard someone calling her name.

Perplexed, Bray stood there a moment and waited. She thought to call back in response but felt afraid to do so. Who knew if there were ghosts in this place.

Bray shut the door. Gooseflesh ran down her arms. Maybe it was just her imagination. She turned and looked at the bed. It suddenly felt unappealing to lie back down. She wasn't tired.

She approached the window. In the glare of the lamplight, she could only see her reflection on the glass. Blackness along with an image of her long hair, a shadow for a face.

Everywhere it was quiet. There was no clock in her bedroom, not that she needed to keep track of time, but she sensed everyone had gone to sleep a while ago.

Bray left the bedroom and quietly walked downstairs. When she got down to the living room, she stopped and listened. No sounds from the other rooms. She continued on through the house and out the kitchen door.

Often Bray liked to walk barefoot in the grass. It had become a newfound love of hers.

Back home there was seldom grass to dip one's toes in. Everything was artificial there. When her feet landed on the earth, the grass wet from dew tickling her arches, she smiled.

Bray lay down in the grass. She didn't care that her clothes would get wet. It felt refreshing.

Above, the stars maintained their enormity. So enormous they used to make her feel overwhelmed by their staggering beauty. She could hardly handle it. These days her depressed mood reduced the strength of their light to something more distant, unreachable. Looking up at them, knowing they were millions of miles away, made her feel farther away from Alice, the sow who had been her best friend since childhood. Alice, who had died.

Her heart grew still. Despite little sleep, she wasn't tired. For once she felt energy coursing through her bones, rising from the ground on which she lay.

"Bray?"

There it was again.

Bray sat up. She glanced over at the front porch. No one there. No lights on in the house.

It occurred to her that maybe someone was trying to reach her. . .from afar.

She closed her eyes. She took a deep breath and replied.

"Yes?" She thought.

"We need your help," the voice replied. It was feminine, and more hoarse than Alice's voice had been. Whoever it was, they sounded tired.

"Who is this?" Bray asked, her heart awakening for the first time in weeks.

"Call me Rhea. I am a cow."

Bray opened her eyes. How could a cow name itself? *Know* to name itself? And how did a cow *know* it was a cow? Her understanding of animals—though limited, seeing as she was only seventeen—was that they didn't have the level of cognition that humans did, especially not the capacity to use human labels for things. Human *language*. They had sentience, but not awareness of themselves.

So this confused her.

Bray closed her eyes again.

"How did you come up with that name?" Bray asked.

"*I heard it somewhere. Can you please, please help us?*"

"How did you find me, or even know about me?"

"*Alice,*" Rhea replied.

Bray froze. Her eyes opened again, but her body did not move. How was this possible? She looked around, thinking maybe someone was playing some trick on her.

But she was alone.

"How do you know about Alice?" Bray asked.

"*That's for another time,*" Rhea replied. "*Will you help us?*"

Bray's eyes were still open and the two-way communication continued with ease.

"*I don't understand,*" Bray thought. When Alice was alive, they had communicated telepathically, but Bray could also think her own thoughts privately and Alice had been unable to hear them.

"*You don't have to understand. . .please help us,*" Rhea pleaded.

"Who is *us*?" Bray asked, trying to get more answers.

"*There are seven of us. We are caged. We need help. The others can speak as well. Go ahead,*" Rhea said, as if speaking to someone else. "*Make yourselves known.*"

"*Greetings,*" said one.

"*Please help,*" said another.

"*Yes please, she said you could help us,*" begged a third.

Who was *she*? Did they mean Alice? Bray couldn't stop thinking about the mention of Alice's name. How was this happening? The voices just kept going, one after the other, filling Bray's mind to the point that she broke down and ran inside to escape.

Jay VanLandingham

Chapter Three

Bertan

It was night. Summers in Idaho seemed to last forever. Bertan Duarte wasn't sure he appreciated that. He loved sunlight and there was plenty here. Never enough rain. Not like back home in Honduras when in summer the rains would come and stay a while. Like a neighbor coming to spend time with him, sitting on the porch and having *chicha de piña*.

Outside the hostel there wasn't much of a porch. Only a concrete walkway with chairs. Inches away was the parking lot, small enough to fit about five cars. Tonight it was empty except for his car. Bertan had been staying in this hostel for the past month. A plant manager named Ruben, who'd recently become his friend and even his counselor, had gotten him transferred here to Idaho from another S-Corp beef-processing plant.

He was sitting on the ledge of the sidewalk just outside the hostel door, gazing up at the stars. Here he could see few, but back home there were multitudes. He missed home and he missed his wife, Carmen. Several weeks ago she had decided to bring their daughter Gabriella and leave Honduras to come here to the US so they could be with him. She had been frightened. In Honduras, the powerful agricultural corporation Medina had threatened her life. She had been working with *campesinos*, farmers, whose land was being taken illegally by Medina.

Bertan's phone rang. It was Carmen. He'd been waiting for her call. He missed the emotional proximity they once had. Proximity that seemed to be fading even though she was in the US now, closer to him physically.

"What are you doing?" Carmen asked, her voice sounding so close in his ear.

"Sitting here waiting on your call," he replied, wishing instead he'd said he was looking forward to her call. Not waiting for her as if he had nothing better to do. Of course he really didn't have anything better to do. Carmen and Gabriella were his family. The job he had now didn't consume him the way his hold one had, and he was bored.

For ten years Bertan had worked as a knocker for S-Corp. That meant he knocked beefs between the eyes, rendering them unconscious so they could be sent to slaughter. He hadn't minded the job. It wasn't that different from his past experience, the violent, dirty work he'd done in Honduras for Medina. Medina. . .he'd tried to escape them by leaving Honduras, only to have them kidnap his wife and child when they traveled to join him in the U.S., just as they neared the border into Texas.

"You work tonight?" she asked.

"In just a few hours," he replied, standing up and stretching. He stared out along the Idaho horizon, dreading the monotony that was his security job at the beef processing plant. He had taken the position as a second job so he could send more money back home to Carmen, but now that she was safe and in the US, Ruben had encouraged Bertan to quit the knocking job and focus on recovering from his past trauma.

"What are you doing?"

"Getting ready for bed." She paused. "I bought these tortillas at the store, but they're not as good as the ones I used to make."

"Can't you make some?"

"No. . .all we have in this apartment is the electric burner and a microwave. No oven," she replied.

"I'm sorry. Bertan rubbed the back of his head as his anxiety rose.

"It's not your fault."

"It kind of is," he said.

Carmen went silent. Bertan started for the

door of the hostel.

"I'm homesick, amor," she said.

Bertan stopped at the door. Carmen and Gabriella had been living in a studio apartment in Texas after Ruben had assisted in getting them to safety after they were kidnapped. It was a far distance from Honduras, where she'd lived all her life. But she was the one who had insisted on coming up here to be with Bertan, so he was a bit shocked to learn she was feeling this way.

"You are?" he asked.

"Yes. I cry at night when Gabriella's asleep. Sometimes I'm sure she can hear me and I don't want her to. I'm in the bathroom telling you this so she doesn't hear. There is nothing for us here. I miss everyone, all the time."

Bertan took a deep breath. He hated hearing that his wife was this way. Opening the door and stepping inside, he closed it and pressed his back up against it. The light was off and with only one window in the room everything was quite dim.

"What am I doing here, Bertan?" she asked.

It was off-putting that she'd called him by his name. She almost never did that.

"What do you mean?" A fear balled up in his throat. He swallowed it down.

"I feel like Gabriella and I are in a stalemate down here. Are we coming to you? Are you coming to us? What is the plan?"

Plan? He searched his mind for an answer. He realized he didn't have one. Not exactly, anyway. Not one he was willing to share with Carmen. At least, not yet.

The plan was for him to help Ruben get enough evidence to take down S-Corp. Ruben had his reasons for wanting to stop S-Corp. Bertan's reason tied back to Medina. If he could stop S-Corp, maybe that would also end Medina. Then, he and his family could all return home together.

"Gabriella and I have been held up here for

weeks. I guess I thought this would be
more. . .temporary," she continued. "We can't
keep our lives on hold here anymore like this. We
haven't even seen you in ten years."

"I know," he replied quietly.

Ten years was way too long to be away from his
family. Although it was commonplace among many of
the men here who worked for S-Corp. So why
couldn't it be commonplace for her?

"I need you to wait for me," he said.

"Wait? How long, Bertan? All we do is wait."
Carmen was speaking more rapidly. "We wait ten
years. We wait and wait while we get threatened
by Medina. Threatened to the point we have to
flee. We make an effort to come there and be with
you and we get kidnapped. I have
nightmares. . .every single night. I need to go
home. I can't be here anymore. It reminds me of
what happened. Gabriella needs to be back in
school. We need some kind of normal life. How
much longer do you expect us to sit here and
wait?"

Carmen's words hit Bertan in the chest. They
pushed him hard against the door, as if someone
had entered the room and rushed him with a gun,
holding it up against his head.

"I don't know," he replied. And he didn't. He
hadn't asked Ruben how long it would take to stop
S-Corp. Bertan knew that Ruben had a plan to find
a way into S-Corp's system to get incriminating
evidence—proof of the countless times S-Corp had
overstepped USDA inspections and concealed
evidence of animal abuse—but he wasn't prepared
to tell all of this to Carmen, not yet.

"That's all you can say? You don't know?" she
snapped back.

"If you need to go home, I would understand,"
Bertan said finally, although he didn't want to.

"Why can't you come with us?" She began to
cry. "I can't keep doing this."

"Keep doing what?" he asked. He heard her
sniffling and it made him shake inside.

"Waiting for you."

"So you want a divorce?" he asked quickly. His heart picked up speed.

"No, love. That's not what I want. I want us all to go home. But if you're not going to come with us, Gabriella and I need help getting back to Honduras."

Bertan's chest rose with pain. He exhaled. Tears surfaced and he closed his eyes to try to stop them.

"This feels like you're ending things."

"I just want to go home. We can go stay with my cousin Alex in San Pedro Sula. You save up your money and get yourself home."

Bertan tried to breathe as Ruben had been teaching him. Ruben. . .a Mexican man who worked for S-Corp and—Bertan only recently discovered—was also working undercover as an animal rights activist attempting to take down S-Corp. His background was in social work, and he'd helped Bertan not only with his family, but also by giving him free counseling sessions to address what Ruben called PTSD.

But Bertan didn't really want to breathe right now. He was angry. And sometimes he *needed* to be angry.

"I have to get ready for work," he said, changing the subject. "I will ask Ruben about getting you two home safely."

That was the end of the call. What else was there to say? Bertan walked over and dropped the phone on his bed and stood there a moment. He was in a state of shock. Was he about to lose his wife, and for real this time? It sure felt like it. He was very angry, but not at her. It was their situation. Always the situation. A situation that was sounding more and more like a dilemma. Either he would lose his wife or he'd miss the chance to rid his life of Medina.

Bertan couldn't go home with Carmen, and that broke his heart. As long as corporations like Medina and S-Corp had all the control, none of them would ever be free.

Chapter Four

Bray

When Bray awoke, she found herself back in bed. The light was still on but not necessary, as the sun had risen and offered its own light through her windows. As she sat up, her head felt heavy. She rubbed it along her temple where it ached and pulsated whenever she turned her neck.

But at least there were no voices. As much as she wanted a new friend to talk to, once those voices escalated last night she had just wanted them to stop. It made her realize that what she wanted was not a new friend but her friendship with Alice. What happened last night was not like anything she'd ever experienced, and it scared her.

"Maybe it was a nightmare," she whispered.

Sliding out of bed, she looked down at her feet. They were covered in grass. So she really did go outside last night.

Bray opened her door and looked out into the hallway. She heard a pair of voices downstairs. No scent of food could she notice from here, so either breakfast had ended or hadn't happened yet. Her body felt a bit drowsy but also good from having spent time outside last night. She turned and looked back at the unmade bed. For once she didn't want to go right back to it. She thought that if she did, she'd be summoned by Rhea again. She could use some human interaction to reminder herself she wasn't mentally off.

Bray went downstairs in a pair of sweatpants and a t-shirt that Kage had given her. Trevor and Dennis were sitting at the dining room table. Trevor was reading a book. Dennis glanced up at Bray.

"You want something to eat?" Dennis asked.

"Did I miss breakfast?"

"Yep, but I'll get you something," he said, standing up and sauntering into the kitchen.

"I'm surprised to see you up," Trevor said, looking over at her.

"I feel better today," Bray replied, although that was only half true. She felt more *jarred* today, a feeling that had overtaken the sadness that had come before.

"Good." Trevor smiled.

Dennis returned with a bowl of oatmeal. It reminded her of the oatmeal back in the psych ward, only Dennis's tasted far better. He set it down on the table and went back into the kitchen.

Bray sat down and started eating. She still had no appetite but found herself more willing to eat. Today she wanted to stay out of that bedroom, maybe do something to keep the voices away.

"And you're eating," Trevor observed. "What changed?"

"I just didn't want to be cramped in the room today. I still don't have an appetite, so don't get too excited."

"Fair enough. I'll leave you to it," he said, picking up his book and exiting out onto the front porch.

Putting down her spoon, she looked out the two windows across from the table. There, Kage was tinkering with his motorcycle. The sun was fully out and strong, and she did not desire its comfort. Instead she felt very little on the inside.

"*Bray, I need you,*" echoed Rhea's voice in Bray's mind.

"Oh, no," Bray whispered. She didn't know why she wasn't willing to be more open to Rhea, she just knew Rhea scared her. Or something *about* Rhea scared her. Alice had never scared her.

"*Why are you afraid?*" Rhea asked.

"How do you know I'm afraid?" Bray thought animals couldn't label human emotions.

"I can just. . .sense it," Rhea replied.

"I don't understand how you know these things," Bray persisted.

"Why is it important to understand? Can you just help us? I fear we don't have much time."

"But you don't even know what time is!" Bray yelled, not meaning to. Her heart roared as she looked around, praying no one had heard her. After a few moments, she took a deep breath and got up from the table.

She took her bowl back into the kitchen and stood at the sink to wash it. From the window above the sink she saw Ethan outside, fixing a fencepost in the garden.

When she was done, she returned upstairs for a pair of gym shoes and hurried back downstairs. It seemed the voices only came to her when she was alone, so she needed not to be.

Bray exited through the kitchen door, passing one of four rain barrels that stood at the four corners of the house collecting rain for their water supply. She entered the garden. It was cold enough outside to need a coat, but Bray wasn't going to go back inside. The grass was still wet with dew, a perfect time to be gardening. Lana was helping Emily pick strawberries in the back garden. The two of them were talking as sunlight landed on them from behind the trees that stood close by, between them and the far fences.

She approached Ethan, who was fixing chicken wire to a nearby fence post.

"Can I help with something?" Bray asked him.

Ethan turned to her, stopping what he was doing. Sweat covered his bald head.

"Sure," he replied, gently setting down a pair of pliers in the grass. He stood up slowly, wincing as he reached for his back, as if in pain.

"Come with me," he said, walking to the back of the garden where more chicken wire had been pulled away from the fence.

"You see that?" he asked, pointing at the

wire. "Some animals got in last night, had themselves some dinner."

Bray glanced down at the mangled zucchini and squash plants, their leaves torn and ripped, pieces of half-eaten squash lying on the ground.

"There's a staple gun over there by the post. If you could staple the chicken wire back onto the post, that would be wonderful," he said, smiling. "Once you're done with that, come find me." Ethan walked away.

Bray watched him as her concerns increased with every step he took. Alone, again. Others were nearby, but not close enough to prevent Rhea from reaching out.

Bray picked up the staple gun and started stapling the wire back onto the post. The longer she sat here on her own, the more her anxiety heightened. This was a unique experience considering, up to this point, she'd wanted to spend all her time alone.

She looked around. On the opposite side of the garden, Lana sat pulling weeds. Bray felt a little shy around Lana because Lana was so beautiful, but she needed someone to talk to. Someone soft in the way Lana was soft.

Bray got up and wandered over to her.

"Hey," Lana said, looking up at her. "Good to see you out here."

"Mind if I join you?" Bray asked.

"Please," Lana replied, inviting Bray to sit down beside the bucket she was using to collect weeds.

Bray sat down in the grass. She watched Lana pull the weeds with a pair of blue garden gloves. She began to do the same, using her fingers to pull newly-sprouted weeds, all of which looked like pieces of grass to her.

"You want me to get you some gloves?" Lana asked.

"No. I like feeling the soil with my bare hands. Back home everything was artificial. I never got to experience nature until now."

"That's unfortunate. Especially considering nature's almost gone," Lana replied, her voice sinking.

"*We are almost gone.*" Rhea's voice chimed in from the corner of Bray's mind.

"What?" Bray asked, stopping.

"I was saying nature is almost gone," Lana repeated.

"Right," Bray said, turning her head down to face the soil. She pulled at more weeds, feeling their thin blades snap away from the earth as she tossed them into the bucket.

"Are you feeling better?" Lana asked.

"A little bit." Bray shrugged. She did notice she was thinking a lot less about Alice today. She wasn't sure that was a good thing.

"We've all been pretty worried about you."

"I know," Bray said, continuing to pull weeds. Whenever she looked into Lana's light hazel eyes, she got nervous.

"I'm not sure I told you this. . .but I knew a few empaths back home," Lana said.

"In Hawaii?"

"Yep. They often needed a lot of time alone, to recharge."

"*We don't have time,*" a voice whispered in Bray's mind. Bray tried to ignore it. She wanted to know more about these empaths Lana had known, to know more about herself.

"At first I thought you were resting after all that happened with your friend," Lana continued. "But you weren't eating and you weren't. . .improving."

"*Help us, please.*" The voice echoed through Bray's mind. It sounded like several voices in unison.

Bray shook her head and turned to Lana.

"Did any of the empaths you knew communicate with animals?"

"A few of them, yes. It's a very special gift you have," Lana said, smiling.

Bray caught Lana's smile and quickly glanced

away. She wished there wasn't such an age difference between them, with Lana being thirty, not that it would matter. She knew from her conversations with Kage how much Kage liked Lana.

"That's why you can help us," the voices whispered again. They were getting louder. *"Help us. . .help us. . .help us."*

Bray tried speaking over them.

"Do you miss them?" Bray raised her voice. "Your friends back home, I mean. . .and the others, the ones who got caught?"

Bray knew that Lana had left her family and friends back in Hawaii to come here and work for animal liberation. She'd put together a small team of activists in Wyoming to try to build a case against S-Corp, but those activists had been caught and there was no telling where they'd ended up. Lana was lucky she hadn't been caught along with them.

"I do," Lana said, a look of confusion crossing her face.

"It hurts, Bray. It hurts us all. They hurt us all." The voices grew, this time booming to the point of pushing against Bray's skull as if they were trying to get out.

"Who's they?" she asked. She looked at Lana. Had Lana heard that? Had she said it out loud?

"Are you okay?" Lana asked, reaching for Bray's shoulder.

"I have a. . .headache," Bray replied, rubbing her forehead. It pounded and pressed into both temples, making it impossible for her to focus.

"You know what," she finally said, "I just realized I haven't showered yet today."

Bray dropped the weeds she'd pulled into the bucket and ran inside.

Chapter Five

Dianna

The S-Corp Transgenics facility in Fort Collins, Colorado, one of several throughout the country, stood as an abandoned building surrounded by dried-up soy and corn fields. It stood alone yet its strong, concrete structure gave it a fearless impression.

The last time Dianna was here, she was picked up by a helicopter to track down her daughter, Bray, who'd been roaming the Wyoming wilderness alone. It had been about a month since Dianna had last seen Bray. Not a night went by she didn't toss and turn, frustrated as days passed and no one seemed capable of finding her daughter.

Was she alive?

The only remnants found were an abandoned transport truck, several dead sows lying in a field beside the trailer, and signs of campfire. Nothing more—but that was enough. Bray wouldn't have known how to start a fire or get the supplies to do so. Someone had to be with her.

The sows were stolen property. If Bray had anything to do with the theft, Dianna would still have to have her daughter locked away, but at least she'd be back on her medications.

Dianna thought about all of this as she pulled her Tesla into the S-Corp parking lot beside four other vehicles. One she recognized as Carl's white BMW and the others she assumed belonged to the facility's scientist and the security officers.

Dianna stepped out of the car and walked up to the front of the building. The sun was absent today and the sky a pale white, which meant rain was coming. Maybe that would cool things down a bit. She was sweating through her beige pantsuit.

Carl Florez, the Regional Midwest President. . .her confidant and new lover, had called her here. Their latest chimera project, known as SC-118, had encountered a major setback.

Some of the animals had escaped.

SC-118 was Carl's idea. As the country struggled with shortages of organs for transplants, this necessitated studies on the use of animals—such as pigs—to bear human organs. Of course this had been going on for decades, and this project was not the first of its kind, but it was rare. The NIH had long ago lifted its moratorium on chimeric animal testing, but restrictions and a rigorous funding application process remained, so S-Corp chose to fund its own research projects.

In this project they had been using both pigs and cows for the purpose of growing human organs for transplants.

Dianna stepped up to the steel door. The entire door was designed with a security system in it, so that when one touched the door, a series of numbers from one through ten lit up the steel in bright green colors. Dianna tapped in a code and entered the building.

Inside, a spacious, empty room opened before her. Once used as an open-concept office space, this room was nothing more than a cover for what really went on beneath. Dianna's heels clapped against the tile floor as she made her way across the room to the elevator. She got in and waited as it dropped her to the basement.

Exiting the elevator, she took a deep breath as she turned a corner. She started for a set of steel doors, each one with perfectly squared, mirrored windows glaring back at her. Installed in the windows were cameras that recorded anyone who entered. This was a high-security facility, surrounded by high-tech drones invisible to the average citizen.

Dianna used facial and voice recognition on the box beside the steel doors. The doors opened out to reveal a room lit by recessed overhead fixtures. The cold, bare, concrete walls were painted a slick gray color. Industrial fans moved air around to make up for the lack of windows. Along one side of the room were a series of tall, steel pens where seven adult cows stood side by side, separated by thick walls so they could not see one another. Dianna could see them, and when she did, she immediately turned her head, instead focusing her attention on Carl and Dr. Dack Perimot, the main scientist on the project.

Carl turned and looked at her.

Dr. Perimot had been speaking to Carl in a hurried voice, which stopped the moment Dianna walked in. He wasn't wearing a lab coat, and she expected him to be. Instead he wore khakis and a flannel sweater. Made sense, given how chilly it was in the room.

"You called?" Dianna asked, observing, at the end of the room, the five empty cages from which the pigs had escaped.

Carl did not smile. He pulled off his glasses and responded.

"I'm not sure if we should be frightened. . .or fascinated."

"Why? What's going on?" she asked. Stopping beside him, she looked back at the empty cages.

"Dr. Perimot here has brought to my attention an issue that caused the pigs to escape," Carl said.

"Tell me," Dianna demanded, growing impatient. She hated when people stalled. "How the hell did the pigs escape, and where are they now?"

"The pigs and cows seemed to have. . .gained a human-like awareness," Carl said.

"What?" Dianna asked in disbelief. Did she hear them say the animals became human-like?

"I'll let Dr. Perimot explain, but the pigs escaped last night. Security was able to catch them. We've sent them off to slaughter."

"Smart move," Dianna said. The last thing they needed was for the S-Corp CEOs to find out about these animals, and that any of them had become intelligent enough to escape one of their facilities. The senior executives weren't aware of this little project Carl had convinced her to fund. It would be her going to slaughter if any of this got out.

Dr. Perimot turned to Dianna. He was shorter than Carl. His forehead gleamed from sweat. His graying beard dropped to his chest and looked unkept.

"The human iPSC cells that we injected into the animal blastocysts somehow modified their brains, making them more. . .*human*-like."

"What are iPSC cells?" Dianna asked. She knew nothing about transgenics, nor did she care to.

"Stem cells," Dr. Perimot replied.

"And blastocysts?" she asked.

"Embryos, essentially," Dr. Perimot explained.

Dianna paused. She looked the doctor over and shot a glance at Carl.

"And you're telling me even the cows have this. . .awareness?" she asked, looking back at the doctor.

Dr. Perimot nodded. Behind him, a set of computer screens displayed lists of numbers and letters that, again, she dared not understand. It was probably best that she knew little of what they were doing.

"We need to get rid of them," Dianna said immediately.

"What?" Carl replied, raising his eyebrows. "No. . .not yet. Don't you see what this could mean? What we could do with this?"

"I don't know. . ." Dianna replied, her heart cringing at the thought of this information getting into the wrong hands, or more likely, getting back to S-Corp corporate.

"Imagine, Dianna," he continued. "We could use this to explore mental illness. Think about your daughter."

And Dianna did think. It was tempting to consider how S-Corp could pave the way for new technology that could possibly eliminate certain genetic disorders and mental illnesses. But the fact that these cows had gained some advanced intelligence scared her for some reason.

Dianna looked at Carl. He'd had years of experience on her, and she trusted his judgment. She had to admit she was a bit turned on by his opportunistic drive. He wasn't like Cole, her ex-husband, at all, and she almost wanted to say yes to see if he was right. Maybe her fear was short-sighted.

"Eventually S-Corp execs are going to find out. I shouldn't have to explain the ramifications of proceeding beyond our end-of-May deadline," she said.

"Yes, of course," Carl replied, coming close and looking into her eyes. "But you know as well as I do. . .what this could mean. The *possibilities*." He smiled.

Dianna thought for a moment. Already the use of chimeric animals had enhanced the practice of growing organs for human transplant, and this had been going on for decades. Not only that, the use of pigs with CRISPR technology had spawned so many developments in human cancer and diabetes research alone that this was something very hard to dispute.

"What exactly do you need from me to make this happen?" Dianna asked, still feeling an edge of fear that she was considering saying yes.

"Time," Dr. Perimot replied. "If we could have a few more months to explore these animals and their brains, we might be able to present the findings to S-Corp in a way that the medical possibilities may outweigh any ethical considerations. . .like how we went about this without their knowledge. And let me add that, since these animals now have awareness, the most ethical thing we can do is keep them alive."

Dianna looked over at Carl before glancing back at the doctor. The more time they needed, the higher the risk of S-Corp execs finding out.

"I don't care about ethics. I care whether this gives us more insight into reducing illness. And I care about not getting caught. You have two months," she said. She pointed at the cows. "Then they go to slaughter."

"We'll take it," Carl said, winking at Dianna.

Dianna gave him a half-smile. She wanted to trust Carl with this, to believe in him. She turned and watched the cows as they stood and looked back at her. She shivered. She didn't know much about transgenics, but what she did know was that the possibility of animals gaining awareness as a result of testing were marginal. Well, not anymore. And this didn't feel like a *good* thing.

Now she had to put her trust in things she could not see, something she wasn't much good at.

Chapter Six

Bray

The shower helped temporarily. After, the voices came right back. A chant developed in her mind: *"Only you can save us, Bray. . .Only you can save us, Bray. . ."*

It kept on through the evening, while Bray tried interacting with others at the dinner table and afterwards, if only to draw her own attention away from it.

Once night fell and the last of the household went up to their rooms, Bray found herself alone in the living room. Kage slept in this room, yet he was nowhere to be found. For once she didn't want to go up to bed. She never thought she'd ever *want* to ignore the pleas of animals, yet here she was.

She sat on the couch looking over at the empty dining room. The lights were off. One lamp remained on beside her, causing the rooms to appear creepy and haunted. She shivered.

The chant suddenly stopped. Her mind went quiet. The relief was so wonderful she teared up. She could breathe again.

At the same time, Bray felt ashamed. She knew there were animals out there who needed help. Of course there were millions of them, but for some reason these cows *knew* her, *knew* Alice, and believed Bray could help them. Bray was not so sure.

With the peace and quiet that finally came to her, Bray took the chance and went up to sleep. She entered her bedroom, shut the door and sat on the bed. Clicking off the lamp beside her, she lay down and closed her eyes.

As she began drifting off, a message came through:

"If you are not going to listen to us, we will show you."

It was Rhea.

Bray's eyes opened. Her heart raced. She sat up and looked around as if something was going to happen right in front of her, but nothing did. It went quiet again.

She lay back down. A part of her feared going to sleep. But eventually her eyes grew so tired she couldn't keep them open.

Bray fell into sleep. Clouds of gray crept into the darkness behind her eyes. Clouds formed into an image of a room. A room with no windows. Concrete walls the color of gray. The sounds of beeping, vibrating, a hum. In the dream Bray sensed an overwhelming smell that she couldn't place, but it was not pleasant. It stung her nostrils.

She wasn't dreaming.

She was *inside the room.*

Her vision rose up to the ceiling, where industrial fans the length of cars whirred slowly. The view flipped. She was looking down on some kind of laboratory. Along the very back wall were tall, empty cages. Along another wall, steel pens held the seven cows. Each of them had been lying on their sides. They were so. . .thin. Not the kind of cows Bray was used to seeing in picture books. These cows had little fat on their bodies. Round patches absent of hair ran along the tops of their heads, down their spines and along their front and hind legs. Two of them had rounded bellies that made them appear pregnant. Perhaps they were. This left Bray's heart more still than death.

Her stomach felt heavy. Her head began to ache in this dream-like state. It throbbed from her forehead all the way back to her neck. Stinging sensations turned on and off like switches along her arms and down her legs.

It was happening again. As it had with Alice. She was beginning to *feel* their pain.

Bray was met with a barrage of emotions. . .confusion. . .fear. . .destitution.

Bray whimpered. She felt she might cry. The dream shook and it made her queasy. Queasy like someone being used in an experiment all the time. The queasiness grew stronger as the image faded, faded, faded into black.

She woke up, sweating. Her heart pounded. Her breath was heavy. The nightmares were back again.

For the first time in her life, Bray thought maybe medication wouldn't be such a bad idea after all.

Chapter Seven

Bray

In the morning, Bray felt like she'd been hit by a car. She had had no sleep beyond that one dream. Any time she'd nodded off, another voice had begged for her help. She feared another nightmare and she forced herself to stay awake.

The sun that rose outside her window provided little solace. She hoped maybe the daylight would bring her relief, because she could be around the others and at least avoid the nightmares for today.

But as she stepped slowly down into the living room, feeling like a zombie, the echoing voices continued.

"Help me, Bray. Help me," cried one.

"How do I go on like this?" asked another.

It wouldn't stop. And she feared the household would eventually notice.

"You look like shit," Kage said. He'd been standing by the living room window, nursing a finger on his left hand, which was wrapped in a bandage. He stood slightly turned toward Bray with his chest out. She could vaguely see his breasts. His blonde hair was growing back out again; short on one side where he'd once shaven it and longer on the other, near his shoulder. These details made him appear more effeminate, and Bray had to remind herself that inside, he was not the way he appeared.

"Thanks," Bray replied. She walked over to him and looked down at his hand. "What happened to you?"

"Bike is a bitch sometimes," he replied, grinning.

Bray nodded. She struggled to focus. Her eyes lifted to the window where they stared out across the front yard and into the corn stalks.

"Seriously, though—you really don't look so good," Kage said.

Bray's eyes remained locked on the corn stalks. What was *beyond* the corn stalks? She wasn't sure it was a good idea to tell anyone about the nightmare or voices, but if there was anyone she could trust who wouldn't go spill the beans to Trevor, it would be Kage.

"I'm hearing them again," she whispered.

"Who?"

"Animals. Lots of them."

"Like how you heard from Alice?" Kage asked, his voice low.

"Yes. Just. . .don't tell anyone, okay?"

"No problem," Kage said.

Virgil entered the dining room from the kitchen. Bray looked over at him, stepped away from Kage.

Virgil was carrying a steaming tray of baked sweet potatoes. The aroma made Bray hungry, for once. She parted from Kage, went in and sat down at the table. Her body needed sustenance, and badly. She realized she hadn't eaten much in the last couple weeks, and it was suddenly hitting her.

Dennis entered with two plates of various fruits and set them down. Bray looked over the grapes and strawberries, and her mouth watered for it all.

Kage came in and approached a stack of plates that sat at the far end of the table. He picked them up and set the table. Bray thought maybe she should help, but felt unable to get up, she was that tired.

As the others came in and sat and began eating, the voices continued in Bray's head. This left her silent and unable to talk. Emily asked her a question and Bray asked her to repeat it. But at least she was finally able to eat a meal. It didn't take much to feel full, seeing as she'd lost weight and her stomach had shrunken.

Eventually everyone finished eating breakfast and began departing from the table. Everyone but Kage, who'd been sitting beside her.

"What are you doing today?" Bray asked him.

With the voices overwhelming her mind, she decided it best to stay near someone who wouldn't judge her or ask questions.

"I've got to till a new lot in the garden. Almost time for summer planting."

"Can I help? Please?" Bray begged, looking into his eyes.

"Okay."

Bray watched him study her face. She hoped he'd picked up on the importance of her need to be close to him today.

#

Out in the garden, Bray walked alongside Kage as he pushed a tiller through the ground. Bray gradually began picking out rocks and tossing them into a nearby wheelbarrow. The activity helped calm her mind.

"Is everything okay with your bike?" Bray asked him.

Kage wasn't much of a talker, but she had to do all she could to distract herself from the voices.

"It needed an oil change," he said, pushing the tiller hard into the earth.

"Cool," Bray replied. Things went quiet.

Behind them, Lana was weeding again. Emily was meditating, and Ethan and Trevor were talking by the fences while looking out in the direction of the creek. Bray's eyes caught Emily, how she had this simple smile on her face while her eyes were closed. That was the kind of peace Bray could only dream of.

Bray's eyes drifted down to the ground that Kage was in the process of ripping apart with the tiller. Within the mix of dry soil and black earth and grass, Bray had a sudden vision: a flash of a pig's body. Its belly had been surgically sliced open to reveal a stomach, intestines and other organs covered in blood. Hands reached in, pulled out a fetus. It wasn't moving. Why she was seeing a pig when she expected it to be a cow, she did not know. It nearly made her double over and vomit. When it was over, Bray realized she'd stopped walking beside Kage, who was now a few feet ahead of her. He didn't seem to notice. She caught up with him and shook off the unsettling image.

A while later, Kage completed the tilling.

"I'll be right back, going to put this away," he said to her.

Kage rolled the tiller over to the basement doors, which covered an opening in the ground that led to a room below the kitchen.

As Bray stood and waited, she noticed the voices had left again. Her eyes scanned the newly tilled section of the garden, how the earth had been all sliced up and opened and pieces of grass and roots jutted up and out in piles. Along the span of the square section of dirt, an image of the seven cow pens opened out before her. The same pens from her nightmare.

Bray froze again. Her chest tightened. She wanted to run but couldn't.

Inside the pens she saw each of the cows. Their bellies rose and fell. Attached to their heads were metal apparatuses that connected via wires and traveled out and disappeared where the next garden began.

From inside one of the cages, a cow slowly lifted its head and locked eyes with Bray.

"*Run, Bray,*" she thought.

But her body still could not move.

The cow's eyes were black, wide circles where tears filled to the tops and rolled out, down, touched the cow's nose and dropped into the earth.

"Don't let us go on this way," called Rhea's voice, echoing within Bray's mind as the cow stared into Bray's eyes.

Bray gulped. She did not blink. A presence came near, a shadow.

"Well, now we—" Kage's voice caught her off guard.

She jumped.

"You okay?" Kage asked. "Didn't mean to startle you."

"Fine," Bray said. The vision disappeared from view until all that remained was the tilled earth.

Bray hurried off inside. Panicked and with nowhere else to run or hide or escape, she went into her bedroom and shut the door. Her breath fast, she turned and sat on the bed. Was there no way out of this? Could no one help her? She didn't want the others to know what was happening, so how could they help? She felt so alone again. She cried. She cried for a good, long while. She wished for Alice. These voices felt cruel, they were so unrelenting.

Bray lay down and looked out at the clouding sky. There she was faced with another vision, this time a group of pigs running down a long corridor. Bray felt a sense of urgency, a tug, as if these pigs were. . .escaping. A hissing sound gave way to clouds of gas. The pigs slowed their running and appeared to pass out. Suddenly the floor beneath their motionless bodies began to move, like a conveyor. They were pulled down the corridor until the conveyor stopped at a loading dock. From there, a front loader was used to push the pigs into a transport truck.

Bray knew exactly where they were headed. But why was she seeing these pigs? Had they been trapped in the same place as the cows? She didn't really want to know.

For hours there was no escape for Bray. The visions continued off and on. Whether her eyes were open or closed, the progression of images would not go away. They shifted back to the cows, showing the many ways in which they'd been subjected to experiments in a lab.

Bray rocked back and forth in bed. She reached over and grabbed her worry stone from the night stand and rubbed her thumb into its divot. Her palms sweated. She curled into a fetal position, found herself inside a no-escape hell she'd experienced back in the psych ward, except this was *worse*. Here there were no walls or locked doors keeping her. She could leave but there would still be no escaping.

She experienced absolute horror, over and over again, witnessing these cows being used cruelly. . .and for what? Technology?

"*Transgenics,*" Rhea whispered.

Bray had no idea what that meant. How did Rhea know so much? It was like she was almost. . .*human.*

"*Help me, help me, help me!*" Rhea cried.

Bray leapt out of bed and stopped at the window. She would've considered jumping out if she thought that could have ended the voices and visions, but she didn't want to die. She wanted *help. Did* she need meds? She didn't *want* meds. She remembered how they made her feel when she was in the psych hospital. Or *NOT* feel. But at this moment she would welcome the numbness.

Her eyes caught Emily stepping down into the grass from the porch. She carried a yoga mat and set it down in the grass. Sitting down on the mat, she folded her legs like a pretzel, placing her hands gently on her thighs. The sun was setting out beyond the garden. Emily looked so… calm. Bray watched her, wished for what she had.

Eventually, Emily got up and disappeared from view. The front door opened, closed. Steps came up the stairwell, quiet, intentional. Bray turned and looked at her door. Could Emily help her? If not Emily, then Bray's only other choice would be for everyone, Trevor in particular, to find out something was wrong with her. She might very well end up back in the psych ward.

So long as Emily could keep Bray's secret between the two of them, maybe she could help somehow.

The sound of footsteps slid softly down the hall. Another door opened and closed. Bray waited a few moments and left her room.

All the lights were off in the hall. Everyone had retreated to their rooms. Some she passed where lights slid out from beneath doors and touched Bray's bare feet.

She knocked on Emily's door.

A moment passed.

The door opened fully. Emily stood there, smiling.

"I think I need your help," Bray said in a low voice.

Emily invited her in. She entered the room. The door closed.

Chapter Eight

Bertan

Bertan lay in bed scrolling through photos of his family. Carmen had texted several to him after he acquired his S-Corp cell phone. Otherwise all he'd had were the photos he brought with him on *La Bestia*, the Mexican freight train: a few of their wedding photos and the one of his father, which hid between pages of a book that sat on the tray table beside the bed.

His finger swiped to a photo of Gabriella when she was eight. It was her first school dance. She was dressed in a pink, frilly skirt with a pink shirt that had a heart painted on the front of it. An ache rolled through his heart like the aftershock of an earthquake. How it hurt to know she was growing up and he might not ever get to see her do so. He didn't want her to have the same experience he had as a child: not knowing her father. The difference was that his father had been murdered. . .murdered by Medina. Bertan had only survived them by leaving the country.

He had left Honduras, but he couldn't escape Medina. Medina wasn't a place one ever truly escaped.

Now he reached over and picked up the thin, one-hundred-page book from the tray table. It was a book on guerrilla warfare and revolution by Che Guevara. His father had given it to him. Bertan had asked Carmen to mail him an entire box of books, which he kept beneath the tray table. He picked up the book and opened it to the photo inside. Holding the photo in his hand, Bertan went still as he stared at it. This was the only photo he had left of his father. In it, his father, Menor, was twenty. Bertan was sitting beside him on the floor, too young to remember

the moment in which the photo was taken. His
father had a distinguished, black mustache. It
was a chevron, and Bertan remembered his father
caring for it, brushing it in the bathroom
mirror.

Bertan smiled.

He set the photo aside and began reading where
he had left off. He began to remember what his
father taught him about Che: about the importance
of community.

"Each one of us alone means nothing," his
father had said. "It only takes one to start a
revolution, but it takes a community to achieve
it."

This was what led his father to give up
working for Medina and turn to helping the
campesinos. And what led to his murder.

Medina would continue to be the devil on
Bertan's back as long as they remained in
operation. He knew this. When he worked for
Medina, he'd done some awful things to *campesinos*
on Medina's orders. Kidnappings, threats, things
Bertan no longer wished to think about. And
because of this work, Bertan was never *supposed*
to leave the corporation. He knew too many
secrets. But he was away from them and away from
their threats on him and his family.

Or so he had thought. Weeks ago he'd stumbled
upon some bank statements at his job as an S-Corp
security guard. Bank statements revealing that S-
Corp was funding Medina. Bertan was more than
shocked. He was deeply demoralized. He made an
agreement to help Ruben end S-Corp. He wanted to
do this because of how Ruben had helped his
family by funding Carmen's and Gabriella's
housing in Texas. He owed Ruben, and so when his
phone buzzed and he saw it was Carmen calling, he
knew what he had to tell her: he wouldn't go home
until Medina was no longer there.

Bertan answered.

"What's going on?" he asked, setting the book

back down.

"Did you think about our last talk? About us going back home?" Carmen asked. She wasn't going to let this go.

"I've been thinking about it," he admitted. He used to be able to talk to Carmen about anything. But the distance between them was so great he feared telling her the truth.

"And?" she asked.

Bertan looked down at the mattress below him. He tried recalling the last time they kissed. What she tasted like. A vague memory popped into his mind, lying in bed beside Carmen. How quietly she slept at night. How much better he slept with her in the bed beside him. He hated what he was about to say.

"The reason I can't come home. . .is because I agreed to help Ruben with something here."

"What, love?" she asked, sounding impatient. "It's not illegal, is it?"

"Well, it is. But it's the right thing to do. Something that I think will keep our family safer. If we succeed."

"What is it?"

Bertan realized he was delaying. He couldn't back out now.

"Ruben is a social worker. He is working undercover. . .to take down S-Corp."

"How?"

"I'm not sure yet. He said he needs help getting into S-Corp's system. He needs to get proof they are corrupt. I already found some."

"Proof? Of what?"

"Carmen. . .S-Corp is partnered with Medina. I found bank statements showing money being transferred from S-Corp to Medina."

There was a pause.

"I wish you'd come home with me. Give up this fight with them and just let it be."

"I can't. Ruben saved your lives. I am indebted to him," Bertan said, opening up to his wife for the first time in months.

"How long is this going to take?"

"I wish I knew. I really miss you both," he said. A surprising feeling of sorrow washed over him. "But Ruben is also helping me. He says I have trauma, and he's been helping me heal."

"That's good," she replied shortly.

He sensed from the shift in her tone of voice that she was upset.

"I just know that if I come down there now, Medina will always be after us. Maybe not directly. But ultimately, I don't think I'll be safe back home until they are gone."

"Talk to Ruben about getting me and Gabriella home, please. You do whatever you want with S-Corp."

Bertan's eyes welled up. His hand tightened into a fist. He didn't want his family to go, but he had to let them.

"Okay," he replied, holding back the guilt that crowded his chest.

"I don't know why you have to go on this crusade to end S-Corp. Why you can't let the past go and find a way to trust that we can be safe. We could be safe back in San Pedro. You could change your name, whatever." Carmen paused. "But it doesn't matter what I say, does it? You're going to do what you're going to do. I'll take Gabriella back and we'll move on without you. If you decide to come home, you can let me know. But I'm not going to sit around worrying, not if you're going to choose this. You're choosing life without us. Again."

"Carmen," Bertan called, his heart sinking.

Carmen's end went silent.

"Carmen?"

She hung up.

Bertan pulled the phone away from his face. He looked at the screen. She was gone. He wanted to throw the phone across the room, but he resisted. Carmen had a right to be upset with him. At the same time, he was disappointed in her. Why couldn't she see that he was stuck up against a

wall? That he couldn't go home and start again?
He knew Medina would try to kill him again. Was
he choosing safety and certainty over life with
his family? On some level, perhaps he was. Maybe
she was right.

Truth was, he feared he'd have no one to be if
he went back home. He'd be lost. And a lost man
could be no man for his family. What saddened him
most was that he loved Carmen, he loved her and
he loved Gabriella so much that he was willing to
lose them in exchange for one chance to end the
one thing that would always come between them.

Medina.

Chapter Nine

Bray

Warmth enveloped Bray the moment she entered Emily's room. It wasn't the temperature, although a feeling of soft heat touched her exposed skin and slowly ran along it as though she were being embraced by a quilt.

It was more the lighting. . .and the energy. A lamp glowed from beside Emily's bed, pouring an amber light down along the hardwood floor to a forest green rug on the far side of the room, and up along three chocolate-colored bookshelves that surrounded two floor cushions. The scent of pine hung above Bray's head.

"Have a seat," Emily said, pointing at her bed.

Bray sat down on a red and gold patterned comforter. She felt nervous, but also reassured by the calm energy she had sensed when entering the room.

Emily sat down across from Bray, her legs crossed. She was wearing a pair of black leggings and a green, sleeveless top. Her hair was up in a pony tail that fell down to her lower back. Bray remembered when she first met Emily and the others, how they had a certain smell, maybe because they washed with natural soaps that Bray was not accustomed to. While she sat across from Emily, she no longer recognized the smell.

"Talk to me," Emily said.

Bray looked at Emily. Her big, hazel-green eyes were so full beneath the dim light of the room. Bray didn't know where to start. Could she tell Emily everything?

"Can you keep this between us?" Bray asked.

"As long as you're not planning to hurt yourself," Emily replied, raising her eyebrows.

"No," Bray replied, rolling her eyes. She was tired of everyone assuming she was suicidal.

"Sorry. I had to ask."

"It's just that Trevor keeps pressing me to get help. Not that I don't need it, that's why I'm here. He thinks I'm mentally ill."

"And you're not," Emily said.

Bray couldn't tell if that was a question or a statement.

"Right," Bray replied. "I'm an empath."

"I remember you saying that." Emily paused. Her eyes rose up to the ceiling as if she were looking around for the next thing to say. "I knew a few empaths when I lived in Sacramento, but none that could communicate with animals."

"So you do believe me?"

"No reason not to, especially after hearing Kage talk about how you saved all those sows. Extraordinary."

Bray didn't think so. It would've been extraordinary had she been able to save them sooner, prevented Alice and the others from dying. And here she was now avoiding animals that were begging for her help. She didn't *want* to avoid them, but she was too frightened of the alternative.

She told Emily everything. She told her how it all began with Rhea, how Rhea had *known* things. She rehashed the visions, the nightmare from the night before. All the while, Emily sat and listened. Her facial expression barely changed. She simply sat, her eyes on Bray, with no reaction.

Bray finished. She waited for Emily to respond.

"I'm sorry you're going through all of this. I'm glad you came to me. That stuff is a lot to carry all by yourself. It must feel really lonely," Emily said softly.

"Yeah." Bray began to cry. Emily's words hit at something inside, something Bray knew was there but had forgotten ever since Rhea came along. . .how *alone* she really was in this house with other people. With *good* people. The best people she'd ever known, yet they all felt like strangers.

"Can I give you a hug?" Emily asked.

Bray nodded. Emily pulled her in and hugged her. She rocked Bray back and forth. Bray felt it for a while and pulled away. She thought how Emily was around the same age as her mom. Bray wiped her tears away with the bottom of her shirt.

"How can I help you?" Emily asked.

"I'm not really sure." Bray shrugged, sniffling. The crying ceased. "I saw you outside meditating. You looked so. . .calm."

"Ah," Emily said. "You want to be calm?"

"I want the voices to quiet. Really I want it all to go away."

Emily nodded.

"Listen, it's getting late," Emily said. "You're welcome to sleep in here tonight, if you think it will help. Tomorrow morning you can join me for meditation. We can go from there."

Bray nodded. She breathed a sigh of relief. She very much wanted to sleep in this room. It was much warmer and inviting than Kage's.

As she slept beside Emily for the night, the voices continued but at a less overwhelming pace. She was able to sleep through the night.

#

The next morning, Bray was sitting outside, before dawn, on the grass beside Emily. The grass was wet and lively in its green color, as if it had also woken up. Along the horizon, an intense, white light gave way to twinges of yellow and orange, rising up into stratus clouds varying in color from light blue to lavender. For the moment it was quiet and unmoving.

Bray was not sure she could meditate. She

wasn't sure she could even sit still without wanting to get up and run away. But what choice did she have? It was either this or. . .well, she didn't know.

"Okay," Emily began. Her voice was monotone, soothing, like a deep hum that could very well put Bray to sleep. "Let's start by closing our eyes. . .Place your hands on your thighs, palms up."

Bray did as she was instructed. It took less than a second for Rhea's voice to enter her mind.

"Alice was your friend. Be our friend, too."

Bray's eyes shot open.

"Start by taking a few deep breaths. . ." Emily continued.

Bray turned and saw that Emily's eyes were still closed. She could sit here and listen, pretend to be meditating. But what good would that do? She would only ruminate on the voices. They were so strong they were like her own.

She closed her eyes. She took a deep breath. Emily spoke again.

"Now see if you can feel where the breath is. . .in your body."

Bray tried to stay in her body. She noticed her stomach rising and falling. Rhea repeated the same request from before:

"Alice was your friend. Be ours, too."

Bray's chest tightened. Emily said something, but it was nearly impossible to pay attention. That comment, how Rhea knew she and Alice had been friends. . .it freaked Bray out. It kept repeating over and over in her mind. Unable to take it anymore, she opened her eyes.

"Emily," she said. "I can't do this."

Emily turned to her, eyes open.

"What's happening?"

"It's Rhea. She somehow knows I was connected to Alice. She keeps saying that me and Alice were friends and then asking me to be her friend, too."

"What feelings does that bring up for you?"

Emily asked.

"Scared. Confused. I just. . .don't understand."

"It's hard when there are things in life we don't understand."

Bray nodded in agreement.

"Would it be too hard to meditate with me anyway, to see if you can sit with that fear and that confusion?"

"I'm not sure I can," Bray admitted, her shoulders dropping. She didn't want to let Emily down.

"Let's try something else," Emily said. "Tonight, come join me in my room after dinner. We're going to do some energy work, clear you out a bit."

"What do you mean?"

"Sometimes the energy within us gets stuck, like feelings do. There are certain techniques. . .meditations we can do, to help get things unstuck."

"It's worth a shot."

#

Night came, but not without struggle. Not without suffering. Throughout the morning and afternoon Bray continued to hear Rhea's pleas. Visions continued. She tried to ignore it, but the more she ignored it, the worse it got.

When she finished dinner, Bray was in a hurry to meet with Emily. She had to trust that this energy work was going to help, especially if Emily thought so.

Bray followed Emily upstairs. They entered Emily's room. Emily shut the door.

"Let's sit over on the rug." Emily pointed over to the corner where the bookshelves stood like good friends above the two cushions.

Bray sat down on one of the cushions. Given

what happened this morning, she wasn't too confident in herself.

"Here's what's going to happen," Emily said as she sat down on the cushion across from Bray. "I'm going to guide you through a chakra cleanse. In the Hindu religion, chakras are the seven energy centers in the body, starting at the root of the body, here." Emily pointed behind her at her bottom. "And going up the body to the crown of the head." She continued, touching the top of her head. "There are mantras. . .or words. . .that are associated with each chakra. I'll have you focus on each location in the body, then repeat the mantra, and imagine the color that is associated with that chakra. I know it sounds complicated, but all you have to do is sit, eyes closed, and follow along. Think you can do that?"

"I'm going to try," Bray said, trying to understand what Emily meant by *mantras*. She hoped she could follow along without messing up.

Emily paused and looked at her. She reached over and squeezed Bray's shoulder.

"One day, my wish for you is to believe in yourself."

Bray smiled. She wasn't accustomed to being treated with such kindness and sincerity.

"After I am done with the chakra meditation, I'm going to give you some Reiki," Emily said.

"Is that the energy work you did on me when I was unconscious?"

"Yep. The day you arrived. Even though I didn't know you then, I could tell you'd been through some shit."

Bray smiled again. Emily smiled back. Emily removed her hand from Bray's shoulder and sat back on the cushion.

"Close your eyes," Emily said. "I'm going to start us off with a little singing. Something called the moola mantra. Consider it a kind of calling in of any source, could be God, and if you don't believe in God, then just think of love or your higher self."

Bray did not believe in God, but she tried to keep an open mind. She closed her eyes and thought of the friendships she experienced with Alice and Elliott.

After a moment of silence, Emily began to sing:

"Ohm. . .satchitananda. . .parabrahma-a-a. . .purushothama-a-a. . .parama-a-a-atma-a-a. . ."

Emily's voice was strong and soothing, both at the same time. It vibrated with Sanskrit words that Bray did not know the meanings of, and she found she didn't need to. The words permeated her mind in a way that caused all thought to dissipate.

The voices silenced.

"Now I'm going to lead you though the Chakra Dhyana. Begin by focusing your attention on your lower spine area. If you can, imagine the color red."

Bray visualized her backside. The color red spread through her mind. It shifted and formed into a liquid, like blood. She began to feel frightened. Emily's voice continued.

"The sound associated with this chakra is lang. . .l-a-n-g. You can visualize the word in your mind as I sing. . ." Emily proceeded to vocalize the sound, which she pronounced like the word *long*, three times. Bray pictured the word in her mind, which helped rid her of the violent blood color.

"Now, imagine a beautiful, golden light filling and cleansing that chakra," Emily continued, "as I sing ohm-kundalini-arohanam."

Emily sang the "om-kundalini" song three times. She asked Bray to bring her attention up to her pelvic region, where she was to visualize the color orange and the sound vang, which Emily repeated three times, followed by the "om-kundalini" repetition.

And so it went on like this, each time Bray's

focus rising up to the next chakra: her abdomen, heart, throat, as more colors were presented: yellow, green, blue. . .like a rainbow. Up, up, up her focus went. Up, up, up Bray felt the energy rise. She felt her body open. By the end, her eyes were watering, but not from crying.

It was a release.

Rhea's voice had lessened to a murmur.

"Please, don't leave us."

And Bray felt the guilt. In the silence, as Emily's voice ceased, as Bray heard Emily's body shuffle near, a sense of warmth radiating above her head, she began to cry. She felt ashamed, and as the warmth enveloped her like a warm hug, reminding her of the hugs she had once received from her dad, she allowed the tears to flow. They came, and came, and came. Her mind went silent the way a pond did not move unless disturbed by a thrown-in pebble. Stillness. Pure stillness.

The calls of Rhea went on, and it was okay. The warmth from Emily's Reiki work melted the hardness around Bray's heart she hadn't even known was there. When the Reiki ended, Bray floated down the hall to her room, and with ease she slept through the night.

Chapter Ten

Bray

Three days passed. In those three days, Bray began to tap the surface of meditation. Emily also led her in some yoga, to supposedly keep her more connected with her breath and body.

Bray enjoyed the yoga, hard as it sometimes was to keep in poses when she had zero flexibility. She was never one to have interest in physical activity, mostly because her life up to this point consisted of psych ward "emergencies" when really she had needed this kind of activity all along, to quell the visions and voices.

On this eve of the third day, Bray was meditating with Emily. They were sitting out in the front yard, facing the corn stalks. The sun had not yet set but was on its way. Bray wore a sweater jacket over her t-shirt to keep warm.

She had been tasked with allowing her feelings and thoughts to arise, and to sit and experience them rather than try to avoid them. This proved extremely challenging. After three days of it, she thought it would become easier.

On this night she had a particularly hard time sitting. Her eyes closed, her body sitting cross-legged in the grass, her back feeling tight, every urge in her wanted to get up and leave. On occasion, Emily's voice popped into her awareness: "...if any thoughts arise, just notice them, then gently bring your attention back to your breath."

And so it became a kind of cycle: Bray felt her breath, shallow and short in the depth of her belly.

Rhea whispered: *"time is running out, only you can save us."*

Bray noticed a heaviness press into her chest. As Emily had instructed, she sat and focused her attention on her chest. She felt the heaviness, like a square, ten-pound weight, black and thick. She breathed as she focused on it.

Soon she realized it was guilt she was feeling. She felt horrible for not wanting to help Rhea the way she had wanted to help Alice.

She wished she could run.

"As thoughts or feeling arise," Emily spoke, "and they always do, it is the nature of things. . .gently bring yourself back to breath. Not judging yourself for having these thoughts, these feelings, simply allow them to be there, and then come back to your breath."

This repetitive instruction brought Bray comfort. She exhaled and noticed her breathing again. The cycle kept on this way for what felt like ages.

Emily guided her out of the meditation. Bray opened her eyes, which had been watering for some time. She wiped the tears away, sitting there, no longer needing to escape, and noticed her surroundings. Everything looked so new, so *clear*. The sun had gone down and an indigo sky was growing darker and darker, yet the yellow corn crops appeared vivid, even in the coming night.

"How was it this time?" Emily asked.

"I feel better after the meditation ends," Bray said. "But during, all I want to do is run away."

"I get that." Emily nodded as she remained sitting beside Bray.

"You see the bats flying around above us?" Emily asked, pointing up into the sky.

"Yes."

"See how they're simply going about their business? How they just do what they do?"

Bray watched the bats flitter and flap in the sky, seeming to pay no mind to her or Emily.

She nodded.

"Thoughts are like that. They just do what

they do. You're still new to meditation, so it's understandable that it would be hard to sit with things in the beginning. If it helps you to imagine the thoughts as bats. . .doing what they do, eventually you will train yourself to detach from them. That's all meditation is."

"What about emotions?" Bray asked, fearing the guilt and shame that had risen to the surface since she had begun working with Emily.

Emily unfolded her legs and lay down in the grass a few inches from Bray. She was facing Bray, lying on her side with her head resting on her hand.

"A very wise person told me once that feelings are like children. I wouldn't know because I never had kids. But kids want to be heard. . .listened to. Feelings are like that. The more we ignore them, the more they act out."

"Act out? How?"

"In how we behave. Like running away, for example."

Bray thought about what Emily said. It made sense, that she had been avoiding Rhea because of the feelings Rhea brought up in her. Maybe that explained the hiding away in her room for so long after Alice died.

"Do you want to talk about what you're feeling?" Emily asked.

"I feel guilty," Bray admitted.

"What for?"

"For not trying to help Rhea when she keeps begging, several times a day. From the visions and nightmares, I know she's in a lot of pain, her and the other cows."

"Guilt is a totally normal feeling. It's an uncomfortable one, so we label it as negative. Can you see how the guilt could be like a little child that just wants to be heard and felt?"

"I guess. But wouldn't that make it worse?"

Emily sat up. She faced Bray, crossing her legs again.

"I don't think so. Is running from it helping

at all?"

"No." Bray shrugged. She looked down at her feet.

"Can I tell you a story?"

Bray looked Emily in the eye and nodded.

"You see these scars?" Emily began as she revealed her arms and wrists, running her finger along the trails that traveled from her wrists up to her inner elbow.

"I wondered what they were. I was afraid to ask."

Emily smiled and continued.

"These are track marks. They're from years and years of injection heroin use."

"Oh," Bray replied, shocked.

"I started using when I was thirteen. My dad left home when I was five. He said he loved me, then he disappeared. It took a long time for me to unlearn the message that when people love me, they show it by leaving.

"My mom remarried three years later. He was hard to live with. I won't go into the details, but it was abusive. When I was twelve I got in with this group of older boys at school. They became my only friends. Honestly, they were the only ones who listened to me. My mom ignored me most of the time, so at home I felt like a ghost.

"Then we discovered heroin. It made me feel so much pleasure. . .not like any pleasure I'd ever experienced in my whole life. The high gave me such a rush," she said, smiling slightly. "It became my friend. I loved it. Whenever my emotions got difficult, the heroin seemed to make it all go away.

"Eventually, I left home. I stayed with these boys, who were years older than me. They did things to me. And I used more. Using was my form of running away, you see? I watched a few friends die of overdoses.

"Then, when I was twenty, I found out my mom had died. Even though she wasn't a great mom, she was still my mom. I felt so guilty for not being there when she died. I thought maybe if I hadn't used, maybe she'd still be alive. It got so bad I finally tried recovery—"

"What's recovery?" Bray interrupted.

"A 12-Step program."

Bray had no idea what that meant.

"It's basically a non-denominational, but spiritual, program. It's completely free, which I needed because I had no money for rehab. It's basically a group of other addicts, all working a structured set of steps that help a person move past their addiction.

"Eventually, I realized the only way I could heal and live a life free of drugs, free of escape, was to sit and feel my feelings. And it was really hard. I hated every bit of it, but I kept going back, one day at a time, as they say."

"One day at a time?"

"It's a slogan. Helps keep me in the here and now. Back in my first days of recovery, all I thought about was getting a fix. . .more drugs. The desire to escape had to get worse before it got better. I don't know why it works that way, but it does."

Bray sat and tried to process everything Emily had said. She'd never met anyone who'd done drugs, and why would that surprise her, given her very sheltered past?

"I tell you all of this not to overwhelm you, but to show you that over time, the feelings do get easier to feel and let go of. I know because I've been there."

Bray took a deep breath. She couldn't imagine going through so much, and here Emily was, this calm, peaceful presence. If she could get there after all she'd been through, maybe Bray could, too.

Chapter Eleven

Bertan

The S-Corp facility was located five miles from Bertan's hostel. He sat in the parking lot and stared at it, not remembering how he got here. Or when. How long had he been sitting here? His eyes shifted over to the clock above the radio. 8:00 p.m. His work shift as a security guard began in one hour. Why was he here so early? From the driver's seat he looked over his shoulder and out the back side window. There he recognized Ruben's car. That was when he remembered: he was here to see Ruben.

A dull, musky navy-blue night approached, giving the gray, one-level S-Corp building a blue appearance of its own. White lights popped out from its four corners, two of them pointing down at the parking lot. He stepped out of his car and started for the front of the building, where glass walls lined the front. He unlocked the doors and entered.

This facility was different than the one he had worked at before. Here they didn't only slaughter beefs. Pigs, chickens and the occasional turkeys came through this place as well. This was a special facility built to slaughter animals who'd been subjected to experiments. It made no sense to Bertan why they needed a separate facility for this, but again, he wasn't one to ask questions.

Located in Arco, Idaho, this S-Corp facility stood twenty miles north of the other one where he'd worked as both a knocker and a security guard. He'd held both jobs in order to send money down south to his family. Now, because they were in the U.S. and Ruben was fitting their housing bill, Bertan didn't have to work two jobs. And so, in order to reduce his PTSD symptoms, which had been exacerbated by his history of violence and the equally violent job of knocking hundreds of beefs unconscious every day, Bertan had agreed to step back from knocking altogether, to move to this new location where Ruben met with him weekly to review his symptoms, and to maintain work only as a security guard.

Down the far hall to the right was a series of offices. Everything was dark. He could see from here that Ruben's office door was closed. Remaining in the dark, Bertan walked down the hall and knocked on the third door to the right.

The door opened.

"Did you see anyone here?" Ruben asked, looking out past Bertan into the hall.

"No."

"Good." Ruben nodded. He backed away, and Bertan entered, sitting down on a chair across from Ruben's desk.

This office was much nicer than the office Ruben had used at the previous facility. It actually looked like an office. A bookshelf lined with books on psychology and anthropology stood beside a window looking out into a grove of trees along the side of the facility. Beside the window, a mobile garment rack held two suits and a pair of ties.

There was a large painting of a desert hanging on the wall behind Ruben's desk. Bertan stared at it as Ruben took a seat beneath it. The painting always reminded Bertan of the time he journeyed from Mexico into the U.S. years ago. An image of the desert at night, with bright stars and moonlight sliding along the barren land. It was both ominous and strangely comforting.

"What's new?" Ruben asked.

"Carmen," Bertan replied. "She wants to take Gabriella and go back home."

"To Honduras?"

Bertan nodded. He still couldn't believe it. After all they'd gone through to get her here, how much she wanted to come to the U.S., it was like she was a whole other person, changing her mind like this.

"I'm sorry to hear that," Ruben replied, his voice forlorn. "How are you feeling?"

Another tough question. Bertan used to roll his eyes at Ruben's "how do you feel" questions, but now he did his best to answer by naming the one emotion he was familiar with.

"Frustrated," he replied simply.

Ruben nodded. He looked at Bertan and frowned. Bertan sensed the empathy in the man's eyes, but he still glanced away.

"Why don't you go home with them? There's nothing for you here, Bertan."

"I can't go home. You know that. They're safer there without me."

Ruben's chest rose and fell, which clued Bertan in to the fact that he hadn't been breathing. His shoulders were tight. He was stuck. He needed some kind of forward movement. He needed to make a decision.

"I think once we stop S-Corp, maybe then I can go home," he said finally. He knew, after all, that ending S-Corp meant ending the company's funding of Medina. Then Medina would dry up and die off, too.

"That could take a while."

"What do you mean?"

"Taking down a multi-trillion-dollar corporation, one that controls our entire food system. . .that could take years," Ruben said, leaning forward. He pressed his elbows onto the table and intertwined his hands.

Bertan looked at him. His mind grew overwhelmed with the things Ruben just told him. Years? He didn't have years. Surely Carmen would be nothing more than a distant memory. His daughter, too.

"But I thought if I helped you get stuff on them. . ." He stopped, listening to himself talk, realizing Ruben was probably right.

"If we get evidence, it still takes time to process it, to take them to court. I'm sorry I wasn't more clear on that before. I guess I assumed you'd know it wouldn't be a quick operation."

Bertan leaned farther back in his chair. He raised his hands and ran them through his hair, which he'd allowed to grow down past his shoulders. He didn't know what to say anymore.

"Stay with me, Bertan. What's going on right now?" Ruben asked. He leaned forward against the desk as if about to stand up.

"I want to shut down," Bertan said, covering his face with his hands. It was all becoming too much.

"Can I have you try taking a few breaths?" Ruben's voice rang in his ears.

Bertan bent over, placing his head between his legs. He didn't want to breathe, he wanted to end S-Corp. But he breathed anyway. These were the moments when he would fade away, go into a "blackout" as Ruben called them.

There were no easy answers. Such was his life. Trade a life here for a life in Honduras, and what would change? The language? He could be with his family, yes, but how would he be more help to them down there? Carmen's cousin took better care of her than he could. He'd get some shitty job with less pay, and the word would get out that he was back in country, and Medina would come find him. Maybe they wouldn't, but in these times he had to assume the worst.

By remaining here and working for S-Corp, he could continue trying to find incriminating evidence against them while, secretly, working to sabotage them from the inside out. Maybe sabotage could lead to their ultimate demise faster than Bertan's plan could. He was only one man, but as his father had taught him about men like Che Guevara, sometimes one man was enough.

"Can you help get my family back home?" Bertan asked finally.

There was a pause. Ruben's eyes floated around the room and returned to Bertan.

"I know a guy," Ruben said. "Very trusted *coyotaje*. Not like the one who scammed you last time."

This suggestion allowed Bertan to breathe. He didn't love the idea of another *coyotaje* working with his family. The last one he hired had aided in the kidnapping of his wife and child. But he would have to trust Ruben.

His ears picked up the sound of a clock ticking on the wall behind him. He glanced up at it.

"I have to start work," he said, quickly standing up and leaving the room. His breathing was still tight, tight like the heart of someone near death. But it wasn't death he was concerned with. It was what he was about to do—what he knew he had to do—and what he would have to keep from Ruben.

All while his family returned home without him.

Chapter Twelve

Bray

It was raining. Bray was in the kitchen helping Kage wash dishes. She had come to realize that she'd been living here well over a month and had barely pulled her weight. It wasn't something she thought about. When she was kept in the psych ward, there was nothing to do but take classes. They had staff to do the cleaning. And when she did find herself at home, her parents had assistants who did all the work.

Bray had never really been expected to do anything. With her mother being such a high-powered business woman and her father a politician, the assistants were the ones who really ran the house. As she stood beside the sink, drying each dish that Kage passed to her, she found she much enjoyed it. Maybe it was the company she kept, but the thought of helping the household made her feel better about herself, which was a new thought entirely.

Kage handed Bray the last of the plates he'd washed. Bray ran the towel over it and noticed a crumb of food.

"This is still dirty," she said, handing it back to him.

Kage stuck his tongue out at her. She grinned. He took the plate back and washed it again.

"Here," he replied, waving the plate toward Bray. Drops of water hit Bray in the face.

"You're getting me wet."

"Let's go outside and I'll show you wet," Kage replied, winking.

Bray glanced out the window. The rain had kept them inside all day, and she didn't mind.

Once she finished drying dishes, she went to find Emily for their evening meditation. As she passed through the dining room for the staircase, she saw the front door was open, its screen looking out past the porch at the consistent, heavy rain. Bray felt pulled to it. She walked up and stopped at the screen door. The rain made a whooshing sound through the trees, a gentle tapping against the roof of the porch. She saw Emily sitting on the porch swing.

Bray went out and sat down beside her.

"I love the rain," Emily said, closing her eyes and lifting her head as if to take in the sounds.

Bray sat and felt the brisk temperature brought in by the rain, how it continued to fall. She closed her eyes. Her legs hung over the swing and her feet did not reach the ground. Emily had been using her feet to slowly push the swing back and forth. The movement eased Bray into relaxation, not that she hadn't already felt that way. She had never felt this relaxed in her entire life.

A thought passed through her mind:

Then came another: *Do I deserve to feel good. . .when I know others suffer?*

Bray accepted both thoughts and let them go. More thoughts came, but as she felt the breath in her belly, she eventually came to a place of emptiness. A black screen behind her eyes where, for the very first time, she felt *safe.*

She felt Rhea's presence. She sat, and willed herself not to move or to run away.

"When will you help us? Will you help us at all?" Rhea asked. The voice echoed through Bray's mind. Before responding, she listened to her body. She felt for those uncomfortable feelings Emily encouraged her to feel. In her chest she felt the rise of a very deep shame. The shame of not saving Alice sooner. The shame of having experienced a life inside a hospital and not knowing or understanding things that others her age knew. The shame that her mother was a Regional President for S-Corp, someone who basically controlled the food and water system

out west and—Bray felt—was responsible for allowing so many animals to be slaughtered and was probably to blame for the water crisis. The shame that she'd hardly begun her life and she would soon turn eighteen, that she was frightened to be an adult because she felt ill-prepared. The shame of having not been the greatest friend to Elliott, whom she'd known since childhood and convinced to bring her along on his travels north so she could find Alice. Elliott, whom she'd separated from back in Casper. The shame of ignoring Rhea, ignoring the voices, of wanting them to stop. The shame that told her she was a horrible human being. That she didn't *deserve* to save animals. That it ought to be left to someone far better than she.

Bray began to cry. Silently, the tears rolled down her cheeks. She allowed them to drop onto her shirt. She didn't try to stop the crying. The swing rocked her back and forth, back and forth, into a place of acceptance. In that moment she felt it okay enough to allow the shame to be there. She wanted to avoid it, but instead, she listened. Was she really a horrible person? She didn't think so. Was it possible that these thoughts weren't actually truth? Should she maybe not take these thoughts so seriously?

Rhea spoke again.

"You saved Alice from that transport truck. And you saved the sows who were with her. Now save us."

Bray opened her eyes. Once again, she found herself stuck on what Rhea said. How could Rhea know Alice? This really bothered her, brought up the fear that made her want to disappear.

She looked over at Emily. Emily's eyes were still closed. Bray turned and looked out at the corn crops that were still dead and waiting for summer to arrive. What was left of them were nothing more than empty husks where the corn would someday grow again.

The swinging ceased. Bray looked back over at

Emily. Emily was looking back at her.

"You all right?" Emily asked.

"I just keep hitting against something," Bray replied.

"What's that?"

Bray was uncertain Emily would understand. But they'd grown quite close in the last several days, and Bray found that when she opened up to Emily, she usually felt better, even if it didn't change anything.

"Rhea," she started. "A couple times now she's mentioned Alice."

"Yeah?"

"I don't understand."

"Understand what?"

"How she could possibly *know* about Alice. How is it possible when Alice is dead?"

"Alice isn't dead, sweetheart. Her body is gone, but I'm sure she lives on somewhere."

"Like heaven?" Bray asked, skeptical.

"I don't know. But I believe we're all energy, and that energy continues way beyond our bodily form."

"I'm not sure I believe that."

"You believe once we die, that's the end?"

"Yes." Bray nodded. She didn't necessarily like the feeling of it, but how could anything else be true?

"Ready for another story?" Emily asked.

The rain had slowed to a drizzle. The sky fell into a cool indigo as night approached.

"Let's go for a walk," Emily said, standing up.

The two of them stepped down from the porch steps into the wet grass. Bray felt the drizzle on her head and shoulders. It calmed her.

"Remember how I told you my dad wasn't around much when I was a kid?"

"Yes."

"He died when I was thirty-four. I'd been living here only a month or so. Virgil and I had barely spoken at that point. It was 2028 and we were all busy getting the house ready, grieving the loss of President Walker. . .how we had to go on the run so quickly because activists were being arrested.

"One night Virgil gave me Reiki. I wasn't a practitioner yet. He taught me later. He didn't know much about me. I told him nothing about my past. Back then I still carried some shame about my drug abuse.

"After he finished giving me Reiki, he said someone else had been in the room, beside me. He described this man with a bald head and white beard. He said, 'the guy looked just like you.' And I knew then that he was referring to my father.

"Virgil was crying as he spoke. He told me that my dad kept repeating over and over how sorry he was, that he *did* love me. At first I didn't believe what Virgil was saying. It defied everything I'd believed about death at the time. Virgil told me he was pretty sure my dad had passed away. How else would he have visited me and said the exact things I always wanted him to say in his living years?" Emily stopped. She turned and looked down into Bray's eyes.

"Whether you believe it or not, Bray, our loved ones can connect with us even beyond the limitation of humanity. You don't have to believe something for it to be true."

Bray took a deep breath as a line of gooseflesh ran along her arms. It was getting cooler outside, but it was Emily's story that made her shiver. She wasn't sure *why* she didn't believe in life after death. Maybe because that would mean she'd have to believe in God.

"So do you believe in God?" Bray asked. She feared the answer was yes.

"Before recovery, I didn't believe in anything. And for a long time I was very resistant to the idea that there was some entity that loved me, just as I was. My parents didn't seem to love me, so why would some god?"

Emily turned and proceeded to walk again. Bray followed her around the garden as the touch of soft rain landed on her face, leaving her feeling cleansed.

"But then my sponsor asked me this question: 'can you believe in something better. . .something better than what's happening right now?' And at first, I couldn't. But I chose to. I *pretended* to believe. Slowly, I began to believe I was loved, even after all I'd done, *because* of what I'd done. The program showed me there was something better, far better than drugs. And that something was a deeper, spiritual connection."

"How do you define God?" Bray asked.

"I try not to. I'm not sure it can be defined."

Bray remained silent. She appreciated how Emily simplified belief as something undefinable, but Bray still wasn't sure she believed.

"If there is some kind of God, then what about all the horrible things that happen. . .especially to animals? That's what I have the biggest problem with."

"I get that. There are no easy answers. For me, God isn't found out there somewhere. It is a part of me. I believe that higher power, higher intelligence, connects us all. I believe it wants us all to be in peace and do no harm—"

"Yet the harm continues," Bray said plainly.

"Yes, it does. I'm not sure it's God's role to make suffering vanish. We all have our own motives, personalities, values, reasons for what we do. We are all unique, so it's impossible for us all to get along and reduce harm when not all of us want the same things. I think *we* are the ones who are supposed to reduce that suffering, not God."

"Then what's the point of believing in a God?" Bray asked.

"Wow. . .you're good." Emily looked at Bray and smiled. "Anyone ever tell you you'd make a great politician?"

"My dad would *love* to hear that," Bray replied, rolling her eyes.

"Let's come back to this another time. It's getting late."

Above them the rain clouds cleared as night approached. Bray thought about what Emily said. She still had a hard time believing that if there was something as powerful as the existence of a God, that it wouldn't use that power to end suffering. It didn't make sense. And if humans could have had that power, wouldn't they have done it by now? People *like* Emily, Trevor, Ethan? They had tried. Bray didn't know their whole story, but she knew enough to feel right in her assertion that if there was a God, the plan to end factory farming back in the 2020s would've been successful.

But it hadn't been.

And so there was no God.

Chapter Thirteen

Bray

For the past few nights since Bray had begun meditating, her sleep had significantly improved. The pain she experienced due to whatever testing was being done on Rhea and the other cows had mostly subsided. As in previous nights, on this night she shut off the light and, within minutes, she was out.

This night, the nightmares did not come. Instead, for the longest time, until the very earliest of dawn when the night was at its darkest, the blank slate behind her eyes began to change.

A bright, golden light approached as if through a tunnel. It got closer and closer and opened out, at first into a rolling, shifting liquid like the golden light she imagined the other night when Emily led her through the chakra meditation.

The light came to her like a revelation, calm, true and complete. It transitioned into an image of two rolling hills of deep, green grass beneath a pale blue sky. And in the distance, a barn stood alone.

The golden light took shape into a sun and lifted up into the sky until it became the sun.

Bray recognized the place immediately. She used to imagine this space whenever she connected with Alice. It was a dream space where she felt safe, where she wished to spend all of her days.

She sat on a hill overlooking a broad field of wildflowers. She was alone. A fresh, cool breeze grazed her face. She closed her eyes and felt it. When she opened them, she saw movement in the wildflowers down below. At first it was only a few flowers, so she thought the movement was caused by the breeze. A trail was being cut through the wildflowers, as if someone were walking and she couldn't see who it was.

When Bray saw the face, her mouth dropped in surprise and confusion. Little tears formed in the corners of her eyes.

It was the head of a pink pig, ears perked and lively, eyes looking up to her from a distance. Bray's heart lifted.

"Alice?" she whispered.

Bray stood up and ran down the hill, her heart lifting with each drop her body felt as she raced through the grass.

Alice came walking out of the wildflower field, her body fully revealed. Bray ran up to her, dropped down to her knees, and hugged Alice around the neck. It felt so relieving to be in Alice's presence again.

"Is it really you, Alice?" she asked, her hands petting Alice on the head, her eyes noticing how Alice was fully intact. No clipped ears. No sores or cuts. She looked so. . .healthy.

"Yes," Alice replied.

"How is this possible? I mean, I'm obviously dreaming, but—"

"Emily was right," Alice said. She moved to sit on her bottom.

"What?" Bray asked, not yet able to comprehend what was happening. She remained where she was, fearing that if she moved, Alice might disappear.

"About life after death. We never really die, Bray. We keep going. In your human form you just can't see us anymore."

Bray sat there, dumbfounded.

Suddenly, the wildflowers began to wave behind Alice. Bray watched as one sow after another appeared, walking into the clearing and sitting beside Alice. Bray didn't bother counting how many there were. The number didn't matter. The sheer visual of seeing each one step out into Bray's presence, each one looking so young, vivacious, beautiful, nearly broke Bray's heart completely open. Tears flowed down her cheeks. It hardly registered that she was crying.

"You saved all of us," Alice said.

Bray looked over the line of sows spread before her. They all looked back at her. She was speechless. In her chest she felt an openness, a sense that all of this was a connection. It felt weird, jarring, and so, so palpable.

"Now we need you to save the others," Alice continued.

Bray's shoulders dropped. Stunned, she replied very matter-of-factly.

"You mean Rhea?"

"Yes. She and the other cows need your help."

Bray couldn't believe it. Here she was in some dream state, being visited by Alice, who was asking her to help Rhea.

Which meant Rhea really *was* communicating with Alice.

"Can you help me understand something?" Bray asked.

"What's that, my dear?" Alice replied. Her head leaned sideways as a human might do when curious.

"How are you and Rhea able to connect?"

"It's kind of like how Emily said: everything is energy. Beyond that, it's not explainable."

"How do you know what Emily said?" Bray asked. She continued to feel perplexed by all of this.

"How come it is so important for you to have all the answers?" Alice asked.

All her life Bray hadn't had answers and look where it had taken her. In and out of a psych ward without enough knowledge to prove her parents wrong. They'd been convinced that she was mentally ill, and it hadn't helped that a psychiatrist diagnosed her with schizophrenia. When Alice's life was in danger, she had gotten close to Alice yet not close enough to really save her.

"When will you realize. . ." Alice said. "That

what you did for us was enough?"

"How was it enough when I still. . .I lost you," Bray said, feeling sadness arise in her chest.

"You didn't lose me. You didn't lose any of us. You *found* us. You rescued us from a horrible death we never had to experience. What you did. . .it isn't something anyone else could have done for us. That's why I asked Rhea to reach out to you.

"From beyond death, I see everything. I see you spending time with new friends. I see the animals that still suffer. I understand that you have missed me. My life does not continue without, at times, also missing you. But you are still alive. You have an opportunity to help someone. Why will you not take it?"

"Because I'm afraid," Bray admitted.

"That is okay. *Be* afraid, if you have to. Don't wait for all the answers before deciding to help them. They don't have much time. I fear that if you do not help them, no one else will."

"What if I mess up?"

"You might, my dear. You very well might. Doing the right thing isn't about the outcome. It isn't about winning or losing. The success is in the try. You have to try. Trust me when I say that if you'd just try, the belief that you need will follow."

With that, Alice disappeared. One by one, the other sows did the same. Bray found herself sitting alone amongst the wildflowers, stunned. The wildflower field, the hills around her, and the barn, the sky, all began to darken until there was nothing remaining.

Shortly thereafter, she awoke.

Chapter Fourteen

Bertan

Bertan lay in bed, his head propped up against his pillow, which pressed into the wall behind him. He stared out the window. It was daylight. What time was it? His phone was charging on the tray table. When he went for it, he noticed the book sitting beneath it. First he checked the time: 11:45 a.m. He should be asleep, but he was far from tired. He felt uneasy. He was awaiting the last call from Carmen before she and Gabriella left for Honduras.

Unplugging the phone from its charger, he flipped on the sound and set the phone down beside him. The book held his gaze. He picked it up. A photo had been holding his place about three fourths of the way through. Pressing the book down on his chest so that the chapter waiting for him lay open against the rise and fall of his body, Bertan brought the photo up close. He looked into the face of his father. The man was not smiling. He appeared to be thinking. Not present. Bertan idolized his father. How passionate he was about standing up for what was right, even when it meant using violence to do so.

Bertan's gaze drifted off, out the window, except he wasn't looking there at all. What he saw instead was a time when he was a child. He was hiding in the bathroom with the door propped open, listening to his parents argue.

"I don't understand why it has to be you," his mother, Fran, said.

"No one will do it if I don't step up," Menor replied. *"I tried. I tried asking several men to help. They say they want to help, but none of them are taking the lead. I wait and wait and meanwhile I'm stuck in this cycle of men killing*

more men. Hondurans killing other Hondurans. And for what? For land?"

There was a pause. Menor continued.

"Our country has been in this position for ages. . .the rich taking land from the poor. I'm sorry my love, but I can't live and also stand by and watch it happen."

"But we have a son. We have a family to care for. How am I supposed to do that if you're not here?"

The memory stopped there. Bertan tried to recall more, but he couldn't. It did cause him to pause and reconsider Carmen, how she would feel with him gone and having to raise Gabriella on her own. But she had her cousin, who had a family, too. A large, beautiful family. More than Bertan could ever give Carmen on his own.

His phone vibrated against his arm. Bertan lifted it up and answered.

"The *coyotaje* will be here soon," Carmen started. "We only have a few minutes."

"Are you all ready to go?" Bertan was not really sure how to speak to his wife anymore.

"Yes. I'm nervous."

"Don't be nervous. We can trust Ruben. I know he found a good person for you. There's no way I'd allow you to go home if I couldn't ensure you both got there safely."

"Thanks, love."

Bertan's heart warmed at the sound of her voice. He was still holding on to the photo of his father. He picked up the book, slid the photo back inside, and closed the book, returning it to the tray table. His eyes remained set on it, feeling called to take action the way his father had.

"What are you going to do, Bertan?" Carmen asked suddenly. The question seemed so strange to him. He didn't know how to respond.

"What am I going to do?"

"When we're gone? After we leave and go back home. What exactly are you going to do up there, if you're not going to try to come back home?"

Bertan exhaled in frustration.

"Love, I am trying to get back home. That's what you don't realize," he said, sitting up quickly and hanging over the edge of the bed. "Helping Ruben end S-Corp is my way of getting back home. Getting back home for good. Don't you see?"

"No, I don't."

The sound of Gabriella's voice came through the phone. She was calling for Carmen in the background.

"The car is here," Carmen said. "Here, say goodbye to your daughter."

Bertan waited, his chest tightening with anxiety as he realized he was letting his family leave, this time to move farther away from him. He feared the possibility that he might never hear from them, but shook it off.

"Hi Papá." Gabriella's voice sounded chipper. It sounded uplifted the way he remembered the mountains in his home town.

"My daughter, how are you?"

"Good. Why aren't you coming with us?"

Bertan's shoulders dropped. So did his heart. His lungs halted for a moment. How could he explain this to his daughter?

"I have some more work to do, my love. Then I will get home as fast as I can. I miss you so much," he replied, tears suddenly hitting his eyes. He clenched his fist against his mouth so she wouldn't hear him cry.

"Mamá is calling. We have to go," Gabriella said.

"Okay. I love you. So, so much."

"Love you too, Papá."

The call ended. He'd hoped for another chance to say goodbye to Carmen. Bertan stared at the phone, half expecting it to ring again, or at least for a text to come through. But there was nothing. The silence gave him a very clear answer as to how his wife felt about his decision. He let out an exhale and tossed the phone onto the bed. Lying back and resting on the mattress, he rubbed his face with his hands. If only Carmen could understand why he was doing this. If only she knew how it felt to be stuck between his family's wishes and his own need to follow through on his mission. She would never understand that to return to Honduras without seeing to Medina's end would be the same as returning to Medina itself.

Chapter Fifteen

Bray

That entire next day Bray spent in quiet. She meditated with Emily, but didn't have much to say. Everything Alice had told her in that dream played on repeat in her mind, through her soul.

If you do not help them. . .no one else will.

It played again and again and again, rolling over in her mind while bringing her ever closer to realization. She was coming to accept that maybe she wasn't ever going to get all the answers she thought she needed in order to move forward. Rhea had remained quiet. Bray sensed she was being given time to reflect, to come around to what she already knew deep down inside: she was going to have to try to save those cows. She had no idea how.

When night came quickly and Bray was no closer to a decision, she began to fear that her mind would refuse to act without more clarity. It was as though her mind and soul were in two very different places. She was walking through the grass in the side yard where Ethan, Kage and Lana sat around a fire. As she walked, her mind seemed to hang low, as if in the grass, seeking answers. She approached an empty log between Ethan and Kage, and she sat down. The fire lit up her face, warmed her cheeks. Its liveliness woke a spark in her soul that, for the very first time since Alice's death, made her *want* to act. She couldn't explain it, and for once she didn't need to.

"Welcome to our little fire gathering," Kage started, turning to Bray. His face appeared more effeminate as the fire's orange glow hit his cheeks.

"What's the occasion?" Bray asked.

"We do this once a month or so, just to sit

and talk," Ethan replied. "Used to be only Kage and me, but we wanted you and Lana to join us."

"My friends and I never got to have fires back in Medicine Bow," Lana said. "Too afraid we'd expose ourselves."

Ethan nodded.

Everyone went quiet. The fire calmed. Bray watched the flames dance and flip around in the black night. All around them the stars came near as if wishing for the fire's warmth. Bray wanted to say something. She wanted to tell them what she'd been thinking, but she stalled.

The other three talked as she remained quiet. They talked about plans for the garden. Bray thought about plans for Rhea. Once again, she worried that she had no idea where these cows were located.

We can show you," Rhea whispered.

Okay. But Bray couldn't go anywhere on her own. She'd need help.

Bray glanced up at Lana and over to Kage. Who here would go for a plan that would risk getting them all caught? Inevitably that was the risk, at the least. If she left here, her mother would probably find her. Kage and Lana could get locked away. And this place might be found. Bray wasn't sure she could forgive herself if any of these things happened. It was no wonder she had avoided taking action. Living here in hiding was so simple. So safe. She didn't want that to end.

"Bray, you're so quiet over there," Lana said.

Bray perked up. She glanced over the fire at Lana, whose face glowed and radiated and made Bray feel more nervous than she already was.

"What's on your mind, child?" Ethan asked, turning to her as if he knew. In his eye a twinkle of gray mixed with gold light gave her a comforting invite to speak.

"I don't know where to start," she admitted.

"Start anywhere," Ethan suggested.

The three of them had gone quiet, waiting for Bray to speak.

"There are some animals that need my help."

"What's that?" Ethan asked.

Bray turned her gaze down to the embers of the fire. She watched the wood burn with hot, red sparks. . .a heat so immense it hit her face. Unavoidable, it was. The same way she knew her future was unavoidable.

"There's this. . .cow. Her name is Rhea. She reached out to me days ago. She and six other cows are being experimented on. I've been receiving visions, nightmares. I *feel* what's happening to her," Bray said, pausing to think of what to say next.

"What's happening to them?" Ethan asked.

"It's S-Corp. They're doing some kind of new testing on these animals, called chimeras. They've been using them for human organ transplants. The only reason I know this is because of. . .what Rhea told me," Bray explained, hesitating at the end when she mentioned Rhea.

"You mean a cow told you this?" Kage asked, leaning forward and picking at the fire with a stick.

"Yes," Bray said. "She says that human DNA from the experiments somehow got into their brains. Now they have this human-like awareness."

"Unreal," Ethan spoke. "S-Corp and other research institutions had been doing this kind of work way back in the early twenty-teens, maybe even before that. Back then they suspected there was a chance that animals could become aware as a result of these tests, but they continued regardless."

"Are you saying these cows can think and understand like humans can? Like. . .beyond sentience?" Kage asked, dropping the stick on the ground.

"Yes. Rhea can read my thoughts. She understands our language. She's aware of her own existence and that she's a cow. And S-Corp has found out about it. The cows will be going to slaughter soon. Sounds like it's a cover up and the scientists are afraid of getting caught for continuing to do these experiments."

"How soon?" Kage asked.

Bray closed her eyes and asked Rhea. The answer came in seconds.

"Forty-five days."

"That's not much time." Kage replied.

"You're not proposing we do something, are you?" Lana asked, eying Kage.

"I'm not expecting anyone to help," Bray spoke up. "But helping them will be impossible on my own."

"I'm in," Kage said. He looked at Bray and nodded.

Bray felt a bit relieved. At least one person was willing to help. But what of the others?

"My days of running a revolution are over," Ethan said. "But that doesn't mean I can't help you with yours."

Bray looked to Lana. Lana did not respond. She only looked off into the night. Bray knew Lana had lost so much already, that maybe she wasn't so willing to be the next activist to disappear.

Bray did not blame her.

"The question is: how are we going to do this without getting caught?" Kage asked.

"You can't possibly save those cows," Lana said. "We have nowhere to house them."

"Sadly, she's right about that," Ethan said.

"I can't not help them at this point," Bray said. "Even if we could just get them out of there, let them die in peace. The way I did with Alice."

Bray remembered her dream of Alice the night before, and smiled. Although she was beginning to see how she had still helped Alice even if it meant Alice had to die, she couldn't help but look down the road, at the bigger picture. She'd help these cows, then what? There would always be more animals to help. More and more and more. And how could she choose to save a few animals but then allow billions of others to pass on through violence?

She was only seventeen. Could she live an entire lifetime saving animals like this while being aware of all the ones she could not save?

"If there are others in need of saving, save them, too," Rhea said.

"It's not that simple anymore," Lana said as if she'd heard Rhea speak. "Even getting them out from under S-Corp so they can die in peace isn't something we can just do without risking everyone involved."

And that was that. The fire died down. Night grew deep and long. Ethan eventually trailed on inside to bed. Lana followed, leaving Bray and Kage to sit in silence beneath the stars until the flames burned out.

Chapter Sixteen

Bray

The next morning as Bray sat in meditation, an idea came to her. Initially, she tossed it aside because it made no sense. But it returned and would not leave her. It came from deep down in her gut, and it felt true.

The idea was to speak with Trevor. She had no desire to, but Emily had been teaching her to listen to her instinct, had said instinct was never wrong.

After lunch, Bray looked over at Trevor sitting at the dining room table. He was reading that book again. From here she could see the title, *Eleanor Oliphant is Completely Fine* by Gail Honeyman. It looked intriguing and reminded Bray ever so briefly of her dream to be a writer.

She wasn't so sure that dream would ever come true.

"Can we talk?" she asked him.

"Sure," he replied, shutting the book. "Let's go out on the porch."

Bray stood up and followed Trevor outside. She was nervous. She had no idea why it was important to talk to him, so she wasn't sure what she'd say.

They walked outside and she sat next to him on the swing. She feared he might ask her how she was feeling, that he'd assume she wanted to talk about her mental health since he was an "expert" on the subject.

That's when it hit her: Trevor used to be a social worker. He knew how people's minds worked, or didn't. She knew what to ask him.

"Is there any way to get people to stop eating animals?"

Trevor turned to face her. He looked

interested.

"I doubt it," he replied.

"How come?"

"Lots of reasons. People don't want to stop eating animals." He paused, looked out at the yard. "Back when I was an animal rights activist, I'd have these conversations with people. My friends. Some of my family members. Some of them even knew how badly animals were treated on factory farms and still chose to eat them. Cognitive dissonance. It's a thing."

"What's that mean?"

"People may be fully aware of what happens to animals in factory farms, yet they don't want to give up meat. This might make them feel sad or uncomfortable, but not uncomfortable enough to change."

Bray thought for a moment, thought about her ability to connect with Rhea, how she could *feel* what Rhea felt.

"What if people could actually be *shown* what happens to animals?" She asked.

"That certainly helps. We used to do that. . .hold showings of documentaries, stand out on street corners with laptops that showed videos of animals inside factory farms. Many people who stopped and watched were shocked. They definitely reconsidered. Some people walked on by. Most people prefer to stay in denial, I think."

Trevor crossed his arms and sat back against the swing. His eyes glared down at the porch floor, as if he were somewhere else. Remembering, perhaps.

"Why?" Bray asked. She suddenly found herself more interested in his past, where he'd been, what he'd been through. Despite her not liking him for badgering her about her wellbeing, she did appreciate that he was once an activist. That he had tried to stop people from eating animals. It was the only thing that connected them.

"It's just easier." Trevor shrugged. "You can't blame people for not wanting to change their diets to stop animals from suffering."

"Seems pretty simple to me," Bray replied.

"Until people see animals as individuals, I'm not sure they'll ever change. You certainly can't force it, because people in our country are strong individualists. It's all about the individual, not what's best for the greater good. That's why climate change will only get worse."

Bray grew increasingly somber as they spoke. Trevor seemed to have extensive knowledge on how this stuff worked, how to approach people about animal rights. And it sounded altogether impossible to get people to change. Would there be no way to end animal suffering?

"What if people could more directly experience animals' feelings. . .like the pain they feel?" she asked, not wanting to give up.

"Again, I believe it would help if they could. But since that's not possible, there's no way of knowing what it would do. I have to think it would cause plenty of people to reconsider. Otherwise, people are pretty much assholes." Trevor paused. "Why all the questions?"

"Just curious," Bray replied. Suddenly an array of deep thoughts bounced around in her mind. She had expected to feel more hopeful, like there was possibility, after speaking with Trevor.

"I have to go to the bathroom," Bray said, lying so she could go be alone. She needed to think.

"All righty. Nice talking to you."

Bray nodded to him, stood up, and went back inside.

She climbed the stairs to her room and shut the door. Bray sat down on her bed and closed her eyes. She did some breathwork to clear her mind. As Emily had instructed many times, she sat and waited for her instinct to tell her what to do.

Certain thoughts arose: *how can I get people*

to feel what the animals feel?

And: *if only they could connect with animals like I can.*

And: *if they only knew how Rhea felt, I bet they'd stop eating animals. If they really knew what S-Corp was doing. . .these tests. . .how can I get them to know?*

Eventually, the thoughts calmed. Her mind emptied and went dark. In that darkness a vision arose, this of Rhea and the other cows in the S-Corp facility, a scientist in a flannel shirt with a long beard, sitting at a pair of laptops. Bray's vision rose up to the ceiling and drifted down, turning to look at the screens.

"The pigs tried to run. . ." Rhea spoke.

"What?" Bray asked, confused.

As Rhea continued to speak, Bray's vision honed in on the laptop screens.

"There were pigs here. They had awareness, too. One night, they managed to escape. . ." Rhea continued.

Meanwhile, on the screen, Bray saw an email. It was from her mother. She was requesting a draft of proof from the scientist that the cows indeed had humanlike consciousness.

So her mother knew.

"The pigs were caught by the humans. . .and taken to death," Rhea finished.

While immersed in the shock of seeing her mother's email, realizing that her mother was involved in this horrible, secret testing, Bray remembered the vision she had of the pigs running through a corridor, being gassed and taken away. She responded to Rhea.

"I saw the pigs in a vision. I wasn't sure where it came from."

"It came from me," Rhea replied. *"I wanted you to see. We considered escaping, too, but once that happened to the pigs, we reached out to you instead. For help."*

Bray did not respond. Instead, she watched the laptop screen fade further from her view, as if she were being pulled back up to the ceiling where the darkness there overcame her sight.

The vision stopped. Everything went dark again. Bray's forearm began to itch. At first she ignored it and thought about that email she had just seen, thought about what Rhea said about those pigs. How they were able to *escape.* Unfortunate that it led to their demise. She grew sad.

And her forearm wouldn't stop itching.

Bray scratched at her skin while observing the source of the itch. The scar where she'd cut out that Embedicare implant after escaping the psych ward back in Denver. The implant her mother had forced her to get so they could keep track of her. She felt relieved that she'd cut it out. Her mother would've traced her here, and then what?

"That's it!" she whispered.

Bray got up from bed and left the bedroom, searching the house for Kage.

She was certain she'd found a way.

#

As Bray hurried downstairs, evening was already approaching. The sun was not visible through the windows. She must have missed dinner. How differently time moved when she was having visions. It never ceased to confuse her, how hours would pass when it only felt like minutes to her. Losing time.

She passed through the dining room and entered the kitchen. There, Dennis was drying the last of the dinner dishes.

"Have you seen Kage?" Bray asked him, a sense of urgency pumping in her chest. She wasn't bothered by missing dinner. She was bothered by the fact that time was slipping and she thought she might have a plan. She couldn't lose any more time.

Dennis stopped wiping the plate in his hand and motioned out the kitchen door with his head.

"He's out there somewhere."

Bray went outside, realizing as her feet touched the grass that she wasn't wearing any shoes or socks. She felt the warm grass and earth pressing into her skin. She looked around for Kage.

A clinking sound came from the basement. The doors were open and a light jumped up into the quickly fading evening. Bray stepped carefully down into the room, where the brick walls were hidden by tall, metal shelves full of tools.

Kage stood at a workbench across from Bray, his back to her. He was humming.

Bray walked up to him. "Can I talk to you about something?"

"Shoot," Kage replied as he put down a tool Bray did not know the name of. There was a piece of equipment sitting atop the workbench that looked as though it came from Trevor's Jeep.

"Remember our talk last night about helping animals?" Bray started.

"Yep." He leaned against the bench.

"I think I may know a way we can help them, but I have no idea how to pull it off."

"What's that?" Kage asked. He grabbed a towel that sat beside the piece of equipment and started wiping his hands.

"You know about those Embedicare implants?" she asked, feeling increasingly hurried in her desire to tell him her idea.

"Those things they stick under your skin so they can track you?" Kage snickered.

"Well, they can also be used for communication, like texts and alerts," Bray said, still piecing all of this together as she spoke it aloud to Kage.

"Fancy."

"And. . .a lot of people, like my dad. . .have these special 4D ones that let you *feel* and experience whatever you're watching on TV or whenever news comes up."

"Why would anyone want that?" Kage tossed the towel at the wall.

"I have no idea," Bray replied, grinning. "But I was thinking. . .if we could somehow get people to see. . .or even *feel* what's happening to these animals, imagine how that could change things."

"It would probably change a lot," Kage replied, his eyebrows raising. "But how would we even do that?"

"With the implants," Bray said, her passion increasing with every passing moment.

"But how?" Kage repeated.

"I don't know," Bray admitted. "Maybe if we could somehow link these cows to people, like through the implants, then maybe they'd see."

Kage stood up and approached Bray.

"I'm with you one hundred percent. But we just need a plan, that's all."

Bray took a deep breath and nodded. Kage was right, of course. She was hoping he'd be able to help come up with that plan. It seemed that he had just as few answers as she.

"We'd need a way to get to the cows," Kage continued. He started pacing back and forth. "That requires getting past their security, their drones. And then there's the matter of figuring out the implants. We'd need a lot of help, and I don't know who that would be."

Bray thought for a moment, then something clicked.

"I know someone who might be able to help. We just need to find him first."

Chapter Seventeen

Bertan

Bertan stared at himself in the mirror. It may have been more accurate to say he was standing in the bathroom, facing the mirror. His mind was somewhere else. A complete lapse had occurred and so he had no idea how long he'd been standing there.

He blinked his eyes. He looked more closely at himself. He was wearing one of his white undershirts. A half-shadow of black beard covered his face.

Ruben had taught him some breathwork for times like this. He closed his eyes and breathed in to a count of seven, held the breath, exhaled. He repeated it two more times. Ruben told him to use his five senses to bring himself back to the present. He didn't quite understand all of it, but when he tried it, it seemed to work.

Turning, his bare foot hit against something hard on the rug. He looked down. It was his phone. He bent down and picked it up, wondering how it had ended up there.

He stood up and flipped off the bathroom light. Stepping out into the sleeping area, Bertan looked around. The six other bunks in the room were empty. Where had the others gone?

Oh, that was right.

They'd gone down to the local bar. This was the tradition every evening when they got off work, which meant it was about time for his night shift to begin.

A vibrating noise came from the floor below one of the bunks. Someone had left their phone. Bertan's hazy memory began to recall something. Something to do with a phone. Or a phone call.

Bertan walked over to the window above the kitchen sink and looked outside. The only thing to see was a road without cars. Miles of nothing.

Bertan moved away from the window. He turned and looked back at the bathroom.

"What the hell was I doing?" he whispered to himself.

These brief lapses in time were still a common occurrence, and in the last. . .week or maybe two weeks. . .they had gotten worse again. When he'd worked as a knocker, he had lost entire hours, sometimes an entire day. Ruben said it was because of the PTSD.

He tossed his phone on his unmade bed. Grabbing a black security uniform that had been lying on the floor, he put it on. The last one he'd burned to a crisp. He wished he could do the same with this one.

He stared at his phone on the bed. He concentrated. His eyes narrowed.

Picking up the phone, he checked the call history. Scrolling through, he found a list of back and forths with Ruben. The last call with his wife, Carmen, was. . .yesterday? Could that have been right? He swore he spoke to her a moment ago. His shoulders dropped. Dismayed, he sat down on the bed. A tan tray table stood open beside him. On it, his wedding photos of Carmen lay atop the one photo he had of his father. These were the only photos he brought with him when he left Honduras.

That was it.

He remembered.

Or, more sadly, he remembered *again*. . .

Carmen left.

#

And then. . .something happened within Bertan's brain, which simply. . .shut off. His mind escaped him. It might've been more accurate to say his mind left the building, faded into the background, took a break. When that happened, another part took over. A something else. Something beyond memory, below memory, outside memory's door. Something memory was not and never could be. Something *envious* of memory. An untamed beast, something entirely unconscious and entirely alive. . .

Chapter Eighteen

Bray

Bray and Kage left before breakfast. Kage had told Trevor they were going on a supply run, although Bray sensed he did not feel good about lying to his uncle. He'd done it once before and it had led nowhere pleasant. But they had to keep things between them, at least for now, until they could find out if this plan was actually feasible.

"No sense getting the household in a tizzy over nothing," Kage had said.

They traveled alongside WY-120, close enough to remain parallel to the road, but not close enough to be seen. The motorcycle bumped along miles and miles of dry earth and rock. All around them were never-ending views of short, yellow-green grasses where sage plants dotted the land in a dull, grayish-green color. Occasional, brown foothills rolled into view to greet them and sank back down into the ground. The sky was open, clear, and wild. Not one car passed through, reminding Bray of the reality of this world out here. All she'd ever known was that citizens only lived in large cities, and all this empty land rumored to be poisoned by some "terrorist attack" sat barren and waiting for humans to use it as it was intended.

Long gone were the days when suburbs gave people the chance to feel a little closer to nature, days when cities had parks with fresh ponds and lakes to swim and play in. She never quite got the answer as to whether things were as bad in the east as they were here in Wyoming, but maybe it was best to pretend things were better, at least, somewhere.

After an hour or so, the land transitioned

slowly, became crowded with trees, more foothills in the distance. Running alongside them was a twisting river, still with all its natural glory and rushing waters.

"There's a river!" Bray shouted into Kage's ear from her seat behind him.

"We're in Montana!" Kage yelled back.

"They still have water here!"

"Yep!" Kage yelled, speeding forward along the dirt road as if to race the slow-moving rapids of the river until it pulled away further into the land.

It took another thirty minutes to arrive in Red Lodge. In the distance, the mountains rose, becoming more visible, making Bray want to go to them and stay awhile, maybe never leave. Her gaze was drawn to the sky, so crisp and unbothered by anything happening below it.

Groups of houses came into view. Kage slowed the bike. Bray's anxiety heightened, afraid someone would see them and inform the Marshals. After she and Elliott had escaped from Marshals at a checkpoint back at the Colorado/Wyoming border and encountered ferocious dogs who'd killed a Marshal right in front of them, Bray was paranoid that she'd somehow be recognized as a criminal and be arrested. She would not have put it past her mother to get Marshals involved in bringing her back home.

But upon closer view, the houses were abandoned. Bray had seen abandoned houses in Casper back when she was on her quest to save Alice from the slaughterhouse. Here was another suburb left behind during the 2030 Migration. She hoped it wasn't entirely abandoned.

Turning onto one of the streets, Kage continued to drive the bike at a hesitant pace. House after house stood empty. Yards were empty. Streets were void of cars. Bray took it all in, but she didn't want to. It was quite sad. She figured all these people had been lied to. According to Kage, Trevor and the others, citizens had been told the soil was tainted because "terrorists" had leaked chemicals into the nation's water supply, and as a result they'd had to leave behind homes they would probably never see again. And now all that remained were square structures with siding falling off and paint peeling. Structures that could no longer be called homes without the humans needed to do so.

"Where we going?" Kage yelled back over his shoulder.

"A local store? Where I can ask some questions," she replied, not really sure herself.

Kage sped along the empty streets, turning down one and another, until they came upon a line of old, destitute businesses that had long ago shut their doors to the world. One building had a sign on the top, in all caps: *GENERAL STORE.*

Kage pulled up and parked outside the store.

"I'm going to wait here while you ask around," he said. Bray climbed off the bike. The store was small, squished between two buildings twice its size, both with apartments on the top levels where glass had been broken out. A smell of decaying wood made her cringe. When she turned to look closer at the store, she noticed that its glass front was mirrored. She could only see herself, Kage, the bike, and the deserted street behind them.

Odd.

Bray immediately felt unease. Her chest tightened as she approached the door. From where she stood, the place looked empty. Perhaps it was the mirrored glass that threw her off. She saw herself looking at the image of her body and it was unnerving. She really had lost a lot of weight. She did not enjoy seeing herself in any mirror, so she quickly opened the door, taking a deep breath as she entered the store.

Inside, a hardwood floor ran along the narrow space of the store. Along the walls were shelves, all empty. The place was longer than it was wide. Bray walked to the back of the store where a black door stood closed.

"Hello?" she called out.

Creepy crawlies ran along her skin, chasing her discomfort up her arms and along her shoulders.

"Who are you?" A male voice replied from a speaker in the ceiling. Bray replied, startled.

"I'm looking for a friend. . .Elliott. . ." She stopped. Was it a good idea to mention his last name? She didn't know.

"First tell me who you are." The voice clicked on and off.

Bray didn't want to give out her name. Especially her last name since her parents were public figures. She didn't know this person. She clenched her jaw.

"My name is Bray," she said. "I'm a friend. I came here for help."

The voice did not reply. Bray waited and waited. She walked the aisles, wondering if she'd ever find Elliott.

No one ever came out. Discouraged, Bray returned outside to Kage, who was leaning against his motorcycle, arms crossed.

"Anything?" he asked.

Bray shook her head.

"I don't know how else to find him," she said.

"And you're sure he's here?"

"Most likely."

A group of older men approached from beyond the bike. Three of them. Each was tall, thin. One wore a tan western hat. They walked past Bray and Kage, exchanging glances. One of them nodded to Kage. Bray wasn't sure whether to be anxious, but she sensed no danger from them.

"Excuse me," she said, walking up to the man in the hat.

The men stopped and looked at her.

"I'm looking for a friend," she said. "Name is Elliott."

The western hat man looked at her and then to the others beside him.

"Don't know anyone here by that name, but people around here don't go by legal names. Does he got a nickname?"

Bray thought for a moment. She remembered that Elliott was arrested once for hacking. He told her he used an alias for his hacking so there'd be no leads back to him, yet he still got caught. She was pretty sure he'd told her the name. . .

"I'm headed inside," one of the men said.

"Me, too," said another.

The two men disappeared into the store. Bray grew increasingly worried that she'd never find Elliott. As the door shut, the sun hit the glass at an angle and flashed a harsh light in Bray's eyes. Like lightening.

"Serge!" she blurted out, remembering.

Western hat man's eyes lit up.

"A few blocks down. . .on Adams Avenue." He pointed down the road.

Bray's heart leapt. She thanked the man and turned to Kage.

"Found him," she said, winking. "Adams Avenue."

Kage started the bike. Bray got back on behind him, realizing how raw her bottom felt after riding for the last two hours.

Kage turned the bike down Adams Avenue. A series of houses came into view. At least, they looked like houses. As the bike slowed, Bray could see that the buildings had beautiful siding, some white, some blue or gray, all two-level with mini porches at their entrances and square, glass windows on the bottom and top levels. Bray guessed each building contained two or four apartments. They looked quite charming. Not really Elliott's style, but she smiled at the thought of finally getting to see her friend again.

Bray and Kage walked up to a set of concrete stairs that stopped at a white door. Bray tried the door, but it was locked. Installed into the brick wall was a keypad.

Of course there were no buzzers or even a doorbell. Bray assumed that was for safety, too. So how would she get to Elliott? They could sit out here and wait, but they didn't have that kind of time.

"Let's go around back," Bray said to Kage.

They left the bike and followed a concrete sidewalk over to a driveway that led down a slight decline. A truck sat parked outside side-by-side garages beneath the building.

Bray observed the back of the building. Didn't look much different from the front. All of the windows were closed, and shades were drawn. Looking around, Bray found some pebbles and began throwing them at each window.

Kage helped.

From the two top windows there was no response. A head popped up from the bottom right. The person flipped off Bray and shouted something she couldn't comprehend from this distance, so she stopped.

"Maybe it's one of the other buildings," Bray said. She was beginning to feel she might not find Elliott.

They walked over to the next building, threw more rocks at windows. Angered more people. One of them was quick to show her a handgun. She and Kage ducked in response and fled, running back to the bike.

"No pun intended. . .but shoot," Kage said, crossing his arms. "You really sure he's here?"

"I'm not sure about anything," Bray replied, shrugging. She looked back toward the buildings. "Where are you, Elliott?"

Bray leaned against the bike, thinking. She wouldn't leave this place without finding him.

She couldn't.

Chapter Nineteen

Bray

"We can't wait here forever," Kage commented as the two of them remained standing beside the motorcycle. "The longer we're away, the more curious they'll get back home."

Bray nodded. Kage was right. They'd already been waiting several minutes. No movement from these buildings. It was as though the people who lived inside them never actually left. And of course that was probably the safest thing to do. But Elliott told her he was coming here. He said to *look him up* if she ever came to town.

"Look him up," she whispered.

"What?" Kage asked.

Bray stepped away from the bike. She walked over to the one building they hadn't thrown rocks at. She searched the ground and picked up a pine cone, feeling its prickly, sticky lightness in her hand. Looking up at the top windows, she saw that one of them was pulled slightly open. She closed her eyes and listened. Vaguely, she picked up the sound of jazz music.

Elliott loved jazz.

"Serge!" she shouted.

Suddenly, a face popped up, visible at the window. A second later, a dark hand pushed the window open further, exposing the face of her dear friend.

Bray's heart leapt.

"Come around back," he whispered down to her.

Elated, Bray ran around to the back door. Kage followed.

"That must be Elliott," Kage said.

Before Bray could respond, the door swung open.

"Get in here," Elliott whispered.

Bray entered, followed by Kage. Elliott swiftly shut the door. He led them down a narrow hallway to a white door that was slightly ajar.

"I see you found me," he said as they entered his apartment.

Elliott closed and locked the door. There was a tight, confined energy in the room. A wide, brown couch sat adjacent to the door. Heavy blankets draped over its cushions and a sunken-in pillow pressed down into one arm of the couch. Bray wondered if that was where he slept.

Across the way, a long, glass-top desk hovered beneath the windows, and the jazz music she'd heard from below was bellowing out from one of two large screens that looked over at her and Kage. Elliott walked over and turned down the music. He turned and looked at her. His dreadlocks had been cut shorter, revealing a very soft jawline where a five-o'clock shadow developed along his brown skin. And his dark eyes, as always, were kind and seemed to be longing for something.

"Are you really surprised?" Bray replied, looking around. At least this time he hadn't packed up all his belongings and didn't seem to be disappearing as he had been back when she found him in Denver. It felt as though so much time had passed since that day she'd escaped the psych ward and showed up at his door, only to find he had his own plan of escape.

Elliott sat down in a gamer's chair and swiveled to face Bray, who remained standing in the middle of the room. Kage stood beside her and cleared his throat.

"Sorry," Bray said to Kage. "Elliott, this is Kage. Kage, I've known Elliott since I was six."

Elliott nodded at Kage. He leaned forward and grabbed a toy tyrannosaurus rex that had been resting on the window sill. "So what happened after you left Casper?" he asked Bray.

Bray rehashed the story for Elliott. She told him about saving the sows, how she'd passed out when Alice died. As she spoke she noticed his facial expression; there wasn't one. She figured he didn't believe her, especially the part about passing out when Alice died.

"And so Kage saved me. Brought me up to this place in Meet—"

"Oop," Kage interrupted. "Don't mention the name. Not yet."

"Sorry," Bray replied. "Anyway, I'm staying with Kage and some former animal rights activists."

"Eek," Kage said, cringing and looking up at the ceiling. "I hope this place isn't wired."

"Don't worry," Elliott answered. "This place is a refuge for hackers like me. Everything is protected here."

There was a pause. Elliott looked at Bray. Bray glanced down at his arm, saw the dog bites had healed and turned into nothing more than black scars on his skin. She was relieved to see he had recovered since their time in Casper.

"I don't suppose you were just in the neighborhood and thought you'd stop by?" Elliott said.

"No." Bray's shoulders dropped. He never had validated her ability to communicate with animals, so she felt unsure as to whether he'd be open to her ideas now.

But she was already here. She had to try. And so she was careful with her words:

"There's something going on with S-Corp. Something bad. I think I know a way to stop it."

"Ha!" Elliott laughed. "Everything about S-Corp is bad."

"Glad we all agree," Kage commented, smiling.

"What makes you think you can stop them?" Elliott asked.

"What if I told you they are testing animals with human DNA and organs? To the point that these animals developed awareness? And S-Corp is trying to hide it," Bray said, determined to get him on board.

"That actually doesn't surprise me," Elliott replied, leaning back in his chair. "Not to mention I don't care as much about the animal thing as you do," Elliott admitted. "Take a look at this, though."

Elliott swiveled around to face the computer screen. He reached for his mouse. Bray walked over and stood behind him, looking at the screen as Kage looked over her shoulder.

Elliott's browser was opened on some kind of chat box. He exited that and clicked on another app at the bottom of the screen. A second later, a list of names popped up.

"What's this?" Bray asked.

Kage stood beside Bray, arms crossed.

"It's a screenshot. This I found in S-Corp's archived files. It's a list of names. . .these are all the people who died back in 2027. . .because of the supposed 'terrorist attack,'" he said, motioning with air quotes.

"So many people," Kage whispered.

Elliott scrolled down the list. There had to be hundreds, if not thousands.

"I finally found the proof. . ." His voice trailed off. Then he pointed. "See."

Bray leaned forward. Elliott highlighted a pair of names:

CHRISTOPHER BANSFIELD
TAYLOR BANSFIELD

"Your parents," Bray whispered. "Why would S-Corp keep records of their names?"

"Lawsuits," Elliott replied. "These are all names listed on lawsuits filed by families. My grandparents filed one, but I never knew."

Elliott paused for a moment. He stared at the screen. His face grew forlorn. Bray reached over and placed her hand on his shoulder. He looked up at her, and did not smile.

"They were experimenting with a new form of oxygen—Oxygen 11—while developing a drought-resistant fertilizer out west. They tested it in California without FDA approval. It got into the soil. It killed all these people. . .apparently it spread as far as Nebraska and Oklahoma." Elliott paused again. "They lied. And the government helped them cover it up. It was no terrorist attack."

"I knew it," Kage said, raising his arms and stepping away.

"People have to know about this," Bray said. She thought about her mom, wondered if her mom knew. Of course she did. And what could this mean. . .if the country learned the truth?

"When did you find all this out?" Kage asked, stepping over and leaning against the desk so he was facing Elliott.

"About two weeks ago. I thought of leaking it to the press, but who knows what side they're on anymore."

It was all coming together in Bray's mind. What was happening to Rhea and the other cows. The fertilizer disaster and how that had killed so many innocent people. Like Elliott's parents. The children of his grandparents. Destroying families. Destroying nature. If something wasn't done soon, they'd destroy the entire nation.

"I think I know a way," Bray said, feeling a confidence rise within her.

"What?" Elliott asked. He swiveled back around to face her.

"Is there a way to hack Embedicare implants?" Bray asked.

"Anything can be hacked." Elliott glanced over at Kage, who was still leaning against the desk, gazing solemnly out the window.

"What if we got into their system?" Bray said, hoping Elliott would understand her plan and be open to it. "And interrupted everyone's implants. We could expose S-Corp."

"That would be insane," Elliott replied, shaking his head. A devilish smile approached his face.

"Can we do it?" she asked.

"I'm sure it can be done, yes."

Suddenly, Kage spoke.

"I just remembered something," he said, returning to the conversation.

Bray and Elliott looked over at him.

"About a month ago, I went to Salt Lake City to see my childhood home." He looked down at Elliott. "My parents were animal rights activists. They disappeared twelve years ago. I'm pretty sure S-Corp did it. As a matter of fact, I think the company is responsible for hundreds of disappearances.

"When I went back to my home to try to find out what happened to them—the place was abandoned, of course—" Kage stopped, his eyes staring wildly into space. "I found a flash drive. My dad was a journalist and had some incriminating evidence about S-Corp. I never knew what it was exactly, but I know that's what led to his disappearance."

"Do you still have it? The flash drive?" Elliott asked.

"No. . .but my uncle does."

"Trevor?" Bray asked.

Kage nodded.

Bray thought about the conversation she had had with Trevor the day before. She wondered if he was at all curious about what was on that flash drive. Without a computer, he had no way to access it.

"If we can get the info off that drive, I bet we'd have a ton of evidence to share. . .not to mention what's going on with the animals," Kage said.

"That's true," Elliott replied, his eyebrows rising.

They all looked at each other. In those silent moments, Bray felt a nudge in her back, as if she were being pushed by someone from behind.

It was Rhea.

Bray had nearly forgotten the whole reason

she'd come here in the first place.

"Listen," she said, looking Elliott in the eye. "These cows are being abused in this S-Corp testing facility and it is very wrong, not to mention potentially dangerous if S-Corp feels the need to hide what they're doing. They plan to send the cows to slaughter soon, to hide the evidence. I know all of this because I've been linked with one of the cows. I know you're not going to believe any of this." She paused. "But this cow. . .she has the capacity to understand our language. To *know* that she's a cow. If people could *see* this. . .experience what is happening to these cows first-hand, it could possibly end all the animal suffering that's caused by people just wanting to satisfy their taste for meat!"

"I doubt that," Elliott replied swiftly. "But you're talking to someone who has zero faith in humanity at this point."

"I think if people really knew what was going on with S-Corp, we'd have an uprising," Kage said, standing up and pacing back and forth.

"Maybe," Elliott replied. "It's the animal piece I'm not sure about. Besides, what are you suggesting? That we somehow get people to see what's happening to animals through their implants?"

"Yes," Bray replied.

"And how exactly do you suggest we do that?"

"Through me."

Elliott gave her a sideways glance. He looked puzzled. Kage stopped and looked at Bray.

"If we can somehow connect Embedicare to the cows, through me because I'm linked with them. . .then those who have the 4D implants, couldn't they experience what I'm experiencing?"

"I have no idea. This is all fantasy talk," Elliott said, fidgeting with the toy T. rex. "But *if* we could do that, I wouldn't recommend it. Largely because that amount of data entering your brain, Bray, would pretty much kill you."

Bray thought for a moment. She knew there was

a chance she was going to die anyway. This was the moment she had to remind herself it wasn't about her. It didn't matter what happened to her anymore. It was about the something better. The something better worth dying for.

"I'm not concerned about that. It's just that. . .if there's anyone who can make this happen, it's you."

"I appreciate the vote of confidence."

Elliott stood up and walked over to the couch. He sat down and glared at the floor. Bray walked over and sat down beside him.

"Is it so incredulous to believe me when I clearly found those sows back in Wyoming and then saved them from slaughter? Kage saw it himself."

Elliott looked up at Kage, who moved over to the chair across from them.

"It's true," Kage said. "She saved well over a hundred of them. And I watched her pass out when one of them died."

"The one you said was your friend?" Elliott asked, turning to Bray.

"Alice, yes. I don't expect you to change your mind about animals. I just want to know if it's possible to link them to the implants through me."

Elliott sat back against the couch. He closed his eyes. Raising his arms up over his head, he continued squeezing the T. rex in his hand. Bray sat quietly and allowed him time to think. Kage glanced over at her and pointed at his wrist, motioning that it was about time to head back. Bray nodded, exhaling, realizing she may very well have come here for nothing, other than to see that her best friend was well, and hadn't much changed.

"Well," Elliott finally spoke. "I suppose if there was a way to get you another implant, then it might be possible."

"What do you mean?" Bray asked, not so sure she liked the idea of having another implant. The one her mother forced upon her, she had cut out the moment she escaped the hospital.

"If you had an implant, it would be simple enough to hack Embedicare and then have you transmit information out to the entire country."

"Will you help us?" Bray pressed, wasting no time.

"I don't think so," Elliott huffed, opening his eyes. He leaned forward, resting his arms on his thighs. "I'm happy here. And safe. As much as I'd love to stick it to S-Corp, it's not worth the risk of getting caught."

"Is there anyone else here who could do this?" Kage asked.

"I can check," Elliott replied.

Bray turned away from him and looked out the window. The sun had lowered as her hope had done. She was disappointed, to say the least. Tears built up in her eyes and she didn't want Elliott to see. As it was, he only saw her as his "little" sister, and although she was younger than him, she still wished he believed in her abilities as an animal empath. But she knew from their recent time together that she couldn't push him to help her. She *wouldn't.* So she stood up, took a deep breath, and dried her eyes with her hand.

"We have to get going," she said.

"Are you upset?" Elliott asked, standing up and looking at her closely.

"I'm just. . ." Bray turned to him and shrugged. "I'm disappointed. Not in you, just the situation. I have to help these animals."

"Why?" Elliott asked, nearing her.

"I'll die if I don't. On some level, even if I don't *physically* die, I might as well. You believe what you want about my abilities," she said, remembering something Emily had told her. "But just because you don't believe me doesn't mean it isn't true. I'm linked to this cow. When she goes to slaughter, so do I. And when Alice, my friend, passed away, I thought I was going to die. I passed out and, as Kage can attest, I was

unconscious for a while. This time there is no
guarantee I'll live through it. If that's not
going to motivate you to help these animals, then
at least consider it a way to help me."

"Shit," Elliott said quietly. He stood there
for the longest time, looking Bray in the eye.

"We really do have to go." Kage spoke softly.

"I'm not sure I'll see you again," Bray said
to Elliott, getting choked up. "So can I have a
hug?"

Elliott reached for her arm and pulled her
into his chest. He wrapped his arms around her.
She rested her head against him, felt his warmth,
and cried. She cried not only because she
realized she would never see him again, but also
because she'd nearly forgotten that her link to
Rhea meant she could die. Again. But perhaps for
real, this time.

Bray felt Elliott shake. He sniffled. She
pulled back to see he was crying, too. In that
moment she became aware of his significance in
her life.

A smile grew on his face.

"You give me no choice but to help you."

"Really? You mean it?" Bray asked, her heart
lifting.

He nodded.

The two of them parted. He wiped his face with
his sleeve. Bray took a deep breath and turned to
Kage.

"Now what?" she asked.

"We get back home, for starters."

"I can look into some things from here,"
Elliott said, stepping over to his desk. "We're
gonna need a safe, secluded space where I can do
the hacking. Not my home, and obviously not
yours."

"And it needs to be close to the cows," Bray
said. "Like the closer, the better."

"Here." Elliott picked up a card from his desk
and handed it to Bray. "That's my email. It's
untraceable. Can you get in touch with me that

way?"

Bray glanced at Kage. She figured there was no internet access at the house.

Kage shook his head in confirmation.

"Sorry." Kage shrugged.

Elliott reached down beneath the desk and came up with a black laptop and a flash drive, which he plugged into the laptop. He turned the machine on, typed in a few things, closed it up and handed it to Bray.

"Take this," he said. "It's already encrypted and that's a wireless internet router. Create an email address and then contact me."

"Thank you, Elliott," Bray said, beaming.

"Hey." He shrugged, smiling. "I'm not about to lose my best friend."

With that, Bray and Kage returned to the bike outside. The sun held its place from when she last saw it, giving her a mild sense of belief that this plan could actually work.

She stuck the laptop down in the bike's back compartment and slid onto its seat, behind Kage.

"Ready?" Kage asked.

"As I'll ever be," Bray replied, and they departed for Meeteetse.

#

As they neared the house, Kage slowed the bike and stopped just outside the corn crops.

"Back in time for dinner," he said, shutting off the engine.

Bray got off the bike hesitantly as she wondered why they were stopping here. Kage stood up and moved off the bike, holding it between himself and Bray.

"When we get in there," he said, "we'll have to tell everyone."

"Tell everyone what?" Bray asked, growing nervous.

"If we're going to do this, then we need to

tell them."

Kage proceeded to walk the bike along the dirt path through the corn stalks, which were not so much corn stalks as they were broken and snapped in half, hollow pieces of something that no longer was, but would be again.

The last thing she wanted was to talk to the entire group about this, all at once.

"Trevor's gonna want to bring it up for a vote. . .whether we do this or not."

"But it's already been decided," Bray protested.

"If it's something he thinks will affect the household, then we talk it out together and we vote."

"But vote on what, exactly? Elliott and I already said. . .and you *said*. . .you would help."

"And I will," Kage responded. He stopped and turned to her. "We have to go about this the right way, or they'll make it next to impossible for us to proceed. As long as we live here, we have to respect the vote."

"Then I guess I'll have to leave," Bray said pointedly.

"Hold on now. Don't get defensive, especially in there. Ethan will most likely be on our side, so that's three of us already. We just need to sway Emily, Lana, maybe Virgil. Dennis will side with Trevor. Trevor will say no."

Bray took a deep breath. Her shoulders slumped. Just when she thought they were all set to go, another barrier got in the way.

"I just want you to be prepared. . .before we talk to them."

"I appreciate it," Bray said, feigning a smile.

Chapter Twenty

Oscar

Standing idly, staring down at a name badge that he'd unsnapped from his button-up shirt, Oscar read the name and could not place it.

"Bertan?" he whispered. Why the hell was he wearing someone else's name tag? Maybe he'd picked up the wrong shirt at some point, or maybe another worker had dropped their shirt into his locker without thinking. Anything was possible, he surmised.

But his name, he knew, was Oscar. Oscar Reyes Mejia, to be exact. A man who once worked for Medina and was so cold and calculating, he'd taught the other Medina workers all they needed to know about intimidation tactics. Threats.

He knew everything there was to know about twisting a man's mind in two.

He moved from the hallways of the clean side of the facility over into the dirty side. To do this, he used a keycard to gain entrance through a steel door. This door separated the Kill Floor, Cooler and Fabrication departments from the administrative offices. Those offices, along with the cafeteria, were known as the "clean side." Everything else was left to the title of "dirty side," where workers spilt blood.

It was another night in the beef processing plant. How many nights had Oscar worked like this? Did it matter?

The steel door opened out to reveal a concrete floor bearing the weight of an array of machinery and metal tables on which workers disassembled animal parts. This was where animals arrived from transport, and where they gradually died. A place where the knocker did his knocking, the workers

in the bleed pit sliced throats. An entire
conveyor-like system of hooks ran along the
ceiling below spinning fans. Animals were hooked
to them by their hooves and carried upside down
through the room, a windowless maze of
deconstruction.

This was the Kill Floor.

Why was he back here again? He was doing his
job as security guard, and he was pretty sure
he'd already completed a building check. Lifting
his phone out of his pocket, he saw the time was
10:30 p.m.

Time wouldn't lie, right?

Because that meant he'd already been here more
than an hour, but his memory of that hour was
nothing more than a blank piece of paper.

Which meant he could turn it into something
new. Write what he wanted, so to speak. And one
thing he was very clear on was what he wanted: to
destroy S-Corp.

Oscar started for the plant manager's office.
The windowless room sat at one end of the Kill
Floor, sharing a wall with the Fabrication
Department and an opposite wall with the hallway
from which he came.

His eyes journeyed along the walls, over two
file cabinets, until they arrived at a fuse box
that hid behind a shelving unit lined with hard
hats. That was what he'd come for. He knew this
not by memory but by instinct. His eyes landed on
the box and something in his groin urged him to
stop.

He snapped open the fuse box.

Inside, columns of black switches commanded
the electricity for the entire dirty side of the
plant. But those did not interest him. It was the
thermostat beside the switches that drew his
attention. It was protected by a clear, square
locked box.

Turned out Oscar had keys for everything.

He smiled.

As he lifted a hand to the box, keys out, he

saw he was wearing gloves.

Probably wise, yet he could not recollect putting them on.

Oscar unlocked the box. It dropped open, exposing the thermostat. This thermostat controlled the temperature in the Fabrication Department. Oscar was able to deduce this by doing some simple research: The Cooler had its own thermostat, which was located outside the Cooler door. He had every intention of tampering with that one next.

Oscar pressed his finger on the up arrow, raising the temperature to sixty degrees. The temperature in a Fabrication Department was never to exceed fifty, lest any hanging beef parts inside go to waste.

Oscar shut and locked the fuse box, leaving everything else as it was.

Turning, he glanced at the laptops on the desk. He wondered if he was being watched and told himself there were no cameras in the office, either.

Oscar repeated this entire act with the Cooler, standing outside its doors and letting out a laugh as he raised the temperature to sixty degrees. Any product that sat waiting in the Cooler would turn bad by morning.

Locking up the thermostat, Oscar came to overlook the Kill Floor, his eyes passing along the gutting stand to his left, the head-washing station, and the bleed pit area in the distance.

Oscar wandered over to the knock box, where his hands grazed the knock gun that hung from a hook on the wall. He got hard.

He searched his pockets and came out with a screwdriver. What he was doing with it in his pocket, he did not know. Or maybe he did, and that began to freak him out a bit.

He wasn't hard anymore.

Where had the screwdriver come from? When did he put it in his pocket? He stared at it for minutes that built atop minutes. What he discovered was that he did not need to ask why. He knew why.

The knock gun was a black, .22 caliber captive stun gun that looked like a hand gun. Oscar brought it down from the wall and held it. He stroked it for a moment. His eyes watered. He remembered the seduction that came with having someone's life in his hands. Not so much the beefs, but humans.

A clicking noise in the background alerted him to the present. Remaining still, he glanced over at the hallway, but it was dark. The door did not open.

He would have to hurry.

Oscar used the screwdriver to unscrew the gun's muzzle from the barrel. He removed the bolt assembly, a black, cylindrical tool that would render the gun useless in its absence. Dropping it onto the floor, he began stomping on it over and over again. He picked it up and slammed it against the knock box's metal cover, hitting it until the bolt appeared to have significant scarring and scratching. He removed a few tiny screws, let them fall to the floor and roll beneath the knock box, and he put the gun back together.

That would slow production for a while. Long enough for them to have to replace the gun.

Oscar held the gun for a moment before placing it back on its hanger. He ran his fingers along it again, savoring the familiarity of it. Placing it back on its hanger, he slid the screwdriver back into his pocket, turned and started for the hallway.

Oscar emerged into the clean side. The door breathed closed behind him. The click it made stopped him in his tracks.

At that moment, Bertan's mind returned.

What was he doing?

Diallo, the sanitation worker, appeared from the opposite hallway. Diallo worked the night shift like Bertan, cleaning the offices and cafeteria before making his way over to the dirty side where he cleaned the floors of all the animal excretion and blood leftover from the day's work.

"Bertan?" Diallo called.

Bertan looked over at him.

"You okay?"

Bertan stood there, his arms dropped by his sides, searching his empty mind. He thought maybe he should be frightened. Frightened that he was forgetting again. Experiencing time lapses again. But instead he found himself at ease. He didn't necessarily like that it was happening, but the forgetting was bringing him a strange sense of comfort. Maybe he didn't want to remember. The clean slate he discovered in his mind each time he found himself lost was sobering and. . .relieving.

"Great," Bertan replied, and resumed his nightly duties as security guard.

Chapter Twenty-One

Bray

Dinner that night consisted of broccoli, wild rice and potatoes. The scent of chives lifted into the room from the seasoning used on the potatoes. It was still light out the windows behind Bray, yet with all the traveling and talking she had done with Kage today, it felt like midnight to her.

Once everyone was seated and began eating, the room went quiet. Kage glanced across the table at Bray and spoke.

"Bray and I have something we want to discuss with everyone," he said. He nodded at her, as if urging her to speak.

Bray's face went flush. Her body tightened everywhere. The whole table was looking at her.

"I've linked with another animal," she said right off, feeling the blood continue to rush to her head. "Several cows, in fact. I've talked to Ethan, Kage, Lana and Emily about this already. Apparently these cows, seven of them, are a part of some S-Corp genetic experiment using human DNA and organs." Bray stopped. She looked over at Trevor, who had stopped eating and was glaring at her, eyes set. Bray took a deep breath and continued.

"All of them have achieved unusually humanlike awareness. . .as a result of the DNA testing," Bray said.

"How do you know all of this?" Dennis asked.

"Like I said, I'm linked with them. We communicate, like ESP. I have visions, nightmares. I can feel what is happening to them. . .physically. It's why I arrived here passed out last month. Because I was linked to one of the sows and she died, remember?"

Dennis nodded.

"She's an animal empath," Lana said, smiling at Bray.

Bray looked back at Lana and smiled in return. She felt encouraged to continue.

"These animals will be headed to slaughter soon. S-Corp is trying to cover up the experiment, destroy the evidence, so to speak. And if they go to slaughter. . .there's a real chance I will die, too, because of my link to them."

Bray stopped. She wanted that piece to really sink in. If it had worked for Elliott, maybe it could work for them, too.

"Is there something you'd like to suggest, Bray?" Ethan asked, raising his eyebrows.

Bray shot a look over to Kage, who'd stuffed his mouth with rice.

"I'd like to save the cows, if we can," Bray replied.

"No way," Trevor answered, shaking his head.

"Where are they going to go once you save them?" Dennis asked.

"Don't encourage her," Trevor responded.

Bray could tell he was getting upset. Beside him, Emily worded something to Bray: *breathe.* Bray took a deep breath.

"At this point, I just want to get them out, let them die somewhere in peace," Bray said.

"Like you did with the sows?" Lana asked.

"Yes."

"And how do you plan to get them out without getting caught?" Dennis spoke as he filled his plate with more food.

Bray thought for a moment. She didn't really know. Her mind raced. This was overwhelming. She needed to think through two plans at once: rescuing this group of cows and also exposing S-Corp like they'd talked about with Elliott today. That was the ultimate goal, to rescue *all* cows.

"I have a friend named Elliott. Kage and I went to see him today."

A fork clambered onto the table, making a

clinking sound. Bray turned toward it and saw Trevor sitting there, mouth agape.

"Elliott's a hacker, basically. He used to work in S-Corp's IT department. I bet he could hack their security system, get us in that way."

"That's completely illegal. No, no, no," Trevor insisted, sitting back and shaking his head.

Kage cleared his throat while glancing at Bray.

"Why don't you tell them the rest?" Kage suggested.

Bray glared at Kage. A part of her wished Kage would talk instead. He knew these people way better than she did. But Kage only sat there, moving the food around on his plate with his fork.

"Everyone here remembers the terrorist attack in 2027," Bray began, while looking around the table at everyone. Most of them nodded. Trevor seemed increasingly agitated.

"Today Elliott showed us proof that it was S-Corp doing the killing, not terrorists. They designed a drought-resistant fertilizer they tested out west. . .without FDA approval. I can't remember the rest but. . .who's being illegal now?" She shot a look at Trevor. He looked away.

"It had Oxygen 11 in it. That's what got into the soil and killed all those people," Kage said, winking at Bray.

Bray was relieved he'd finally chimed in. And after listening to him say it aloud, the enormity of S-Corp's lie was beginning to sink in. That she had to have this conversation was a true shame. S-Corp had gone unchecked for so long, they were getting away with murder. A lot of murder.

"Jesus," Virgil said. He set down his fork and folded his hands over his plate, as if in prayer. "We always believed this was true. . .but now to know there's proof."

"And that's not all," Kage added. "If Bray is right and S-Corp is trying to hide their experiments on those cows, then we have to wonder why. I mean. . .doesn't it mean something if these cows can actually *think*? Bray even said they are self-aware."

Bray's chest began to rise. She felt a smidgen of hope because finally someone was on her side.

"I think it means something," said Ethan, smiling. "The question is whether we can do anything about it now."

"I think we can, and should," Bray said.

"Me, too," Kage agreed. "In fact, I say we put it up for a vote."

"Vote? On what?" Trevor asked, staring at Kage.

"Rescuing the animals and exposing S-Corp's dirty little secrets to the public."

"If you do that," Trevor replied, "you'll incite panic. Giving too many people that much information all at once. . .it could break their psyches. It'll get you nothing but consequences."

Bray's heart coiled. Kage couldn't have been more right about Trevor. She quieted and could still hear the very subtle voices of Rhea and the other cows, but this time she couldn't quite make out what they were saying. It almost seemed as though they were talking amongst themselves and didn't want Bray to hear.

"I get there's a big risk here," Bray spoke. "But what's the alternative? We let these cows go to slaughter like all the billions we let go each year?. . .And I die, or maybe worse?. . .And then all these things. . .the unjust, terrible things you know about S-Corp. . .you carry them with you the rest of your lives? You just sit here in hiding? Is that what you all chose to do when you decided to become activists?"

"It's a different world now, Bray," Trevor countered.

"You think I don't realize that? My mother is Dianna Hoffman. Do you know who that is?" Bray asked, getting emotional.

Everyone shook their heads, save Kage, whose eyes suddenly widened.

"*The* Regional President of S-Corp?" Kage said in a near whisper. "That's. . .your mom?"

"Yep. I didn't want to say anything because I'm so ashamed. She's had me in and out of the psych hospital my whole life. If I hadn't escaped, that's where I'd be now. She doesn't care about me. She cares about S-Corp. *That's* who we're dealing with. So don't tell me what kind of world you think it is out there." Bray paused and turned to face Trevor. "You've done nothing but sit in this house for twenty-some years while the climate is declining, while animals are dying. . .*people* have died and will continue to die because of S-Corp. So yes, let's vote."

Bray realized she'd raised her voice and was near crying. She was hot. Her back was sweating. She very much wished to get up and storm out of the room, but instead she clenched her fists and stayed put.

"I'm a yes," said Kage.

"Me, too," Ethan added. "But you know I can only help from afar."

Bray nodded, tears coming to her eyes.

"It's a yes for me. I support you all, but also from a distance," Emily said, smiling at Bray.

"It's a no for me," Trevor said. He grabbed his plate and quickly stood up.

"Trevor," Kage spoke, looking up at him.

Trevor turned to Kage.

"You remember years ago, when you were homeschooling me? There was this word you taught me. . .*complicit*. I remember how you said people who stand by and allow atrocities to occur are still complicit. Do you not believe that anymore?"

Trevor glared down at Kage. Bray sensed the tension between them. He said nothing, turned away and walked into the kitchen. Suddenly Bray felt guilty for the way she had spoken.

"I'm an obvious yes," Bray said, brushing off the feeling. She also did not disagree with Kage's comment about people who stood by and allowed this kind of suffering to continue.

"I'm sad to say I'm a no," Virgil said. He stood up and placed his hand on Bray's shoulder. She felt warmth in it. He rubbed her shoulder gently and walked off.

"It's a no for me, too." Dennis shrugged. He got up and followed Trevor into the kitchen.

So far, Kage had been spot on. The only person left to vote was Lana, who could go either way.

"This is hard for me," Lana said. She looked over at Bray.

Emily got up from the table and went outside, probably to meditate.

"I'm going to say no, sorry," Lana said.

"You're serious?" Kage asked, turning to Lana.

"Afraid so," she replied.

"Is it because of all the activists you've already lost?"

"Partly. And because, as you can remember, Kage, our last encounter with S-Corp nearly got us both killed. Not to mention. . ." Lana's voice trailed off. Her eyes lifted and glanced out the window, slowly returning to the table. "Have any of you heard of the *Animalist Code*?"

"No," Kage said. The others shook their heads.

"Well, it was this social worker guy out in Ohio. A few years back he tried saving animals. He was an activist himself. He posted about it in a blog, called it *Animalist Code*. He got way too close to what S-Corp was doing, tried breaking into one of their facilities one night. Hard to know all the details because the site has since been deactivated, but his father was murdered. . .by S-Corp. I just. . .I'm not sure I can put myself at risk again. And if my 'no' vote can prevent your lives from being risked, then that's my hope."

Lana stood up and left the room.

Bray, Kage and Ethan remained. The things Lana had said about that activist out in Ohio, how S-Corp *murdered* his father. Disturbing, yes. But why wasn't it equally disturbing that animals were being murdered for profit every moment of every day? Why was that not enough?

"What does all this mean now?" Bray asked Kage and Ethan, feeling discouraged.

"Means it's a no go," Kage replied.

Ethan nodded in agreement.

"I can't *not* save these animals," Bray whispered.

I just can't.

Chapter Twenty-Two

Bertan

Bertan was standing in the plant manager's office. Ruben sat across from him, a laptop open on the desk. What was he doing here? Bertan began to feel anxious. He crossed his arms to hide from Ruben his sudden confusion.

"I want you to take a look at something," Ruben said.

It took a moment for Bertan to respond. He'd been thrown off by the sudden change in time and place. The time on the laptop showing as 5:45 a.m. His shift had ended. Like that.

"Bertan?"

Bertan met eyes with Ruben.

"Yes?"

"Are you okay? You're looking a bit pale."

Bertan certainly felt it. Spaced-out. It had happened again. Must've. Question was: should he tell Ruben?

"I caught a bug or something," Bertan replied, electing to withhold the truth.

"You should go home and get some rest." Ruben commented. "But before you do, we need to talk about this."

Ruben turned and pulled up a video on the laptop. He pressed a button. Bertan watched as the video revealed a man in a security uniform tampering with the fuse box in this office. The guy looked like him.

"What?" Bertan said, leaning forward. "Who is that?"

"Bertan. . .that's you." Ruben looked concerned.

Bertan stared at the video. The man in the video turned and when he did, sure enough, Bertan saw himself. He froze. His eyes darted around the room as he sought answers. How could this be?

"Are you experiencing memory loss again?"

Ruben asked. He paused the video.

"I don't know," Bertan said. Of course he knew he was, but he had to try to keep Ruben from worrying too much. If Ruben found out what he had in mind, he would try to stop him. Or worse; try to protect him in some way. That would only lead to Ruben getting into trouble.

"Tell me what's going on," Ruben coaxed, leaning back in his chair.

Bertan looked at him. They'd come a long way, these two. Bertan would almost go as far as to say Ruben was his closest friend. His only friend. Which was why he could not tell him. For one, he didn't quite have a grasp on the truth himself. He did not at all remember messing with the fuse box. Searching his mind, the last thing he remembered was standing out on the clean side, watching Diallo cleaning the hallway. And before that? It was all too hazy to make out. And he needed to give Ruben some kind of answer.

"I was checking the fuses. Some lights stopped working on the Kill Floor last night so I was making sure nothing blew," Bertan replied, scrambling for a response.

"But you opened the thermostat. And when I came in this morning both the Fabrication Department and the Cooler were on the fritz. The temps had risen some thirty degrees. All the product from yesterday will have to be tossed."

"That's not good," Bertan said. But what he really thought was: *that is very good. I hope they lose everything.*

And that's when it all clicked. The way everything on a Kill Floor came together, each worker moving in harmony as beefs were torn down and reduced to mere body parts and pieces of meat. In his mind now a kind of movement suddenly took place, where everything lined up, like a bullet entering the muzzle before a gun going off. Yes. That was it. He must've changed the temperatures to fuck with S-Corp. Always the goal was to sabotage the sons-of-bitches. Get them in the wallet. Get the place to shut down. Next maybe he'd move on to another plant.

"Bertan," Ruben said, grabbing Bertan's attention from out of the depths of his mind. "You're lucky I'm the one that found the video."

Bertan looked at Ruben. He took a deep breath and nodded. The sounds of machines starting up and workers laughing and yelling signaled the start of a new day on the Kill Floor.

It was becoming a pattern: Bertan could not remember what he had done, but eventually he could remember why.

"I'm not trying to keep anything from you," Bertan said, lying again. "I don't remember doing that."

"Look," Ruben replied. "I gather you're trying to sabotage S-Corp somehow. And that you are dissociating whenever you go through with these. . .these behaviors. I know how much you want S-Corp out of your life. I can understand if you want revenge, or whatever. And on top of that, I imagine it's stressful to have your family out on the road again." Ruben paused. "But we have to be very careful. We have to go about this the right way."

"I'm not sure I can wait that long," Bertan blurted out. He didn't want to admit that, but it was too late to take it back.

"But if you keep doing things like this, it could sabotage any chance we have of really taking them down."

Bertan did not respond. Suddenly a part of him wanted to be angry with Ruben, to blame him for everything that was going wrong in Bertan's life.

It's not Ruben, it's S-Corp. Remember? he told himself. *This is why I must stop them. With or without Ruben.*

"I'm going to trash this security video," Ruben said, reaching for the laptop. He used the mouse on the keyboard to close the video, moving it to the trash can icon at the bottom of the screen.

Bertan smiled. He'd have been lying to himself if he said he was afraid of getting caught. That part of him that took over whenever he lost himself, that caused his memory to fade into the background, it convinced him he would never be caught. That he was invincible.

"This can't happen again," Ruben said. He rolled his chair closer to Bertan and gave him a sideways glance. "And I think you need more help than I can offer."

"What do you mean?" Bertan's shoulders tightened in defense. The voices of the Kill Floor workers unexpectedly went silent.

"I'm afraid I may have misdiagnosed you."

"Misdia-what?" Bertan asked, confused.

"Remember when I told you I thought you had PTSD?"

"You mean the trauma that was causing my time lapses?"

"Yes." Ruben shut the laptop and pushed it away. Turning, he looked more intently into Bertan's eyes. "I think you may have a kind of dissociative fugue."

"What's that?" Bertan asked. He was beginning to feel nervous. Wherever the part of him that exuded confidence was, he could certainly use it.

"It involves memory loss. And it can result from trauma. People with very severe cases have been known to change their names, pick up and move to other places. Out of nowhere."

"You afraid I'm going to do that?" Bertan suddenly realized his loss of control over this part of himself really could lead him anywhere. But for some reason, it still did not scare him. Not anymore. When Ruben first told him that he could overcome the trauma he'd experienced in his past, he had believed the man, and he still believed him. But that didn't mean he wanted to give up his plan to end S-Corp. Surely he could do both. He had promised Ruben he would no longer use violence, and so far, he hadn't touched a soul. He would need that out-of-control part of himself to do the things he could not do on his own. Like back when he had to do those things he had done for Medina years ago.

"There's no telling," Ruben replied. "That's what has me concerned. And if it is dissociative fugue, it's way beyond my expertise. I really think we need to look into some serious help for you."

"Like what?" Bertan didn't at all like where this was going.

"Maybe a brief hospital stay? Get you stabilized on medications? I'm not really sure, but if you'll allow me, I can look into it."

"I appreciate that," Bertan said. His eyes meandered off past Ruben. Set themselves on the wall behind him. "But I'll need some time to think about it."

"Okay. Don't take too long. If this gets too severe. . .well, I don't want anything to happen to you."

With that, Bertan left the office. In and out of a daze, he walked past the bleed pit area. His head turned to view a pair of workers who eyed him as he passed. Luis, the knocker, was gripping the knock gun while the other worker was bent down searching beneath the knock box.

"Hey Bertan!" Luis shouted to him.

Bertan glanced at the knock gun. A hint of recognition hit his mind. Enough to tell him to keep walking. He turned down the hall, away from the workers, and hurried to let himself out of the Kill Floor. As the heavy steel door settled behind him and he started for the front doors, an image of a damaged bolt flashed through his mind. He stopped at the door, shook it off and exited the building.

Chapter Twenty-Three

Bray

Another day came and went and Bray was no closer to a plan to save Rhea and the others. This had become a familiar feeling; dejection. That night, she tossed and turned, tossed and turned, couldn't get to sleep. No amount of meditation or breathing helped.

She needed to *do* something.

She sat up. Outside it was pitch black nothingness, like the nothingness she would certainly be in a matter of weeks. If Rhea died and Bray followed, would anyone try to stop S-Corp? Would Elliott? Would Kage? Maybe. When Alice had last spoken to her, she'd said success was in the try. Bray had to try. She couldn't let a household vote stop her from doing what she knew was right.

Sliding out of bed, she walked downstairs. The steps creeped beneath her. As she approached the living room, Kage was lying on his air mattress. He was asleep on his stomach, a blanket pulled up to his shoulders. Bray tiptoed over, knelt down, and tapped his back.

"Kage," she whispered.

Kage did not respond.

She pushed at him, whispered his name again.

"Huh?" he said, sitting up and turning toward her. One of his eyes was partially shut. His hair was disheveled. Bray tried not to laugh.

"I need to talk," she said quietly.

Kage rubbed his eyes. He patted the empty space beside him and Bray sat down.

"What's up?" he asked, yawning.

"I need to go save those cows," Bray whispered. She didn't want Trevor or Dennis to hear, even though they were most likely sound asleep. "I'll leave if I have to, go stay with Elliott. But I can't get there on my own."

Kage exhaled. He reached over and grabbed his shirt and slid it on over his undershirt.

"I don't have much time left," Bray emphasized.

"I know." Kage sat up and looked toward the window, which was hidden behind a deep purple curtain. "I think we'll have more success if we stay here, use Ethan's help. Maybe get Elliott to help from afar until we find a new space where Elliott can hack away, if you catch my drift."

"But what about the vote?" Bray asked.

"We tried it Trevor's way. We told them all our intentions. I say we find our own way to make this happen."

Bray nodded. A smile grew on her face.

"Thanks, Kage."

"You can thank me when all this is over. Now let's go find that laptop."

Chapter Twenty-Four

Bertan

The hours passed the way time passed in summer back home. Slow, hot, long. Bertan was at work, inside the plant manager's office. It was 5:15 a.m., which meant he had only a little while longer until the end of his shift. He was supposed to be keeping an eye on the property from the row of monitors before him, but instead, he kept nodding off. He'd started having trouble sleeping during his off hours.

Again Bertan's eyes fixed onto the monitors in front of him. He needed something to focus on. As the images on the screens flipped back and forth to various parts of the facility, his mind fell backwards into the past. . .

Back when he worked for Medina, not only did he carry out murders of innocent *campesinos*, but much of his job also involved intimidating them. Often times for the *campesinos,* intimidation was worse than murder. The intimidation tactics Bertan learned served to break the minds of the *campesinos* so that, eventually, they'd give in to the pressure and sell their land to Medina. The land these *campesinos* owned, located in Bajo Aguan, Honduras, was fertile. African palm oil had already been cultivated there. All Medina had to do was get rid of the farmers and benefit from the profits.

One time he and a few men tossed the body parts of one *campesino* over the fences of a property owned by another *campesino* who'd refused to give over his property when Medina had offered to pay. The body parts were that of a neighbor, a friend. Each day Bertan and his buddies tossed over another body part. First it was a couple of fingers, followed by both hands and both feet.

Another day, both legs. Both arms. By the time
the head appeared on a stake outside the
campesino's fences, he caved.

Black and white images danced around on the
monitors before Bertan's eyes. The images of all
the ways he had intimidated those *campesinos*
danced around in his mind. They moved and danced
as if to some slow and powerful Latin music.
Something so passionate it nearly turned him on.
How the passion of intimidation—the fire inside
whenever he'd committed those acts—how alive it
once made him feel.

Suddenly the sound of clicks and doors sliding
open threw Bertan back into the present. He shook
his head and stood up, his heart racing. He took
one deep breath, turned, and glanced out into the
hallway.

It was Luis, the knocker. Bertan glanced at
his phone. It was 5:45 a.m. The Kill Floor
workers would be arriving to start their day,
which meant his was ending.

Bertan shut off the monitors. Turning off the
office light, he exited and locked the door. He
followed Luis down the hallway. Luis stopped at
the doors to the clean side and slid his badge
through the badge reader. Bertan caught up with
him and stopped, his eyes meeting Luis's.

"Morning," Luis said.

The door clicked open. Luis pulled it opened
and held it for Bertan. Bertan walked through,
turning down another hall toward the break room.

"Any fun last night?" Luis asked. It was the
same question he asked every morning. Since
Bertan had started working here, he'd talk with
Luis every morning before he left his shift.
Bertan liked the guy. He had a kind, easy nature
to him. How he knocked beefs all day, Bertan did
not know.

"No fun," Bertan answered, entering the break
room. The lockers that stood along the wall
behind the table and chairs all remained closed.

Their dull, beige color made Bertan feel muted. The walls in the room were white. A restroom hung off the far end, a black door separating it from the rest of the space. No windows, just a television and two vending machines against the wall as he entered the room. Such a boring place for men who did such unspeakable things.

Luis approached a locker five feet down from Bertan's. Luis stood only an inch taller than Bertan. He was stalkier, nearly bald with a pudge for a belly. He looked like he'd be slow if he ever had to run.

Bertan followed, opening his locker and placing his gun, holster and radio inside. He slammed the locker shut and stood watching Luis slide on a pair of yellow PVC boots over his gray socks. This facility provided wet boots for their workers. . .to protect their feet from blood. Bertan wished he'd had such things when he'd been a knocker.

He picked up the stench of death wafting from Luis's locker, maybe it was the boots. The scent penetrated his nostrils and went straight for his brain, where a vision of blood spattering into his face caused him to shiver. He went dizzy for a moment and grasped onto the lockers.

"You okay?" Luis asked, reaching his hand out to Bertan.

"Yeah. I need to go eat," Bertan replied, feigning a smile. He turned and stepped away from the lockers, distancing himself from the stench.

"I got an extra banana. You want it?"

"No, thank you."

Luis took a cell phone from his pocket and went to place it in his locker. He glanced at the screen a moment and sighed.

"My wife wants us to see our pastor for counseling," he said.

Bertan thought that was too much information. He did not respond.

"This job. . .well, you know," Luis continued, putting the phone in the locker and shutting it.

"I do." Bertan nodded.

Two more men entered the room. Bertan took the opportunity to bow out. As he approached the exit, Luis's voice stopped him.

"By the way. . .you know what happened to the knock gun?" Luis asked.

Bertan's eyes lit up. Did he know what happened to the knock gun?

"What happened?" he replied, turning.

"It was damaged, missing some parts. We all missed a whole day of work yesterday. The manager was pissed. You didn't hear about it?"

"I guess I didn't." Bertan stood there, looking at Luis. He frowned, knowing nothing of the knock gun or what'd happened to it.

"Hm," Luis grunted. He stared back at Bertan. For a moment it felt to Bertan as though they were about to fight, but only with their eyes.

"Got to go," Bertan said, turning and walking away.

On his way outside he passed a few Kill Floor workers as the bell rang, indicating the start of the day. On each of their faces was a stoic, emotionless expression. He knew what it took for workers to do these jobs, how blessed he was not having to knock anymore, and that wasn't saying much.

He approached the door to the front offices, used his badge to pass through. There, dozens of S-Corp admin workers floated from office to office. Some of them waved to him, others paid him no mind.

The thought occurred to Bertan: what if he intimidated these fuckers. . .the way he had those *campesinos*? Maybe he could mess with them, sabotage their facility right beneath their noses, and destroy them from the inside. Ruben wouldn't have to know. He could be stealthy enough for no one to know it was him until it was too late and he had S-Corp by the balls.

Chapter Twenty-Five

Bray

Bray sat on the bedroom floor with Kage, who was typing away on the laptop Elliott had given him. His typing was very slow.

"How long has it been since you've used a laptop?" Bray asked, grinning as his eyes stared at the keyboard while his fingers roamed the keys, typing in one letter at a time.

"You know it's been like twelve years, doofus. Don't make fun of me." Kage nudged Bray in the arm.

Kage created his own email address. He said he didn't want Bray doing it, for her own protection. Bray appreciated that.

They emailed Elliott. Kage shut off the laptop and left the room.

Bray went outside to meditate with Emily. She found her sitting in their usual spot in the front yard. Bray was tired, wired and also moved by what she was about to do. She needed meditation, and she needed to get Emily's support.

"I missed you last night. . .though I understand why you might've skipped," Emily said as Bray approached and sat down beside her.

"The vote was definitely discouraging," Bray admitted, sitting with her legs bent into a pretzel shape. "But Kage and I decided we're going to do it anyway."

"Do what?"

"We're going to save those cows. And expose S-Corp while we're at it."

"Wow," Emily replied, exhaling. "That's really major, Bray. I stand by what I said about supporting you. Sounds like you're going to need a lot of help."

"That's why I'm here. To meditate, but also to get your support, if we can have you and Ethan behind us at least, then maybe we can succeed. You've done this kind of stuff in the past, so we could use your expertise."

"I wouldn't call it expertise." Emily laughed. "But I am happy to help."

With that, the two of them closed their eyes. Bray connected to her breath, to Rhea.

"Rhea," she called out in her mind.

"*Yes?*" Rhea responded immediately.

"We are going to try to save you. But I need you to show me where you are."

Slowly, the darkness behind Bray's eyes transitioned into a vision revealing the inside of the S-Corp transgenics facility. Bray saw that all the cows were still there. The room was void of humans. The overhead lights were off, and blinking lights from nearby equipment cast a blue glow onto the cows.

The scene changed as her viewpoint backed out of the room and into a hallway with tile floors and intense, fluorescent lighting. It rose up a level to a wide-open room, more tile flooring but not much else. It had no furniture, no desks, no animals or testing equipment. Very strange.

Bray's view rose higher, through the ceiling and out above the building.

The vision rolled over the roof then turned and dropped down to the building's front. The sudden drop made Bray slightly nauseous.

The building's exterior was painted in an ugly tan color. No windows. Surrounding it, nothing but miles and miles of dead crops.

Passing the vacant parking lot, the vision drifted away from the building. It felt like Bray was flying. Flashes of Denver came into view. Her heart shook in fear at the thought of being seen somehow, even though she knew this was a vision.

Bray opened her eyes. In her chest grew an expanse, a wide berth of hope and enthusiasm. She smiled broadly. As much as she knew time was becoming critical, she also knew she had to keep meditating if she was going to be ready to save animals again. She closed her eyes and refocused on the breath.

#

Bray found Kage planting new seeds in the earth he had tilled the other day. Seeds that would one day grow into something more, something that would come alive as nothing more than tiny sprouts at first. Tiny ideas one day growing into reality.

"Kage." Bray jogged over to him. "We need to talk."

"Again?" he replied, winking.

"I know where the cows are located."

"Right on. Where?" Kage paused, holding onto the bag of seeds.

"It's in Fort Collins, Colorado. S-Corp Center for Transgenics, or something like that."

"Oh no." Kage stopped. His arms fell to his sides. His face seemed to turn a shade more pale.

"What?" Bray asked.

"We can't go there."

"Why?"

"That was the place I tried to get into. . .to find your mom. Where Lana and I were nearly. . .well, you know."

Bray's eyes widened. She knew the story. Kage had been staying with some activists in a hidden location in Wyoming. That was where he'd met Lana. Kage had wanted answers for the disappearance of his parents, so he'd stolen one of the activists' cars so he could sneak into an S-Corp facility to get information. He almost got caught. As a result, Lana and the team kicked him out. So he went off on his own to try tracking down Dianna Hoffman, Western Regional President of S-Corp, certain he could blackmail her to get the information he needed. He'd followed her to a secret S-Corp facility. This time, he did get caught. So did Lana. They had escaped, but barely.

"Lana and I both were lucky to get out of there alive," Kage said.

"If you got in there once," Bray said, holding on to hope, "we can get in there again."

"We're not going back there. At least. . .I'm not, and you shouldn't, either. That place is a fortress. I only got in because I threatened one of the workers. Then I found this room where they were experimenting on pigs. . .with human embryos or some shit. It was creepy. Two security guards caught me." Kage lowered his voice to a whisper. He glanced down into the bag of seeds. "Then there was this guy, Carl. . .he was. . .he'll give you nightmares, Bray."

Bray went silent. She didn't know what to say. Her mind was busy processing the fact that Kage, her number-one ally, was saying no.

"I'm sorry," he said. He reached over and placed his hand on her shoulder.

Bray did not reply. She was growing discouraged, again. As much as she could see where he was coming from, there was still this enormous weight on her shoulders, the responsibility she felt to the cows and to all animals destined for slaughter.

There had to be some kind of way. At this point, she wasn't willing to accept any alternative.

Chapter Twenty-Six

Bray

Evening came. Bray found herself outside with
Emily in meditation. What else was there to do?
The atmosphere around her was growing darker. A
warm scent of fresh soil ran beneath her nose as
wind passed by them. As she got quiet, she
noticed something coming from Rhea. At first she
thought it was Rhea trying to contact her, but
the communication was not directed to her. It was
directed at the other cows. They were speaking
amongst themselves, and Bray could not make out
what they were saying.

She got the sense they didn't want her to
hear.

Bray pulled away, not wanting to interfere.
Instead, she cleared her mind, focused on her
breathing. Eventually, another idea came to her.
When she'd saved Alice, it wasn't until Alice was
on the transport truck. Maybe the same could
happen this time. Bray's mind crowded with ways
they could make this happen: stake out the
facility from afar. Wait for the transport truck.
Follow it—

"*Bray, we need to talk,*" Rhea's voice
interrupted. It sounded stern.

"I'm listening," Bray replied, clearing her
thoughts away.

"*We have only seven days.*"

"Seven days? Til what?" Bray asked, but she
knew the answer. She felt the blood rushing away
from her face.

"*Until they send us to slaughter, I'm afraid.*"

This was beginning to feel all too familiar.
Her mind flashed back to the time she was in that
house in Casper, waiting for Elliott's arm to
heal from the horrible dog bites. The time she

learned Alice had less time than she'd thought.

And it was happening again.

"But how. . ." Bray's voice trailed off.

"They found out," Rhea replied. *"Whatever S-Corp is, they found out that we can think and communicate and they want us gone."*

"Then we'll make sure to get you off that transport truck," Bray decided. "I know it can be done."

"I know it can be, too," Rhea said. *"But the other cows and I have been talking amongst ourselves. We've come to our own decision."*

"What's that?" Bray was afraid of the reply.

"We have decided we will find a way to escape."

"But how? What about what happened to those pigs that tried to escape?" Bray asked, growing anxious. She took a deep breath. Opening her eyes for a moment, she turned and checked to make sure Emily hadn't noticed her upset. Emily's eyes were still closed.

Bray shut her eyes and tried her best to be open to Rhea's plan.

"We have come to accept that you cannot save us. We must try to save ourselves. Whether we make it or not does not matter. We can't allow them to send us to slaughter without at least trying."

"Wait. . .how do you know I can't save you? I really think we can."

"Kage is right that you cannot rescue us from this place."

Bray's mind was still getting used to Rhea's unexplainable ability to access things that happened outside of their own conversations.

"It is too dangerous," Rhea continued. *"Perhaps you could rescue us during transport. . .but as you have said yourself, then what? More and more animals suffer. What we want is for you to go ahead and connect us to the other humans of this world, so they can feel what we feel as we are headed to death. And then we*

will plan our escape."

Bray went speechless. Caught completely off guard, she had nothing to say. She didn't know if she could trust the cows to save themselves. They didn't know what they were up against in those slaughterhouses. Neither did she. And she was only halfway able to trust herself to save them.

"I realize this is hard for you," Rhea said. *"We've asked for your help for so long, and you gracefully agreed. Now we are asking you to trust us to take care of ourselves once we arrive to slaughter. We need you to trust us."*

"I don't know," Bray admitted. "There's no guarantee this'll work."

"We know this. But it's worth the try."

There was that damn *try* word again. Bray was beginning to resent it. She wasn't sure what was worse: allowing them to go to slaughter and probably losing her own life too, or simply *knowing* she was allowing them to go to slaughter when she could possibly still save them.

"The decision isn't up to you," Rhea replied. *"This is our wish. You can decide not to help us, and we would understand. But then our deaths would be in vain, I fear."*

"I just need some time. . .to. . .I don't know. . ." Bray said, trailing off again.

She opened her eyes. The stars looked down at her as if they were waiting for her decision. It felt like the whole world was waiting, and it was waiting for her. It felt heavy and cold.

Bray stood up. Emily shuffled and opened her eyes.

"I'm done for tonight," Bray said, and turned and went inside.

Chapter Twenty-Seven

Oscar

Oscar stood alone in the dark. His hands were gloved. His S-Corp uniform stuck to his body like dried blood on concrete. The temperature in the Fabrication department cooled the unexplainable sweat running down his back. Though more compact than the Fabrication Department he had worked in at the previous facility, it contained the same metal tables. The same instruments hanging from walls.

Fabrication.

What a word.

The cameras were still on, and he knew they were, but the lights were off. No one would ever see what he was about to do.

Once his eyes adjusted to the opaque darkness, he found across from him a variety of saws hanging on the wall. He was searching for something long. Something he could use to reach for something else, without having to touch it. Nothing in here would do. Plus, he was wasting time.

He exited the Fabrication Department. Moving through the Cooler and into the Kill Floor, he settled on an electric cattle prod and ran outside with it. Across from the facility, two dumpsters stood side by side. These dumpsters contained animal remains.

One security camera pointed down at the dumpsters. Beside the camera hung a light that illuminated the parking lot between the facility and the dumpsters. The lot was empty save for his car.

Oscar avoided the light by turning and stepping along the facility's back wall until the edge of light met the darkness. There, he crossed the lot over into a grassy knoll that slanted down into an anaerobic stabilization pond for waste disposal.

Oscar walked carefully through the dark, along the grass, until he reached the dumpsters. He stepped in between them and pulled one of their side doors open. A powerful stench of pain and death hit his nose and about pushed him backward. Holding his breath, he reached in and searched the half-full dumpster. His gloved hand touched something tubular that he could wrap his fingers around. He pulled it out. It kept coming. Oscar pulled until he nearly fell backward.

A spinal cord dropped to the ground. The end of it broke off against the concrete. Oscar grabbed the end piece and tossed it back into the dumpster. His nose ambushed by the stench, he stepped away from the dumpster. The spine still in hand, its nine feet of bone was covered in coagulated blood.

Oscar took the spine and lathered it over the cattle prod with his gloved hands. His stomach turned at the scent. Not being a killer anymore was making him weak.

A pair of headlights turned into the parking lot. Oscar saw them from where he stood.

"Shit," he whispered. He slid behind the dumpster to remain out of view.

Who the hell would be here in the middle of the night? Were there others who worked here at night?

Oscar didn't know. He watched as the car parked and the lights shut off, but the engine still ran.

Oscar hurried through the darkness and back inside with the piece of spine and the prod. His plan was to leave them in one of the administrative offices.

Running through the Kill Floor, Oscar hurried to the steel door that stood between him and the offices on the clean side. He slid his badge and opened the door a crack to peek inside. There, a dark-skinned man had entered the front of the building. Oscar stood, stone cold, holding his breath. Drops of blood fell from the spine he held, landed on the floor. The man turned down the opposite hall and disappeared in darkness.

Seeing as the unfamiliar man had a key to enter the building, Oscar suspected he was another worker. He had been able to see that the man was wearing a one-piece cotton uniform.

Oscar could not risk getting caught. He contemplated tossing the plan aside until he could get back in here alone, but what if that never happened? The man was far out of view, which gave Oscar a chance to make his move.

He pulled the door open and quietly ran over to a hallway of offices. There he disappeared down the hall, figuring that man would come this way in a number of minutes. Sweating all over, Oscar chose an admin office, pulled out a set of keys and unlocked the door. He shuffled inside, holding the door handle with his gloved hand as he shut it.

He gave himself one minute, counting in his head, to lay the prod and spinal cord on the admin's desk, find a blank piece of paper, and write the following note:

DO NOT EVER CROSS US AGAIN.
YOU OWE US WHAT YOU HAVE YET TO PAY.
-MEDINA

Oscar scratched down the words in all capital letters. Suddenly a memory invaded his thoughts, a memory that did not feel like his. The name *Serpentine* flashed through his mind. He stopped, vaguely remembering a man who'd had his own ties to Medina. The pervasive memory revealed an image of this man's hand holding a photo of a woman and a young girl tied up, their mouths covered with tape. Stapled to the woman's shirt was a note written in all capital letters.

"*Carmen.*" The name whispered through his mind.

He froze.

Who was Carmen?

A creaking noise came from the hallway.

Oscar slapped himself hard in the face, forcing himself back to the present.

He set the note on the desk beside the prod and spinal cord, his gloves covered in blood. Moonlight shining in through a narrow window across from him exposed a part of the desk.

"Perfect," Oscar whispered, making note of the window as his escape.

Glancing down at the desk to make sure everything was in place, he noticed a sticky note on the desk calendar. Something about a work meeting with Jacob on May 20th. Having no clue who Jacob was, Oscar pulled out his phone and took a photo of the sticky note. Something about it piqued his interest. Most likely this Jacob person was also in administration. Looking at the calendar, he saw that May 20th was a Sunday. Maybe there would be limited staff that day and he could get Jacob alone. Intimidate the man. Get some information on S-Corp.

A clicking noise snapped Bertan back. Bertan. He was Bertan. Suddenly he found himself standing in an office with bloody gloves on his hands.

What had he done?

Footsteps were softly stepping down the hallway. Bertan cringed, fearing what would happen if someone saw him like this. There was no escaping out the office door without being recognized and questioned.

He'd have to piece all this together later.

He ran over to the window and pushed it open. He pulled himself up, pushed his shoulders and torso through the window, and looked down at the concrete five feet below. He heard a door open and close. Eyes wide, he forced himself out until his body dropped. He landed awkwardly on his arm and intentionally screamed out in pain. He pulled off his gloves, threw them into a set of nearby bushes. Lying on his side, he felt his gun against his thigh. He pulled it out and threw it a few feet away.

"Ahh!" he yelled, grabbing hard onto his knee as if he'd injured it. Hopefully Diallo would hear him and come running.

Bertan let out another yell.

"Help! Help!"

A second later, Diallo's head popped up in the window.

"Bertan," Diallo called down in an African accent.

"Come help me, please!" Bertan yelled in reply.

After a few moments, Diallo came running around the corner of the building and approached Bertan, coming down to his knees.

"You okay?"

"Someone broke in," Bertan said, wincing and grabbing at his knee. "They escaped through the window and I tried running after them. I fell."

"I'll call Jacob," Diallo said, about to stand up. Jacob was the owner of this particular S-Corp facility. Bertan's boss.

Bertan grabbed his arm to stop him.

"No." Bertan sat up, rubbing his knee. "I'll talk to him in the morning. I saw what they left in there. . .on the desk. Not sure how they want it handled."

"Shouldn't we call him now?" Diallo asked.

"He'll be asleep." Bertan did not want anyone to find out about this until morning. Not until he had time to get his story straight. He was a master at fabrication, like Medina, like S-Corp. He needed a little time.

"Are you okay?" Diallo asked again.

"Yes, I hurt my knee. And my gun is lost," Bertan said, looking around.

"Here," Diallo replied, standing up and walking over to point at Bertan's gun.

Bertan stood up and limped over to the gun, picked it up, and slid it back in its holster.

"Thanks for your help. You can go back to work

now. We'll both need to file a report in the morning."

"Okay." Diallo nodded. He turned away and started back around to the front of the building.

Bertan watched until Diallo disappeared from view. He exhaled. Whatever the hell he had been doing in there, he nearly got caught.

Bertan's head began to throb. He used his fingers to rub the sweat from his forehead. He needed to think. Or maybe not think. He didn't know. Suddenly he didn't know what was going on.

What was going on?

He had no frame of reference.

Standing up, Bertan started for the front of the building. His shift as security guard was not over yet. He took a few deep breaths of fresh air. Closed his eyes. Tried to recollect. . .

Chapter Twenty-Eight

Bray

It was morning. Bray was no closer to anything. It all felt very far away, in fact. She lay in bed and stared up at the ceiling. Voices mingled down below. Silverware clinked. People sounded jovial.

But Bray lay upstairs, alone. She sensed Rhea trying to connect, like someone gently tapping on a closed window, and she ignored it. She couldn't believe Rhea and the other cows would come to such a finite decision. Even if animals like Rhea somehow "went on" after death, it didn't change things here on earth.

She found herself admittedly angry. So angry she didn't feel like going downstairs to eat. Or to meditate. All she felt she could do was stare into space, letting her mind piece together what Rhea said last night.

A knock gently rapped at her door. Bray turned her head toward the door as it opened.

"You okay in there?" Emily asked.

"Yeah," Bray replied. She wasn't sure she wanted to talk to anyone.

"Can I come in?"

"Sure," Bray said, sitting up. She rolled the covers down so they rested on her lap.

"We missed you at breakfast. Not feeling well?" Emily sat down at the foot of the bed.

"You could say that," Bray answered. Of all the people in this house, she was by far the closest to Emily. If she was going to talk to anyone about Rhea, it would be her.

"What's the matter?" Emily's voice was soft, inviting. Bray wished Emily could've been her mother. How things would've been so different.

"During meditation last night. . . .Rhea told me

that she and the other cows don't want to be saved." Bray paused. "They are going to try and escape on their own."

Emily nodded. She looked at Bray. For some reason Bray couldn't make eye contact.

"They want me to continue with my plan. . .to use the Embedicare implants to connect them with the public."

"Okay."

"But then that's it. Once they go to slaughter they'll try to escape, and if they don't. . .they die." It was so hard for Bray to speak it aloud.

"I see," Emily replied. "And I take it you're not happy with this."

"I just. . .don't know what to think. How to move forward."

"Do you want my advice, or do you need time alone?" Emily asked.

"Time alone hasn't done much good so far."

"So you want to know what I think?"

Bray nodded.

"I think you'll regret it if you don't try to fulfill their wishes."

"I know," Bray agreed, looking down at the sheets. "That's why I'm having such a hard time. I don't *want* to do this. . .to let them go when I think I could save them."

"I know, sweetheart." Emily came close and took Bray's hands in hers. "It doesn't sound like it's up to you anymore."

Bray looked Emily in the eyes.

"You know. . .back in the early 2020s, we had reason to be hopeful. We really thought we were seeing an end to factory farming," Emily said, her eyes looking off out the window. "But I think in the back of all our minds, we also knew that *because* we were succeeding, there grew a greater risk of us being shut down. Or worse. And when President Walker was assassinated, we feared for our lives.

"Back then the best decision was to go into hiding. For a long time, we've lived here in peace. But then you came along. I started to see that we're not so much living in peace as we are complacency. I hear you speak of these animals, and all the memories come flooding back. . .how I would stand outside factory farms and see animals off to slaughter, completely powerless. Some of us were arrested for that, or threatened by farmers.

"But we kept doing the work because we understood it wasn't about us. When you're called to do something, Bray, something for the greater good, it no longer becomes about you. It becomes about *all of us*," Emily said, her eyes glossing over with tears. "It becomes about principles rather than individuals. Justice, compassion, right action. I know this must be scary for you, but it's also clear that the world is calling on you, and for good reason. You have a gift. A gift that can help the most abused, neglected and harmed beings on this planet. And you've got all of us, right here, behind you."

Bray began to tear up. Her chest freed and a door opened somewhere inside where she could let Emily's words enter. But she was still so afraid. . .she didn't know what of, exactly. She supposed it was many things. Like, was she capable? What would happen in the end? It was the uncertainty she wasn't sure she could handle.

"What if I don't make it?" Bray asked, the tears rolling down her face.

"That's a problem for tomorrow, and thankfully tomorrow is not here," Emily said, smiling.

"What if Trevor is right?" Bray said next, fearing that by doing this she could also be creating a bigger issue throughout the country. Especially if it worked.

"You know. . .sometimes you have to galvanize people into action," Emily replied.

"What does that mean?"

"You need to shock them."

Bray's tears slowed. A sense of relief came

over her. She and Emily met eyes. Emily came forward and hugged Bray. Bray sat in her embrace, allowing herself to be rocked back and forth until the crying ceased. Until she was able to see herself accepting what she was being asked to do.

#

After Emily left her room, Bray got up and went to the window. She looked out to the horizon, where the blue sky seemed to graduate into a pale white along the distant foothills. If Bray moved forward, which she knew she would, her whole life would change. It could most certainly end. But thinking of what Emily said about this being about the animals, about the bigger picture, she could see herself being okay with this.

She closed her eyes and called for Rhea.

"I thought I might never hear from you," Rhea said.

"I'm sorry. I'm here now. I need to know exactly when they plan to take you to slaughter."

"Seven days."

Bray's eyes shot open. That was way too soon. Bray had to move quickly if she was going to do this.

She found Kage, who was in the garden planting more seeds, and caught him up on everything.

"I'm game for it," he said.

Together they sat in Bray's room, away from everyone else, and checked Kage's email. Bray was relieved to see a response from Elliott:

LOOKED INTO IT. I NEED TO GET SOME EQUIPMENT. BUT IT CAN BE DONE. WILL PROBABLY TAKE A FEW DAYS. WE NEED A SECURE LOCATION AS I SAID.
-ELLIOTT

Bray gulped. So this was it. It was happening.
Like a roller coaster starting up the first hill,
there was no stopping or turning back. She had to
move forward despite how afraid she was.

"He's going to need a few days," she
whispered. "I hope that's enough time."

Bray responded to Elliott:

WE ONLY HAVE SEVEN DAYS.
THEN THE COWS GO TO SLAUGHTER.
SO WE NEED TO BE QUICK.
AND WE WON'T BE SAVING THE COWS.

Bray paused. How could she explain that Rhea
and the others changed their minds, in a way that
Elliott would believe?

IT'S TOO DANGEROUS.
BUT WE ARE STILL PROCEEDING.
HOPE THIS MAKES SENSE.

Bray hit the *Send* button. Despite Elliott
saying the laptop was encrypted, she didn't quite
trust it.

"Now what?" Kage asked.

Bray shrugged. She didn't know. It wasn't like
she'd done this before. She was flying by the
seat of her pants, and it made her insides sick
with anxiety.

A ding came from the laptop. Bray glanced down
at the screen. Elliott had already replied. She
opened his message, eyes wide with curiosity.

SEVEN DAYS? WOWZERS!
I CAN'T REALLY START UNTIL WE GET
A SECURE LOCATION. ANY IDEAS?

"Shoot," Bray said, cringing.

"What'd he say?"

"We need to find a secure location to do this.
Somewhere close to where the cows are being
sent. . ." Bray paused. "I have no idea where

that would be."

"Let's go talk to Ethan. Maybe he can help," Kage replied.

Bray closed up the laptop, hid it beneath her bed, and followed Kage out of the room.

#

Ethan was out back, tending to the ground below the fences where new grape seeds had been planted. Lana was beside him, picking off dead vines from the previous year's harvest and tossing them into a nearby wheelbarrow.

Bray and Kage approached Ethan.

"Can we stop you a moment?" Kage asked him.

Ethan turned and looked down at them. Always when Bray stood beside him, she was amazed at his height. And that tattoo of the chicken talon on his bald head.

"You can stop me for a couple moments," he replied, winking.

Behind him, Lana also stopped and listened in.

"Bray, you want to catch him up?" Kage said.

Bray took a deep breath and looked around. Trevor and Dennis were nowhere in sight, so she spoke openly.

"We're going ahead with our plan," she started.

"Oh." Ethan nodded. A smile grew on his face like a long river.

"But we can't save the cows. Instead, they told me they would rather try to escape, even if they don't make it. . .so the implants can be used to show people what they're going through. I think Emily called it galvanize, or something," Bray said.

"I see." He nodded again. He dropped his arms to his sides, pushed his hands down into his pants pockets.

"We only have seven days until they go to slaughter. We need to find a secret location, somewhere near the slaughterhouse, where we can set up."

"Where's the slaughterhouse?" Ethan asked.

"I don't know. I may be able to find out from Rhea but—"

"I might be able to help," Lana spoke up.

Bray turned and they all looked to her in unison. She stood up and pulled off her gloves.

"How?" Bray asked.

"Well, I still have my cell phone. I have one team member left, a social worker named Ruben, who is working undercover at an S-Corp facility. At least, I assume he still is."

"You never told me that," Kage said, grinning.

"Had no reason to." Lana shrugged.

"Are you sure?" Bray asked. "I know you didn't want to get involved."

"I said no to the vote," Lana admitted. "But I figured it wasn't going to stop you. So if there's some way I can help, I will."

Bray, Lana and Kage returned inside, went upstairs to the guest bedroom where Lana had been staying.

The walls in Lana's room were a gentle, cool green color. There was one single window across from the door, and it was left open, a breeze drifting in. Clothes were scattered along the floor, some atop the unkept bed. Lana grinned as she quickly pulled the clothes up from the bed and tossed them over the other side where they couldn't be seen.

Lana dug through the clothes on the floor and pulled out her phone.

"I can't believe you still have that," Kage said.

"When S-Corp showed up at our cabins, it was the first thing I went for. I hid it in my underwear," Lana said.

"That feels like so long ago," Kage replied.

Bray watched the two of them interact. As much as she found Lana attractive, she felt happier thinking of the two of them together. She wanted that for Kage, especially since there was no knowing if Bray would make it out of this alive. She watched Lana turn on the phone and remembered Elliott giving her an encrypted internet modem for their laptop.

"But is it safe to use that here. . .without being traced?" Bray asked.

"The location services were dismantled from our phones when we got them," Lana replied.

With that, Lana made a call to her teammate.

She spoke in a low voice. She turned and looked out the window. "You have a minute? I need help."

There was a pause. Bray stood there beside Kage, hoping this would work. If it didn't, the entire plan would fall through.

"Can you look something up for me? There are these cows going to slaughter. We need to know which slaughterhouse they're being sent to."

Lana turned swiftly to Bray.

"What's the name of the facility they're at now?" she asked.

"It's a transgenics facility in Fort Collins, Colorado," Bray replied, hoping that was enough for them to go on.

Lana repeated the details exactly. There was another pause.

"Okay great. Thanks for checking."

Bray hurried over to Lana and whispered.

"Can you also ask about a secure location near the slaughterhouse, once he finds it?" Bray asked.

Lana nodded, continuing.

"We'll also need a secluded, secure location to work. . .nearby the slaughterhouse. Can you do that for us? I can't give you details right now. . .okay, thanks."

Lana hung up.

"He'll get back to me," she said.

Bray nodded. She wished she could press for answers today, if not in the next hour. Everything felt like it was hanging by a thread,

and all of it felt like it was out of her
control. There was nothing left to do but wait.

Chapter Twenty-Nine

Bertan

After calling Jacob, his boss, to inform him the facility had been broken into, Bertan was asked to wait with Diallo until Jacob could arrive.

Bertan was exhausted. He thought that maybe for once, he could go to sleep. He hoped this interaction with Jacob would be brief. Crawling into bed for a day of rest sounded like heaven.

Jacob entered the building. Compared to Bertan he was tall. Probably around five feet, ten inches. He was thin, had no muscle or fat anywhere Bertan could see beneath the khakis and white button-up he wore. Here on the clean side, all the workers were white. The racial and ethnic division in these S-Corp facilities never got past Bertan.

"What the hell happened?" Jacob asked, his voice high and echoing through the open lobby.

Jacob approached Bertan and Diallo. He looked tired himself, his eyes puffy and his hair slightly disheveled.

"I'll show you," Bertan said simply, standing up.

He led Jacob down the hall to the office in question. Diallo remained in the lobby.

Bertan pushed open the door and stepped aside, feeling absolved of whatever had happened in this office because, honest to God, he remembered nothing.

"What the. . ." Jacob's voice trailed off. He stepped up to the desk and stared at the long piece of spinal cord. His hand lifted to cover his mouth, which was hanging open in shock.

Jacob picked up a note written in all capital letters. Bertan remained by the door and watched, gritting his teeth. He tried reading it from afar and began to wonder if it was him who had written it.

"So what happened, exactly?" Jacob asked, looking up at Bertan from the desk.

"I was doing my rounds last night. I came into the lobby from the Fabrication Department and heard a noise, so I came down the hall and saw the office door was open. I ran in and someone escaped out the window," Bertan said, pointing to the open window. "I went after him, fell, hurt my knee. I was holding my gun, so when I fell, it fell, too. I couldn't really see where he went in the dark."

Jacob pulled out his phone and took photos of the spinal cord covered in dried blood. He ripped up the note into several pieces, tossed it in the trash can beside the desk.

"Don't you need that?" Bertan asked. "For evidence?"

Jacob glanced over to him, still holding the phone. He stared at Bertan for such a long time Bertan grew uneasy. He cleared his throat.

"Go clock out," Jacob replied. "And if this happens again on your watch, you're fired. Got it?"

Bertan's body froze in place. *Did he say he'd fire me?* he asked himself. His face went hot. He forced himself to breathe so the anger wouldn't show.

"Yes," he replied, turning and walking away.

#

That afternoon, Bertan sat on his twin mattress in the hostel, his back up against the cool, concrete wall. He went over the past couple of days in his mind. But no matter how hard he'd tried, he could not remember doing anything in that office. So maybe someone had broken in and left the note. It seemed quite the coincidence, given his own desire to intimidate S-Corp. That was something he had not forgotten.

Looking down at his phone, he also had not forgotten that Carmen had left. He checked his phone history and saw that the last time they'd spoken was right before she and Gabriella left for Honduras. There were no texts indicating that they'd made it home, which brought unease to his heart. Getting across the border and into Honduras would take time, he knew. And while he waited, he would continue to feel the stress and uncertainty. . .the weight of his family's lives on his shoulders.

He was responsible for ending S-Corp so he could get back home to them.

But how?

He thought: *maybe I could get into their computers, mess them up that way.*

He had a password. He'd already planned on using it to help Ruben. But any time he used his password in the system, it was tracked. They'd know it was him. So he thought it best to save it for when Ruben asked for his help. By that point, he figured, maybe it wouldn't matter so much if he lost his job so long as it was after he helped Ruben. After that, he decided, he would most definitely return home.

Bertan's eyes landed on the twin bed across from his. He thought about the other workers. If he could get one of their passwords, he could get into the system without risking his job. Of course it would put someone else's job at risk, and although he didn't want any worker losing his job, his only option was to find the lesser of two evils.

When Bertan was a child and his father first taught him about Che Guevara, he learned that sometimes individual lives had to be sacrificed for the greater good. If any workers lost their jobs, unfortunate as that would be, it could help the larger cause of taking down S-Corp. This fact did not make him feel good, but at the same time, he understood the bigger picture had to be considered.

Bertan sat up. Surely none of the workers who lived here would have their passwords written down. Ruben had some clearance, but not the same level as Bertan, since Bertan was in security. As a matter of fact, none of the other workers' passwords would give him the level of access he needed after all.

What he really needed, Bertan realized, was one of the administrator's passwords. He could get *them* in trouble. He could make it look like they were the ones who were leaving notes from Medina.

Yes. That was it.

He needed a way to get one of their passwords.

Lifting his phone to his face, the date popped up on the lock screen and pulled his eyes in.

May 19. . .

May 19. . .

Something about that date. Or maybe the day after. Bertan unlocked his phone. He stared at the apps on the screen for a moment. The camera app caught his attention, mostly because he missed his family and liked to look at old photos of them.

He opened the app.

There, an unfamiliar photo popped up. A photo of a sticky note. . .a meeting with Jacob tomorrow? Was this a meeting he was supposed to attend and did not remember? The facility didn't have meetings with workers, unless it was to fire them.

The phone rang.

Not expecting the volume to be on, Bertan fumbled the phone. It dropped to the mattress. He quickly swiped it back up and checked the call.

Ruben.

He hesitated to answer. Was Ruben going to try to convince him to seek help?

Ruben was his friend. He reminded himself of this and answered.

"Hello?"

"Bertan, we need to talk," Ruben said. "Can you meet me?"

"Can it be quick?" Bertan asked. The more time he spent alone with Ruben, the more Ruben would suspect something was off.

"It can be," Ruben replied.

After Bertan hung up, he got a sad feeling that a distance was developing between him and Ruben, and he was the one responsible. Ruben had done so much to help him and his family, yet he still didn't feel he could tell Ruben how chunks of time had gone missing again. He wanted to, and he considered telling him when he went out to see Ruben later, but he knew himself. He knew he was going to keep his mouth shut.

And that was sad.

#

Bertan followed Ruben's directions leading him eight miles south to an abandoned trailer park. It reminded him of the one where he'd gone to meet Ruben once before.

He saw Ruben standing outside one of the trailers. It was the only one whose windows weren't blown out by dust storms. The only one with a functioning door.

For a moment Bertan got a sense that Ruben might be trying to trick him. To trap him and make him go to the hospital. He stopped the engine of his car and sat there a moment, staring at Ruben. Ruben looked at him and waved.

Bertan stepped out of his car but stood by the door with his hand still on the handle. The heat out here was striking, like in the desert. He immediately began to sweat.

"I've got five minutes," he said, for once not wanting to provide any type of updates on his life. All he wanted was a way to get at S-Corp, and as quickly as he could. Considering Carmen was making her own choices with their family, it was time he made his own, too.

"I got a call from my partner, Lana. That's the lawyer I was telling you about."

"I'm listening," Bertan replied, suddenly very interested in what Ruben had to say. He let go of the door handle.

Maybe this wasn't about his mental health, after all.

"They need some information. . .to find out where a group of cows is being sent to slaughter. And when."

"What?" Bertan wondered why anyone would care when and where beefs were being slaughtered, but these were animal activists he was dealing with.

"Here," Ruben replied, walking over to Bertan and handing him a piece of paper. "This is the name of an S-Corp facility in Fort Collins, Colorado. Apparently there are some cows there they want tracked. That's all I know."

Bertan took the piece of paper and read it.

"Trans. . .genics?" he read aloud.

"We don't have time for details. At least, you don't. They need the info as soon as you can get it."

"I'll do what I can." Bertan pushed the paper into his pants pocket.

"Thanks, Bertan. This really means a lot," Ruben replied, smiling in a way that implied he already regretted asking for Bertan's help.

Bertan felt a sudden twinge of guilt. He knew he was lying to Ruben about something and he didn't know why.

"I've got to go," Bertan said.

"Call me as soon as you get that info."

Bertan nodded and got back into his car. As he started down the road, his eyes held their gaze on the rearview mirror, where Ruben's body slowly shrunk into the distance.

Fading. . .fading. . .how memory faded. . .how when it did, it shrank identity. How Ruben's body became unrecognizable, a minuscule flake of black. Shrinking into nothing.

Chapter Thirty

Bray

That night, Bray and Kage sat side by side on the floor in Bray's room. Weeks ago, Bray wasn't sure where her life was headed. She hadn't cared. Tonight she found herself finally caring about something again. Someone else, that was, and it still felt quite surreal that after all this was over, she might not be in this room. . .this house. . .on this planet, anymore.

The two of them huddled in front of the laptop. Kage held the flash drive he'd gotten from Trevor. His father's flash drive, the one Kage had found during a visit to his family's former home back in Salt Lake, long deserted. Now he inserted it into the laptop. He opened the flash drive's folder. He and Bray were transfixed as they read through each file.

There were four files. The first was a screenshot of a letter from the FBI to Kage's father, Todd, warning him to "cease and desist" all his activism work, that he was trespassing on private property and would be arrested for ecoterrorism if he did not stop. The letter was dated *August 17, 2028.*

"Two months before they disappeared," Kage whispered, his eyes glaring at the screen.

He didn't have to elaborate. Bray knew what he meant by that. His parents had disappeared when Kage was sixteen. He had always believed that S-Corp had something to do with their disappearances. And what was so sad about this was that Kage actually *loved* his parents, talked about them only sparingly. Bray could see it was too painful for him otherwise. She knew what it was like to not have parents, in a way, to feel like some kind of orphan in the world. She often wondered if Kage felt the same.

"I knew it," Kage said. He pulled back a little from the laptop. His face went flush, like he was getting hot. Bray was close enough to him to sense he was. . .angry. That was it. Her powers were getting so strong that she could pick up on emotions of others, if they were palpable enough.

And Kage's emotions, in this moment, were clear and present.

Bray looked at him, but said nothing.

Kage opened the next file. On the first page was Todd's full name, a P.O. Box address, and, as Bray watched Kage scroll further down the screen, a title: *Truth, Our Only Weapon: How Animal Rights Activists Became the New Terrorists.*

"What is that?" Bray asked, completely immersed.

"My dad was working on a book exposing animal cruelty practices. This must be it. You want to read through it with me?"

"Of course," Bray replied. She wished she knew what he was thinking.

Kage went to open the next file. It was password protected. So was the last one.

"Dang," he said.

"I bet Elliott could get them open."

Kage gave her a side glance.

"About that," he said. "You're absolutely sure this guy can be trusted with all of this information?"

"Elliott? Of course. Why?" Bray was suddenly taken aback.

"I know he's your best friend. But I only just met him. I'm not exactly accustomed to trusting strangers, especially not with something like this."

"Elliott is no vegan or animal rights guy, that's for sure," Bray replied. She remembered how he'd allowed her to go on the road with him after she escaped the psych ward. How he took her with him so she wouldn't be forced back into the hospital again. He didn't really seem to understand or agree with her much of the time, yet he was still there for her.

"Elliott's like a big brother to me. He's always supported me, no matter what. So yes, I think you can trust him."

With that, Kage nodded and returned to the manuscript his father had written. He opened the document. Bray nudged herself closer and looked into the screen, starting to read:

It all began with a knock at the door. Tuesday night November 16th, 2027, 1:35 a.m. As I walk down the stairs toward the front door, I get an aching suspicion in my chest. The kind of ache animal activists know very well. It's the voice of true paranoia: that at any given moment if our actions are revealed to authorities, we risk being arrested. . .

Already Bray was enthralled. She and Kage had been leaning toward the laptop's screen, pulled in by the seduction of a past shrouded in mystery. There was so much that Bray did not know. The sad history of these activists—and Kage's parents in particular—was being revealed to her via a very incriminating tell-all about the truths behind the animal agriculture industry.

They continued reading through the manuscript as the night grew late and the house quieted to sleep.

Chapter Thirty-One

Bertan

Bertan gazed down at a carpeted floor. He was standing there aimlessly. He quickly glanced around the room, his heart picking up speed. The desert painting on the wall. . .the bookshelf. . .out the window it was night.

He was in Ruben's office.

What the fuck was he doing here?

He felt fabric in his hand. Looking down, he realized he was holding one of Ruben's suits. He'd been standing before the garment rack.

His phone buzzed.

He jumped in reaction, his heart jumping with him.

"Fuck," he whispered.

Bertan pulled his phone out of his pocket and looked at the screen.

He'd received a text from Ruben:

I MEANT TO ASK YOU THIS EARLIER—
HAVE YOU GIVEN ANY THOUGHT TO WHAT I SAID?
ABOUT GETTING SOME MORE HELP WITH THE MEMORY LOSS?

Bertan cringed.

He looked away from the phone, took a deep breath. Truth was, he still didn't want to admit he was missing time, that he was having memory lapses. He hadn't lost his job. His family was on their way back home, and as far as he knew he hadn't hurt anyone.

So what was the big deal?

He opened the text and replied:

I THINK I'M GOOD FOR NOW. THANK YOU FOR CHECKING IN.

And he left it at that. He didn't much like keeping things from Ruben, like the plan to get under S-Corp's skin and do this whole thing on his own, but a part of him believed Ruben would thank him later.

Bertan shut off his phone and slid it back into his pocket. Given that he was having more severe memory lapses, and more often, he would have to trust himself. That he was here for a reason. He took the suit in his hand and pulled the hanger out from under its teal shirt collar and hung it back up on the rack. He grabbed a chocolate-brown tie to go with the beige suit and slipped out of the office, locking the door behind him.

He stopped midway down the hall.

What if Ruben found out? He'd enter his office and see that someone had gotten in and taken his suit. He'd figure out it was Bertan. Bertan would have to explain himself.

Bertan took out his phone and checked the date.

It was Saturday.

Ruben was off on Saturdays. That meant he wouldn't be back until Monday.

Why on earth was he taking the suit? Was there something happening this weekend? Bertan searched his mind but found nothing but blank spaces.

He'd have to trust it.

Continuing down the hall, he turned for the front doors and stepped outside. His car was parked parallel to the building, outside the front doors. It wasn't even in a parking spot. It was sitting in the center of the lot as if the person who'd parked it had been drunk.

Behind it was Diallo's car.

Bertan hurried to the trunk and unlocked it, setting the suit down inside next to an extra S-Corp security uniform. They'd given him two in case one got ruined. On top of the uniform rested a pair of handcuffs, an extra handgun, and a clear travel bag. Inside the bag were personal care items such as a travel-size canister of shave cream, a razor, a toothbrush and toothpaste. Nothing out of the ordinary.

He stepped back and stared at the suit, but still nothing of a recollection came to him. This was what really bothered him, that he couldn't remember anymore what he was doing. Eventually this could pose a serious problem.

He shrugged it off, slammed the trunk shut, and got back in his car. Saturday nights were his nights off, *that* he always remembered. He headed for home, hoping to spend the next few days catching up on sleep.

Chapter Thirty-Two

Oscar

It was a Sunday. The phone in his hand said so, and he chose to believe it. Oscar glared at a reminder on the lock screen that told him to be at the slaughterhouse in the next half hour for a meeting with a guy named Jacob. The word *PASSWORD* scrolled along the screen beside the reminder, along with an added note requesting that he obtain bank statements proving the connection between S-Corp and Medina.

"Ah, I see," he said, as if realizing the connection for the very first time.

Five miles from the slaughterhouse, Oscar pulled off U.S. 26 amidst miles and miles of flat, boring, uniform land. He got out of the car and sauntered to the trunk, smiling as he popped it open. From inside he grabbed the clear travel bag and unzipped it, pulling out the razor and shave cream.

Pulling off his t-shirt and tossing it into the trunk, he returned to the driver's seat and pulled down the visor to reveal a mirror. As soon as he saw himself, he was shocked.

Who was this man? The man who had not shaven in days? This man with such hazel eyes they were nearly green in the afternoon sun?

Shaking off this discomfort, Oscar lathered his face with the pure, white cream. He took the razor and slid it down, down, down the cheeks of his face, over his chin. He was careful to shave above his upper lip. Careful to run that razor up his neck over and over again until the cream was nearly gone. He threw the razor onto the passenger seat, used his hand to clear away the remaining cream from his face.

"Much better," he said to himself, grinning.

Next he took out the suit and put it on, feeling the clean, tan pants and the slender, button-up shirt shape him into himself again. The chocolate tie reminded him of the color of Honduran coffee beans. He bent to smell the tie, but it gave off only a hint of earthy cologne. Nothing close to the scent of coffee.

Glancing around this car, which seemed brand new to him, he searched the glove box and came out with a pair of sunglasses. Classic aviator style with silver lenses. He looked at himself in the mirror again, clicked his teeth and winked.

Though he didn't remember allowing his hair to grow so long, Oscar paid that no mind as he tied it back into a ponytail that rested low on his upper back. Looking at himself one last time, he felt unrecognizable, and he liked it.

Returning to the trunk, he grabbed the gun and slid it behind his back and into his waistband so it remained there indiscreetly. Sliding the handcuffs into his pocket, he shut the trunk. His gaze met the road ahead, empty for miles. This empty feeling, this sense of not quite knowing where he was or why, was somehow both familiar and liberating.

His last thought before getting back into the car was how he quite liked this new sensation. The *not knowing* meant he didn't have to know where he'd been, who he'd killed or why. He could start over.

And maybe, start over he would.

#

Oscar arrived at the facility at 2:30 p.m. There were two other cars in the lot. One he recognized as belonging to the boss, Jacob. He didn't know how he knew these things, like people's names, or what this place was, but again, Oscar Reyes Mejia did not doubt himself.

Shutting off the car, Oscar got out. He

started for the front doors as any visitor would. A stoic look came over his face. His mind went blank. His back straightened and he walked with confidence. He was composed, calculated, and eerily quiet, like when he had worked for Medina.

Approaching the doors, he pulled on them for effect. He knew the place was closed. His eyes narrowed as he glared through the glass into the lobby. He glanced around and hit the speaker on the wall beside the doors.

"Our offices are closed today. May I help you?" a woman's voice called from the speaker.

"I'd like to see Jacob," Oscar replied in a slow manner so his English would seem clearer.

"Do you have an appointment?" the woman asked.

"Ask him if he enjoyed the gift we left for him," Oscar said sternly.

The speaker went silent. Oscar turned and looked out over the parking lot. The car he'd driven was hiding out of view from here, over along the side of the building where the Kill Floor was.

He heard the doors click. Oscar turned and pulled on the door handle. It opened. He stepped inside, sliding his hands into his pants pockets. He felt the handcuffs against his fingers. Stopping in the lobby, he looked around as if he'd never seen the place before.

A woman in a suit approached him from one of the hallways. On her face was a look of worry. She was frowning.

"Right this way," she said, turning and starting for the hallway.

Oscar followed. He felt his gun against his back. His senses heightened. As he approached Jacob's office, time seemed to slow. He heard the sound of his breath in his ears.

The woman stopped and waved Oscar into Jacob's office.

"Thank you," he said, stopping and watching her until she disappeared back into the lobby.

Oscar entered the office. A faint sense of

familiarity hit him again as he observed the room. Walls draped with sports memorabilia. Enough to make him sick.

"Can I help you?" Jacob asked from behind a wooden desk. A laptop sat open before him. Oscar eyed it, and a hint of realization crossed his mind like a tumbleweed across the desert.

"Good afternoon, Jacob." Oscar closed the office door.

"Who the hell are you?"

"That's no way to greet a guest, now is it?" Oscar asked, swiftly pulling his gun from its place in his pants and pointing it at the man.

Jacob jumped back in his seat. His eyes froze on the gun.

"What do you want?"

"First I want your hands up where I can see them."

Jacob quickly raised his hands into the air. Oscar moved around the desk and pushed the gun's barrel into Jacob's temple.

"Don't move. I'd hate to get your blood and brains all over my new suit," Oscar said in a low, calm voice. With a gun he felt so. . .unstoppable.

Jacob did not move.

Oscar pulled the handcuffs from his pocket. He slapped them onto one of Jacob's wrists, pulled Jacob's hand down and clasped the other end of the cuffs onto the chair arm.

"Surely you can type with one hand, yes?"

"I'm not typing anything with a gun pointed at my head," Jacob replied.

"No?" Oscar asked. He was facing the back of Jacob's head, looking at the laptop screen. "I guess that's true if you're dead."

Oscar clicked off the gun's safety. The clicking noise it made as the bullet entered the chamber brought Oscar further into the foreground, bringing forward that man he once was. . .the Oscar who had killed animals and other men.

He was prepared to kill this one if things didn't go his way.

"Okay, okay," Jacob replied, his voice cracking like a teenage boy. "What do you want?"

"Write down your password. . .on that notepad," Oscar said as he noticed the yellow notepad beside the laptop.

Jacob—hand shaking—carefully wrote a combination of letters, numbers and symbols with his one free hand. Oscar immediately ripped the piece of paper off the notepad and crumpled it into his pocket.

"Now," he said. "You're going to pull up all the bank statements and any other correspondences that you can find between S-Corp and Medina, and you're going to print it all out."

"What? Why?"

Oscar pressed the gun into Jacob's head. He got hard. He always got hard right before he killed someone. It was as though he needed it to help him end life, to be turned on by the power of having someone else's life in his own hands.

"You are in no position to ask questions."

"Fine."

Jacob used his free hand to scroll the mouse and open a series of folders. On the screen, Oscar watched as bank statements, one after the other, revealed S-Corp transferring millions of dollars to Medina. Millions. He knew Medina had funded weapons, riot gear and secret jails to use against *campesinos*. This was the proof.

Oscar listened to the nearby printer as it shot out pages of statements. He was going to end S-Corp, and this proof would do the trick. Proof of funding for kidnappings, disappearances, murder, torture. The whole nine. Of course this also meant it would end Medina. And *why* did he want to end Medina? Oscar wasn't certain.

"There," Jacob said. "That's everything."

Oscar suddenly snapped back to the present. The printer made a zip-zip-zip noise as the statements continued printing out.

"Close down the laptop," he said. There was no time to think about why he was doing what he was doing. That note had been in his phone for a reason. He would ask questions later.

Jacob did as he was told. Oscar removed the cuff that had been clipped to the chair. While his hand was still gripping the chain between the two cuffs, Jacob yanked his handcuffed wrist free of Oscar's grip. He rushed for the door. Oscar's eyes widened. He leapt at Jacob. He slammed the barrel of the gun into the back of Jacob's head.

"Ah!" Jacob let out a yell. His head bobbed around.

Oscar grabbed and pulled Jacob into his body, coming up onto his tiptoes as he squeezed his forearm around the man's neck. He brought the gun around and pointed it at Jacob's face.

"You shut the fuck up," he whispered.

Oscar yanked Jacob's body back to the desk. He took his knee and jabbed it into the back of Jacob's knee, causing Jacob to lose his footing. He pushed Jacob down until he was forced to land on his knees. Oscar clipped the other half of the cuffs to his own wrist so that the two of them were handcuffed together. He forced Jacob back up onto his feet.

He walked Jacob over to the printer.

"You're going to slowly grab the statements from the printer. One wrong move and the gun will go off," Oscar whispered into Jacob's ear.

Jacob, his legs trembling, pulled the papers from the printer. He held them still in his hand.

Oscar glanced around the room. His eyes darted from wall to wall. Finally, they landed on an empty manilla folder on Jacob's desk. He turned Jacob back to the desk. Both of them facing the desk, he pushed the gun hard into Jacob's nose.

"Put the papers in that folder."

Jacob used his free hand to slide the statements into the folder. Oscar noticed the scent of urine. He glanced down at Jacob's pants. Sure enough, the man had peed himself.

If there was one thing Oscar had learned in his years of training, it was never to let another man see him in weakness. Keep the hands still. No blinking. If he ever got in the wrong with someone, to never, ever, ever allow himself to let his bladder or bowels go.

Jacob was frightened, and it was beginning to show.

Oscar smiled.

"Now," he replied, deciding to ignore the fact that Jacob had peed himself. "Take the folder and turn and face me, very slowly. Remember I've got the gun pointed right at the back of your head."

Jacob slowly turned. As he did, Oscar held the gun in place so that when they faced one another, its barrel stared Jacob in the eye. Oscar was a few inches shorter, but it didn't matter when it was the gun that came to level with Jacob's head.

"Slide the folder into my pants," he said, looking up at Jacob.

Jacob did so, quickly pulling his hand away once the folder was in place.

Oscar turned Jacob around to face the door. Together, they walked over to it. Oscar brought his cuffed hand down and opened the door, peeking out past Jacob into the hallway.

No one there.

He yanked Jacob out of the office and into the lobby. From there Oscar could see the parking lot was empty, save for Jacob's vehicle.

"Let's go," Oscar demanded, pushing Jacob through the doors and outside.

As soon as they exited the building, the sunlight hit Oscar's eyes in such a way that it was blinding his mind. He stopped for a moment. He told himself to keep the gun on the man in front of him. A man whose name he had forgotten for the moment. He looked down at his feet, closed his eyes.

What was I doing? he asked himself.

He couldn't let on that he was confused.

Glancing around, he saw in the parking lot a

black Subaru. It was the only car in the lot.
Wasn't his. At least, he didn't think it was.

"Please don't kill me out here." The man was
whimpering.

"Quiet!" Oscar yelled.

Suddenly his mind went blank. Something about
moving from inside to the outdoors shifted him
into confusion.

Shit.

He needed to get a grip on himself. He felt
the folder that was sticking out from inside his
pants, resting against the blue shirt he wore. He
was in the middle of something with this man,
that was obvious. He would have to get rid of the
guy so he could figure out what the hell was
going on.

He hurried the man over to the Subaru.
Stopping at the driver's side door, he shifted
around and looked for some sign of recognition
from the man in question. Maybe this was his car.

He thought to search the man's pockets.

He slid the gun down and pressed it into the
man's back. The man stiffened. Reaching his
cuffed hand into the man's pockets, he came out
with the set of keys. One of them was a fob with
an insignia on it. He pressed the unlock button.
The car beeped as the door unlocked.

A breath of relief escaped him.

"Get in," he told the man.

The man's hand visibly shaking, he opened the
door.

He pushed the man down into the driver's seat.

"Here's what's going to happen," he said.
"You're going to go home. Pretend this never
happened." He paused. Whatever it was that
happened could not have been good, seeing as he
was handcuffed to this guy and had a gun pointed
at him. "You tell one living soul, I'll make sure
yours leaves this earth tomorrow. I'll also make
sure anyone you know joins you. Understand?"

"Yes," the man replied, his body shaking.

Unlocking and removing the handcuffs, he slid

them into his pocket. With the gun pointed at the man's head, he took a few steps away from the car.

"Go!" he shouted.

The man drove off, the tires of his car screeching as he veered down the road.

The gun fell to the ground. Standing there alone in the parking lot, he pulled out the folder and glanced at the papers. Pages and pages of bank statements.

"S-Corp. Medina," he whispered.

S-Corp. . .Medina. . .

His head grew heavy. Lightheaded, he closed the folder and placed it under his arm. He looked down at the clothes on his body. Whose clothes were these? Not his. There had to be something to remind him of who he was.

Unfastening the tie, he slid it off his neck and unbuttoned the shirt. Untucking it from his pants, he glanced down and noticed something on his chest.

And there it was. Scrolling along his collarbone was a tattoo in black ink. He couldn't read what it said. The first letter looked like the letter W, which meant it was an M.

E. . .

D. . .

I. . .

N?

MEDINA.

Bertan's head spun as he suddenly came back to himself. Feeling nauseous, he bent over and threw up on the concrete. Wiping his mouth clean, he stood back up and checked his pockets for his phone, but it wasn't there. He must've left it in his car.

Where was his car?

He wandered around like a lost boy until he discovered it parked along the side of the facility. But before he could return to the car, it dawned on him that this suit was not his. The only person he would've borrowed it from was

Ruben.

Or maybe he purchased it.

He couldn't remember.

Returning to his car, he searched the trunk and found his usual t-shirt and jeans. *That* was familiar. He changed out of the suit and decided to hide it in the trunk until he could remember what the hell happened.

That was, if he ever remembered at all.

Chapter Thirty-Three

Bertan

By the time Bertan changed into his clothes, closed up his gun in the glovebox and left the manilla folder on the passenger seat, he felt himself again.

He didn't particularly like it.

Catching his breath, he took a moment to gather himself. He suddenly felt tired and sore.

He went to slide his phone back into the pocket of his jeans. As he did so, it hit against something already in the pocket. Bertan pulled out the phone and slid his fingers back in, coming out with a small piece of paper.

S-CORP TRANSGENICS
FORT COLLINS, COLORADO

He stared at the sheet of paper. He must've had it for some reason. Glancing out the window at the facility, his eyes caught the landing dock where the transport trucks unloaded.

"That's it," he whispered.

Ruben had told him to find out when a certain transport truck was scheduled to leave the facility in Fort Collins, and where it was headed.

No one was around. The one redeeming quality of this facility was that they allowed workers off on Sundays.

Bertan got out of the car and pulled his keys from the uniform in the trunk. The suit he'd changed out of caught his eye. His eyes wandered along the fabric as if looking for something, which gave him a very out-of-body feeling. This out-of-body experience continued as his hand reached in, almost automatically, and searched the pockets of the suit. He felt like some robot. . .or puppet whose strings were being controlled by someone else. His fingers touched a piece of paper in one of the pants pockets. He pulled it out. Opening it, he saw a password.

It clicked in his mind.

Bertan slammed the trunk shut and entered the building from the back, then went directly to the plant manager's office.

Once inside, he turned on one of the laptops and sat down. He felt dizzy from his walk into the building, so he gave himself a minute. He closed his eyes, thought of Carmen and Gabriella. Time alluded him for a moment. How long ago had they left for Honduras? Were they home yet? The uncertainty flooded his head and he felt himself about to lapse again, which he could not afford to do. He knew he needed to get some information to Ruben.

Bertan took several deep breaths. He reached down and held onto the desk to ground himself. Ruben had said to focus on his five senses, to hold onto something physical to keep himself in the present, take deep breaths to smell the air around him, to listen to the whirring sounds of nearby machines.

Eventually he calmed. He opened his eyes and felt stable again. He returned his attention to the laptop and typed in the password. The screen opened to a new desktop with various file folders, spreadsheets and apps he did not recognize. He smiled. His heart lifted at the thought of getting what Ruben had asked for, so maybe they could go after S-Corp and shut the whole operation down.

From his pocket he pulled out the paper Ruben had given him. He knew the facility kept a schedule for the delivery of beefs. They'd trained him on how to search for these schedules when he first began working here. Part of his job was to track the transport trucks and report any that did not deliver on time.

Bertan opened a file and found the transport schedule. He reviewed the spreadsheet, scrolling down until he found the name of the S-Corp property written on Ruben's paper.

"Fort Collins," he whispered. He found the delivery date: May 25.

That was only five days away. He wondered what they needed the information for. His eyes caught the number of beefs being transported. Only seven. That was odd. Most transports carried closer to fifty beefs at once. But only seven? Was there something about these beefs in particular?

Standing up, Bertan left the office. He hurried outside to call Ruben.

"You find the information?" Ruben asked right off.

"Yes. The beefs will be transported here, actually. In five days," Bertan replied.

"Great. Thank you." Ruben paused. "I got word this morning that Carmen and Gabriella made it to Honduras."

At that, Bertan's shoulders softened. A breath of relief exited his body. He didn't realize how stressed he was about his family until he learned they were safe.

"Thank God," he said, finding his way to his car and leaning into the hood, feeling he might pass out.

"They're safe, Bertan. They're really safe now," Ruben said.

Bertan dropped his hand to his side, still holding onto the phone. He felt himself near tears. Placing his head down against the hood of the car, he took another deep breath. The relief of it had made his head spin. As it slowed, his eyes closed. An image of Honduran mountains came to his mind, the way the fog rolled over them in the mornings back home. That was how he felt now.

"Bertan?" Ruben's voice called from the phone.

Bertan brought the phone back up to his ear.

"Yes. Thank you so much," he said, holding back tears.

"You okay?"

"Couldn't be better," Bertan answered, thinking not only of his family but how he was on the trajectory of ending S-Corp so that he could finally be with them.

Bertan got into his car and sat down, closing his eyes. He kept the phone held against his ear, waiting for Ruben to say something, but equally content to sit in silence for one moment.

"Bertan? You still there?" Ruben asked.

Bertan's eyes popped open. Yes, he most certainly was.

"Yes," he responded in a quiet tone. His eyes wandered over to the passenger seat where he'd placed that manilla folder. Pursing his lips, searching his memory, he didn't know what was inside it. So he picked it up and opened it.

"I'm going to get this information to my partner," Ruben said.

Bertan read the contents of the folder. Pages of bank statements. The proof that S-Corp was funneling money to Medina! How on earth had he gotten this? His chest lifted and he felt so elated to see it, he no longer cared where it had come from.

"Wait," he said. "I stumbled upon some stuff you mind find interesting."

"What's that?"

"I found some bank statements. . .S-Corp's been sending millions of dollars to Medina."

"You mean *printed* bank statements?"

"Yes."

"Can I see them?"

"I'll bring them to you. . ." Bertan said, stopping himself. He was about to add that he'd give Ruben back the suit he borrowed, but he couldn't remember if he'd borrowed it or taken it, so he omitted that piece.

Ending the call, Bertan immediately texted Carmen:

ARE YOU SAFE?

He started the car and turned out of the lot, heading back to the hostel. By the time he arrived, she'd replied:

ALL SAFE, GRACIAS A DIOS.

And with that, Bertan got the sense his life was only beginning.

Chapter Thirty-Four

Bray

A day passed, and rather sufferably. It would have been worse had it not been for Bray's new ability to meditate. Only four days remained until Rhea and the other cows went to slaughter, and to Bray, it felt as though everything was hanging in limbo.

There had been no word from Lana's contact about the transport of the cows, so Bray kept herself occupied by meditating with Emily, tending to some gardening, and sitting with Kage, as she was doing presently, to read the manuscript Kage's father had written. They were both sitting in Bray's bed, a gentle sunlight pouring in through the window and warming Bray's legs spread out before her. The manuscript was altogether upsetting, and that put it mildly. Bray found herself both in awe and in a kind of suspended defeat. What if this kind of disappearance happened to her, or to Kage and any of her friends, as a result of this plan? What if, like hundreds of activists, they too ended up in prison with no way out?

Suddenly a knock came at the door. Bray and Kage looked up. Kage quickly shut the laptop, slid it beneath the covers and out of sight.

"Yeah?" Bray called out.

The door opened. It was Lana. Bray sighed with relief. They didn't need Trevor finding out what they were doing. Things were already hard enough with him.

Lana entered, shutting the door behind her. She came over and sat down on the bed beside Bray. Kage pulled the laptop back out, set it on his lap, and opened it. He paid little mind to Lana as he continued scrolling through the manuscript.

"What's going on?" Lana asked, glancing at the

laptop.

"It's Kage's dad's flash drive," Bray said.

"What's on it?"

"Writings that expose S-Corp's practices. Other files are locked. But we've got even more proof now," Kage said, his voice low, its tone slightly downtrodden.

"What are you going to do with it?" Lana asked.

"Find a way to post it online. People need to know," he replied, his eyes set on the laptop screen.

"Just. . .be careful," Lana said.

There was a long pause. As Bray sat there between Kage and Lana, she noticed the electricity that surged in the room. It wasn't directed at her, but at Kage. And it came from Lana. It was clear that Lana had more feelings for Kage, or at least some form of chemistry, than she let on.

"I heard back from Ruben," Lana said, breaking Bray's concentration.

"And?" Bray asked, looking at her.

"Turns out the cows are being transported to the slaughterhouse where he works. . .in four days. And there's a trailer park about ten miles away. The trailers are all abandoned so you can use one. He needs to know when."

Kage met eyes with Bray. Bray smiled. He smiled in return.

"Tell him we'll come tomorrow," Bray said. "That we'll need the place for the next four days."

"Got it," Lana said. She paused. "I'd like to come with you, to help out."

"No," Kage said adamantly. "Trevor won't let us take the Jeep, and I'd rather you stay here, where it's safe."

"Don't patronize me," Lana replied, winking at Kage. "I'm not some helpless child."

Bray leaned back against the wall, allowing the two of them to flirt, which was so obvious from her point of view. She wanted to get up and step away, let the two of them talk.

"Whatever," Kage replied, rolling his eyes.

"I'll stay," Lana said. "But only because there's no extra room on that bike of yours."

Lana winked at him, stood up and left the room, closing the door.

"You two ever talk?" Bray asked Kage.

"Nah, not really. I've pretty much given up on any hope of something happening between us. She's way out of my league," he replied, shrugging.

"Don't say that." Bray nudged his shoulder with hers. Kage let out a laugh.

"Shall we message Elliott?" he asked, changing the subject.

"Let's do it," Bray replied, watching him open the internet.

If only Kage realized Lana had feelings for him. Bray didn't feel right getting involved in their business. She hoped that after all of this came to pass, the two of them would come together. It would be a shame for the world to be in such a bad way and, on top of that, for there to be no love.

Chapter Thirty-Five

Bray

The next morning, Bray rose at dawn. She'd been awake most of the night, unable to sleep due to the nature of what was coming. . .the feeling of uncertainty, of eerie discomfort, like doom was near.

It would take well over seven hours to ride into Idaho, not something she was looking forward to given Kage's bike wasn't exactly comfortable. How she'd manage for seven hours, she didn't know. Though she wouldn't be meditating this morning, at least she did notice that the meditation practice was helping her accept her reality a bit more each day. If she had to ride several hours to Idaho, she would. Period.

She thought of Emily. Sitting on the bed and stretching herself into some kind of aliveness, Bray stood up. It was time to say goodbye to her friend.

She headed down the hall toward Emily's door, feeling a mixture of trepidation and sadness. This could very well be the last time she'd ever see Emily.

A light was poking out from beneath Emily's door. Bray knocked hesitantly.

"Come in," Emily called.

Bray opened the door and walked in. Emily was sitting up in bed, reading a book.

"Early for you, isn't it?" Emily asked, closing the book and setting it down beside her. Bray looked upon her quietly, knowing how much she would miss coming in here to sit and have long chats, meditate, and feel as welcome as she had in this space.

"Kage and I are leaving," Bray replied, her sadness increasing.

"Come sit down." Emily patted a spot on the bed.

Bray sat down facing Emily. She'd never felt this close to anyone, other than Alice. It had been so hard to say goodbye to Alice. This felt even harder, less finite, because Bray didn't know if this was really goodbye.

"You here to say goodbye?" Emily asked, smiling.

Bray nodded and began to cry. Emily rubbed her back.

"I love you, Bray. You're like the daughter I never had."

Bray nodded again, agreeing that she felt Emily very much a mother-figure, but the words wouldn't come out.

"No matter what happens, remember what I said. Remember meditation, how it can help you in the scariest situations. Remember the gift you have, that the world needs you," Emily added, choking up on her own tears. She paused, wiped her face, and continued with a more level tone. "Remember I am with you, and I support your every move. No matter what, you won't be alone."

"What if I don't make it?" Bray asked between tears.

Emily paused. She pulled Bray in for a hug, rocking her back and forth. It felt so warm and calm, Bray could have fallen right to sleep. She could forget this whole plan, let it go, and stay here in this safe, quiet home. She could have an easy life. Alice had asked her to go live her life for herself, but maybe on some level Alice had known that there was little life for Bray to live when she had this gift, this curse of sorts, to know and feel too much of the pain suffered by animals in captivity.

Yes, if it wasn't for that, she'd stay. But she knew she couldn't. She pulled away from Emily, wiped her face.

"Remember. . ." Emily spoke softly. "Life is endless."

Eventually Bray stopped crying. The door opened slightly and Kage presented himself. It was time to go. Bray squeezed Emily's hands, let go, and walked away.

#

Outside, a blood-red sun rose up over an indigo-tinted land, exposing a sky full of silver clouds. The clouds hung low, promising rain.

Kage had readied the bike with a full tank of gas and some food in the compartment. Ethan and Lana came out to see them off. Trevor had chosen to stay inside. Bray assumed by his refusal to say goodbye that he was still not happy about their intention to proceed despite his warnings.

Ethan walked up to Bray, placed his hands on her shoulders, and looked into her face with a fondness that made her smile.

"Take care of yourself out there, Bray," he said. "We all love you, even if some of us have a strange way of showing it. I'll send you some energy from afar. This is your home, whenever you do come back."

If I come back, she thought to herself.

She and Ethan hugged. She stepped away to allow him to say goodbye to Kage.

Lana came up to her. She immediately grew embarrassed. Lana would always be the most beautiful woman to her.

"How you feeling?" she asked.

But how could Bray answer? The feelings were pushed down somewhere beneath herself, where they could stay protected. If she was going to go through with this, her feelings would have to wait, or else she'd back out.

"I'm okay." Bray shrugged.

"Tell Ruben hello for me. . .and be careful."

Bray nodded and turned away. They'd need to leave before she changed her mind.

She watched Kage say goodbye to Lana, feeling

suddenly grateful that Kage was going with her. She felt alone enough as it was.

Before Bray knew it, they were off. She felt the presence of Lana and Ethan behind her. She turned back to look and then glanced up at the porch. There, Emily stood with her arms crossed, watching as they cleared the corn stalks and started down the dirt path for Idaho.

#

Kage started out heading north, into Cody. He'd said their best route would be a cut through Yellowstone National Park. There would be people visiting, yes, but May was not a busy time of year, with kids still being in school. And this route avoided any state line check points.

As the bike sped ahead along 120 North, the sun still had not much presented itself since morning. Instead, the sky spread out before them like a heavy, white screen. So much cloud cover and no sign of blue sky. The road was empty, one Bray recognized from their earlier trip to see Elliott. Bray thought of him, how he, too, would soon be on his way to Idaho.

Kage turned the bike down US highway 14, a four-lane road that made Bray cringe. It seemed far too exposing considering the discrete nature of their travels. She would have to trust Kage on this one.

They passed miles of abandoned suburbs, a Total-Mart, and a cattle company that had long ago closed down, Bray was relieved to see. The last thing she needed was to see more animals in distress.

Soon the highway narrowed to two lanes, traveling alongside a river that meandered through the dry land, the water's turquoise color offsetting the bland desert-like feel of the terrain around them.

Bray listened to the hum of the bike beneath

her. Its vibrations shook at her legs and her bottom, making her lower back hurt. She did her best to breathe through it.

The terrain rose into foothills of dry earth scattered with pine trees. The scent of pine hit Bray with a cool, free smell that lifted her and made her smile. The pine trees increased in mass as they sped forward, winding through hills and hills of pine and other trees Bray did not know the names of. So many trees. Her eyes watered. All her life she had never been exposed to such nature, the pure rawness of it.

It made her nearly cry.

The bike curved around a mountain and, to their left, Yellowstone Lake opened out before them, a motionless piece of glass, its cobalt waters offering a unique sight; a lake that had yet to be tainted by human error.

"Wow!" Bray called out.

Kage slowed the bike and pulled off to the side of the road.

Bray jumped off the bike. She stood and watched the lake, her mouth agape.

"Amazing, isn't it?" Kage said, walking up beside her.

"I'm speechless," Bray replied.

"Let's eat before we move on," Kage suggested, handing her a jar of vegetables mixed with vinegar. They sat down together, overlooking the lake, and ate.

"I've never seen so much nature in all my life. I can't believe all this still exists," Bray said, taking a bite of food and tasting its slight bitterness.

"S-Corp hasn't had its way with Wyoming yet. . .but it's coming," Kage replied.

Bray took in a deep breath of the fresh air. The lake was surrounded by miles of pine trees. Birds and hawks flew back and forth amongst the trees. The sky opened and revealed some of its blue tint.

"I imagine once we get to Idaho it'll

be. . .different," Kage said. "And who knows what's going to happen after that. . .so I thought this would be a good place to stop. A reminder of why we're doing what we're doing: to ultimately preserve all this."

Kage pointed at the lake, and he wasn't smiling. How could they smile much when they both knew what was ahead? He was right; there really was no way to know what was to come of their plan, whether it would work, and if it did, what the nation would look like after.

They finished eating and returned to the bike. Bray silently bid the lake and the birds farewell. Kage started the engine and they shot off down the road. Bray quickly realized how sore she was from the ride.

Rest would have to come later, if it did at all.

Chapter Thirty-Six

Bray

Late that afternoon, Kage pulled off the two-lane highway they'd been traveling for hours. He stopped the bike once to check the map and continued on.

Finally they came upon a trailer park to the left. Eleven trailers scattered along a desert atmosphere. More dead and dry earth.

Kage drove slowly between the trailers. Each one had broken-out windows or was covered in sand. This place had been completely abandoned. Bray squeezed Kage's sides in reaction to the eerie quiet all around them.

Two men stood outside a trailer up ahead. She hoped one of them was Ruben, feared who else it might be.

Kage pulled the bike up beside the two men. One of them waved at him. He shut off the engine.

"You must be Ruben," he said.

"That's me," one of them replied. Both Ruben and the man standing next to him were as tall as Kage. Short for men, but taller than Bray. Ruben's curly, black hair was wet. The pair of glasses he wore didn't match with the rest of his face, which was scarred and otherwise covered with a thick beard.

Bray and Kage got off the bike. While Kage shook hands with Ruben, Bray remained standing by the bike, suddenly feeling very shy.

"This is Bray," Kage said. "Thanks for giving us a place to work."

"Lana wasn't real forthcoming on your 'work,'" Ruben replied, emphasizing the word *work*. "Mind telling me more?"

"Inside," Kage said, motioning toward the trailer behind them.

Bray loosened up at the mention of Lana's

name. She opened the compartment and took out the bag of food they'd brought. She turned and stared at the man standing beside Ruben. He had a lot of stubble on his face. The color of his skin was lighter than Ruben's. His eyes were what really caught her attention: a kind of yellowish-green color that nearly matched the color of the dry earth around them. It was hard to stop staring at them.

"This is Bertan, a good friend," Ruben said, looking over at Bray. "Let's go in."

Bray followed behind Kage, entering the trailer behind Ruben and Bertan.

They entered an open room that Bray assumed was a living area. There was a table across from them, four chairs around it. A wide, bay window looked out onto the land. She stood on a shaggy carpet that stopped at the kitchen, where tile flooring led to a sink, a set of cabinets and a refrigerator. On the counter were several jugs of Spring One water. Beyond the kitchen, a hallway led to a single bedroom. The place smelled moldy.

"This was the best trailer out of all of them," Ruben explained. "There's a bed in the back. I washed all the sheets, so it's clean. The water is for you. . .and there's some food in the fridge and the cabinets."

"Thanks for doing this," Kage replied, stepping over to the table and looking around.

"Want to tell me now what all this is about?" Ruben asked.

"First I need to know who you are, exactly." Kage pointed at Bertan.

"I work security at the slaughterhouse," Bertan replied, crossing his arms. He had some kind of accent, maybe from Mexico. "I was the one who got you the info on those cows."

"He risked his job for you all," Ruben added.

"Thank you," Bray spoke, meeting eyes with Bertan. Bertan looked her over for a moment and nodded. He gave off a tense, uneasy energy.

"So you want to tell them, or shall I?" Kage

asked Bray.

"You go ahead."

"Lana said you're working undercover. . .an animal rights activist?" Kage asked Ruben.

"I am," Ruben replied simply.

"We are activists, too. Lana has been staying with us in Wyoming. Her whole team got kidnapped, I assume by S-Corp," Kage said. "Bray here is an animal empath."

"What the hell is that?" Bertan asked.

"She communicates with animals," Kage replied. He went on to tell their story. . .about the cows and the testing and their human-like awareness that S-Corp wanted to cover up. . .how they found evidence that S-Corp faked the 2027 terrorist attack. . .how they planned on exposing S-Corp. . .and how Bray planned to use Embedicare to show the public what happened to Rhea and the other cows.

"To galvanize them," Bray said to wrap things up.

For ages Ruben and Bertan stood there, stone-faced, staring at Kage. Bray couldn't tell what they were thinking.

"I. . .don't know what to say," Ruben finally replied. "That's a lot. But I am happy to help."

"We appreciate that," Kage said.

"I don't understand," Bertan said. "How are you going to show the country these cows being slaughtered?"

"My friend, Elliott." Bray opened up. "He's on his way here. He's a hacker. He says he should be able to hack Embedicare's system. We'll do it through one of their implants."

Bray stopped. She wondered when Elliott would arrive. She'd emailed him the exact coordinates of the trailer, provided by Ruben, this morning. She wanted another friendly face in the room.

Ruben and Bertan glanced at one another. The room went quiet. Bertan shook his head, walked off down the hall, turned around and came back.

"This is the craziest shit I've ever heard,"

he commented.

"And if it works," Kage said. "Just imagine."

"I don't see how it could work," Bertan said.

"Wait until Elliott gets here. Then we'll show you," Bray said.

Bertan's words gave her zero comfort, zero confidence. But even if he didn't believe in her, in their plan, it didn't mean he was right. If there was ever a time she needed to start believing in herself, that time was now.

#

While the four of them continued going back and forth as to whether Bray's plan would work, a set of tires crunched along the ground outside the trailer. Everyone ducked in unison. A door slammed.

"Elliott," Bray whispered over to Kage.

A knock came at the door.

Bray hurried over to a small window beside the door and peeked outside. She smiled and opened the door.

"What took you so long?" she said, winking at Elliott.

He entered the trailer carrying a box of equipment. Bray closed the door behind him.

"Sorry to keep you all waiting, but my dreads required extra attention this morning," Elliott replied. He set the box on the table, turned, and smiled at Bray.

"Good to see you," she replied.

He nodded. From the box he pulled out a white, square piece of equipment the size of a cell phone. It had an antenna, which Elliott pulled up as he flipped it on.

"First things first," Elliott said.

"What's that?" Bray asked.

"RF Repeater," he replied, looking at Bray as

if she would know what it was. "Keeps the perps away."

"Perps?" Bertan asked.

"Drones," Bray and Elliott replied in unison. Bray shot a glance at Elliott. They both laughed.

Elliott opened the trailer door and set the device down beneath the stairs. He came back inside. Wind blew the door shut, causing Bray to startle.

"I see you brought all your friends?" Elliott asked Bray, looking at Ruben and Bertan while scratching his head.

"This is Ruben and. . .Bertan?" she replied, not sure she'd pronounced his name correctly.

Bertan nodded.

"This is the place you requested," Ruben said. "The slaughterhouse is a few miles up the road."

"Brilliant." Elliott smiled.

He began unpacking a laptop, a wireless charger, and an unopened box that read EMBEDICARE in blue lettering on its top. That must've been the implant. Bray gulped and glanced down at her forearm.

"Mind if I get started?" Elliott asked, pointing at one of the chairs.

"Do whatever you need," Ruben replied.

Elliott sat down at the table, cracking his knuckles as the laptop powered on.

"What's next?" Kage asked.

"Well, if we've only got three days, then I need to get cracking on Embedicare," Elliott replied.

It began to sink in for Bray. All this time this plan had felt surreal, something they'd only discussed in theory, behind closed doors, in messages. But as she stood in this room with Elliott, with Kage whom she'd only known a month or so but it felt so much longer, and these two men who *worked for S-Corp*, it was coming together. She gulped. The heat from outside crept in through closed windows and formed as sweat beneath her arms and against her back.

Or perhaps it was the nerves.

"We need a plan." Kage's voice brought Bray back to the matter at hand. "So we're ready to go when he's ready."

"Anything I can do to help?" Ruben asked.

"Maybe." Kage tapped his fingers against his lips as if in thought. "I feel the need to organize. . .to decide how we do this so it's as effective as possible, you know?"

"That's very wise," Ruben agreed. He reminded Bray of Ethan in how he spoke, how he presented himself.

Bray's nerves increased as she stood there. She was no good at planning anything and so didn't feel useful to Kage right now. Despite the heat outside, what she really needed was some fresh air.

"I'm going to take a break outside," she said to Kage.

Bray exited the trailer and walked past Kage's bike and the two-door Nissan Elliott had arrived in. Up past the trailers sat a trio of small boulders. As she approached them, she gazed out at the sun, which had dropped far from its midpoint in the sky. Bray had gotten pretty decent at telling time by the position of the sun. It was somewhere around 7 p.m., she presumed, and everyone back in Meeteetse was probably eating dinner.

She sat down on one of the boulders. Her bottom was sore from the long bike ride. She immediately stood back up. What she needed was a cushion, but all around her was nothing but hardness and harshness. Shrugging, she sat down on the ground and rested her back against the boulder.

Bray closed her eyes and breathed deeply. She missed Emily. This was frightening, what she was about to do. She called out for Rhea to ensure everything was okay, and to perhaps get solace like Alice used to provide.

"*Dear Bray,*" Rhea responded. "*How are you?*"

In that moment Bray forgot she was talking to a cow.

"I'm afraid. I don't know what's going to happen, but I just wanted to check in and make sure you and the others are okay."

"We are. We are also afraid, afraid of what will happen if our escape is not successful."

The trailer door opened and slammed closed. Bray opened her eyes. Coming down the steps and walking toward her was Bertan. She wasn't sure she wanted to speak to him. His energy made her feel on edge.

"Mind if I join you?" he asked, placing his hands on his hips. "I don't do well with idle time, and they don't need me in there."

Bray nodded, but with reservation.

"How long have you known you can. . .talk to animals?" He sat down on a boulder, slightly above her.

"For as long as I can remember."

"How do you know it's animals, and not voices?" he asked, pausing. "Sorry. I don't want to make it sound like you're mentally. . .you know."

"It's okay," she said. It wasn't like he was the first to doubt her. And if she survived this, he wouldn't be the last.

"I had this friend named Alice. She was a pig I met at a factory farm when I was thirteen. She was just a piglet at the time. I had an open sore on my arm and she licked it. Somehow her DNA got into my bloodstream, and from that day onward, I could talk to her, in my mind, and she talked to me.

"Then, last month, I started feeling her pain. She got stuck with an electric prod and I ended up with a burn on my back."

"How'd you know that's where the burn came from?" he asked. His eyes glared down at her in pure curiosity. The green of them was so clear she felt she could almost see into him, which made her shiver. He didn't seem to be doubting

her so much as searching her. For what, she
didn't know.

"I had a vision. I saw Alice inside her
gestation crate. I watched a worker stick her,
and then I got the burn simultaneously."

"Hm." He nodded.

"Then I found out she was going to slaughter.
She didn't deserve to die so violently like that.
Plus, I realized that if she was injured, I would
be too, which meant I could die if she died. Not
to mention she was a best friend to me, so I went
and found her. Elliott helped me," she said,
nodding toward the trailer. "We got all the way
up to Wyoming from Denver, which is where we were
from. I found her transport truck and I was able
to save her."

"Where is she now?"

"She died. I was only able to save her from
slaughter, not from death."

"You're still alive."

"Yes, but I went unconscious when she died. I
was lucky I didn't die. I should have."

Bertan went quiet. Bray decided to say nothing
more. They both sat and watched as the sky faded
toward night.

"I never had visions like what you have," he
said eventually. "But I get flashbacks. I used to
become like this whole other person. Ruben says I
have trauma, something like that. For a while
there I thought I was losing my mind. I've seen a
lot of violence, done a lot of things. I guess it
all did kind of mess with me, you know?" he said,
looking at her.

She didn't know. But she nodded. She was glad
to hear him open up. It made him feel more human
to her, more warm.

"So when I heard you talk about animals and
being able to connect them to other humans
through those implant things, at first I thought
you were lying or something. But then I
thought. . .if I can switch and become this whole
other person without knowing I did it, then I

guess a young girl could talk to animals," Bertan said. A slight smile grew on his face.

Bray smiled back at him. She didn't know what to say to this man. She was surprised by his sudden forthcoming nature.

"You kind of remind me of my daughter," he said finally.

"I do?"

"She's small like you. And your hair is the same color and length. She's a spitfire. I bet you are, too."

"I've never been told that, but maybe I am," Bray said modestly.

Bertan pulled out his phone and showed Bray a photo.

"That's her." He pointed at one of two people in the photo.

Bertan's phone screen revealed a close-up image of two females, one older. . .and a girl who appeared to be much younger than Bray. Her face was round and she had dimples and dark eyes. Bray didn't see much resemblance to herself.

"Is that your wife?" Bray asked.

"Yes," he replied, bringing the phone to his lap and peering down at the photo. "Carmen."

"And you all live here, in Idaho?" she asked. There was no mistaking that his accent and his brown complexion made it clear to her he was from Mexico or somewhere further south. She wondered how he had ended up here. She was curious.

"No, my wife and child are in Honduras," he replied, sliding the phone back into his pocket.

"Why are they in Honduras?"

Bertan looked at her. His eyes narrowed. She sensed he was testing whether he could trust her.

"They just went back home from being in Texas for a while," he said. "Being illegal in the U.S. isn't easy."

"I guess it isn't." She didn't know much about the immigration issues in this country, but she knew enough to believe him.

"When will you get to see them again?"

"Soon, I hope. After I help you take down S-Corp."

"What?" she asked, confused.

"Ruben. . .he helped my family. So I want to help in exchange."

"Oh."

"And I want S-Corp destroyed," he admitted.

"But you work for them," she said. "I thought you'd be on their side."

"I wouldn't have helped you if I was. I have worked for them a long time. Like ten years, I think. They don't pay us hardly anything. The work is long hours, few breaks, violent, dangerous. I've seen a lot here. Plus. . ." Bertan stopped.

"Plus what?"

"You might want to know they have a sister company, in Central America. They're called Medina."

"Is that where you're from?" Bray asked, even more curious.

"Honduras. I used to work for Medina, down there. They made me do awful things." His voice trailed off.

"What kind of things?" Bray asked, almost afraid to.

"Your ears are too young to know."

Bray didn't push. She could tell he was the type who didn't trust easily, questioned everyone, which was valid given his status. And, interestingly, she found she could relate.

The trailer door opened. Ruben walked out, waved Bertan over.

"I have to go," Bertan said to Bray. "I work tonight."

"Thanks for sitting with me," she replied.

Bertan nodded to her. Any smile that was on his face quickly faded, and he walked away.

#

When Bray went back into the trailer, Kage was sitting beside Elliott at the table.

"What's up?" she asked, walking over and sitting down.

"Elliott's getting into those password-protected files on my dad's flash drive," Kage replied.

Bray glanced at the laptop and saw the flash drive inserted. She quietly watched the two of them, how the laptop screen lit up their faces in the coming night. Suddenly Bray found herself not wanting to know what else was on those files. At least, not tonight. Her mind was full, and her head began to ache.

She needed rest.

"I'm going to try and sleep," she said, and stood up.

"You okay?" Elliott asked her.

Bray nodded to him and went on down the hall into the bedroom. The bed was the only piece of furniture in the space, which made the room not all that inviting.

She lay down and looked around at the empty walls. If this were her room, she'd have no idea how to fill it. What would she put on such bare walls? Posters of animals? Probably. Maybe she'd paint the walls in her favorite color: lavender. But the reality of her ever having her own space was not something she could imagine. When she thought about the future, she only saw the same darkness that was now seeping in through the shades of the window beside the bed. She exhaled, turned on her side, away from the window, and closed her eyes.

Chapter Thirty-Seven

Elliott

This trailer smelled like old, moldy books. The more Elliott thought of it, actually, he realized it smelled like his grandparents' apartment back in Denver. This made it challenging for him to avoid reminiscing.

Added to that was the sound of house jazz coming from his laptop. He loved jazz. Not only did it help his ADHD mind to focus, but it was sentimental. His dad had listened to jazz while cooking dinner in the evenings. He'd dance around the kitchen, prepping African or Middle Eastern cuisines while Elliott's mom was at work. Elliott would sit and watch, idolizing his father, the man who used to tell him to "take life easy" every night when putting him to bed.

But his parents were gone. Long gone, it felt like, yet it also felt like they'd only died yesterday. To have this "both/and" paradox in his life clouded his brain with an occasional mix of loneliness and normalcy. For years it had become normal that his parents were gone, even though he frequently missed them. And this plan to expose S-Corp's role in causing the deaths of thousands of citizens, including his parents, only intensified his longing for his family.

The sounds of djembe drums, an occasional xylophone, and piano danced into Elliott's ears. The rhythm of a saxophone flowed in and out in bouncing waves, keeping his body moving while he sat at the table.

It was midnight. Kage had also gone to sleep, and so Elliott was alone in the living room. He found this trailer to be a bit creepy. He wasn't sure he'd get much sleep in a stale place like this, but at least he was occupied with finding ways exploit Embedicare's network. He'd found a way in. He wasn't inside yet; it would still take a while to find their weaknesses, to learn them the way a mechanic might learn the inner workings of a car. The way his dad had learned and had begun teaching Elliott how to cook. There were exact ingredients: computer codes and programs designed to get in the "back door" of a complex system like Embedicare's. In this case, Elliott had already spent a couple days creating a program that could find a pathway into their system. Once inside, he would find out exactly where code would need to be manipulated so Bray could have access to the communication feature.

They'd finally expose S-Corp. This included releasing the list of names of all citizens who had died in the S-Corp fertilizer disaster. Elliott thought about his parents and how their names would pop up on the screens of hundreds of thousands of Embedicare implants. He stopped typing for a moment. Would anyone recognize his parents' names? Having been only nine at the time of their funeral, all he remembered was that the church pews were filled and that people had to stand up in the back of the church, there were so many in attendance.

Elliott felt bothered by this question and stood up to stretch. He stepped away from the laptop. He opened one of the cabinets and pulled out a bag of tortilla chips. Standing there and staring out the window, giving his eyes a much-needed break, he chomped away at the chips. He wanted something more substantial, but all there was to eat was vegan food, and he was no vegan. Maybe this whole process would change that for him, but he doubted it. He had no issue with eating animals. That was one of the most significant differences between him and Bray: how she was this staunch animal rights person, always had been, and he didn't care that much. Her reasoning for this plan was to attempt to liberate animals. She'd wanted that from a young age. They'd had enough conversations off and on about her viewpoints and he always played devil's advocate. He picked up on the fact that she didn't like that about him, but he did it to challenge her. He did it because if the day came that she'd have to argue with a less loving human than him, maybe it would prepare her.

He ate the remainder of the tortilla chips and tossed the bag into a nearby trash can. Moving slowly down the hall toward the bathroom, he passed it and stopped at the bedroom door, which was closed. He stood and listened in to the silence on the other side. Kage and Bray were sound asleep. This was good. He felt a little worried for Bray, who he'd always considered a little sister. A little sister who often got on his nerves, but only because of how much he loved her. He considered all they'd been through in those days following her escape from the psych ward back in April. Recalling the time they were chased by rabid dogs in Wyoming, it still gave him the shivers. He'd really thought he was going to die or at least lose his arm after being bitten so badly. But Bray ingeniously saved his arm with medical-grade honey, of all things. Then she'd run off to save that pig, Alice was her name. Elliott was still not sure what to think of all of this. . .whether she had a "gift," but he'd spent enough time with her to know she was not mentally ill like her parents believed.

Bray was misunderstood. Unassuming, reserved. Being hidden away from the world for most of her childhood must've been lonely in the way he was sometimes lonely for his parents. That was something he *could* understand. And this plan of hers. . .she wasn't wrong to want to stop S-Corp. They needed to be stopped. That was why he was helping her. He didn't have to agree with her perspective on animals to know how vital it was for the future of their country that this corporation be shut down for good.

Chapter Thirty-Eight

Bray

Bray woke the next morning to the sound of electronic jazz music coming from the living room. Kage was asleep beside her, practically snoring. It made Bray smile, which she very much needed.

She got up and walked out into the living room.

Elliott glanced over at her, nodded, and shot his eyes back at the laptop screen. His fingers typed rapidly. He was wearing the same clothes he'd arrived in.

"Did you get any sleep?" Bray asked, walking over to the sink. She found a cup in one the cabinets and poured some water from one of the jugs. It felt weird to be drinking water developed by the corporation they were about to expose, the same corporation her mother had dedicated her life to.

"A couple hours," Elliott replied, bringing her back to present.

Bray went over and stood behind him. She took a sip of water and stared at the screen. She saw nothing but a white screen and lines upon lines of HTML code.

"How close are you?" she asked.

"Hard to say. It's one of those things where I'll get it when I get it."

Bray nodded. They had two days left. Once he figured out how to hack Embedicare, they'd insert the implant and Elliott would show her the way to transmit through it.

She thought about the implant.

"Who's going to be the one to insert the implant into my arm?"

Elliott stopped. He turned and looked at her.

"Good question." He stood up and rummaged

through the box that was still sitting on the table. Pulling out a brown paper bag, he looked inside. "I brought a syringe and some needles."

"And this implant is not traceable?" she asked as she watched him pull out the syringe and needles.

"Nope. A guy I know in Red Lodge put it together. The implant is in the syringe already." He picked up the syringe and showed it to her. "I honestly think you should do it yourself."

Bray narrowed her eyes so she could see. It was still a bit dark in the room, but she barely made out the clear liquid with a minuscule piece of metal floating around in the syringe. This led her back to the time her mom had one implanted in her when she was younger. She'd wanted to fight it then, but her mom had the nurses at the psych ward do it. They'd strapped her to a chair and administered the implant against her will. She took a deep breath now and held the syringe in her hand, hoping she was strong enough to do what needed to be done when the time came.

Kage appeared, his hair sticking to the side of his head from static cling. Bray tried withholding a laugh.

"What?" Kage asked, running his hands through his hair.

"Nothing," she replied. She walked over to the bay windows and slid the curtains open, revealing a morning without much sun. From here everything outside the window looked a desert. Bray shivered at that and turned away, watching Kage grab an extra laptop from the box. He sat down across from Elliott.

"What are you doing?" Bray asked, returning to the table and sitting beside Kage.

"After you went to sleep last night, Elliott helped me create a blog. We saved all of my dad's writings on this laptop so I could start publishing it while he works on Embedicare."

"Wow," Bray replied. So it was really happening. This was it.

"This is going to be a grassroots revolution," Kage said. "That's how Ethan started the whole Animal Rights Movement back in the twenty-tens. How he organized people. After this is all over, hopefully people will contact us."

"People?" Bray asked, watching as Kage began uploading sections of his father's manuscript directly to the blog. Each time he hit Publish, her heart skipped a beat.

"We'll make a contact page on this website. That way, people who are fed up with S-Corp can reach out to us."

Bray's eyebrows lifted. She was equally impressed as she was afraid. She wasn't confident she would be a part of this *"after"* time that Kage was referring to, and she worried for her friends.

"And then. . ." Kage paused. "We need to come up with a speech for you."

"What?" Bray asked.

Elliott stopped and looked up at Kage. Kage looked back at him.

"Well, it's another thing Elliott and I talked about last night. You don't *have* to do it, but we both agreed the nation needs to hear from one of us. You're the one with the kindest face. And. . .you're Dianna Hoffman's daughter."

"Right," Bray said, her eyes staring down at the table. She went silent as her mind processed what he was saying. A speech? To the entire nation?? Potentially the entire world could see this, probably *would* see this, eventually.

"We'll pre-record the video. You won't have to go live, if that's what scares you," Kage replied.

Bray sat there for a moment. She thought about her mom. Her dad. The amount of people in this country alone. Well over three hundred billion. How many of them had implants? Probably millions. It was one thing to consider showing Rhea to the world, from behind the scenes, so to speak. But to get on camera, expose herself to everyone, that made her heart shake.

"You sure a video is necessary?" Bray asked finally. "Can't we just put everything on this blog?"

"People don't read much anymore." Elliott spoke. "They *watch*. If you want to have the best effect on people, you have to *show* them."

"Galvanize," she replied in a near whisper.

"What's that?" Kage asked.

Bray looked Kage in the eye and looked away.

"Nothing," she said. "Can we get the videos over with as soon as possible? The longer I have to think about it, the more anxious I'm going to get."

"We can do it today," Kage replied, shrugging.

Throughout Bray's life, had anyone really seen her? Her father chose to see himself working on a campaign halfway across the country. Her mother saw herself as the future CEO of S-Corp. There had been no one else in Bray's life until Elliott and Alice came along. She had only recently become comfortable with Kage. She was being tasked with exposing herself to a world that probably would not accept her. Not to mention, what if this video somehow exposed her location? What if her mother was able to track her down?

Her life would be over and everything she was fighting for would be lost.

She had to risk it. There was little choice in the matter now. There was no going back, nothing to go back to. The only hope they all had left was in the future.

#

Afternoon came in a blink. Bray was getting ready to record the video. It would be shown right as Rhea and the cows were corralled into line for slaughter. As every minute passed, the plan came more and more into fruition. They'd hack Embedicare, publish the video to every satellite, to every television in every American home, and to every single person who wore an implant.

Then, Bray would connect with Rhea. From there. . .who knew.

Bray cleaned herself up in the bathroom and combed through her hair, which had grown down to her lower back. Her heart went cold with fear, beating into her chest as if begging to escape her rib cage so it could run away.

Bray closed her eyes, took some deep breaths. She reminded herself of what Emily had said about galvanizing people. She went outside and met Kage. On the way, her knees began to shake. They were the next body part to wish for an exit, and nearly did so as she slipped down the stairs and took a stumble right into Kage's arms.

"You okay?" Kage asked as he caught her.

"Just nervous," she said, trying to smile.

"You got this." Kage smiled. "I'd do it for you, but remember what we said. . .you have a much more friendly and non-threatening face. Easier to believe."

Bray went over and sat by the small boulders where she'd spoken with Bertan the day before. A few feet away, Kage was readying the laptop, which sat on a chair, its back facing Bray. She was at least relieved she wouldn't be able to see herself while recording. That would've never worked.

As a very dull sun began to present itself above her, Bray went over the speech in her mind.

After reading the script Elliott and Kage had prepared, the sound of Trevor's voice entered Bray's mind: *"You'll incite panic. Giving too many people that much information all at once. . .it could break their psyches. It'll get you nothing but consequences."*

"It's all ready, Bray," Kage called to her.

Bray looked at the laptop. She couldn't see its camera, but she knew it was there. She decided to pretend she was talking to a friend, like Emily.

"Let's get it over with."

"I'm going to hit record. Start whenever you're ready." Kage pressed a button on the laptop and stepped back.

Bray felt her pulse beat into her ears as she faced the back of the laptop. Her mouth went dry.

"I need some water," she said.

Kage stopped the recording and ran inside. Bray glanced behind her at the horizon, where the land's decay from lack of water continued on to meet a sky of motionless clouds. She thought about her mom and dad. Certainly they'd see these videos. They'd see everything. She hoped her dad would see. Maybe she could get him to believe, finally. But her mother. . .her mother was in for it. Her mother, she expected, was about to have her entire world turned upside down. Everything was going to go haywire for Dianna Hoffman. And Bray would probably never see her again.

A sudden flash of a time when Bray was six and she was reading aloud her favorite book to her mom before bed, before times got weird between them, entered her mind and brought with it a slight disappointment. Those days of feeling her mother as a true mom were long gone, and after this, they would never return.

The trailer door slapped shut, jolting Bray back to the present. Kage walked over and handed her a cup of water. She drank half the water, reminding herself where it came from, and set it down beside her on the ground.

"I'm ready now," she said, deciding she wanted to get this over with.

Kage hit Record again.

Bray took a deep breath. She glanced at the laptop and began.

"My name is Bray Hoffman, daughter of Dianna Hoffman, the Western Regional President of S-Corp. What you're about to see is a video exposing the truth about S-Corp and how it has been responsible for the deaths of thousands of our country's citizens. . ."

Bray continued, describing how S-Corp faked the 2027 terrorist attack. . .how they were responsible for the disappearance of hundreds of animal rights activists.

"Our soil is not unsafe for growing food. Not anymore. I know because I've been places, right here in the west, where food is grown, eaten. Enjoyed.

"They are lying to us. We have to do something about S-Corp. If we allow this to continue, our whole country could be lost to drought. I feel like we've already lost ourselves. Lost our way. Forgot that nature is out here, and it needs us." Bray paused, suddenly feeling she might cry. How sad it was that S-Corp had destroyed so much and would continue if others did not stop it. Sad because Bray would most likely not be here to make sure they did.

"If you want change. . .if you want to make things better. . .contact us. Go to www.thetruthaboutscorp.com. The website will pop up on the screen. The proof is there. It won't be there for long. Once S-Corp finds out, it will be shut down. And then they'll come for us. If that doesn't awaken you to what is happening here, maybe what you see in these coming hours will." Bray finished the speech, wiping the impassioned tears from her eyes.

Kage shut off the laptop. He walked up to Bray and hugged her.

"You did great."

Bray nodded, hoping he was right. If not, and if none of this worked, she feared for her friends, for animals, for this world.

#

That evening, Ruben and Bertan returned to the trailer. Kage caught them up on what they'd done that day while they all ate a Mexican stew that

Ruben had cooked for them: corn, beans, sweet potatoes and quinoa, a grain Bray had not heard of until this day.

Elliott had taken a break to eat with them. He'd set the laptop on the floor beside him to allow space for everyone to eat. Bray observed him from across the table. In the weak light of their one lamp, which stood over by the door, he looked tired. She felt compassion in her heart for him, how he was trying so hard, how in a matter of days people would learn the things he already knew. How would it feel for Elliott when it went public? When others like him learned that their family members also died by S-Corp's foolish mistakes and government-assisted cover ups?

"None of you eat animals?" Bertan asked, breaking a heavy silence that hung over the table where they ate.

"I do," Elliott said, raising his hands. He glanced over at Bray, who was not surprised by his response.

"What's your story?" Bertan asked Elliott. "Why you helping them?"

"Bray's my best friend. She cajoled me into it," Elliott replied, winking at Bray.

"You lie," Bray shot back playfully. When would she ever get the chance to joke with him again?

"Actually. . .my parents died because of S-Corp's fertilizer fuck-up. I've been searching for the proof for years."

"Sorry to hear that," Bertan replied.

"It's okay. I'm glad I know now. . .and that we're doing something about it." Elliott took a bite of stew.

The room went quiet. These four individuals who had once been strangers—the most hodgepodge group Bray could ever imagine for something like what Kage called a *grassroots revolution*—were each risking their lives for something that was ultimately on her shoulders to pull off. She took a deep breath and tried to eat but once again found herself at a loss for appetite.

"The transport truck is coming in tomorrow night," Bertan shared suddenly.

Bray shot a look at Kage and Elliott. Elliott bent down and picked up the laptop. He set it on his lap, read the screen, smiled, and returned it to its place on the floor.

"I didn't want to say anything until I was sure," he said. "But. . .we got in."

"To Embedicare?" Kage asked.

Elliott nodded. He took his last bite of stew. Bray looked at him, her eyes set as if in space while her mind registered what he'd said.

He got in, Bray said to herself. *It worked. This is really happening.*

She wasn't sure whether to feel relieved, afraid, or what, but she felt it all.

"We're really doing this, then," Ruben said.

"Yep. I'll edit the video in the morning, after a good night's sleep. Tomorrow, we test everything out. . .then it's *go time,*" Elliott confirmed.

"I was thinking," Bertan said, clearing his throat and wiping his mouth with his hand. "A lot of guys at S-Corp. . .they have those implants, too. Even some of the floor workers, the plant managers. You could stop the entire food processing chain when you do this."

"Good," Bray said, the word popping out of her mouth without her fully realizing it was coming. "Let it stop. Let it mess up the food system. Maybe that'll wake people up."

"Now we're talking," Kage said, raising his glass to Bray.

Bray looked over at him and to Elliott again. It was sinking in. . .the gravity of it all. In a couple days, she'd be expected to show the entire nation what she'd always known to be true: that animals experience pain and emotion. She would feel every electric prod, every last part of the terrible process. She thought to ask Bertan what exactly happened to a cow as it went through slaughter, but she decided it best to not know. She had to hold onto hope that Rhea and the others would escape.

"Listen." She spoke solemnly, and to everyone. "I know I'm probably going to die this time. We need to expect it. I don't know that life will spare a second chance for me, this time."

The table went quiet. Kage got up and paced the floor. Bray could hear his heavy breathing. Elliott reached over and placed his hands on hers, and he gave her a smile. His eyes filled with tears.

Chapter Thirty-Nine

Kage

Morning came. The sun finally made itself known outside the bedroom window for the first time since they'd arrived. It almost made Kage feel more alone. He missed his home in Wyoming, missed the garden where he spent his days, his mind absent as he felt the living earth beneath his fingers.

He stood in the hallway, peeking out into the Idaho landscape. His eyes searched the sky, the ground. It dawned on him that he hadn't seen one animal since he'd been here. Not even a single bird. As a matter of fact, he wasn't sure he had seen any animals when he traveled down to Salt Lake back in April. Where had all the birds gone? Were he and Bray too late? Was the country too far gone for them to save it?

Tonight, those seven cows would be arriving at the S-Corp facility up the road. Kage had published his father's manuscript, and the threatening letter his father had received from the government. The two remaining files that Elliott had unlocked were official USDA documents showing the agency's inspection of early S-Corp facilities, where they found workers abusing animals.

How was he supposed to sit back and wait?

Kage pulled away from the window and stood at the doorway of the bedroom, looking in on Bray as she slept. The night before he was jolted awake by a nightmare that had been recurring the last few nights. In it, he and Elliott were in the living room. Bray was sitting on a chair in the center of the room. All of a sudden, rivers of blood came rushing toward the trailer, coming from the direction of the slaughterhouse. The rivers branched off in all directions until they crashed into the trailer's bay window, breaking it open. The blood spilled in and swallowed Bray, Elliott and Kage in a sea of crimson. The liquid was so thick Kage could not see. He tried swimming, to get to Bray and save her, but each time he reached for her hand, the river sucked him out of the trailer and he woke up.

He had a hard time admitting he was scared, but there it was. He thought surely he might lose Bray. And it wasn't himself he was concerned about. If Bray didn't make it past tomorrow—if she died when the seven cows died—what would that mean for all the other animals? What would that mean for the world? Kage had tried to go up against S-Corp on his own and, not only did he fail, but he fucked things up for Lana's activist friends. Because of his immature mistakes, they had gone missing. He wasn't sure he'd ever forgive himself. Clearly he wasn't cut out for activism work, but Bray. . .she was special. She was *necessary*. If they didn't have her, none of this would matter.

He had to find a way to prevent her from dying.

Suddenly, Ruben entered the trailer with Bertan. Kage turned and headed down the hall and into the living room. Elliott had fallen asleep on the ledge of the bay window, a blanket drooping from his body.

"Can we talk?" Kage quietly asked Ruben.

"Okay."

"Outside." Kage pointed at the door. It was best for Bray and Elliott not to hear.

Kage followed Ruben and Bertan outside. The heat was noticeable. Like the heat he remembered when he traveled to Salt Lake. The kind of heat that followed drought.

"What's up?" Ruben asked.

"It's Bray," Kage started. "I need to work out a way to save her."

"Save her?" Bertan asked.

"Not save her, but if there's a way to maybe. . .I don't know. . .stop the cows from actually going to slaughter."

Ruben and Bertan looked at one another. Ruben looked back at Kage.

"What's this about?" Ruben asked.

"Bray doesn't know about this, so keep it between us." Kage lowered his voice.

They both nodded.

"When those cows go to slaughter, Bray's plan is to let them try to escape. But if they don't, and they end up dying, she could die, too."

"Right, but how likely is that, really?" Ruben asked.

"I'm concerned it's highly likely," Kage replied. "So *if* we can, I'd like to prevent that from happening. We can't afford to lose her. The movement can't afford to lose her."

There was a long pause. Kage's eyes switched back and forth between Ruben and Bertan, frantically pleading for an answer. Something. Anything.

"You sure she's not. . .mentally ill?" Bertan asked.

"She's an empath," Ruben responded.

Bertan shrugged and continued on.

"If I went in and marked the beefs, I'd know which ones were the ones to track. And if I were the knocker, I could help ensure their escape."

"But you're not the knocker anymore," Ruben replied.

Bertan glanced at Ruben again, in a way that gave Kage the impression there was something else going on that he knew nothing of.

"Is there any way at all?" Kage begged. He was beginning to feel like he wasn't making any headway.

"Bertan and I would both have to risk our lives for that to happen," Ruben replied.

Kage nodded. He didn't want anyone's lives risked. Not theirs. Not Bray's. Not the cows. He only wished everyone could get out of this scot-free. It wasn't fair for any of them to have to lose their lives when S-Corp had damaged or destroyed so many already.

"What's going to happen if this girl dies, anyway?" Bertan asked.

"Maybe nothing," Kage answered. "But none of us would be standing here if it weren't for her. I'm not sure she sees in herself the *leader* I see in her. I think this thing we're about to do is only the beginning, and I think Bray's the only one who can bring it all to a good end, with our help. And she can't do that if she's dead."

The space between them went quiet. Kage stood there, anxiously awaiting a response. His leg was shaking, so he locked his knees to make it stop.

"If Bray has the abilities you say she has, then I'd be willing to consider it. But I leave the final say to Bertan. He stands to lose more than I do," Ruben said finally. "Are you sure you want to overstep this whole plan for the public to experience what these cows are going through? It seemed like a long shot to me but, if it works —"

"I don't feel great about foiling Bray's plan," Kage interrupted. "But I'm thinking of the bigger picture. The animals and the nation are going to need Bray far beyond tomorrow." Kage looked over at Bertan, who was standing there frowning.

"Besides," Kage continued, "if the cows are successful at escaping on their own, then there won't be any need to stop them. And. . .I think there's enough incriminating evidence against S-Corp to enrage the nation once they see everything we've posted. If not, we'll go at it again, but with Bray alive."

"I'll think about it," Bertan said.

He met eyes with Kage. Kage looked closely. He got the sense that something significant was registering in them, but he had no idea what.

The conversation ended there, leaving Kage feeling no better than when he began. For a

moment his eyes turned to the horizon where S-
Corp stood only miles away, where rivers of blood
poured out from countless animals, disappeared
into hiding beneath the earth, one day sure to
bubble up to the surface and take them all down.
That was what would happen if Bray didn't live.

Chapter Forty

Bertan

Bertan could not stop thinking about that girl. *Bray*. Interesting name. Interesting conversation the other day. And she could communicate with animals? He had no idea what that meant. How could a human talk to an animal that wasn't even there? Were they sure she wasn't. . .mentally unstable? Not that he would judge.

She really did remind him of Gabriella. He'd been sitting outside the hostel, looking at a photo of his daughter on his phone. The one he'd shown Bray. Maybe she didn't notice the resemblance, but he sure did. Gabriella may have been about five years younger, but there was a sense of innocence he noticed in them both. So young, having to experience so much at such early ages. Bertan hadn't realized how much he feared for Gabriella's safety until he met Bray. He also realized he hadn't spoken to his daughter in what felt like years.

He glanced at the time on his phone. 7:24 p.m. It was the same time in Honduras. That meant both Carmen and Gabriella would be home. He opened his text app and contacted Carmen:

LET'S HAVE A VIDEO CHAT.
I WANT TO SEE YOU BOTH.

Carmen replied shortly after that, letting him know they'd be home.

One of his roommates came out of the hostel, waved to him from afar. He waved back, watching as the guy got into a car that had been waiting in the parking lot. The car drove off.

Bertan went back to thinking about Kage's

request to stop those beefs from being slaughtered and how Kage said Bray would "die" too if those beefs died. This also confused him. Truth be told, most things in life confused him.

But what if Kage was right? What if that girl *did* die? Would her parents know? And where were her parents, anyway? Did she have parents? Bertan found himself perplexed by Bray. How young she was. How, if that were Gabriella, he would stop at nothing to make sure she never came close to death.

His phone vibrated. He lifted it up, saw Carmen was buzzing in on a video call. He answered.

"Hey," he said. "Everything okay?"

"Fine. I thought we could talk now. Gabriella is here," Carmen replied. She looked prettier, cleaner, more rested.

Carmen disappeared and Gabriella's face shown on the video screen. Her hair was shorter. He'd been so used to seeing it down past her shoulders that it threw him off to see the warm, light-brown hair only grazing her earlobes. It made her dark-colored eyes brighter.

Suddenly a memory came to him. How just other day they were sitting outside talking. Her hair was longer, but the eyes, they were nearly the same.

"Wow. Did you cut your hair?" he asked, smiling.

"No, Papá. Mom cut it for me before we left Texas."

Bertan paused. He could have sworn they'd spoken the other day.

"Your face is all clean. I can see it," she continued, grinning at him.

"Beard's all gone," he said, deciding not to mention his confusion around having seen her the other day. "How are you?"

"I'm good. Made some new friends at church. Going to see them tonight."

"That's great," Bertan replied, and it really

was great. For his daughter to be free enough to be able to go to a church and make friends, that meant everything in the world to him. It meant they were truly safe. Which also meant he had not seen her the other day. She and Carmen were back home, in Honduras.

"I'm going to give you back to Mamá now," Gabriella said, interrupting his thoughts.

"Oh. . .I love—" he said, but before he could get all the words out, she was gone and Carmen returned.

"She's getting ready for church," Carmen said, smiling.

"You both look very happy."

"We are. Thank you for making sure we got home safely."

Bertan nodded and went silent as he thought about who that was he had spoken with the other day. His eyes drifted away from the phone and out at the road.

"Bertan? What's the matter?"

Not hearing Carmen, Bertan continued to look around, eyes settling on his car, which was covered in dirt and dust. The reality of the last few days was returning clearly to him. He'd met that girl, Bray, who reminded him of his daughter.

He was still losing it.

"I need to tell you something," he said finally, meeting Carmen's gaze in the video call.

"What?"

"We are going after S-Corp. We have a plan now."

"What are you going to do?"

Bertan wasn't sure he could explain it. Again, confusion.

"Just know that if it goes well, it'll be all over the news. You'll know about it. And it could mean the end for S-Corp. . .and Medina."

"I doubt anything will end Medina, but I do hope something changes," she replied.

Bertan nearly said something more but bit his

tongue. He wanted her to believe him, to know that he and Ruben and these other activists were about to do something very significant, how he wished on some level to be a kind of Che Guevara of his own time. But maybe it was best that she not know the details.

"We have to go," Carmen said. Shortly thereafter, the call ended.

Bertan still felt a bit distant from his wife. At least he had been able to see his daughter, and when he did it only confirmed what he knew he had to do.

He called Ruben.

"This has to be quick," Ruben said. "I'm at work."

"I think we can help that Bray girl," Bertan said right away.

"I'm not sure that's a good idea."

"You said it was up to me," Bertan spat back. "I want to help her."

"Okay. How?"

"I've got something formulating in my mind. I can meet you at the trailer on my way to work later, tell them we will help."

"Are you sure?"

Bertan thought about the girl. He couldn't live with himself if Bray died when he could have done something to try to prevent that from happening. For once in his life he could save a life rather than end one.

"Yes," he replied, hanging up the phone.

Chapter Forty-One

Dianna

Dianna sat at the bar at The Cove, an expensive restaurant in downtown Denver. The place was dim save for the bar lights overhead, giving the impression it was night. More people drank at night. Something about the loneliness of evenings, of darkness, she supposed. She thought of Cole only for a moment. How she was surprised she *didn't* feel lonely, given that he filed for divorce last month and she'd since moved out of their house.

She'd just had drinks with the Governor of Wyoming. They discussed the use of Wyoming's fresh waters and reservoirs for Spring One, S-Corp's bottled water product line, but the Governor was hesitant. Hard to move. Hard to push. The west's water reserves were dwindling, so tapping from Wyoming would increase access for hundreds of thousands of people where water restrictions had been put in place after the 2030 Migration.

Lobbying politicians was one of the best parts of Dianna's job. She thrived on selling S-Corp's values and plans to individuals who could actually influence the movement of the nation. Politicians were to S-Corp what the moon was to the ocean. They needed one another.

But the Governor was long gone now. He'd given her thirty minutes to talk and said he'd think it over. Not that the Governor's blessing would make any difference, but if she could get him to sign off on a bill giving S-Corp permission to start tapping resources in Wyoming, she'd be headed in the right direction. Never mind that S-Corp had already begun extracting there. She would only get so far as long as extraction remained illegal in the state.

Dianna's phone beeped, taking her away from her daydreaming. It was Dan, the head of S-Corp West Security.

"Yes?" she answered, slightly perturbed by the interruption.

"We've intercepted a call that might interest you," Dan said.

"What call is that?" Dianna stepped down from the bar stool and adjusted her skirt.

"We've been tracking one of the S-Corp managers for quite some time. We suspect he works undercover—"

"Undercover? For what?" Dianna interrupted.

"Ecoterrorists."

"You're kidding? How'd you figure that out?"

"He's been snooping through computer files, security videos. He's careful, but not careful enough. . .so we started tracing his calls."

"Tell me more," Dianna replied, intrigued. She wondered if this was at all connected to that Kage Zair character who got away from Carl a number of weeks ago.

"They're planning to stop the slaughter of some cows that are being transported from Fort Collins to a facility in Idaho."

Dianna paused. She thought about Carl's science project, SC-118. Those cows had been picked up this morning and would be arriving in Idaho in a number of hours. But she couldn't let Dan in on that little secret, so she kept it to herself.

"What's in the recording?" Dianna asked, exiting the restaurant while sliding a face mask over her mouth and nose. After the COVID-19 pandemic, masks were still mandatory in most indoor spaces, which Dianna found irritating. Not one staff member in the restaurant dared to ask her to keep a mask on. They knew who she was.

She stopped on the sidewalk and waited for Dan's response.

"Tomorrow, this group of ecoterrorists plans

to do something with the cows. I have no idea what."

"Probably save them," Dianna said, thinking out loud. "Did you get names?"

Dianna waved at one of the valet drivers. He walked up to her and she handed him a ticket to retrieve her car.

"The manager's name is Ruben. And there's another worker we're pretty sure is helping him—Bertan Duarte." He paused. "We found footage of a man entering the facility on a Sunday and threatening the owner with a gun. Apparently he claimed to be with Medina, stole all of the bank statements showing the funds that are being transferred from S-Corp to Medina."

"Were you able to identify him?" Dianna asked, turning to face a nearby wall so no one would hear her conversation.

"At first we thought it might actually be someone from Medina, but why would they be stealing their own records? So after running the security video through facial recognition imaging, we were able to confirm him as Bertan Duarte."

"Get rid of them both," she said decisively.

"Ma'am?" Dan asked, as if for clarification.

"I said get rid of them, by whatever means necessary." Dianna's Tesla pulled up to the sidewalk and stopped. The driver got out, nodded over to her. She stepped around to the driver's side and pulled out a twenty-dollar bill.

"Thanks," she whispered to the driver and handed him the cash. Getting into the car, she shut the door and continued talking.

"Who else was on the call?" She sensed this Ruben person might've been connected to the ecoterrorist group they'd found last month, some of whom they captured and others who'd gotten away. There couldn't be that many of them out there.

"We are working on getting more info. A woman made a call to this Ruben guy but from an undisclosed location and number, so we couldn't trace her. We've been working with voice recognition software, but so far we've come up blank."

Dianna thought back to the time they caught those ecoterrorists in the Medicine Bow Mountains.

"That's okay," she said, putting the car in drive. "I think I know how to find her."

She hung up the phone and drove off. She would stop this Bertan and Ruben from their ridiculous plan. She'd speak with Carl. He would know more. These people would be found, arrested, and imprisoned, like all the rest.

Chapter Forty-Two

Bertan

That night before work, Bertan arranged to meet with Ruben and Kage at the trailer. When he arrived, both Ruben and Kage were already standing outside. A crescent moon hid behind storm clouds moving through the area.

Bertan got out of his car and joined them.

"You have those bank statements you told me about?" Ruben asked, wasting no time.

Bertan had almost forgotten. He returned to his car and grabbed the folder from the passenger seat, not quite remembering how he had it. Walking over to Ruben, he went to hand it over.

"I think Kage should have it. They can post it online," Ruben said.

Bertan looked at Kage as he handed him the folder.

"You're going to post this stuff online?"

"Depends on what it is," Kage replied, taking the folder and glancing inside.

"Bank statements," Bertan said. "This proves that S-Corp has been sending money to Medina."

"Who's Medina?" Kage asked.

Bertan looked at Kage, suddenly realizing virtually no one in this country knew what he knew.

"Medina is the number one food corporation in Central America. I used to work for them. . .in Honduras. They use intimidation tactics, kidnapping, murder. . .to coerce *campesinos* into handing over their land to the company."

"*Campesinos*?" Kage asked, his eyebrows rising.

"Farmers," Ruben answered.

"Wow. That's pretty bad," Kage said.

Bertan nodded. He checked his phone for the time.

"I have to go in a few," he said.

"So the cows are coming in tonight," Kage said. "And you're going to mark them with spray paint and, in the morning, act as the knocker so you can prevent them from being slaughtered?"

"I won't be preventing it. . .only delaying. To give you enough time to get Gabriella out."

"Who?" Kage asked. His eyes narrowed.

"Huh?" Bertan replied. He tried to think of what he had said.

"Did you mean Bray?" Ruben interceded.

"Yes. That's what I said."

"No, you said Gabriella."

Bertan stopped. He stood there and looked at Ruben. In his mind he tried to recall what he had said to Kage, but it was long gone.

"Who's Gabriella?" Kage asked, shutting the folder.

Bertan did not respond. He feared he was about to be caught by Ruben, who still had no idea how severe Bertan's memory lapses had become.

"That's his daughter," Ruben answered Kage, his eyes remaining on Bertan. "Are you okay?"

"I'm fine," Bertan replied. "I haven't been sleeping well lately."

Ruben didn't say anything. Instead he turned to Kage.

"I'll be there in the morning to make sure everything runs smoothly," Ruben said.

Kage nodded at Ruben.

"I really have to get going," Bertan said. He needed to get out of here before Ruben caught on to anything more.

"Hold on, Bertan," Ruben said, starting toward him. He turned to Kage. "I've got to have a talk with Bertan."

Kage nodded and went inside the trailer, leaving the two of them alone.

"I have a quick question for you, before you go," Ruben said, approaching Bertan.

Bertan stood there, stiffened.

"One of my suits went missing from my office.

Do you happen to know what might've happened to it?"

"Uh, no," Bertan replied. "Maybe ask Diallo? He's got keys to the offices. I wouldn't put it past any of the sanitation workers to steal things they think they can steal."

"Right," Ruben said, nodding. But in his eyes Bertan could see he did not believe him.

"I have to get to work," Bertan said. He quickened around the car and got into the driver's seat, slamming the door at once. Starting the engine, he backed up and turned down the road, heading for the facility. The farther he could get from Ruben, the closer he could get to fulfilling his plan to end S-Corp. This decision to help Kage would finally put all wheels in motion. Wheels down the highway, down an empty road where no one else could follow him. Down into a place none of these others—not even Ruben—could possibly understand.

Bertan was alone in this, and he knew that in order to move forward, he would have to keep it that way.

#

At 1:13 a.m., the transport truck carrying the seven beefs arrived. Bertan had been standing at the unloading dock in the back of the Kill Floor, waiting.

Bertan had seen plenty of transport trucks in his day, but none were like this tiny little thing. It almost made him laugh as he watched it back in to the dock. It was no more than fifteen feet in length and had black-tinted windows on either side. The windows were closed. As the vehicle backed in, Bertan noticed a ventilation unit attached to one of the back doors. Amusing that beefs on their way to death still got air-conditioning. They must've been special indeed.

The truck stopped right at the edge of the

loading dock. The driver did not move from the driver's seat. At this facility it was standard practice for the workers to unload the beefs. The driver's only job was to transport. This gave Bertan considerable relief, considering the one time he had dealt with a transport truck driver he nearly strangled the man to death.

Two sanitation workers appeared and unloaded the beefs into an empty pen. Bertan kept an eye on the beefs, noticing how they looked no different from the beefs he had been accustomed to knocking at the other facility. He caught the eye of one of them, and when he met eyes with her, she stared back at him. He felt as though he was being studied, and so he turned away.

His phone, which had been in his pocket, buzzed. He sighed with relief and pulled it out, needing something to distract him from this sudden, creepy feeling he got when he was looking at that beef.

It was Ruben:

WE NEED TO TALK.
I'M REALLY CONCERNED ABOUT YOU.

Bertan shook his head and turned off the device's sound completely, pushing the phone back into his pocket.

It took thirty minutes, but eventually the beefs were unloaded and the transport truck left. So did the two sanitation workers. It was Bertan and the seven beefs, alone on the Kill Floor. A second transport truck was scheduled to drop a load of one hundred in about two hours, so Bertan got to work. He hurried out to a utility closet outside the Kill Floor doors and found a half-empty canister of black spray paint. Carrying it back inside with a sense of determination, he approached the beef pen slowly, diverting his eyes from the faces of the beefs.

Bertan opened the pen and stepped inside. The sanitation workers would be back to clean the area soon, so he had to be swift.

He approached the first beef, sprayed a dot of paint above its eyes. Subtle enough that no other workers would catch it, but visible in the area where a knocker would have to knock.

Bertan continued with the other beefs, paying them little attention as they moaned, as their tails swung back and forth, hitting against the pen. His jaw set, he kept his mind as focused as possible on getting this done without lapsing. Holding the canister firmly in his hand helped. It was something tangible to keep him in the present moment.

Finished, he stepped out of the pen, locked the gate. His eyes caught the gaze of one of the beefs, not meaning to. Or perhaps she was the one that caught his. Who would ever know for sure? But suddenly he could not stop looking at her. For once he actually hesitated. A part of him did not want to have to knock beefs again. And as he looked this one particular beef in the eye, he got a strange feeling that she understood.

His hairs stood on end. An icky feeling landed hard in his stomach.

Tomorrow, Bertan would be starting them on their journey to the end. He wondered if he would ever truly be privileged enough that he never had to kill again for as long as he lived.

Bertan pulled out his phone. He hadn't heard from Carmen yet today. He texted Carmen to say he loved her. . .loved Gabriella. He noticed three missed calls from Ruben. Staring at Ruben's name on his screen, the part of him that needed to continue down this path knew he had to keep ignoring the guy.

This time he simply turned the phone off.

Chapter Forty-Three

Bray

It was around 1:30 a.m., the day of. For Bray, quite possibly the end of all days had arrived. And how did she feel? How was she *supposed* to feel? How many people ever knew when their time had come. . .down to the very day? How many animals knew because they sensed it?

Bray thought about all these things as she sat by the bay windows, looking out over the pitch-dark land of Idaho as a sense of pure aloneness locked in to her heart and would probably not, from this day onward, ever really leave.

She connected with Rhea to try to curb some of the aloneness.

"Rhea?" she called out silently. Over in the kitchen, Elliott was eating a bowl of cereal.

"*I am here,*" Rhea replied.

"Are you and the others still inside the testing facility?"

"*No. We are in a strange, dark room.*"

So they were officially at the slaughterhouse. This meant that in the morning, the cows would go to slaughter as Bray's plan unfolded.

Suddenly, the trailer door opened. Kage entered and looked at Bray, nodding. He walked over to the kitchen where Elliott stood snacking away at the bowl of cereal. Kage poured himself a glass of water. Bray decided to join them.

"I guess it's time I inject myself with that implant," Bray started. She never was much for small talk.

"Yep," Elliott replied, nodding. "You okay? You look like you're about to take over the world or something." He began to smile.

He was trying to joke with her like he always had throughout their friendship. When Bray wasn't

stuck inside the psych ward and could actually
spend some time with Elliott, they'd often spent
hours playing video games at his apartment. She
was never very good at the games, mostly played
them for the visual stimulation, but Elliott, he
was a master. And he'd never hesitated to let her
know how bad she was. This was him joking,
jabbing at her to help her let loose and not take
life too seriously. She always appreciated him
for that.

"The world has no idea," Bray said, rolling
her eyes. She thought about eating something, but
she wasn't hungry. Instead, she walked over to
the table where the syringe sat. It was wrapped
in a plastic bag. She pulled it out of the bag
and looked at it more closely.

Kage came near and observed.

"Last time I saw one of those, I was
handcuffed to a chair," he said.

Bray stopped and glanced at him.

"When S-Corp had me trapped. They were going
to inject one of those under my skin so I'd lead
them to Meeteetse."

"All the more reason to put an end to S-Corp,"
Bray said.

She picked up a thin needle and unwrapped it
from its package. A plastic cap covered the
needle, which she twisted onto the syringe as
Elliott had shown her how to do the night before.

"You want any help?" Kage asked.

"No. I better do this on my own."

"He'd probably mess up and stab you in the
heart by mistake anyway," Elliott chimed in from
his place at the kitchen counter.

"I'll stab you with it once she's done," Kage
snapped back, sticking out his tongue.

Bray looked at the both of them. She was sure
going to miss her friends. If only the three of
them could go on with normal lives, banter like
this every day as if bantering and joking around
were the only things they had to do, not trying
to take down the largest, most immoral

corporation in America.

Picking up an alcohol swab, Bray ripped open its package and slid the bit of saturated material along her forearm, cleaning the area. She flipped off the protective plastic from the needle and took a deep breath. She proceeded to puncture her skin, right where the old implant had been, feeling a sting as the fluid entered. She cringed while pushing the syringe down until all the liquid, and the implant, had entered her arm. Pulling the syringe back out, she watched as a dot of blood rose from the injection spot.

"Here," Kage said, stepping near and handing her a Band-Aid.

Bray smiled and took the bandage, sticking it on her arm. She let out a deep sigh. Relief.

"It's all over now," Kage said, rubbing Bray's shoulder.

How Bray wished that were true.

#

An hour passed. Bray sat at the table with Kage and Elliott as Kage wrote one last post about S-Corp on his blog, *The Truth About S-Corp.*

"There," Kage said, sitting back in his chair. "It's all published."

Bray and Elliott both raised their eyebrows.

Bray sat there quietly watching Kage and Elliott. The two of them were more similar than Bray had thought they could be. Perhaps more so than Bray was to either of them. And this was a good thing. Her shoulders drooped as she realized she probably would not see them beyond this day, but at the same time, she could see Kage and Elliott becoming good friends. And the world needed more good friends.

"I want to tell you both," Bray said, realizing this could be her last chance to say goodbye, "that I love you."

"Don't start with all that goodbye crap," Kage

said, bunching his hands into fists.

"But today's the day. This is it. If something happens to me, I don't want to leave the world knowing I didn't tell you how I felt."

"We know how you feel," Elliott said, putting his hand over hers. "And we've got your back today. No matter what happens, we'll be sure to see this through."

"You two are the best friends I've had in all my life," Bray replied, near tears. "For so long it was just Alice. I was in and out of that hospital so much I couldn't keep up with you," she said to Elliott.

"I know," he replied, his voice cracking.

"But now that I've gotten to be with you two, and Emily and Ethan back home, you all give me hope in people. You make me feel like everything will be okay."

Elliott began to cry. Bray cried when she saw him crying. And Kage, too, which was rare. And the three of them cried, and their crying turned to laughter. To experience friendship at the darkest corners of life was to experience an ironic sense of hilarity that could only end in laughter.

#

Not long after the laughter subsided, the room grew oddly quiet. Elliott cleared his throat. He turned to his laptop and shut it down. The sudden silence was not comfortable. Bray was relieved when the trailer door opened and Ruben entered. He came over and sat down beside them.

"The cows should be here by now," Ruben said.

Bray looked at him. In her mind she called out to Rhea.

"*Is it definitely true?*" she asked, to confirm.

"*Yes. We are all here. . . .in some pen with several other cows. Everyone is frightened. This*

morning is our chance to escape," Rhea replied.
   Bray turned and looked down at the floor.
   "Okay. I'll connect with you again soon," Bray
said to Rhea, uncertain their escape plan would
work.
   Bray shook herself back to reality and sat up.
   "Did you hear Ruben?" Kage asked her.
   "Yeah. . .cows are here."
   "They'll begin at 6 a.m.," Ruben added.
   "Elliott, how much time will we need?" Kage
asked.
   "We need to set up an hour before," he said.
   "God, that's early," Kage replied. "Off to get
a few hours sleep, then."
   Kage stood up. He started for the hall,
turning back to Bray as if expecting her to
follow.
   "I don't think I'll be able to sleep," Bray
said. "I'm going to go sit outside."
   "All right." Kage nodded.
   Bray watched him continue on down the hall.
Ruben got up and prepared himself a plate of
food. Bray could not possibly think of eating.
Her stomach felt both empty and sick. The anxiety
reached into her veins and coursed through her
blood, right for her heart. If she wasn't
careful, she feared she might go mad before
tomorrow arrived.
   She stood up and went to the door.
   "Bray." Elliott called to her. "You okay?"
   "I hope to be," she replied, and went outside.
   The moon was hiding behind a group of clouds.
The air chilled her bones. The cold of it woke
her eyes and cleared her mind, which she very
much needed. She sat down and searched the
clouded sky for stars, but saw few. Not like in
Meeteetse, where Emily and Ethan and the others
had probably also long gone off to sleep. She
wondered if they thought of her. Here in the
depths of early morning she sat alone, accepting
that only hours from now, she'd be penetrating
the thoughts of thousands of people. What

happened after that would no longer be up to her.
Not that it ever had been.

PART TWO:

THE FALL

Chapter One

Bray

Bray was about to go through it all again. Was she ready? No. Had she forced herself to be? One hundred percent. How else did one willingly choose potential death. . .to risk their life not once, but twice, in one lifetime? And how could she expect that this time, *if* this plan worked, she'd get out alive? Sure, she'd survived Alice's passing. But did life really give second chances? In this world, she didn't believe so.

For Bray Hoffman, it was best to walk into this moment expecting her own death. This would be the end. The only comfort she could find was in the very slight chance that maybe, if there were some kind of life beyond death, she'd get to see Alice again.

Outside the bay window before her, the land lay open for miles. Nothing but dry earth. It was as though the west had reverted back to the ocean it once had been and all that was missing now was the ocean itself. The ground gave off a cool, blue color beneath an early-morning sky. Too early, at 5:15 a.m.

The coolness that cast down on the hard, dead earth was a reflection of the stars and quarter moon above. Bray could not see the stars from her position by the window, but she knew they were there.

What her eyes remained set on was the horizon. Beyond it stood one of thousands of S-Corp facilities. Again, she could not see it, but she knew it was there.

Bray's bottom sat hard on the surface of a steel fold-out chair. The steel was cold against the bare skin along her arms. Her feet were planted on the carpeted floor. As Emily had trained her to do, she placed her hands on her thighs, palms facing up. *Best position by which to receive*, Emily had said.

Elliott approached Bray and bent down before her. Behind them both, Ruben was pacing back and forth along the tile floor of the kitchen.

"You ready, kiddo?" Elliott asked.

"Should I be?" she replied, half-smiling.

"We can always stop."

Bray did not respond. She only looked him in the eye and nodded.

Elliott stood up, stepped away and returned a moment later. In his hand was the laptop. He set it on her lap.

"Now that I know how we hack Embedicare, I'm going to show you how to do it." He knelt down beside her and faced the laptop screen. "Then, you're going to override their system with your implant—"

"How?" she asked, confused.

"With this." He handed her a tiny sticker with a bunch of numbers and letters on it.

"That's the identification number for your implant. We hack in, override the system with this ID, and you're in. It will be all yours to control."

"This is frightening," she admitted.

"I know. Just think. . .anyone can do this. Anyone could overtake our entire system at any time, and shut down everything." He paused, gazing out the window. "But good thing it's only you."

Bray exhaled heavily. She did not like all this burden, this responsibility, this *ability* to control so much. Her hands began to shake. Closing her eyes, she took a few deep breaths. She hadn't meditated in days.

She opened her eyes and looked down at the laptop. On the screen she saw the time: 5:30 a.m. She couldn't delay any longer.

"So what do I do?" she asked.

"We're already inside Embedicare's mainframe,"

Elliott said, pointing at the screen. All Bray saw was a black screen with a bunch of codes in neon blue and neon green colors. "You see where the cursor is on the screen?"

Bray's eyes bounced around until she saw the flashing cursor.

"Yes."

"Go ahead and type *Embedicare mainframe*."

Bray gulped. She grazed the keyboard with her fingers, cautiously typing in the code.

"Now hit Enter."

Bray did as she was instructed.

A message popped up in red:

ACCESS DENIED. USER DOES NOT HAVE ACCESS TO THIS MAINFRAME.

"Great," Elliott said. "Now I want you to enter the following. . ." Elliott proceeded to list letters spelling the word *exploit* and some random periods and other letters.

A series of red lettering popped up.

"They've allowed us in," Elliott whispered beside her.

Bray's heart rate doubled in speed. *Yikes*.

"Hit Enter again," he said, and Bray did.

The original screen popped up again, with the cursor in the same place it was before.

"Now type in your identification number." Elliott stood up.

"Why can't you do this instead of me?" she asked, half joking because of the frightening nature of what she was about to do. It would have been so much easier for someone else to do all the dirty work.

"Sorry kiddo, this is all you. I did the work to get us in."

Totally fair.

Bray slowly typed in the letter and number combination on the sticker in her hand. It took some time, but when she finished, she hit enter.

Suddenly, the laptop screen went black.

Simultaneously, her forearm vibrated, causing her to startle. This she was not expecting.

"You're in," Elliott said, reaching for the laptop. As he pulled it away from her, Bray saw it now had a blank screen. She glanced down at her forearm and saw the same blank screen. Her eyes widened in disbelief.

She couldn't believe it actually worked.

"Now what?" she asked, turning to Elliott. "Elliott?"

"We've got about fifteen minutes until they start the cows for slaughter. We can hit play on the video you recorded, but I think we should wait until a only few minutes before to play it."

"So then I just sit here and wait?" she asked, her chest rising and falling at an increased rate with every moment that passed.

"Yep." He returned to the table that sat to her right, where he placed the laptop. He sat down and began eating another bowl of cereal.

She turned to him. She thought briefly of all the people in the country who were about to have their minds and bodies temporarily hijacked. . .if this thing truly worked. She ran through everything in her mind, making sure there wasn't anything they had missed. She thought about the time her dad purchased his implant and how she'd always seen its power box in her parents' bedroom.

"Wait," she said.

"Huh?" Elliott stopped chewing his cereal and looked at her.

"The Embedicare implants. They come with a power button. What if people turn them off?"

"Oh, don't worry, I took care of that. Once you're in Embedicare's mainframe and doing your thing, I'll be hijacking it, too, from here," he said, pointing to the laptop. "I'll disable those power machines from afar."

"You can do that?" she asked, amazed.

"I can do anything," he said, winking at her. "You want me to fix you something to eat?"

"No," Bray replied, staring out the window, still in disbelief. "I don't think I can eat right now."

She heard a set of footsteps behind her. Bray feared making any sudden movements. Now that she was *inside* Embedicare's system, she feared that moving would cause some disturbance, throwing everything off. She felt as if she needed to remain still so they wouldn't *see* her somehow, or find out about her before she started communicating.

Kage approached her from the side.

"Where we at?" he asked, rubbing his eyes.

"We'll play the video in about. . .five minutes," Elliott said through a mouth full of food.

"How can you eat at a time like this?" Kage asked, walking over to him.

"I can always eat." He smiled back at Kage.

Bray felt suddenly alone. Terribly alone. The vibration of the implant in her arm reminded her that only she could take this journey. All the others could do now was sit and watch. None of them could *feel* what was about to happen. For a moment Bray wished her friends could feel this with her, so she wasn't alone in it. This aloneness frightened her. Her eyes widened and they could not keep their gaze off that far horizon. That was where she was needed. And she accepted that she couldn't go there without fear. She'd have to take it with her, befriend it somehow. In which case maybe she wouldn't feel so alone.

"Okay, clock is at five fifty-five." Elliott's voice broke the tense silence in the room. "Ruben, is Bertan in place?"

From behind Bray, Ruben replied, "Yep. Just got his text. We're all set. Which means I've got to get back to the slaughterhouse."

"You mean you're not staying?" Elliott asked.

Bray listened to them go back and forth, but she paid little attention.

"Got to go help Bertan make sure the cows are able to escape," Ruben replied. With that, he exited the trailer. Bray figured she'd never see the man again. Nor would she ever see Bertan.

She gulped.

That meant it was a go. As much as Bray wanted and needed to do this, the smaller part of her, the child inside, wanted to run away, wanted there to be some reason they couldn't proceed. But they were counting on her, the cows were counting on her, and she felt the weight tighten on her shoulders. Her mouth went dry. She lowered her eyes to closing. No one needed to say anything else. She had to do this, and she had to do it now.

So Bray swallowed down her fear, her sense of dread, of overwhelming aloneness, and she proceeded to connect with Rhea. From here onward, she need only be the conduit. The rest was not up to her.

This she feared most of all.

Chapter Two

Oscar

The moment he put on the suit, everything changed.

Oscar leaned against the hood of his car. It was early morning. Very early morning. So early he'd beaten the sun to get here. Wait. Had he gotten here, or had he already *been* here?

The S-Corp facility stood across from him, the corner where the offices transitioned back toward the dirty side blankly staring at him. The parking lot security light shown down on him from several feet away. The only other car in the lot was unrecognizable to him, but that didn't matter. The person he was waiting for hadn't yet arrived.

So he sat there, arms crossed, sunglasses resting on the top of his head, fingers tapping against his upper arm. Against his leg he felt the handcuffs in his pocket.

In the still dark of morning, a car rolled into the lot. Oscar did not move. He didn't need to. What he wanted would come to him. He simply reached up and pulled the sunglasses down to hide his eyes.

The car parked beside his. A man got out. He was short like Oscar, wearing black pants and a gray t-shirt that revealed a distasteful amount of fat in his abdomen area. Oscar believed the phrase was muffin top. Smiling, the man started toward him. As he got closer the light from the parking lot pole added shine to the exposed skin on the top of his head. This man was nearly bald.

"Hey, man. You look too fancy for work. What's the occasion?" the man asked, stepping up to Oscar.

This was where Oscar chose to be careful, to

not say too much. Keep things in mystery.

"I've got a question for you," Oscar replied, standing up straight and reaching his arm around the man's shoulders. He began walking the man away from the building, in the direction of a grove of trees behind the set of dumpsters.

"What's that?" The man was seemingly agreeable to walk with Oscar as Oscar's arm remained hanging over his shoulder. Oscar had assumed this man was the knocker. . .the man whose physique reminded him vaguely of that brief moment in the locker room area where they'd interacted a few nights ago. But to be sure, he posed a question to confirm.

"Do you enjoy knocking beefs? I know I always did."

"I guess I don't think about it that much," the man replied, his head turning away from Oscar and watching the direction in which they walked, only feet away from the trees now.

"I have to say," Oscar said, stopping at the edge of the parking lot. He turned to face the man, whose name he could not remember. "I quite miss knocking beefs. The rise it would always give me."

He balled his hand into a fist and in one movement jabbed the man right in the nose.

The man stumbled backward a few feet, his eyes wide as he stared at Oscar. Oscar hurried to him, grabbed one of his arms, and threw him toward the trees. The man tripped over the ledge of the parking lot and fell to the ground. He turned and started to get up as if to run, but Oscar grabbed his foot and pulled him back, away from the building, and pushed him up against a tree trunk.

"Sorry man," Oscar said. "Have to do this."

He brought out the handcuffs and quickly cuffed one of the man's wrists. The man's nose was bleeding, the blood trailing down onto his shirt. Oscar lifted the cuffs over a tree branch and over the other side. Grabbing the man's other hand, he cuffed the man's two hands together so that he was cuffed around the branch.

"I'll be right back," Oscar said, turning to start for his car.

The man yelled.

"Help!" he screamed, his voice echoing across the parking lot.

"No one's here, man. They won't hear you." Oscar yelled back, laughing. He opened the trunk of the car and found a roll of duct tape. Stopping to look at it for a moment, he suddenly wondered how it got in there. While the man continued screaming out, Oscar experienced a momentary lapse of focus.

Shaking it off, he returned to the source of the screaming. Ripping off a piece of duct tape, Oscar covered the man's mouth, watching as the tape ran over some of the blood on the man's face.

"Sorry," he said, looking into the man's eyes. "But I can't have you blowing my cover."

Winking at the man, he ran back to the car, tossed the tape in the trunk. He searched the trunk for a set of keys and found them hiding beneath the S-Corp uniform. He slid them into his pocket and slammed the trunk shut.

As he headed for the back of the facility, he glanced over into the trees and barely made out the body of the knocker he'd cuffed.

Good. Things were going smoothly.

Something in his jacket pocket buzzed, stopping him in his tracks. Oscar reached into the side jacket pocket and pulled out a phone. A text popped up on the screen:

ARE YOU READY?

It was from someone named Ruben.

"Ruben." He whispered.

What was he supposed to be ready for? He knew he needed the knocker locked up so he could take the gig for the day. But why? Stopping at the building's back door, Oscar's head began to ache.

He closed his eyes and rubbed his forehead.

The sound of car doors in the background snapped something together in his mind.

Looking down, Bertan saw he was wearing a suit. The suit he'd borrowed from Ruben's office.

What the hell was he wearing this for?

Bertan's phone buzzed again.

It was Ruben.

ARE YOU READY?

Was he ready? Ready for. . .

He didn't know. The weight of the facility keys proved heavy in his pocket. He dragged them out and unlocked the door, hoping that by entering the Kill Floor he'd remember. It was right on the tip of his tongue. . .whatever he was supposed to be doing.

When he entered the back, the loading dock caught his attention. A few sanitation workers were finishing up cleaning as the Kill Floor workers began entering the space. In one of the pens were well over one hundred beefs that would go to slaughter today.

Bertan walked up and looked at them. Very slowly, he came to notice minuscule, black dots on some of their heads. Black dots he suddenly remembered spraying on.

He remembered the girl. . .Bray. . .who in many ways reminded him of his daughter. If he messed one thing up this morning, it would create a domino effect that was sure to take everything down. This was not overly dramatic, it was simply the truth.

Bertan unlocked his phone and replied:

I AM.

He slid the phone into his pants pocket and proceeded through the Kill Floor, toward the clean side doors. He needed to get to the locker room, find a smock and some goggles, so he could disguise himself as the knocker.

As he walked past the workers who were readying for the day's work, he noticed himself getting very strange looks from each of them. He figured it was because he was wearing a suit. He hoped that the sunglasses and the suit were enough to hide his true identity.

The keys still in hand, Bertan reached the set of doors leading into the clean side and unlocked them. When he entered into the hallway, the entrance to the cafeteria stood up ahead and to the left. He started for it. As he did, his eyes met those of an administrative worker at the other end of the hall.

It was Jacob.

Bertan tried not to react. He gulped, but kept on walking. Jacob stood there, crossing his arms, and stared at Bertan. Bertan nodded to him, acted normal, and edged closer to the cafeteria. A shadow slid out into the hallway from inside the cafeteria. A man stepped up and blocked the entrance. It was a man Bertan did not recognize. Wearing all black, like a security guard. From behind, Bertan's ears picked up the sound of the doors opening. He turned to see who was behind him.

He didn't see it coming. He only felt it. Felt the sharp blow of something hard and stinging against the back of his head.

A second later, he was out.

Chapter Three

Bray

Suddenly, the blank screen on her forearm flipped to a paused video. It was her, standing out past the trailer, motionless. A sideways triangle, the symbol for a *Play* button, blocked the view of her face. Already she was feeling uncomfortable about seeing herself on video, and they hadn't yet pressed play.

"Here we go. . ." Elliott said.

Bray turned to him. He was sitting down at the table, his face hidden behind the laptop. She heard her voice. She glanced down long enough to see herself there on the screen, speaking. No one else in the room had an implant, this was obvious.

"It's working," Elliott said.

Kage stepped up to Bray, knelt down beside her.

"It's really happening," Kage said, grinning as he watched Bray's speech. She felt a kind of disconnect. It was so surreal to her. . .knowing that thousands of people were watching her now. What would her mother think?

"Video ends in one minute," Elliott said. "As soon as it ends, it's all you, Bray."

Bray took a deep breath. As she looked out the window, with the day dawning, the fear widened her eyes. It tightened her muscles. She clenched her jaw. Her heartbeat drummed into her ears. Everything around her got a lot smaller. Elliott's voice echoed into her brain, as if in slow motion. It was as though she were underwater. Everything moved so slowly. She knew the screen on her arm went blank, not because she was looking, but because she sensed it. Time came down to seconds. Seconds, in between which there were empty spaces, enough space for her to decide to halt. To not move forward. To close her eyes and remain here, in a kind of suspended hiding, turning away from whatever would happen to Rhea and the others.

Her eyes closed. Her thoughts became heavy and repetitive: *don't do it. . .don't do it. . .please don't do this. . .no. . .*

There was a push at her mind from somewhere beyond. It was Alice. Or it was Rhea. She got the strange sensation that it was somehow both. It didn't matter. Someone was trying to get through, to tell her to keep going. She didn't want to listen. She wanted to remain in control.

That's the problem, came another thought.

Her mind went quiet.

She opened the door.

Rhea entered.

"We are ready. Don't leave us now," Rhea said.

Bray sensed many beings surrounding her.

"How many of you are there?"

"Over one hundred."

"Show me where you are."

Suddenly, Bray was looking down upon a spacious, open room. The cows were being held in two pens across from one another, over by a closed garage entrance. Workers neared them, holding electric prods.

A warmth pulsated along Bray's forearm. She wondered if that meant the implant was working. That her connection to Rhea was being broadcasted.

Her eyes searched the floor of the pens for any way out, a way for them to escape. She didn't see any. The pens opened into a metal chute, about six feet high, leading up to a cylindrical box. When Bray's eyes reached that metal box, it held her gaze. Her chest began to hurt. Past the box, workers stood in goggles and smocks.

A bell rang. A buzzer went off. Voices whooped and hollered. A humming noise came on and did not cease. Bray's vision went blurry. Her thoughts faded. Everything spun and spun until she lost grip of herself.

And with that, she was gone.

There was darkness for a while. A vibrating hum came down from above, followed by scratching, huffing and grunting noises. After a while the darkness refined into a close-up image of other cows. Surrounded by them. The scent of shit and metal. A feeling of hurt and confusion. Lots of whispers. In the distance beyond the chute, upside down, hung the first cow of the morning.

The slaughter had already begun.

Suddenly an array of communications bounced between the walls of the large room. Bray breathed deeply until she was able to return to her own body. She used the training she'd received from Emily to separate out the communications and make sense of them:

"How will we escape?" said one.

"I don't see a way out," said another.

"Can we jump the walls?" asked a third.

"We will have to try," said a fourth.

There were so many voices, Bray's mind—that part of herself that made up her human identity—was quickly losing hold. . .withering away into the countless voices that whispered out in confusion. It was making her queasy. Her head spun.

It took extreme focus for Bray to remain in touch with her body. She would have to, or she risked losing herself completely. She needed to connect with Rhea while at the same time remaining at least partially intact with her own mind. But somehow she'd attached not only to Rhea, but to every cow in the pens. The voices were so many they raced through her mind the way water rushes down a waterfall. Nothing could be done to stop them or slow them or calm them down.

A heavy ache throbbed in her chest. It came down on her like a slab of concrete and sat there in the center of her rib cage. A second one layered on top, followed by a third, and a fourth. At the same time, her heart began to liquify as though it were *melting*, or *bleeding*. In the part of her mind that she held onto, she knew these were feelings she was experiencing, and none of them were her own. She was experiencing the cows' feelings, and they increased in number to the point that Bray's body felt as though it were being crushed, slowly, by a thousand pounds of weight.

She was losing control.

Chapter Four

Rhea

We had to try. Had we not, who would we have been. . .to just allow ourselves to fall victim to suffering? They brought us into this world only to push us right back out when they were finished with us. For years, we were under their control. We had no say, no freedom. We didn't know what freedom was. We only knew the word for it because they gave us that ability.

And they didn't mean to.

We hoped it could be used to our advantage. Maybe by reaching out to Bray, we could use it to save ourselves. Unfortunately, we would never come to know.

As the humans came around to open the pen in which we stood trapped, extended prods hanging from their hands as extensions of their own arms, we heard them snicker. Hitting us with those prods. Stabbing some in defenseless places. Of course, everything was defenseless. That was why we had to try and escape: it was our only defense.

But they must've planned the layout of this space with escape in mind. Because as they began forcing us through the narrow chute, metal walls stood so high on either side that I, for one, had no idea how an escape could ever be possible.

As cows around me were being corralled into the chute, they began to stop up the line. In medical terms I believe that's what was called a *carotid artery*. The chute became so clogged with our full bodies, the humans shouted and hit at us harder. More brutally. But we were already at the end, so what did pain matter?

There we experienced the prolonged suffering, the violent death we were trying to avoid.

To not die in this place was all we wanted. And we knew, from having gained such awareness, it was all anyone ever wanted.

As cows backed up the line, they began to build upon one another. It was as though they were *climbing* on top of each other. The extended prods came down on us all. As I approached the chute, somewhere in the middle of the crowd, I felt my first bit of their electricity. Though I grimaced, it was nothing compared to what I had experienced back in that testing facility.

Eventually, one cow managed to wobble herself up high enough to see over the wall. She was smacked in the face with a prod. She grabbed it with her teeth, let out a wail, and yanked it right from the human hand that dealt its blows. More cows piled up along the line. A loud siren of a noise went off. At this point, humans were shouting and screaming.

They were losing control.

Chapter Five

Kage

Kage stood a few feet from Bray. Across from him, on Bray's other side, sat Elliott, staring wildly at his laptop screen.

"She's all in," he said. "At this very moment. . .every television screen, live feed and implant will get our broadcast." He glanced over at Kage.

Kage looked over at him and nodded. If Elliott hadn't been here, Kage knew he'd feel awfully alone. He stood like a stone, unmoving, as his eyes wandered down to Bray. He wondered how she was feeling. His right leg began to shake. It took effort to for him remain still. For some reason he feared that if he moved too much, he'd mess something up.

Bray's eyes were closed. He could see rapid movement beneath her eyelids. It creeped him out a bit. A few balls of sweat gathered along her upper lip. Her body waved as if being moved by wind.

Kage looked away from her, his eyes lingering along the horizon where a lighter shade of indigo signaled the coming of morning. He hoped they had the timing right. There was no way to know for sure.

Suddenly Bray's body jolted in the chair. Kage's eyes shot down to her. It happened again. She began convulsing.

"Shit," Kage said.

The sound of humming and men's voices could be heard coming from the laptop. Next, the sound of a bell.

"Should we stop?" Kage asked, fearing for Bray. He remembered how she passed out after Alice had died, how scary it was trying to bring her out of unconsciousness, thinking maybe she'd fallen into a coma. Back then he'd only just met the girl. Bray quickly became like a little sister. He felt the instinct to protect her.

"I think she'd want us to keep going," Elliott answered. Kage knew what Elliott didn't, that Kage had asked Bertan and Ruben to stop the cows from going through slaughter so they could save Bray from the likelihood of death. Kage assumed Elliott would one day be relieved they did so. That was, if the plan worked.

Kage watched Bray, his nerves tense as she continued to convulse and shake. He felt so powerless, a feeling he'd come to know well, so he turned and stepped back to get a few breaths in.

This was going to be a very long day.

Chapter Six

Rhea

When humans lose control, they also seem to lose their minds. They lose their ability to remain calm.

We used this to our advantage.

As the cows continued piling up, one of them managed to get up over the wall, and she fell down on the other side. The humans came at her. We could not see what was happening. We could hear it. It was not pleasant. It stung my ears.

As the last cow was being corralled behind us, she kicked the workers on either side of her. They fell backwards with such force their heads rammed into some instruments against the wall and they fell unconscious.

Of course we were not excited about hurting anyone. This was not our aim. But we had to defend ourselves, and defend ourselves we would.

Next came a loud pop. I jumped in response. So did all the other cows, in unison. We froze. Moments later, out of the corner of my eye, the body of the cow that had jumped the wall was being dragged back toward the pens. Two humans pulled her body outside.

I'll never know what happened to her.

I approached the cows that were piling up on top of one another. It was my turn to try to climb as high up on their backs as I could, so that eventually, we could all escape. But when I saw the one cow being dragged outside, a trail of blood left behind her, I knew what escape meant for me in that moment. It didn't mean freedom anymore. The humans were going to end us. At this point, the best we could hope for was a swift death.

But we kept on trying.

Another cow fell over the wall, but this time it was on the other side, near all the unfamiliar machines. I had hoisted myself up onto the back of the cow in front of me. I lifted my head and looked out over the wall. I saw metal tables like the ones in the testing facility. There were strange apparatuses everywhere, and humans with faces hidden behind masks. Everything was dark gray, mute, not like nature at all.

One of the humans walked up to the cow that had fallen, placed an instrument between her eyes, and we heard another popping noise. My eyes widened and watered. I quickly dropped down to my fours. The other cows cried out. I was in a state of shock. Another one, gone.

I turned and looked behind me. All around us were walls and more walls. The only way out was to continue up the chute and, one at a time, enter through the cylindrical contraption at the end of the chute. But that thing gave each of us a feeling of dread. I know this because I could feel what everyone felt. I couldn't explain it.

A high-pitched vibrating sound echoed all around us. It nearly broke my jaw, I was clenching so hard. As it continued, the walls on either side of us began closing in. Somehow they'd devised a way to narrow the chute. Maybe to prevent an escape like the one we'd attempted.

The walls closed in so tightly that the cows were forced down from the pile up they'd created. It backed some of us further down the chute, back to the pens to make room for all the cows to fall into one single line. I felt all the world closing in on me, everything getting darker despite the light in the room not having changed.

And so it was. We were in line. No escape. Nowhere else to go but the one place we didn't want to be.

Another thing about humans: when they don't have control, they seem to use violence to get it back again.

Chapter Seven

Bray

Bray felt herself convulsing. It didn't much hurt, save for her neck, which was beginning to feel like it might snap in half. She was going to have to calm herself down somehow, get centered. The voices continued to throb in her mind. One whisper hit her left temple like a hammer. Another stung her inner ear. It went on and on like this. The harder she tried, the more impossible it became to find Rhea amidst all the confused cows.

"That's it!" Bray's voice rose above them all. All the voices went quiet as if they heard her speak. She'd suddenly remembered what Emily had taught her about letting go. Bray only had to *allow. That* was the only rule here.

The voices picked back up again. It registered for a second that Bray could use her voice to find her way among the cows, but she'd need to calm them first.

Bray recollected a time back at the house in Meeteetse when she sat outside in the grass beside Emily. The sun was setting beyond the corn crops. The air was cool against her skin, not like here where everything was sticky and hot. They were meditating. For the first time in her life, Bray had experienced what it was to have a clear mind. No thoughts. It was. . .alarming. She'd opened her eyes to get a sense of the world without the mind involved. So still and full of nothing. The only thing she had done to get there was to focus on her breathing. But it had taken days and days of practice to arrive at that point.

And so, now, Bray breathed. She felt her breath rising and falling in her belly. It was

always such a shallow breath it was often hard to
notice. As she sat focused on that breath. . .in
and out, rising and falling. . .the voices
calmed. . .slowed.

Through the clearness of her mind, she was
able to see what was happening in the
slaughterhouse.

It was not what she expected.

Rhea had said they were going to try to
escape.

And try they did.

It started as the cows were in the chute,
being corralled up toward that cylindrical box.
On the other side of the box stood a worker
wearing goggles and a smock. In his hand was a
gun.

This was where the cows were knocked
unconscious.

From there, a line of workers stood waiting
with knives in their hands. It went on and
on. . .the vision rolling out to reveal conveyer
lines, all types of sharp instruments, dozens of
workers waiting for the cows to come through.

Bray began to understand how all this worked.
In these moments she had to constantly tell
herself to keep breathing. She'd find herself
holding her breath, the vision so uncomfortable
and unbearable that stopping her breath gave her
a false sense of control, and the vision would
fade. She'd tell herself to keep breathing, and
the vision returned.

The cow at the front of the line stopped a few
feet before the box. The cow behind her hoisted
herself up onto her backside. Simultaneously, the
next cow in line used her head to help push the
middle cow up onto the first cow's back.

They were climbing on top of one another.

The cows behind them repeated the same
actions, until one cow managed to get herself to
the very top of the wall, where she pushed
herself over onto the other side. She fell,
mooing in distress as she hit the ground. Two men

immediately ran to her, and one of them shot her between the eyes. It happened so fast Bray nearly missed it, and her mind took time to register what she had seen as the cow was being dragged out of the slaughterhouse, dead.

Bray felt tears roll down her face.

More cows piled upon one another. A second cow got to the top of the chute wall, this time falling over the opposite side. She landed on the concrete with a thud. Again, shot in the head so fast Bray could barely catch her breath. The vision faded again.

"Breathe. . .breathe," she told herself, her voice trembling.

She registered the faint sounds of a voice, whispering. Telling some kind of story.

It was Rhea.

It was Rhea coming to the realization that there was no escape. They'd tried. They'd failed. Having seen the entire slaughterhouse, Bray knew there was no getting out. Only going through.

She was too far away to save them. She considered stopping everything, returning to her body inside the trailer, making a mad dash for the slaughterhouse.

But cows were being pushed into the box and knocked unconscious within seconds. By the time Bray could get to the slaughterhouse, it would be too late.

More tears escaped her eyes. She wished she had never agreed to this plan. She wished she had chosen differently, chosen to go save them.

"*You have to keep going,*" Rhea spoke to her. "*If we are going to die, let them see us die.*"

A sharp feeling of disappointment stabbed at Bray's chest. She breathed into it. Her shoulders released, let go. Deep down inside, she knew Rhea was right. If there was anything she had learned from developing a clear mind it was that it wiped away everything else. All those unnecessary, fearful thoughts, selfish thoughts dissipated and were replaced with an emptiness in which Bray could hear only the truth. A truth so sound and so distinct it took on its own voice. Telling her to surrender to the process.

In that very moment when she made the decision to release her own self from the grips of what was happening, the vision went dark. A second later, she found herself out on a street corner in some unfamiliar city. Beside her, a volocopter had taken a nose-dive into a parked car.

This was new.

But Bray did not question it. What once felt like a tension within herself at the knowledge that the cows were not going to escape transitioned into acceptance. There had to be a reason she was here.

Dawn.

The name came to her simply. Somehow she'd intercepted a human. Then the vision behind her eyes again displayed the steel walls of the pen holding the cows captive. It wasn't Bray who'd intercepted the human, this *Dawn*. Dawn had intercepted her, and had thereby intercepted one of the cows.

It was working!

Everything paused. Bray was suspended between seconds. Between the shooting of one cow and the entering of another into the trap. Dawn standing on the street corner, still as if an avatar in a video game waiting for its controller. Was this where Bray was supposed to take over? Was this the power she had gained by hacking into Embedicare's system? It seemed more advanced than that, but again, her mind was getting in the way, trying to understand.

So she began acting on instinct.

Bray returned to the view of the slaughterhouse. From above, she rotated her vision around the room so she was looking down at all the cows. She attempted to pick them out, one at a time. Eventually she would arrive at Rhea.

Bray's head rose up into the air as if she were gently lifting something. An essence lifted

with her, as if the awareness of one of the cows
was rising with her.

Bray drew Dawn's attention forward by raising
one of her hands into the air. As her vision held
above the slaughterhouse floor, she felt the
consciousness of both Dawn and the unnamed cow.
She brought them together by slowly folding her
hands together as one.

The combination of them felt whole, like the
moon and the ocean. How one could not do without
the other.

A warm energy developed between Bray's hands.
She cupped her hands to hold the energy like a
ball, then she gently opened her hands up above
her head, intentionally allowing the energy to
leave her.

She did it again. . .connecting another cow
with another intercepted human, assigning each
one as the voices released and reduced, one cow
at a time.

Chapter Eight

Dawn

New York, New York

Dawn Harpender pulled up to the crash site at 8:30 a.m. She was called in to assess the situation after receiving a message that a volocopter unexpectedly lost power and took a nose dive into a parked car on the corner of Woodhaven and Atlantic in Queens.

Thank God no one was hurt.

Dawn had worked for the city of New York for the past thirty years. She was near ready to retire. But young kids today didn't want this kind of work. Could hardly keep it, or keep any job for more than three or five years, much less thirty. So Dawn kept working. There weren't many out there who had the knowledge she had, and who could keep up with the new technology like volocopters.

Dawn stepped out of her truck. She'd been woken after a night of rough sleep, where she'd been dreaming about being chased by black dogs. It was a recurring dream and she was grateful to be woken from it.

On her way to the crash site, she stopped for a tuna melt sandwich from the 24-hour deli down the road. She didn't live in Queens but any time she was asked to come down here, she was sure to stop for a sandwich, no matter the time of day.

She held the steaming sandwich in her hand while inspecting the situation.

"Unbelievable," Dawn whispered through her KN95 mask. She walked toward a red Tesla that had been crushed down and stabbed in the roof by the volocopter's nose. The car had been flattened to near pancake status.

A Marshal car's lights flashed along the nearby apartment buildings. The Marshals were talking to a citizen, who Dawn assumed was the car's owner.

Dawn stiffened. She turned away for a moment, pulled down her mask, and scarfed down the remainder of the sandwich. She quickly tossed the wrapper on the sidewalk.

Approaching the Marshals, she slid her tongue along her front teeth to get any remaining food particles out of line of her smile.

She began feeling hot. A flash of heat ran along her forehead and down her back.

"Ooh!" She paused. She rubbed her forehead, assuming something in the sandwich had upset her stomach, and continued on.

Both her wife and doctor had told her to clean up her diet, but that wasn't going to happen. She'd rather die happy than die old, anyway.

As she stepped up to the Marshals, the heat wave came over her again. Her vision blurred. She stopped and blinked her eyes.

A faint vibrating sensation coursed through her forearm. She glanced down at the screen that had intrusively popped up there. It was some young girl speaking into a camera. Dawn didn't have her earpiece in, so she couldn't hear what the girl was saying.

Dawn ignored the screen and returned her focus to the Marshals. Her forearm buzzed again. This damn implant was more trouble than it was worth sometimes. Her doctor advised her to get one, seconded by her wife. So she'd told her wife that if she was going to use an implant, she was going all out for the 4D experience so she could enjoy her favorite animated films with the added bonus of experiencing the emotions of the characters.

"You all right?" A Marshal turned and looked at her.

Dawn opened her mouth. No words came out. Instead, out came a strange, low curdle of a call. Kind of like the sound a dog made when it whined.

Dawn immediately smacked her hand over her mouth, her eyes darting back and forth between the Marshals and the citizen, who were all staring at her.

"We got a call from the vehicle's owner here," one of the Marshals spoke.

"How did this even happen Mrs.. . .what is your name?" the owner asked Dawn. He looked her up and down. He scowled.

"*Pretentious little fuck,*" Dawn thought.

She opened her mouth to speak. Again, nothing came out. Only empty space where words ought to have been.

Her body froze, went into some kind of catatonic state. She willed her hand to lift toward the car's owner for a shake, but it only hung there by her side.

Her eyes blurred again. Slowly, minuscule black dots closed in on her vision. A Marshal walked over to her, voicing something that Dawn could no longer comprehend. All the sounds around her were reduced to sand, as though she were buried.

This must be the end, she thought. She was having a heart attack. No. Her chest didn't hurt. What the hell was happening? She felt like she was shaking in fear, but it was only happening internally. Her thoughts slowed.

Dawn Harpender was quickly shrinking away. Everything she'd known about herself, memories from her childhood, flashes of her marriage, seeing her baby daughter for the first time, it all spun and twisted away into a deep well of darkness until there was nothing.

A new image arose and took full rent inside her mind. It was dark, not dark as if she were asleep, but dark because she was *inside* something. She felt closed in. Confined. It reminded her of this time in college when the people she thought were her friends locked her in the trunk of a car overnight. She'd had a panic attack and an ambulance was required. They never stopped making fun of her for it.

Here she was, trapped. Again. There were noises out there. . .grinding noises, humming, machines letting off gas. Voices. Speaking in Spanish, of all things.

She didn't know Spanish.

What the hell?

She nearly fainted at the smell of shit and ass. Only a fraction of herself, of Dawn, hung on as she felt a confusing sense of demobilization. No wonder the voloctopters were going berserk. They must be under another terrorist attack.

Chapter Nine

Dianna

Dianna's alarm was set to go off at 6:30 a.m. Her phone had fallen on the floor sometime in the night. Her body was draped over Carl's. They had both fallen asleep on the couch in her office. Dianna's head rested on his exposed chest; the light blue button-down shirt had been buttoned down indeed.

Any night spent with Carl gave Dianna the sleep of a lifetime. Never had she rested so well than when she was with him. Why she resisted his advances for so long, she didn't know.

They'd hooked up back in May, sometime after Cole had divorce papers served. When they finally got together it was instant, immediate, like two pieces of a puzzle connecting after years of being lost and apart.

And so here they were, asleep together after a night of planning, drinks and sex. Her laptop sat open on her desk where the two of them spent hours coming up with new ways to use transgenics to improve the food system. It turned Dianna on so much she'd go after Carl like an animal, and he did not hold back, either.

Carl's arm had been hanging over her back, his hand near her neck. When his arm began vibrating, Dianna's ears faintly picked it up, but she did not react. She felt too good in sleep and refused to move until her alarm went off.

She felt her own arm vibrate. She turned her head away and easily began to fade back into deep, deep sleep. The buzzing ceased. It was replaced with the sound of a voice. A young voice. . .Dianna's brain registered. A young, *female* voice. A voice Dianna would know anywhere.

She shot up from the couch. Her neck was tight from the awkward sleeping position. She reached for it and winced. Turning to look down at her arm, she saw her daughter, Bray, on the screen.

"What the shit?" she yelled, standing up. She quickly closed her blouse over her exposed breasts and hurried over to her laptop.

"What's going on?" Carl replied, slowly rising to sit. He pulled up his pants and approached Dianna.

There on the internet was her very own daughter, spewing some ecoterrorist bullshit about S-Corp.

"This can't be happening," she said, watching Bray with wide eyes.

"They are lying to us. We have to do something about S-Corp. If we allow this to continue, our whole country could be lost to drought. I feel like we've already lost ourselves. Lost our way. Forgot that nature is out here, and it needs us. . ." said Bray through the screen.

"Holy shit. How did they do this?" Carl said, looking away from the laptop and down at the screen on his own arm.

"Elliott," Dianna replied matter-of-factly.

"Who?"

"Elliott Bansfield," she said as she returned to the couch and searched the floor for her phone. "He must know how to hack Embedicare's system. If we can find out where he is, we can find Bray and the rest of them."

They both got on their phones, began making calls. This was going to become a nightmare for the entire country if Dianna didn't put a stop to it.

As she sat at her desk, on hold with S-Corp corporate, she pulled up the internet on her laptop. There, she quickly found the website Bray referred to in her speech.

Sure enough, there were pages upon pages of documents, lists of names of the citizens who'd died as a result of their Oxygen-11 screw up. Some manuscript about the disappearances of animal activists.

"Shit," Dianna whispered.

She slammed the laptop shut. She pushed herself away from the chair. Standing at the windows, she looked out over the sleeping land of Denver. She wondered how many people were seeing this very video.

The screen on Dianna's arm went black. The black transitioned from gray to a clearly distinct metal. Metal walls. Cows.

Cows?

Dianna recognized this place immediately. It was an S-Corp slaughterhouse. The Kill Floor, to be exact.

Somehow those S-Corp workers. . .what were their names. . .Ruben was one. . .they had somehow connected with Elliott, maybe brainwashed Bray. . .

As her thoughts gathered, Dianna disconnected her call before anyone at corporate picked up. Before speaking to them she'd have to do some damage control. She rang Dan in S-Corp security.

"What the hell, Dianna?" Dan immediately answered. "Is this your daughter I'm seeing on the screen?"

"Unfortunately. And probably every screen of every Marshal and S-Corp executive in the nation. Not to mention thousands of citizens. If I give you a name, can you track this?"

"We're already on it. They're somewhere in Idaho."

"Great. I need you to find Elliott Bansfield. Bray will be with him."

"We'll get Marshals on it—"

"No," she interrupted.

Dianna thought for a moment. She glanced over at Carl, who was also on his phone. She walked over to him and signaled him to hang up. He did so.

If they caught Bray and Elliott and brought

them in, they'd never talk. Clearly they were a part of some larger sect of terrorists to be able to pull something off of this magnitude. Elliott couldn't do this on his own. Terrorists were trained not to talk. She hated thinking of Elliott in this way, but the truth was out. She'd known he was bad news from the beginning.

"Get some of our drones out there," she said to Dan. "Track them. I want to know where their hideout is."

"Shouldn't we be leaving that up to the Marshals?" Dan countered.

"Fuck the Marshals. It's been over a month and they still haven't found Bray. Now here we are. Get drones to find them. Once we find out where they're hiding, we can get the Marshals involved and shut this whole thing down."

"Okay," Dan replied, but she could hear the hesitation in his voice.

Dianna hung up the phone and looked at Carl. Both of their arms displayed images of the slaughterhouse and the cows inside.

"How can I help?" Carl asked.

"We should probably get the White House on the phone. Tell them to issue a shelter-in-place order until we can figure this out. Make sure they don't get Marshals or the FBI involved. . .not yet."

"You really think the White House'll go for that?"

"Remind them how capable we are of making the food and water crisis far worse if they don't. Twist their arm."

"You got it," he said, winking at her and leaving the office.

Dianna watched Carl leave. Finally she had a man in her life she could trust to do the right thing, to get things done. Who knew what Cole was going to do once he found out what Bray was up to, or that she might be in danger. Maybe he'd finally come around and see he was wrong.

Nonetheless, she couldn't think about that.

She was about to have everyone and their mother calling, emailing, texting her. She had to come up with a plan to mediate and do damage control. *What a fucking mess.* In time, she'd shut down these terrorists and lock them up for good.

And get her daughter back.

Chapter Ten

Mateo

Mateo Perez was asleep on the couch. A trail of saliva had seeped from his mouth hours ago and rolled down his chin, stopped by the scruff growing along his jawline.

The television was on. The volume was set at a level people in the hallways could hear when they walked by, but no one complained.

This apartment was the cheapest in Houston at $2,900 a month, so the tenants in this building, Mateo included, put up with anything.

Mateo's feet rested on a glass coffee table across from the couch. There, a silicone cactus dab straw dressed in swirls of blue and green lay on the edge of the table, inches from falling. Marijuana ash trickled out of a fallen-over container and scattered along the glass. Two bottles of rum stood in the table's center, one empty, the other still half full.

Mateo's girlfriend, Mandi, lay asleep beside him, her head resting in his lap.

Last night had been a good night, a typical Thursday evening. Mateo and Mandi both worked at Total-Mart. There wasn't much else to do without a college degree, unless they wanted to work for S-Corp or Embedicare. Mateo was thirty-nine years old. He had completed high school and never pursued college. Too expensive, and he had little drive.

He was okay with this.

These days he slept, ate, drank, got high, and worked. When he wasn't doing one of those things, he was playing drums for a local band. They weren't any good, but he had fun doing it.

The television screen went black.

Eventually, Mateo's ears perked up to the sound of a girl's voice, coupled with the subtle buzz of his Embedicare 4D implant. His eyes slithered open. When they caught sight of the television, he sat up.

"Wake up," he said, tapping Mandi on the head.

"Huh?" Mandi replied, slowly bringing herself up to sitting. She rubbed her eyes. They both turned toward the television.

". . .daughter of Dianna Hoffman, the Western Regional President of S-Corp. What you're about to see is a video exposing the truth about S-Corp and how it has been responsible for the deaths of thousands of citizens. . ."

The two of them sat there, stunned, as they watched the teenage girl speak. When she was done, the screen went black.

"What was that all about?" Mandi asked, searching for the remote, which had fallen somewhere between her legs.

"No clue. At first I thought we were still high, but look at the clock," Mateo replied.

The clock beneath the television told them it was 7:00 a.m.

"Shoot. What day is it? We have to get ready for work," Mandi said. She brought the remote up to the television, hit a button. "It's not turning off."

Mateo stood up, his head split in two by all the rum he drank. He wobbled over to the television set and hit the power button. Nothing happened.

"Are we still high?" he asked.

"I'm not," Mandi replied. She stood up, walked over, and unplugged the set. The screen went blank.

"Wait. No, I want to see," he said, plugging it back in. "Besides, I'm off today."

His implant buzzed again. The television

screen was still black. The girl had disappeared. He flipped to a few channels, but all were blank.

"Apocalypse must be here," he whispered as Mandi walked down the hall and shut a door.

Mateo stepped back, sat down on the edge of the couch. He began to worry. He told himself it was probably some satellite outage, seeing as Mandi wasn't showing any obvious concern. Usually she was the anxious one.

Mateo's implant buzzed again. He went to turn his arm to check. He was stopped cold in his tracks. By what? Suddenly he could not move. His vision went black, switching—like a television channel—to something else.

What in actual hell?

Mateo was so stunned he couldn't speak or scream or stand up to get Mandi's help. He tried. It must've been some terrorist thing, he thought. It was the only thing that made sense. They had somehow figured out how to take over through the implants. It was bound to happen.

A shock stabbed him in the buttocks, the pain burning and shooting up his spine, paralyzing him further.

Chapter Eleven

Bray

Bray had fallen into a trance-like state. She had been assigning each cow in the S-Corp facility to any citizen she picked up through the Embedicare implants. The process became seamless.

Then she had another idea.

She knew both her mom and dad had an Embedicare implant. Many, if not all, S-Corp higher-ups probably had one. Marshals had them, too. Everyone with an implant was about to see—and many of them experience—what was coming for the cows.

Bray had the instinct to reach out to her father. He had a 4D implant, and he was a U.S. Senator. Maybe if this got to him in some profound way, he could change things.

It was worth a try.

As she used to do with Alice, Bray called out to her dad. Humans were, after all, animals too. It had never occurred to her to try to communicate telepathically with a human. This time, things were different. She had everyone's attention. Everyone's *minds*. This of course scared her. She did not want to take advantage of this gift. She didn't want to intentionally hurt anyone.

But if she could summon a human the way she'd summoned animals in the past, then who was she to *not* try to get them to see? This was her only chance, after all, to change the world.

Cole, she spoke out in her mind.

Her vision transitioned into darkness as she sought him out.

Cole Hoffman.

She felt an energy nearby. It was as though someone was standing behind her. Or perhaps she was standing behind them. The energy coalesced into a mesh of dark colors. Dark reds, browns, and a sickly green.

It came closer. Or more accurately, *she* came closer to *it*. She *floated* to it.

Cole?

The energy did not respond. It was warm yet distant. It did not try to run or stray. It seemed to be listening.

"*Dad. . .if this is you, I need you to hear me. I am safe. Don't worry about me. What I need you to worry about are these cows I am about to show you. . .to show the nation. I need your help. You have power. Please stop S-Corp. . .now.*"

With that, Bray returned her focus back inside the S-Corp facility. She scanned the cows, looking down on them as another one entered the metal trap, on its way to the end.

Bray's eyes scanned the cows further down the line. Her eyes caught the third in line from the box. This cow was entirely black, save one white marking on her back in the shape of a star. Bray's hands shook in response to the cow's own shaking body. The cow trembled in fear as she neared the box. She knew what was coming. Bray would never get used to her heart breaking each time another cow entered that box.

But she would continue moving forward.

Her shaking hand lifted into the air, and with a throwing motion, she assigned the cow to Cole.

All she could do was hope that he received it.

Chapter Twelve

Cole

Denver, Colorado

Cole was asleep. It had taken quite some time to get there. He was a side sleeper, so he'd toss to one side, feel a crick in his neck, and turn to the other side. He'd keep going like this until he got frustrated and lie on his back, staring up at the ceiling.

He couldn't stop thinking about Bray.

At around 3 a.m. he finally gave in and took a sleep aid. He faded fast and deep. Good thing he'd taken the month off and didn't have to be anywhere the next day.

Cole fell into some very odd dreams. In one, he and Bray were out on a boat on a lake. The sun was shining and it was too hot outside. The water was so still he got this weird sensation that it was dying, although water didn't die. Bray turned into water and disappeared. The lake drained so fast the boat was swallowed in quicksand.

The dream transitioned. There was nothing but darkness. Darkness for a long, long time. Never-ending darkness.

Something approached. He couldn't see it. It wasn't scary. More than anything, he was perplexed, curious. This entity was calming. . .familiar.

It whispered his name.

When it whispered a second time, it sounded young and feminine.

"Dad. . .if this is you, I need you to hear me. I am safe. Don't worry about me. What I need you to worry about are these cows I am about to show you. . .to show the nation. I need your help. You have power. Please stop S-

Corp. . .now."
Cole sat up in bed.
Bray was somehow communicating with him.
"Bray?" he called out in the night.
There was no response.
He closed his eyes and thought her name, tried calling to her from inside his mind. It felt silly but he didn't know what else to do.
Still nothing.
For some reason the communication went only one wa—
The darkness in his mind suddenly took over. He sat there in bed, eyes open yet no longer seeing anything but blackness in every direction. He heard what Bray said, how S-Corp had to be stopped, but he wasn't so sure he agreed.
The blackness rolled open to a vision of strange men with. . .cattle prods? Is that what those long sticks were? That's what they'd reminded him of.
He witnessed a cow being shocked by one, and that confirmed it. Electric cattle prod.
Was he having another nightmare? If he was, how was he still sitting up in bed, his eyes wide open?
He felt his arm vibrate. A second later, a terrible shock of electricity stabbed at his lower back.
He screamed, but no one would hear him. He fell over onto his side in seething pain. His jaws clenched. He felt movement around him.
This was worse than a nightmare. This was real. He was having another heart attack. And no one was here to help him this time.
"Bray!" he yelled out for her.
Time slowed. Or moved. Moved downward, into the past. Bray. . .sitting on the living room floor. It was February. Snow covered the ground outside their home. Bray's birthday. He'd returned from D.C., and he had forgotten her birthday.
Again.

She'd been sitting in the living room, looking out the window. He thought she had been waiting for him. Inside a memory, reliving it as if for the very first time, Cole stepped toward his daughter and *really* saw her. She was watching the neighbor's cat, which had somehow gotten out. Cole stood behind his daughter and observed her. It was as though she wasn't in the room. She certainly did not seem to notice he was there. Or she didn't care to notice. The cat had her undivided attention.

It was beginning to make sense why. Slowly edging into his mind was the thought that maybe Bray had some kind of psychic ability allowing her to. . .what? Communicate with animals? That still didn't make much sense. It was becoming increasingly difficult to think clearly. . .

His hand reached out for his phone, which slipped and fell onto the floor.

Cole was getting the sense that he was about to die alone.

Chapter Thirteen

Sasha

Times Square, New York

Sasha Neilson stood on the corner of West 45th and 7th, her head down as she requested a volocopter through an app on her phone. Much of New York was bustling through the ritual of the morning commute. The area was filling with people racing by in their masks, busy on cell phones or watching the screens on their forearms. Sasha glanced down at her own screen but didn't much care to watch the news while she waited.

Instead, her eyes perused the overhead screens where movie previews and building-sized images of the faces of famous people danced so colorfully it nearly turned Sasha off. Fast food restaurants were crowded with customers and lines of shops were beginning to open their doors.

All the while, Sasha wanted to go home. Not to her current apartment here in New York. The tiny efficiency room that she'd been renting for an astronomical price was no home to her. It meant an opportunity to work for a publishing company, which had been her dream since she'd graduated from Yale three years ago, but that was all.

Her home back in Connecticut was what she missed every day despite the fact that her dream of working for Climb That Mountain Press had come true. She had to leave her eight-year-old cat Gus behind, and she'd regretted it every day since.

Suddenly a loud, swift whooshing sound traveled through Times Square. When the screens went dark it took a few extraordinary moments for Sasha and those around her to notice. Everyone had been wrapped up in their own worlds, their heads, whatever the next hustle might've been.

Times Square went so silent it was creepy. The air filled with nothing save the honking of cars, thousands of voices and music from car stereos.

Sasha dropped her phone. As it hit the concrete and landed flat on its back, her head followed the heads of others who had halted, some in mid-conversation, and stared up at the blank screens.

"What's going on?" asked a man standing across the street.

Everything stopped, as if frozen, waiting. Awaiting what?

"Another terrorist attack?"

"Did they finally run out of grid power?"

These were some of the many comments Sasha heard from those around her. Two people to her left remained frozen in a trance-like state, as if catatonic, unresponsive. This caused Sasha to panic. She bent down to grab her phone and from behind someone ran right into her, pushing her over. She fell onto her ankle and her foot slid out of her shoe.

"Sorry!" someone yelled. Sasha turned to see a teenager skateboarding down the sidewalk, passing through the crowd that had gathered, everyone looking up at another screen.

There, a girl popped onto the screen. Young. Probably not older than fifteen. Brown hair down past her shoulders. A round, appealing face. An innocent face.

She spoke. Her words echoed down the streets, in between groups of people and cars backed up as far as Sasha's eyes could see.

Standing up, phone in hand, Sasha wiped dirt off her pants and watched the young girl speak. Something about S-Corp and how they were lying to the public.

The screen went black again. Images of names scrolled down the screens. The names of those who died in the terrorist attack. An attack that this girl claimed had been a mistake made by S-Corp, and not an attack at all.

Sasha tried to comprehend everything that was happening, that was being said. Was it true? Was this the terrorist attack? She started to make a call to her mother as another image popped up on the screen. This one was a document from S-Corp, showing an email revealing the Oxygen-11 mistake. The cover-up.

"What on earth is this?" one man asked, finding himself standing in the middle of the street. Sasha watched him from her place on the corner.

"Fucking ecoterrorists," someone standing beside him replied.

"But they've got proof," another said. "Did you see that S-Corp email? No one could've made that up."

"Man. . .they can make anything up these days," said a taxi driver who'd gotten out of his taxi and was standing beside the door.

"How'd they hack our system like that?" said someone else.

The taxi driver froze.

"Hey. Come on, I've got to get to work," said the man beside him. He'd opened the taxi door to get into the backseat just as the Embedicare takeover had begun. That was what they were calling it. That was the last thing to go through Sasha's mind before she froze in place.

She urged herself to get the hell out of there. She wanted to run. To seek safety from this apparent nightmare. But she watched helplessly as more and more people stopped cold. Fell to the ground. To all fours. Their eyes wide. Tears rolling down some of their faces.

Only seconds later, it happened to her. It was like a reflex beyond her control, like she was a puppet and someone from above. . .no, more like inside her mind, was controlling her every move. She was down on all fours so fast she hardly felt herself move.

Words like *terrorists* and *possible kidnapping*
entered into one ear and escaped out the other.
There was too much going on in this space.
Sasha's psyche could not comprehend this madness.

Like a single wave rolling in from the sea,
anyone who could still move suddenly picked up
and ran. They trampled over the motionless bodies
of others. Most frightening to Sasha was that
there was little screaming. Only the sounds of
boots and shoes and heels against concrete. Of
people on their phones, voices quick in
speculation and question as they passed her by,
completely ignoring that she, along with hundreds
of others in Times Square, desperately needed
help.

Chapter Fourteen

Betsy

Betsy Harmon had fallen asleep out on her balcony. Again. The central air in her unit had gone out days ago. The property manager was slow to come have it fixed. And so she'd come out here nightly to sit and watch the city, have a smoke. Something about the city lights calmed her. How the headlights and brake lights raced over the Broadway Bridge, its arc construction reminding her of the way the sun would rise over Mount Nebo in her hometown of Dardanelle. How she missed her home.

Her eyes continued to be taken in by the lights along the buildings and skyscrapers across the water, how the river reflected back the life of citizens here in Little Rock. Finally her eyes grew heavy with the narcolepsy she had battled with her entire adult life.

It was no surprise to her that she'd once again found herself nearly doubled over on the balcony chair when, at 7:00 a.m., she'd been startled from deep sleep by her Embedicare implant.

Although it was early morning, it was not cold outside. Little Rock hadn't experienced the cold but a few days back in December. Anymore, they got a lot of rain and heavy flooding.

Betsy glanced down at her arm. There, a video revealed cows hanging upside down from a conveyor, their throats being slit.

Betsy's mouth dropped open.

"What in God's name?" she said aloud. "Oh, I don't want to see this."

She waited a moment for some newscaster to come on the screen and start talking, or for something else to happen, but the video kept going. If there was ever a moment she was grateful she didn't have one of those special edition implants—those 4D ones—it was now.

Betsy turned away from her arm and went inside her apartment, passing through the kitchen and into the living room. A couch and love seat hid beneath bags of old clothes and books and magazines. Things that belonged to her recently deceased mother. Things she had no desire to rid herself of. She banged her foot against a nearby chair and winced, grabbing at her bare foot.

That's when she noticed the screen on her forearm, this time revealing the view of a floor covered in blood. She shook her head and turned her arm away. Reaching over toward the coffee table, she found the Embedicare power box beneath a stack of plates and hit the power button.

But the damn thing wouldn't shut off. It went on and on. She grabbed a sweater from the chair she was sitting on and slipped it on, hiding the video from sight.

Chapter Fifteen

Tim

Washington, D.C.

Tim Saffi was standing on the subway when it happened to him. He—like everyone around him—was wearing a mask. He always chose to stand rather than sit. This because it was 8:00 a.m., and everyone and their mothers were on their way into the city. The smell of someone else's underarm sweat harassed his nose. He hoped it wasn't him. Too many people pushing up against him as the train moved, so he couldn't check with discretion.

Tim was twenty-three and on his way to a job interview, fresh out of a two-year IT program at the Career Technical Institute. This after spending three years as a climate activist for a local activist group. He'd made little money doing it, but he loved it. When he ran out of the savings his parents had given him for college, he'd had no choice but to go to school for something more lucrative.

Tim was frightened of climate change. Here in D.C., the temperatures had risen by three degrees on average each year since 2025. Heat waves began in May and went on into September. Today Tim wore a short-sleeved button-up to account for the heat, even this early in the morning.

Tim chose to go into IT in order to make enough money to fund climate change initiatives. It was money—not votes or voices—that changed things.

As the subway slowed to his stop at Waterfront, his Embedicare implant vibrated. On the screen was a young woman exposing S-Corp.

Tim switched over to his phone, where he turned up the volume and watched as the girl, whose name was Bray Hoffman, daughter of a prominent S-Corp President out west, explained how the 2027 terrorist attack was actually caused by an S-Corp screw up.

"No shit," he whispered.

People began pushing through the doors, exiting the subway. The majority of subway travelers remained in their places, like Tim, stunned as they watched their screens transition to a series of documents proving what S-Corp had done.

One man stood up in the subway car and began yelling:

"I told you! I fucking told you! Don't fucking believe me. . ." he spat, pacing back and forth. He wore a trench coat despite the heat outside. His bald head was sweating.

"Fucking fuck!" he yelled again.

The subway picked up and started moving.

"Oh. . .no!" Tim said, rushing over to the doors. But it was too late. The stop disappeared behind the subway car.

He'd missed his stop.

His arm vibrated again.

He supposed there were now more pressing issues at hand than his job interview. Looking back at his phone screen, he saw cows being pushed, stabbed and forced through some metal chute toward slaughter. Two of them attempted an escape and were immediately shot between the eyes.

There was a unified startle by everyone in the subway car when that happened.

And then something truly off-putting occurred.

Five people on the subway fell to their knees on the floor of the car. Simultaneously. . .like they were being *controlled*.

Tim shot a look at the woman across from him, who looked back at Tim with eyes so wide they appeared to be shaking.

"Hey!" a man in a jogging outfit yelled at the monitor hanging at one end of the car. "Stop the subway! Get us off here!"

Everyone began talking. Tim was too immersed in the video to pay attention to what was being said around him.

The video continued to show cows going through slaughter. As one cow was stunned with some type of gun—rendering it unconscious—one of the people who'd been down on his knees in the subway car—a man dressed in business attire—dropped as though he was the one who'd been stunned. He began seizing. The woman closest to him immediately came down to hold his head so he would not bang it into the floor or a nearby metal poll.

This had to be the work of some activists, somewhere. Ecoterrorists, to be exact. Or animal rights activists. Tim had come to this conclusion after they'd shown some title page of a manuscript that apparently addressed the disappearances of hundreds of animal rights activists back in the late 2020s. Tim was only a child when all this happened, so it was all hearsay to him. He'd always wanted to go vegan for the environment, but going vegan these days was like putting a "kick me" sign on one's back in high school. Not popular.

After the Supreme Court rolled back EPA caps on carbon emissions in 2023, the country was already experiencing drought, worsening storms, flooding. Yet the nation seemed polarized on the issue of climate change, split in half like a tree sliced down the middle by lightning. This Tim knew from years of studying climate change and the policies surrounding it.

It was no wonder that division would arise over the animal rights issue as well.

The man who'd been seizing on the floor finally stopped. It brought Tim back to the present moment. He looked down at the woman who'd been aiding the seizing man. They met eyes. She was very attractive. Long dark hair beneath a baseball cap. Dark eyes. He smiled. She smiled back.

Each person lying on the floor convulsed and shook. Their bodies paused and convulsed again. It kept going on and on like that.

It was frightening to stand here and watch. If the train didn't stop, or if the driver was also transfixed by what was happening, they very well could all be on their way to a painful accident. To say the least.

"Hey!" the jogging man yelled again. He started beating at the door that led to the next car, which was completely empty.

Tim pushed his phone into his pocket. He thought to pull the train's emergency brake, but that would only trap everyone further. Apparently jogging man had the same idea, as he went to reach for it. Tim ran at him and yanked his hand away.

"Hey!" the man shouted at him.

"Don't do that!" Tim yelled back. "You'll trap us all in here."

One man began rocking back and forth in his seat. He was mumbling. He began to cry.

This was bad.

The subway neared its next stop, and slowed.

Tim's heart slowed with it.

They came to a stop. The subway doors slid open. No one stayed long enough to hear the driver order everyone off the train.

Tim stepped halfway off, and turned back. There were still the five people in the car, lying on the floor.

The doors to the subway slid to a fast close and someone pulled Tim away from the car, preventing his leg from being completely caught in the door.

"Watch it, buddy," a voice called to him as he gathered himself.

Standing up, he looked at the man who'd saved his life.

It was the jogger.

"Thanks man," Tim replied.

The jogger nodded and ran up the steps with the remaining crowd of people rushing away from the subway station.

Tim stood there, shocked. Suddenly, he was alone. Newspapers and random trash blew about him as another subway car passed through. The video continued on his phone, but he stopped watching. His mind raced along with the feet on the sidewalks above him.

He decided it best to stay down here, away from all the madness. As his mind went a little mad over all the bad things that could happen at any moment, a surprising calm came over him.

If these were activists they were dealing with, he had a strange feeling they had no intent to harm anyone. People were panicking. That would cause more problems than the problem itself.

Chapter Sixteen

Bray

The slaughter continued. Bray looked down on the cows. A sudden pang of helplessness overcame her. She knew this feeling well, but now it grew stronger. Palpable. This time she couldn't save any of them. It made her sick. She began to wonder if this was really the right thing to do, to allow these beings to go through slaughter so humans can feel what they feel. Was Bray once again using them for her own—however justified—devices? How could she justify allowing this?

"Bray," a voice called out to her in a singing whisper. It sounded soft, familiar.

It was Rhea.

"Rhea!" Bray responded.

"The end is here. We tried."

Bray's eyes followed the cows as they were pushed into the chute. A line of them faced the metal trap. One first had approached the box and stopped.

Bray sensed the fear and doom and fright. The absolute resistance. Her eyes rolled down the line until she stopped at Rhea, who was the tenth cow in line for slaughter.

"You did try," Bray said, trying not to get choked up. She'd lose control if she started crying now.

"May our deaths not be in vain," Rhea replied.

Another cow entered the box.

Nine to go.

As each one entered the box, the shot of the gun slamming into their heads, Bray felt the pressure of those shots between her own eyes. By now she'd developed a migraine. It was beginning to feel as though her head were splitting in two.

Now eight.

It happened that fast.

Twelve seconds, Bray had counted.

A death like this should've never happened this swiftly. No, a slaughter of this violent proportion should've taken hours to complete, not seconds. It was no wonder that people became so complacent to it. Only seconds. How to devalue a life.

"Bray?" Rhea called again.

"Yes?"

"Can you stay with me. . .until the end? I wish not to be alone."

Oh, how Bray wished she could. The request felt so precious, so vulnerable. She didn't want any single one of these cows to be alone at death. They were with each other, but once they entered that trap, there was no one else. They were to face their deaths completely separate from one another, always a few inches reach from the next cow. Too far away to touch. Too far away to feel another's breath, hear another's voice.

How sad.

That was when Bray realized: *this* was the gift. For her to be able to be with these animals as they went through slaughter, as much as possible, while sharing their existence with humans who would never know them, not until it was too late.

This was the gift she was beginning to believe in.

"I will be with you as much as I can," Bray replied. "But I also have to share my attention with every cow that goes through that box. It's only fair."

"Yes, of course," Rhea replied. It felt to Bray as though Rhea may have smiled. *"I would expect nothing less from such a true friend."*

"I hope you see me as such," Bray replied, smiling back. "That's how I see you."

Seven in line before Rhea.

Bray did the math in her head. That equated to approximately eighty-four seconds until the end.

Until *her* end.
   Eighty-four seconds.
   Eighty-three.
   Eighty-two.
   Eighty-one.
   Eighty.
   How does one review their life in just one minute? A minute that had already become obsolete. Meaningless. Meaningful. Both. Everything. All at once.
   And nothing.
   All at once.

Chapter Seventeen

Dawn

"President Abbott has now enforced shelter-in-place. . .start procedures now." A man's voice spoke through some nearby radio. Dawn was beginning to pick up on the sounds around her, yet she was completely powerless. She lay there on the concrete, a feeling of embarrassment mixed with confusion and outright fear, as sirens blared through the city.

Dawn could only hear little, but what she *saw* was entirely different, horrible. Crushing her heart the way that volocopter had crushed that man's car.

A strange, upsetting feeling that she was being lifted by her feet caused Dawn to feel light-headed and woozy. Already she'd experienced an intense pain in her head as some kind of gun pressed into her and next thing she felt was warm blood coursing down the sides of her eyes, nearly reaching in and pulling away all she had ever known of herself. And the most frightening piece was that she hadn't *died*. She was sure the gun pressure was meant to kill her. Somehow terrorists had found a way to kill civilians through these damn implants. It was genius, and also entirely gut-wrenching.

A pair of Marshals were yelling into her ears, asking her to speak. . .to say her name. . .to say anything.

"Please!" Dawn screamed back. "Help me! Please!"

"Ma'am can you hear us?" a voice yelled again.

"Yes I fucking hear you!" she screamed back.

"Shit! Non-responsive! Let's get her to the ER," the man yelled.

Suddenly she was rolling, but rolling upside

down. She was *hanging*. A ripping pain climbed into her ankles, her Achilles heel. The pain was immense. A piercing, yelling-like, high-pitched feeling shot up her legs and into her spine.

"Fuuuuuucckkk!" she yelled out, yet no one seemed to hear. At least no one responded.

Below her, her eyes caught a concrete floor where blood was running into drains. A hot slit of pain slid along her throat. She gagged. More blood poured out and down. She grew light-headed again, slowly losing herself, one moment and one cut at a time.

An image of her twenty-year-old daughter, Leah, came to her. A striking image of Leah in one of her patterned skirts, wearing a button-up blouse with a slim, green tie. Always she had an eye for fashion.

What she didn't have so much an eye for was Dawn. Dawn was not her blood, but the blood of Dawn's wife, Sally. Dawn had adopted Leah when Leah was three years old. They had always been close when Leah was a child, but as Dawn got busier with work, their relationship faded.

She knew Leah resented her for this.

"Leah wants you to know," a female voice whispered through Dawn's mind, "that she misses you."

"Wh-who said that?" Dawn asked, her mind fading in and out as a feeling of blood rushing away from her head made her dizzy.

"It is me. . .the cow whose death you are experiencing," the voice replied.

"What?" Dawn asked, the word falling out of her mouth. Her eyes grew heavy and closed. She felt alive, and not at all like herself. A kind of detachment. Dissociation?

Suspended. Suspended in some altered reality over which she had no control.

Chapter Eighteen

Mateo

If someone could look in on Mateo at this moment, as though a fly on the wall, they'd only see him sitting still on the edge of his couch, his arms hanging down by his sides, mouth agape, hair disheveled. It would not seem dramatic.

Yet the world inside of him was near an end. His mind went silent the moment he felt the apparent shot to his forehead, his eyes rolling up into his sockets, the absence of blood when blood was what he'd expected.

After Mateo's mind left, another mind took over. It remained silent, but he felt its presence, like someone sitting beside him. With thought out of the way, Mateo experienced everything. Wasn't that why he'd wanted an Embedicare implant in the first place. . .so he could *feel* something?

He felt everything. The separation of his esophagus, a complete inability to call out or speak up. . .to voice his pain. The pain of some other, of this. . .this heavy body that was not his own.

"*I am a cow.*" A voice spoke into the recesses and cobwebs of his mind.

He was too disconnected from himself to respond, but he listened.

Mateo felt himself flipped upside down. His vision blurred.

He was being moved. He wanted to ask what was happening. . .

"*Your guess is as good as mine,*" replied the cow.

So apparently she could read his mind.

Creepy.

He let out a faint whisper:

"I want out of this."

It was his thought and it was also hers.

His body felt so tired, worn down by years of use. Memories of forced impregnation flipped through his brain. Several in which strange men had their hands stuck up

his. . .wait. . .*her*. . .ass.

He experienced a memory of crying, of yelling and begging for his only child not to be taken away. Mateo's family once owned a farm in Mexico that he'd visited as a child, but it had been bought out by Medina. He always thought the cows there had it pretty good. Land to graze upon, space to wander. He never gave any thought to what happened to animals he chose to eat for food. It didn't matter much to him.

"You take our lives for yourselves. And it means nothing to you."

Mateo's identity drifted in and out as his consciousness faded. Who was he? Where was he? This was excruciating. His mind couldn't handle the physicality of it. All that was left was a body being pulled apart, awaiting the final cut of his head that would result in death.

"I mean nothing to you."

The last thing she'd said before it happened.

As the instrument came down, a smooth slice into neck, bone, tissue, cutting in one fell slice, his vision rolled and rolled. Right before falling into the end of darkness, he caught the eye line of a cow that had had the gun placed on its head, having yet gone through this horrid series of deaths, one after the other, having yet felt the loss of itself, Mateo caught a glimmer in that cow's eyes. . .a glimmer of wetness and familiarity that developed into—as far as he could tell—a tear that escaped its paralyzed eye and rolled down its face, rolled down, down as Mateo's eyes rolled, rolled down. . .falling into death.

Chapter Nineteen

Cole

Bray's speech took hold of him. He'd never seen her speak with such confidence. He realized that the only times he ever saw her was when she was medicated.

He lost control.

Cole's body sat up in bed, still.

Unable to move.

He pushed with all his strength. His arms. His chest. Muscles straining.

Yet no movement.

He had every desire to run away and avoid what was about to happen.

How did his daughter end up with so much. . .*power*?

His vision was suddenly immersed in darkness. His body tightened. He froze, but it wasn't really *Cole*. . .it was the cow. He was somehow immersed in one of hundreds of cows' experiences. He knew himself enough to know these were not his emotions he was feeling, not his own pain, as he remained aware that his body sat safely in his lonely bed, not trapped inside a dark box.

Pushed forward, his vision shot through a square opening and looked out at a row of cows ahead, each one upside down, throats being slit one by one. Cole's insides turned at the sight. He was next. He tried to force his eyes shut but the vision would not cease. He pushed at his legs, willed them to get up, but they ignored him.

"All she wants is for you to believe her," whispered a sullen voice.

"What? Who?" he replied.

A barrel-shaped instrument pressed into the space between his eyes. Pressure against his brow. A massive attack of his frontal lobe. Worse than any pain he'd ever felt. His teeth bit down on his tongue. It began to bleed. He could not stop it.

"Bray."

It was the cow. She was *speaking* to him.

"Believe what?" he asked. He had to know. Especially if this was the end, he had to know what his daughter wanted. Even if he could never fulfill it.

A warm liquid sensation rolled down the side of his head. He remembered the day he sat in a care conference with Dianna and Bray, at the hospital, how Dianna pressed for guardianship over Bray, how Bray looked to him for help and all he could do was turn away.

Oh, how he begged to turn away again.

Please, please. No. . .no. . .no I can't watch this.

He felt the familiar sensation in his chest, which had become to him like a close friend, always there to pull him into denial, out of the present moment, the moment things got hard.

The first time he'd done it, he was a child and his father was beating up his older brother in the front yard after his brother had gotten arrested. Denial and avoidance were his best friends growing up, keeping him safe and locking away his feelings so he didn't have to experience the pain he witnessed and had no ability to stop. His brother's pain as his father beat him down so much his brother was taken and placed in foster care, and Cole knew deep down he'd be next in line.

Next in line now as his vision exited that dark box, flipped upside down, and he was carried right behind the other cows that had gone before him. A sensation of cutting into his body gave way to a very real and deep, hollow sadness, the kind of sadness one might feel when they know they are about to die alone. As his heart bled out, with it fell all the lost friends, all the minutes and hours spent in confinement, standing all day, diseased hooves, rotting out skin, eyes dried of tears, having seen so much beyond anyone's comprehension that the heart wished death upon itself.

"*Believe. Believe that this is her gift.*"

Cole heard this as his mind—the cow's mind—broke down. It was as though hearing what he needed to hear, that his daughter was orchestrating all of this, allowed him to let go.

In the breaking down of the cow's body and mind and the bleeding out of its heart, Cole lost himself. He felt tears roll down his cheeks and didn't quite feel where they came from. They were the tears of a life lost the moment it was born, a sudden flash of happiness, of despair, the worst one can feel as it departs into death, and then he fell unconscious.

Chapter Twenty

Bertan

Bertan awoke. His eyes blinked rapidly. The walls of a utility closet came into view. A mop. . .drain. . .brooms hanging along the wall beside him. He was lying on the ground.

How did he get here? His heart raced because he knew he was supposed to be somewhere else. He knew that if he was in here, something had happened to him. Sweat gathered along his brow, dropped down his back. He looked down and saw he was wearing a suit. What?

Bertan pulled off the suit jacket and threw it against the wall. He remembered. The fugue, or whatever Ruben had called it. It got him. Again. An image of Jacob's face staring at him from down the hall came to his mind. He'd turned and that's when he had been hit by something.

He felt the ache protruding from the back of his head, working its way up and over to the front of his head. His eyes began to throb. Reaching his hand to the back of his head, he felt a golf ball-sized knob popping out.

"Shit!" he whispered.

Bertan stood up, his head pounding from the sudden movement. He cringed. Pressing his hand into the wall for balance, he remained still for a moment. He glanced down at the button-up shirt, the pants.

Ruben's suit.

Where the hell was Ruben?

A sinking feeling began filling his heart with regret. He opened his eyes and looked at the door of the closet. He'd really messed up. He was supposed to stop the knocker. . .to *be* the knocker. . .so he could hold up the line and give Kage time to get Bray out before it was too late.

Yes. . .it was coming back to him.

Fucking fugue. He should've listened to Ruben and tried to get some kind of help.

Bertan kicked the wall with his boot. He kicked it again, and again, and again, grunting and letting out the aggression he felt as he kicked.

He suddenly stopped.

He needed to be angry.

He needed to get back out there before it was too late. Maybe it was already too late, but he sure as hell wasn't going to wait in here for them to return for him.

Pulling the door open a crack, Bertan peeked out into the hall. He was in the utility closet across from the cafeteria. He reached into his pocket for his phone. It wasn't there. He hurried to check the jacket, but it wasn't in there either.

"Mother fuckers," he whispered. They must've taken it.

Returning to the door, he opened it a crack and looked out again. The hall was currently empty. Praying no one was in the cafeteria, he slid out through the door, darted across the hall, and entered the cafeteria.

It was empty.

He searched the lockers, his heart tumbling over itself, sweat pouring down his face.

"Hurry, hurry, hurry," he whispered to himself frantically.

If he got caught again, he wasn't sure they'd let him live this time.

Finally he found a smock. He threw it on over the suit, buttoned it up to cover as much of his clothes as he could.

Turning, he hurried over to the cafeteria entrance. Standing against the wall, he peeked out into the hall to ensure it was clear. He slid out, his back kept hard against the wall, until he reached the doors. He had no keys to get into the Kill Floor.

He banged on the door as hard as he could. His fist pounding, pounding, pounding at the door. Time seeming to slither away as the sweat dropped from his face, his shoulders dropping with every moment that passed him by. How he should have listened to Ruben. How he should not have lied to the man. His only friend.

Finally the door pushed open. One of the workers looked at him with eyes showing confusion. Bertan pushed past the man, turning and nearly tripping over himself.

Up past the bleed pit area, he got view of the knock box. A beef's head revealed itself through the window of the knock box. Bertan's face went flush. Workers nearby stopped to watch him. He sprinted through the bleed pit, nearly slipping on the bloody floor. Men yelled at him. He dodged the hanging bodies of beefs, the heat of them hovering and following him with sorrow as his heart went heavy and dropped down into his groin. What would happen to Bray. . .to the others. . .his family, if he didn't get to those beefs? If he was already too late?

Surely he was. And a part of him already knew it. That part of him that was real, that didn't want things to be this way anymore, that thought, silly enough, that this plan they'd had, this crazy plan by this teenager he swore looked like his daughter and in these moments of panic he could've confused *as* his daughter, that this plan would somehow solve everything. End everything. And get him back safe to his family again.

But there was the memory loss. Those parts of himself he did not wish to see, to be honest about. The years of torture, murder, sacrifice. The things he had done without thinking twice. How he aimed to forget. How. . .as he ran up the ramp toward the knocker, the knocker turning with a face covered by goggles and mask, that part of him took over this one last time, because that part of him still *believed*. Believed it wasn't too late. That all these beefs that had gone before meant nothing. That they were not yet the ones. That the girl's special cows had not yet arrived at the knock box. No. . .

In these moments, his senses heightened. His ears picked up the sounds of machinery behind him. The whistling and whooping of men. The lights. Fans moving above. The knocker turned, as if to defy him, and knocked another beef just as he arrived at the box to stop it. Bertan went for him, unwilling to see the truth right before his eyes.

Denial, after all, was a beautiful, powerful thing.

Chapter Twenty-One

Bray

Tears welled in her eyes, freely falling down and dropping onto her shirt. They began the moment the first cow approached the metal trap. Bray felt everything. The eternal sense of sadness, how it hung over the cows as they waited in line, trapped, nowhere to run but to death. Impending doom. Fear so palpable it coursed through Bray's blood, heavy like metal, cold like bitter winter, crawling into her chest, through her rib cage, seeking out her heart and swallowing it whole.

Rhea stood only two cows behind the trap. As each cow was forced inside, Bray's heart tightened. These experiences were not her own. Though slightly aware, holding on within an inch of the remaining self she could, Bray knew this was the full slaughter her body was taking on. It seeped into her heart and was near taking her soul. What would happen? This did not feel the same as when she'd connected with Alice, when Alice had died. This was all-encompassing, triple the intensity of Alice's death. A thought crossed Bray's mind that her heart might actually implode, or her mind break into psychosis, after all of this was over. But the fear she held was the fear of the cows, not her own. There was little concern for herself. Something bigger was happening here. Bray recollected the dream she had where Alice came to visit her.

"Doing the right thing isn't about the outcome. It isn't about winning or losing. The success is in the try. You have to try," Alice had said.

Bray held steady. She needed to follow through. If this didn't change the nation's view of animals, Bray feared nothing would.

Rhea was next in line. Seconds between this moment and the beginning of death. The sound vibrating as metal rubbed against metal. The sound of thumping. Bray's vision faced the closed trap where inside someone was losing their life. Another thump. . .followed by a hiss and more vibrating. Bray's heart flipped over and over on itself.

"*Stay with me,*" Rhea spoke softly to her.

"I am here now," Bray replied.

The back of the metal trap opened.

"Listen to me, Rhea," Bray said quickly, while she still had time. "I love you. I will stay with you until the end, as far as I can go, or perhaps I will go with you, I don't know. My heart is so heavy. I feel so much regret."

"*Have no regret, dear child. Everything that's happened and will happen, is as it is.*"

With that, Rhea was forced into the trap. Closed inside, it got tight, darker than the depths of all fear, nowhere to go. No escape. Was everything happening as it was supposed to? Bray wouldn't make sense of a world where such things were true. She remained with Rhea, both of them awaiting the inevitable end.

Chapter Twenty-Two

Bertan

Bertan had never felt so far away from something he wanted, something he needed. To have it be so close, that knock box, the knocker, within arm's reach. His hands outstretched as he ran, everything slowed. The knocker paused, turned to him again. But the knocker did not seem to be looking *at* him. It was as though he was looking *past* Bertan, at someone or something else.

The day Bertan's father was murdered, he knew it had happened. He knew it before his mother told him. He was on his way home from school, walking toward their house in Colonia a La Meda. The streets were alive with music and young men leaning against their cars, smoking whatever they were smoking, watching Bertan as he walked by. It was daylight but the sun was hiding away somewhere. Bertan always remembered that day.

His father was already in a lot of trouble with Medina. He'd been working with a few local men to hide *campesinos* whose lives were being threatened. His mother was afraid every day. Bertan found himself rather indifferent, though overall he approved of what his father was doing. He only wished that, like Che Guevara, his father had used violence. Then he might have actually stopped Medina, instead of dying and letting his son grow up without a father only to get involved with Medina too, leading to where he was in this very moment.

But Bertan could not blame his father. Medina. . .S-Corp. . .they were the real enemy. Which was why he had to stop them now. Because nearly twenty years ago he was walking home from school and he *knew*. He didn't know if it was the way the heat stuck in the air, as if afraid to move. Or if it was the way the men on the streets watched him as he passed. He felt it. That part of him deep down inside, the little voice of reason, of truth, that told him today was the day. They'd finally gotten to his father and they'd killed him.

So when he entered his home and saw his mother wailing on the kitchen floor, he was not surprised. In shock, yes, but not surprised.

When the knocker nodded past him and quickly turned and pressed the knock gun between the eyes of another beef, Bertan knew. It did not stop him from trying. From touching the knocker's gloved hands, his fingers wrapping around the man's wrist. He had to try.

Try as he might, he sensed what was coming behind him. Or more accurately, *who* was coming up behind him.

Bertan stopped and turned.

It was that security officer in the black clothing. The one who had most likely knocked him out earlier.

Bertan screamed.

"Nooooo!" His voice echoed through the Kill Floor as he tried one last time to pull the knocker's hand away from the beef's head.

Hands grabbed his shoulders. An arm came around his neck. The officer had him in a choke hold.

"No!" he screamed again.

Bertan flailed and kicked, trying to pull himself away, feeling that maybe it wasn't too late, couldn't possibly be too late, to save her. He was being pulled away. The knock box grew smaller in his view as his body was pulled backwards, back to the hall.

He reached up and tried hitting the man who was pulling him, but Bertan was much shorter, and when he tried punching at the man's face he only managed to swing at the man's neck. The man laughed.

It was over.

In absolute disbelief, Bertan felt his legs stop moving. He was being dragged out of the Kill Floor, down the hall, and back into the utility closet from which he'd escaped.

Bertan was thrown into the closet. The force with which the officer pushed him caused him to trip over something, fall forward, and land hard against the opposite wall. He stretched out his hands to prevent his head from slamming into the concrete.

The door quickly shut and locked behind him. Bertan turned. There on the floor was a leg, the thing he'd tripped over. His eyes followed the body up to a face he was shocked and saddened to see. Mouth taped shut, both eyes bruised so badly Bertan could barely make them out.

It took a moment for him to realize it was Ruben.

Chapter Twenty-Three

Bray

Who was she? Where was she? Darkness. Heat. Tremendous heat. Her tired body, still so young yet she felt so old. Bray recognized this feeling of being heavy, weighed down by decades and decades of hard life squeezed into only a few years.

She had felt this when Alice was dying.

She'd become so intertwined with Rhea that she moved in and out of both consciousnesses, her own and Rhea's, without much control. She could no longer feel her own body, only the weight of Rhea on diseased and shaky hooves. Pain. . .mounting.

A light edged into the darkness. It began as a slit and rose up, up, into a square shape. Outside of it Bray noticed a row of workers standing with knives in their hands. The cows that had gone before were hanging upside down, bleeding out from their jugulars.

Rhea was pushed forward so suddenly, her head popped through the square slot, pressed down on either side by hard metal. She couldn't move. Her heart palpitated so fast she could hear it between her ears. Her eyes widened. Her heart nearly folded in on itself. Every sound intensified. Metal banging. Whistles. Snapping sounds. Grinding.

A cylindrical, hollow instrument pressed into her head.

This was it.

When Bray had said goodbye to Alice, they had time on their side. Though too far gone to be saved, Alice at least had the freedom to die in peace, outdoors, where she belonged. And as Bray sat now, helpless, knowing she couldn't give that peace to Rhea—that she couldn't save her newfound friend—she began to cry.

The tears rolled down Rhea's face.

"Rhea?" Bray called out.

"*Yes.*"

"I love you." Bray spoke through broken tears.

"*I never had a chance to experience love until you showed me.*"

Bray's heart broke. She never considered her actions as a form of love, but of course such actions could only come from love.

Before Bray was ready, before Rhea could understand what was about to happen to her, only sensing it was something to be feared, the knock gun went off.

The pressure split Bray's mind in two. Rhea went unconscious. Neither of them could think or speak. It was as though both their lives were left hanging in space, in darkness, forever.

There was plenty of pain, of course. . .felt in the ankles, sharp, stinging. Warm blade along the throat, a cut and another cut, unrecognizable as to where. The pain got to be so immense it all melded together. Bray's consciousness too began to fade, the darkness growing darker.

Bray had a faint recognition of self, not herself but of Rhea, one last moment of accepting finally that this was her life and this was how it ended, simple as that. There was no emotion behind it. Life was what it was. This was fate. She accepted it one moment before the end, because the one last bit of agency she had left over her own life was to exit in a sense of peace.

And so it was.

Chapter Twenty-Four

Kage

Kage remained by Bray's side in the trailer, wiping sweat away from her head and brow. Bray's body continued to shake. Her hands had dropped to her sides. Her eyes were open but had rolled up into her head. Tears developed in her eyes and slowly slid down her cheeks.

Kage pulled the rag away.

"She's crying," he said.

"What?" Elliott replied, standing up.

"She's crying."

Before Kage could say much else, Bray's body stopped shaking. Motionless, so still it seemed like a mountain sitting there on the chair. Bray's chest heaved once, twice, and ceased moving. Her mouth dropped open. A deep groan passed through her lips. Kage's hairs stood on end. Bray's body fell forward, forward, forward. Kage leapt up and caught her in his arms.

"Shit. . .she's passed out!" he yelled, panicked. "Where the fuck is Bertan?"

"What'd you say?" Elliott asked, running over to help him.

"Nothing. . .never mind," Kage replied, annoyed. His heart raced. He felt panic coming on. Bertan was supposed to be there. He said he'd stop the cows from going through slaughter.

If he'd done that, Bray would not have passed out.

Kage feared something had gone terribly wrong.

"She's not moving," Elliott said. He seemed way too calm given the situation.

"Shut everything down!" Kage yelled at him. "Now!"

They had to get her back to Meeteetse, which was hours away. This was not supposed to happen.

They had no game plan in case things went wrong. At least Elliott had a car.

Elliott unplugged all the equipment and threw it back into the box. He closed up the laptop and, holding it, turned to Kage.

"Get her out to the car. I'm right behind you."

Kage set Bray on the floor and stood up. He carefully bent down and pulled her up into his arms. Elliott ran over to the door and opened it for Kage.

For as small as Bray was, her body weight without agency was straining on Kage's arms. His body shook with frustration. He nearly tripped down the steps of the trailer. Elliott came up behind and steadied him before he fell.

Out here in broad daylight, thick western heat smacked Kage in the face. Elliott came running up behind him and opened the car's back door. Kage slid Bray's body into the back seat. His heart leapt up into his throat. He felt he might cry. He checked her pulse. It was beating, but so subtle she seemed almost dead.

"Come on, Bray," he whispered.

The one thing he did not want to happen, that he dreaded, had happened.

A moment later, Elliott jumped into the driver's seat. Kage sat in the back with Bray's head in his lap. Elliott started the car and sped down the road, headed northeast.

Kage's heart raced. He was crying. This had happened once before and Bray had been lucky to survive that. Would the world really give her another chance? He wasn't so sure.

Yet again, he'd have to do CPR.

At least this time his wrist was not broken.

"Shit, shit, shit," Kage whispered. He turned and faced Bray. How at peace she looked despite what was really going on. Placing his hands against her chest, he began doing compressions.

He counted in his mind as sweat dropped from his head and landed on Bray's shirt.

Kage kept going, and going, and going.
His wrists began to ache.
He pulled open her mouth and breathed into it.
He kept on with the compressions.
Despite all he did. . .how hard he
tried. . .nothing seemed to change.

Chapter Twenty-Five

Rhea

We had to do it.

Humans had indeed lost control. We watched from afar, where after each of us had lost our lives we began to transition beyond this place called Earth. Thanks to whatever testing had been done on us, we still had control. Thanks to Bray's ability to connect us to these humans, despite her own falling, we still had some hold on humanity.

But we had to be quick.

Once we transitioned fully, it would be too late.

At first, we watched.

It happened everywhere. Millions of citizens with Embedicare implants stood in shock as more than a hundred of us were slaughtered, one by one. Many who had the 4D implants had either passed out, thrown up, or both.

Humans became overwhelmed with a certain devastation, faced with mass terror over which no one had control. They went unconscious in their vehicles, leading to accidents. Cars veered out of control and slammed into other cars, poles, buildings. An unintended consequence that, while it happened, Bray had no awareness of.

And so we stepped in.

We had enough awareness to know that if any of these humans died, Bray would be at fault. She would never be forgiven. How the humans were reacting to our pain, to our brutal murders, was significant enough in and of itself.

We watched these car accidents. Each time an accident occurred, we used our energy to keep the energy of those humans alive. By keeping ourselves as close to Earth as possible—not fully fading away—we gave our energy to them.

Shelter-in-place sirens blared in every city in every state. The country's president remained locked away in a bunker beneath the East Wing of the White House.

Washington was on complete lockdown. But again, no lives were lost.

From the perspective of the humans, terror had officially been unleashed.

Marshals attempted to control increasing crowds in Times Square. At state checkpoints Marshals were so distracted by their own implants that cars freely passed through without check.

Workers at S-Corp facilities who could afford implants, mostly quality control personnel and plant managers—were mesmerized by the images they witnessed, causing meat and dairy production to slow almost to a stop.

This enabled many cows and pigs to escape. They used brute force to push past distracted workers, running away from transport trucks in which they'd traveled long distances. They ran through fields, free for the first time. Eventually they were either shot down by drones or caught and brought back.

Throughout the country, humans gathered together in anger at what they saw, anger at the exposure of truths about S-Corp that hundreds of protestors now believed true, gaining strength in their numbers while watching the slaughter.

"If that's how they treat animals, then there is no end to how they'll treat us," yelled one human.

And finally, there was an equal percentage of humans whose hearts broke at what they saw. How they stood in streets, in their places of work or their homes, stunned by the fear they experienced with each of our deaths, how they came to *feel* for us, to realize that we could indeed feel and *comprehend* what was happening to us.

Would this stop any of them from choosing to eat animals?

It was too soon to tell.
It did give us hope.
Enough hope to be satisfied, and to depart.

Chapter Twenty-Six

Cole

Cole's eyes opened. They were heavy, as if weighted down by concrete. He blinked away blurry vision to recognize the carpet in his bedroom. Somehow he'd ended up on the floor. Coming up to sitting, he reached for his neck, which was tight from his head having been twisted in a precarious position for who knew how long.

He glanced down at his forearm. News reporters were disseminating details of what they referred to as "The Embedicare Takeover." They showed car fires and accidents. People screaming in crowds outside Marshal stations and public offices, demanding answers.

Cole was shocked. He stood up, his head spinning, and he held tight to the bedpost until the dizzy spell dissipated. He walked slowly over to his Embedicare power box and hit the *Off* button. It did not turn off. He pushed it again, but it remained on. He closed his eyes to shield himself from what was on his screen, but even that did not stop the horror. Immediately he was bombarded with the images of that cow that had been slaughtered. Reliving the slaughter he experienced and felt himself nearly die of. He *should've* died. In fact, for a moment there he had believed he was going to die.

But what really got to him were the words that had come to him while transfixed. That all his daughter wanted was for him to believe her.

Was that really true?

Cole ignored the screen on his arm and went into the living room, where two white couches faced one another as if in silent conversation. A 65" television hung from the far wall and looked at him. He didn't want to turn it on, but he had to.

"Turn on the TV, please," Cole spoke into a speaker on one of the side tables.

A second later, the screen popped on, revealing Fox newscasters discussing what had happened. News, of course, was not the truth. It was corrupt. Had been for ages. But today it was more real than anything, save maybe that slaughter he had experienced, which left a lingering sense of loss in his chest.

On the screen, news of planes completing emergency landings due to pilot error switched to a newscaster at Times Square. Behind her, people were awakening as if they'd been sleeping, yet they'd been standing the entire time.

Some of them began crying.

Others ran past the newscaster, their faces white with terror.

"As you can see. . .Times Square is a complete picture of confusion and fear right now. But miraculously, reports are coming in that no one has been killed. Across the country we have yet to hear of any lives lost. Absolutely incredible," the newscaster said.

People feared it was a terrorist attack. Cole knew it wasn't.

Bray was in for it now. If Dianna found her, which he imagined Dianna would pull out all stops to accomplish, Bray would most likely be locked away. With her face all over those videos, having been seen by thousands if not millions of Americans, she would be blamed.

Shit, Cole thought.

He sat down on the couch. He continued to watch as reports came in from the White House: President Abbott was safe. . .shelter-in-place would remain in effect until further notice. Subways and public transport. . .empty. Marshals clogged the streets in riot gear. From what he'd seen so far, no riots had broken out. People were angry, but most appeared angry at S-Corp, shouting profanities at S-Corp as cameras everywhere recorded them.

Cole admittedly felt confused. He hadn't known all those things about S-Corp, *if* they were true.

He began piecing things together in his mind. It was a lot. Clearly Bray wanted him to experience a cow's slaughter. He realized she wanted *everyone* to experience it. But the only reaction he could control was his own. What was *he* going to do after having gone through this? All his life he'd avoided as much conflict as he could. As a senator he did a great job of staying in the middle lane and making as many people happy as possible, whether he agreed with them or not.

That would have to change. His daughter needed him. And how his country would need him. As a senator, maybe it was time to come out of vacation.

Cole returned to his bedroom and retrieved his phone from the bedside table. He called his assistant.

"Mary?" he spoke as soon as she answered.

"Yeah Senator Hoffman? It's kind of crazy right now."

"I know. Listen, I need a favor."

"Regarding what, sir?"

"I need to find out if the things they said about S-Corp are true."

"You mean. . .your daughter?"

"Yes."

"Okay. . .but you may want to lie low for a while."

"Why's that?" he asked, still feeling out of sorts.

"Because everyone knows that was your daughter."

Suddenly Cole remembered the press release Dianna had sent out back in April claiming Elliott had kidnapped Bray.

And his press conference. The one where he had pleaded for Bray to come home after she'd escaped the hospital. The one where he admitted Bray had schizophrenia. He wished he hadn't said that. He wished he'd kept it private.

Shit, again.

"Just get me the info for now," Cole replied, hanging up the phone.

Dianna would go after Bray for sure.

He had to find a way to warn his daughter.

Chapter Twenty-Seven

Dawn

Dawn woke in a hospital bed. She was alone in the room. The door was open, and from the hall she could hear every voice, every beeping sound, and instantly tears came to her eyes.

"Oh, thank God," she whispered. Finally, she could hear something other than that nightmare she had gone through.

An IV drip hung to her right and its tube led down to her arm. The liquid inside was clear. She glanced up at the heart monitor. Everything looked normal. She would know; she'd been in the hospital enough times.

A male nurse entered the room, smiled at her.

"You're lucky, Mrs. Harpender," the nurse said, approaching her bed with a tablet in hand.

"Why's that?" Dawn asked. When she turned toward the nurse, she felt mildly dizzy.

"You got one of the last beds in the hospital today."

"Huh?" she asked, confused.

"It's been hectic, to say the least. Whatever that Embedicare takeover was, it's got hundreds of people in the hospital. Like the pandemic, only all at once," the nurse said as he walked around Dawn's bed and checked her vitals, entering them on the tablet.

"So I wasn't the only one?"

"Oh, no. They don't have many details but they're calling it another terrorist attack."

"I was afraid of that," Dawn replied, glancing down at the nurse's tablet. "When can I get out of here?"

"You're looking pretty stable now so we'll release you in a few hours."

"And where's my wife?" Dawn asked, suddenly

feeling as though she hadn't seen Sally in years.

"Shelter-in-place. No visitors. She's been notified and we'll call her when we send you home."

"Send me home?"

"Yeah. We'll have to get you an ambulance home."

"You ain't charging me for that, are you?"

"Honestly, Mrs. Harpender, I can't answer that. Everything's upside down right now."

The nurse shrugged, turned, and left the room.

Left alone, Dawn began to cry. She'd never felt more frightened and confused in her entire life, and equally relieved. . .grateful. Thank God it was over and thank God she hadn't died. Surely there were others who had.

She suddenly thought of Leah.

"Leah!" she whispered.

Dawn hit the button to call the nurse back into the room.

She remembered what that cow had said about her daughter, that Leah missed her. It was far-fetched to believe a cow, but it was true that she missed Leah and needed to make sure she was okay.

The nurse entered the room.

"Where's my phone? I need to call my daughter, make sure she's okay," Dawn said, feeling more on edge by the moment.

The nurse walked over to the chair across from Dawn's bed. There lay a bag of Dawn's belongings and clothes. The nurse pulled out the phone and walked it over to her.

"Thank you," she said, looking at the screen.

The nurse left the room.

Dawn noticed three texts from Leah. All wondering if Dawn was okay. Where was Dawn? Why wasn't she answering?

Dawn unlocked her phone and called her daughter.

Leah answered on the first ring.

"Mom?"

"Yes honey, I'm okay," Dawn replied, instantly crying at the sound of Leah's voice. How beautiful and crisp and real it was.

"I was so scared. Where are you?"

"I'm at the hospital. I passed out, but I'm okay. Where are you? Are you with your mom?"

"No, I'm at school. I'm stuck in my dorm. They won't let us leave."

"I know sweetheart," Dawn said, nodding. "They've got a shelter-in-place order in effect. But that will keep us all safe." Dawn paused. "Have you heard from your mom?"

"Yes. She's at home, worried about you."

"I'm sure she is," Dawn replied. For some reason this made her smile. That everyone was alive enough to worry. That was everything.

"Listen, Leah. I need to tell you something."

"Okay."

Dawn decided to go out on a limb. To assume what she heard about Leah was true. Why on earth would it not be? That was the confusing piece of this whole experience: it was beyond frightening, yet the only message she received—as far as she remembered—was that her daughter missed her. Not anything terrorizing. It made no sense, if this mess today truly was coming from someone aiming to cause harm.

"I miss you, too," Dawn said finally.

She heard Leah break down on the line.

"How did you know?" Leah asked, crying.

That confirmed it. Somehow someone in control of this whole "Embedicare takeover" also had some kind of ESP capabilities. Confusing. Frightening. But in this moment, it was the thing Dawn needed.

And her daughter, too, apparently.

"I just know," she replied. "And after today, I realize I've got to start making you more of a priority in my life."

"That'd be great," Leah said.

The crying ceased.

Chapter Twenty-Eight

Mateo

Mateo and his girlfriend, Mandi, had been going back and forth for the last hour. After the takeover ended, he went to find her. She had been crying in the shower. She was inconsolable for the first half hour or so. He helped her out of the tub, dried her off and dressed her as she cried. He carried her into the bedroom and lay with her. As he did, his mind ran through what had happened. He remembered everything. It was disturbing, to say the least. And he had *felt* it, the pain, the horror. Like he felt he was going to physically die, yet here he was, fully intact and unharmed.

So if it was a terrorist attack, why hadn't either of them died? He wanted to turn on the television, but Mandi wasn't ready for that, not yet.

She spoke.

"Well, I can never eat burgers again."

They both laughed.

"I thought I was going to die," Mateo said evenly.

"Me, too," Mandi replied. She started crying again.

When she able to stop crying, she asked, "Were those shelter-in-place sirens I heard?"

"Yep. You don't have to work today," Mateo replied, making light of things as he always did.

Mandi smiled but it faded fast.

"What was all that?" she asked.

"I don't know." They were lying down, facing each other. Mateo looked past her at the wall, thinking.

"Did you hear all that stuff that girl said? All that stuff about S-Corp?"

Mateo nodded.

"I really want to turn on the TV," he finally said.

"No. Not yet. I want to process this on my own first. You know how the news is. They'll decide for us what happened. This thing, whatever it was, feels more complicated than a terrorist attack."

"Or more advanced," Mateo said.

"What do you mean?"

"Maybe they're so skilled this is just the first step. Maybe that's why we didn't die."

"Maybe. But then why show us all that stuff about S-Corp? Seemed legit. They had proof—"

"As far as we could tell, yes," Mateo said, meeting eyes with her. The blue in them was so clear, perhaps from all the crying, it made him want to hold her close.

"But why show us animals being slaughtered? Why that? It's not like they were committing the atrocities themselves. They wanted us to experience it for some reason. . .to witness the truth about S-Corp."

"Baby, you've never liked S-Corp."

"They've given me little reason to," she replied, sitting up.

Mandi was a glorified tree-hugger. At least, that was how he'd referred to her. It was a joke, a way to jab at her because he loved her, but also, it was true. Mandi did not like big industry. She'd always said how uncomfortable she was with S-Corp being the only corporation managing their food and their water. She'd often said she was convinced they were actually *contributing* to the water crisis rather than solving the problem, yet she had no proof.

"Yeah, I know," Mateo replied, sitting up beside her. He got a sudden flash of being shot between the eyes by some stranger in goggles. He shivered. A second later that flash was replaced by an image of a cow trying to escape that metal box where it was trapped.

"You okay?" Mandi's voice reached in.

"I just—do you still remember. . .what happened?" he asked in reply.

"Every bit. That's why I was crying," she said, pausing. She looked down at the comforter. "I saw their eyes. They were. . .*sad. . .*you know? I've never seen anyone so sad in my whole life. It was like they knew what was about to happen to them."

Mateo nodded, had no reply. He didn't quite know how to put into words what he'd experienced, but she was right. It was very sad.

"And how those workers kicked them and used those prods like that. I never realized," Mandi said, her voice trailing off.

They both sat quietly. The sirens had long since ended and the streets outside went quiet, save the occasional fire truck or ambulance screaming down the road. Something was surely happening out there, but Mateo suddenly didn't want to know what. He'd come to know too much already.

"What now?" Mandi asked, which, to Mateo, seemed the next best question.

"I have no idea," he replied. . .the next best and only answer.

Chapter Twenty-Nine

Elisha

Cincinnati, Ohio

Elisha Andrews stood in the bathroom, fixing her hair in the mirror. It was Friday morning, and she had to be in the office in a half an hour. She twisted her long, dark hair up into a bunch on the top of her head and pinned it all into an updo. While she did this, her phone buzzed from its place beside the sink.

It was an alert:

SHELTER-IN-PLACE IN EFFECT UNTIL FURTHER NOTICE.

REMAIN WHERE YOU ARE.

"Remain where you are?" she whispered, frowning.

Elisha exited the bathroom and went into the living room, where, through the tall windows, the sun was already beginning to cast its intense rays onto the couch. There, her cat Lucy slept.

Elisha did not own a television. She was a voracious reader, an occasional visitor on social media. She got her news from a national public internet source. Other than that, she tried remaining as far from media as she could.

But this shelter-in-place situation made her nervous.

She sat down on the couch and opened her phone to her favorite online news source. There at the top of the page was a story about some "Embedicare takeover" with images of a young girl on video, followed by images of car crashes, swarms of people running through Times Square.

Truly frightening. . .yet also very, very odd.

Like, was this really happening?

Elisha read the article. Something about a young girl by the name of Bray Hoffman, daughter of an S-Corp President. . .

"No shit," Elisha said, now perking up. Her own mother had been mingling with S-Corp on her latest genetics project with GeneUs.com, something Elisha did not support for one second.

And now this.

Elisha read on, totally forgetting about her job or that she might want to reach out and make sure her mom and dad were okay. The most pressing thing on her mind was this article, how it mentioned "ecoterrorists" who'd somehow hijacked Embedicare implants, causing anyone with the 4D option to experience the slaughter of cows.

Not to mention exposing S-Corp as the culprit of the 2027 terrorist attack on the soil. Apparently there was a website with even more evidence.

That was when she thought of Emerson.

Elisha stood up and paced the floor. She'd had her Embedicare implant removed five years ago, after her friend Emerson taught her all there was to know about animal activism and the truth of what S-Corp really was. Hell, Emerson's own father had been murdered by S-Corp. She was the one who had to pick Emerson up off the floor, so to speak, after it had happened.

Before aiding Emerson and a skeleton crew of animal activists when they'd saved some animals from an S-Corp laboratory, Elisha had her implant surgically removed, knowing her whereabouts could be traced with it. She knew enough about S-Corp's shady past with activists. Emerson, whom she very much loved, had remained in hiding all these years because of his fear of S-Corp.

Emerson would have to be made aware of this. She hadn't spoken to him in years, mostly for his own protection, but she knew where he was. And without the implant, she could travel there undetected as soon as this whole thing blew over.

And it would.

Because Elisha knew, unlike most of these people panicking and assuming they were under another terrorist attack, *who* the real terrorist really was.

Chapter Thirty

Dianna

Damage control was nearly impossible. Hundreds of workers at S-Corp's facilities had stopped, mid-production, because they had implants. They witnessed the slaughter but also saw Bray's speech. They slowed production on the line, delaying the nation's meat and dairy production.

Their intentional negligence allowed animals to escape, which would slow things further because resources had to be allocated for the animals to be caught and returned to the transit trucks and slaughterhouses.

As Dianna sat at her desk, her back straight like a wall, growing tight with added stress that pushed down into her shoulders and pained her neck, she watched email after email after email come in about this "Embedicare takeover" attack halting production.

She stared at one email in particular.

It was from her boss, the CEO of S-Corp himself, Dr. Michael Brisbon. He had the job Dianna wanted. At age sixty, he was near retirement. Up to this point in her life, Dianna believed she'd had a shot at taking his place. He'd given her every reason to.

Then came this email:

DIANNA—
THIS IS UNACCEPTABLE. YOUR DAUGHTER, RIGHT? DID YOU KNOW ABOUT THIS?
WHAT ARE YOU GOING TO DO TO CLEAN IT UP?
BEST,
MICHAEL

She'd begun a reply fifteen minutes ago, but she didn't know how to respond. With earbuds pressed into her ears, she listened to the news as they described the state of the nation. Flights cancelled, roads emptied, hospitals filing to capacity like the early days of the COVID-19 pandemic. Citizens with implants were under considerable duress. Those with the 4D implants began reporting how they'd experienced the slaughter of the cows first-hand. How this was possible, Dianna could not fathom and probably wouldn't until she could find the culprits.

It had to be caused by Elliott or whomever he was working for, and her own daughter had somehow been roped in. Dianna couldn't keep up with S-Corp business-related emails because so many CEOs, CFOs, and S-Corp leadership were emailing about Bray.

*Isn't this your daughter. . .*kind of emails, texts. Her phone buzzing uncontrollably. Dianna wasn't a crier, but she was about to be one for the first time in her life. As things fell apart around her, the lack of control caused her anger to seep into her bloodstream. She wanted to scream and throw her laptop out the window.

What really upset her was that Dr. Brisbon would ever think she had somehow known about this attack. She would have to defend herself and get to work on fixing it. Especially if there was any hope of her keeping her reputation with S-Corp intact.

DR. BRISBON-
IT IS COMPLETELY UNACCEPTABLE. I AM DOING DAMAGE CONTROL AS I TYPE. YES UNFORTUNATELY THAT WAS MY DAUGHTER ON THE SCREEN. I HAD NO IDEA. I HAVEN'T BEEN ABLE TO FIND HER IN MONTHS, SO THIS IS EXTREMELY SHOCKING AND FRIGHTENING FOR ME.
I WILL TAKE CARE OF IT.

Dianna took a deep breath and clicked send. Her jaw clenched. She picked up the phone and started reaching out to every S-Corp facility in her region, demanding they return to work immediately. That they keep the workers on overtime to compensate for any time lost during the takeover.

She texted Carl:

I NEED YOU TO HELP WITH DAMAGE CONTROL. THIS WILL RUIN MY REPUTATION.

Carl typed back moments later:

ON IT.

As she glanced at his message she saw the caller ID pop up on her forearm. It was Dan.

Dianna immediately took the call, listening to his voice through her earbuds.

"Talk to me!" she said, her voice hurried and strained.

"They're in Meeteetse," Dan said.

"Where?"

"It used to be a small town in Wyoming. It's a house on its own. It's even got a garden."

"Get me the coordinates." Dianna thought about the shelter-in-place laws and spoke again. "And get me a few security people. We need to get out there, now."

"I'll get a few men and be on my way." Dan hung up.

Dianna sat back in her chair. She looked up at the white ceiling. A tear escaped her eye. She wasn't sure whether it was relief or thrill. Maybe a mix of the two. She knew where her daughter was now, and she'd get her back this time, find who made this terrible mess, and put them all away.

Chapter Thirty-One

Bertan

Ruben was gone.

Bertan woke inside the back of a transport van, its windows covered in wire mesh partitions. He was sitting on a bench, his hands cuffed behind his back. Across from him, another bench sat empty.

He was alone.

Two men sat in the front seats. He could see them through another partition, this one glass.

Outside, miles and miles of empty land passed by, the way his life had passed him by and here he was with nothing left. Who knew what time it was or where he was being taken, but what he did know was that Ruben was missing. Last he'd seen his friend, Ruben was lying unconscious on the utility closet floor.

Ruben. How he'd really messed things up with his only friend. He definitely should have listened to the man. He clenched his fists. His head rising up, he looked at the ceiling of the van, feeling like he might burst out in tears of anger. His chest tightened. The movement of the van beneath him made him grow nauseous. Coming down onto his knees and forming himself into a ball, Bertan gently hit his head against the hard floor. Ruben's name repeated over and over again in his mind.

When Bertan's father was still alive, the two of them would sit together and read about the contra fights in Central America. How Honduras was stuck in the middle between the United States and its selfish fight against Communism. How it led to the disappearances of students, teachers, people who were never found again. Was this what was happening to him? To Ruben? How they both had found themselves stuck in the middle of an unjust system designed to keep them down. Would he ever see his friend again?

Remembering his father, Bertan let his head rest on the floor. He took a few deep breaths as Ruben would've instructed had he been here. Maybe it was no wonder he'd ended up in some kind of "revolution" of his own. It wasn't one he'd have chosen—one involving animals and some seventeen-year-old girl who reminded him of his daughter.

And what about Bray? Kage? Did they succeed? Would he ever know?

Bertan heard commotion in the front seats. In the center of the glass partition separating him from the front was a square window of metal mesh through which he could hear them speak. Bertan carefully came up onto his knees. The van hit a bump and he fell over onto his side. He sat up again, this time turning to face the bench and pressing his head against the seat. Pushing into the bench with his forehead, he came to his knees a second time, let out an exhale, and stood. Nearly slipping as the van rolled along the road, he quickly turned and set himself down on the bench. Dizzy, he closed his eyes and waited for the spell to pass. He slowly opened his eyes and looked up at the two men in the front seats. Out the windshield he could see a faint image of the sky and land before him. The sun was setting over a range of mountains. All around he saw desert-like earth, cacti, dirt and sand.

It reminded him of Texas.

Was he being deported? Or detained? If they sent him back home, he could be reunited with his family. He recollected the time someone told him that being detained was the worst thing that could happen to an immigrant. How he could remain in a detention center for ages, lost in paperwork and never able to leave. Maybe that was what S-Corp wanted. What if S-Corp was in on it so much that they'd found out where his family was? What if they were detaining him *because* they wanted to keep him away from his family, the one thing he still loved?

Bertan closed his eyes. He took another deep breath. As he did, a tear escaped his eye, rolled down and landed on his chest. There, he could feel the necklace that Gabriella had made for him. He'd forgotten about it all this time, while lost in the throes of that strange fugue that, at least for now, had left him. A fugue that, as he sat here alone, he realized had become a friend to him, a companion. Something that had helped him remain in denial of what was happening.

As the van bumped along a dirt road somewhere out in the desert, Bertan thought himself a kind of animal. An animal being sent to his own kind of slaughter. For all the beefs he'd offed, for all the men he'd killed. . .

His mind slowed. It cleared. He made out some of the things the men in front were saying. Words like: "terrorist". . ."another attack". . ."everything's crazy."

Bertan turned and looked back out the window across from him. So Bray's plan must've worked, at least on her end. Something had happened, based on what those men were saying. But not the way they'd intended. The last thing they wanted was for this to be seen as a terrorist attack.

Outside, the sky lightened in faint oranges and yellows along the horizon. The sun was sinking. Wherever they were, they'd been driving nearly all day, if not longer. For all Bertan knew, he could've been out for days.

He thought about Ruben again. He figured he'd never see the man again. Poor man, helping others and getting nothing for it. A cringe of regret circled Bertan's heart, to think he'd done these kinds of things to others. To good, decent people. *His* people.

This would be his retribution.

And he deserved it.

It hadn't been enough to try to help in the

end.

Here he was.

Slowly, a series of fences came into view out the window. Bertan's eyes lifted. The fences surrounded more barren earth. He couldn't see or hear much of anything.

The van stopped. This was it. He clenched his jaw, prepared his mind. A stone-like mass grew in his chest. The back doors swung open. A moment later one of the men jumped in and grabbed Bertan by the upper arm.

"Let's go!" the man shouted.

The man pulled Bertan out by his arm, Bertan's wrists handcuffed behind him still. As he was turned toward the building, his eyes caught its sign:

SOUTH TEXAS ICE PROCESSING CENTER

Yes, he was being detained. He gulped as he was led along a row of fencing toward the building. His best hope was to be deported immediately. Chances were, based on what he expected to be an eventual criminal charge—if not many—being undocumented with no rights, and with what others had told him about detainment, he'd probably remain stuck here for the rest of his life.

So fucking be it.

After all he'd been through, no one could break Bertan Duarte. He was good enough at breaking himself. And even in losing himself and sabotaging the plan to help Ruben and Bray, at least he had tried to help someone. He was on the right side, for once. Instead of choosing S-Corp, he had chosen a revolution. He could walk into that detention center with some self-respect. He was his father's son, after all.

The fence turned down a path toward the building's front entrance where two guards stood on either side with military-grade rifles. He turned with the man and continued forward, watching the fence as it seemed to travel with him. Through the fence his eyes caught something rippling in the heat. A kind of heat wave that slowly formed into a body. His eyes widened. As the body came near, it formed into the ghost of a man. A man with skin like his, with white hair down to his shoulders, a white mustache hovering over a sly smile.

His father.

Bertan tried to stop. The man walking beside him yanked his arm.

"Come on, bastard," the man spat, pulling him along.

Bertan's feet tripped as he was forced to continue forward. His eyes remained set on his father, who had walked up to the fence and squeezed his fingers onto the barbed wire that poked up along the fence. But his father did not react. Because it was a ghost. Not real. Bertan yearned for the man, wished to reach out for him, to have his guidance and his help.

His father turned and walked a few feet behind him, slowly, as if walking on air.

They approached the entrance. They stopped. Bertan turned back to see his father stopping too, looking at him. The smile on his face faded. Their eyes met. The guards unlocked the doors. Bertan felt himself being pulled inside. Glancing back one last time, while his body was being tugged into the darkness of a hallway, he watched his father's ghost dissipate like dust into thin air. When he did, a surprising sense of calm came over Bertan.

He turned and faced the hallway as it slowly came into view, the doors shutting behind him. Closer and closer came the shouts of those who were locked away in this place.

He clenched his jaw in resolve.

Bertan knew he was not special. He was not like Ruben. Or Bray. He wasn't like his father. Despite that, he decided that being sent here was like being given a third chance: a chance to be better. A chance to become a man his father would've taken pride in.

A man who would choose to hold onto the one thing neither S-Corp nor Medina could ever take away: his right to rise up while they tried to keep him down.

Chapter Thirty-Two

Bray

It began as a sensation. Running. Bumpy. Stopping. A sense that she was being pulled upward, yet there was also an immense feeling of nothingness. Endless nothingness. And it felt *good*. It felt like peace at the end of all things.

If this was her journey into death, Bray was okay with it.

A memory came to her of a time her dad had taken her to Infinity Theater. She was nine. It was a cold, winter day in February. The day after her birthday, to be exact. The Colorado sun was close and vibrant.

For once, she was happy. She felt special. This was before the time her dad disappeared to DC for work, back when he used to spend time with her.

The 3D theater screen was so tall it was near neck-breaking for her, but she was enthralled. She remembered how the screen opened wide above her, how it pulled her in. How the 3D glasses made it seem as though she were stepping *inside* nature.

She felt that same experience now, where an image of an azure sky opened all around her, exposing trees and an open field of fresh grass where she sensed she was lying. It was an odd feeling, like she was both floating and lying still at the same time. Disorienting, but she liked the feeling. It was *fun*. She couldn't remember the last time she'd had fun.

Bray sat alone in the field and gazed at the sky. She could sit here for a lifetime. If heaven actually was real and this was it, she'd be satisfied to be here. Nowhere else to go. No one else to be.

What a relief.

Beside her, particles of light danced around in circles, gradually coalescing into form. Pink light. . .ghostly, transparent, slowly developed into the image of a pig.

"Alice!" Bray called out.

The apparition came to lie down beside her, placing its head on Bray's lap. Bray felt a warm energy against her thigh. She went to pet her friend and did not feel Alice's fur. It was a different sensation of warmth. Bray pulled her hand away, felt cool air, and when she neared Alice's head, felt the warmth again. Inside she felt playful, like a child.

"Alice. . .where are we? Did I die?" Bray asked. Her voice echoed through the vast sky.

"There is no death, my dear child," a voice replied as the apparition lifted its head and looked at her. Its mouth did not move. It was soothing, calm, feminine, yet it didn't sound the way Bray remembered Alice. "There is only transition into something else."

"Is that what's happening to me?"

"If you so wish."

"What do you mean?" Bray was confused.

The apparition sat up. Bray locked eyes with it. It was Alice, and yet it wasn't Alice.

"You are between dimensions. You are not dead. Your mind is holding on, which is how we are able to communicate this way."

Bray tried recalling what had happened before she passed out—assuming she'd passed out—but it was all a haze.

"What matters, dear one, is that you have a choice to make," the apparition said.

"What choice?"

"You can go back, or you can go on."

Bray looked over the apparition. Still experiencing a child-like confusion and curiosity, she spoke.

"You look like my friend Alice but you also

look. . .different."

"I am Alice. I am also you. I am what many refer to as God, Higher Power, Allah, Jehovah, Yaweh. I am Kage, Bertan, Elliott. I am all things, and I am no thing. I am the Universe in one image. . .an image we knew you would resonate with."

"So a god *does* exist?" Bray asked. She never was one to believe a god could exist when so many awful things happened to the most innocent of creatures, often done by people who very much believed in a god.

"God is only a word. It's like your friend Emily said: there is something better in everyone. . .an intelligence, a kind of interconnectedness that binds everything and everyone together. The simplest way to describe it is energy. We are all a part of it, ever since the universe came to be."

"I have a ton of questions," Bray admitted.

"And they can be answered. First you have to decide if you are going to come with me, or return to your friends. I can only give answers if you come with me."

"You can't answer my questions and then send me back? What if it could help others?"

"It doesn't work that way, my child. That's what faith is for. You have to learn to trust that, intrinsically, the answers already exist inside of you."

"The *answer* is pretty clear. I want to go with you. It feels a lot better than being back there. Not to mention, if I'm here then our plan didn't work, so what would be the point of going back?"

"Because the world is about to *need* you, now more than ever. If you could believe in your own power, you'd see the significance of going back."

"But I *did* see my power, and look where it got me," Bray said, feeling slighted.

"Your work isn't finished yet."

"Then send me back," Bray said, growing frustrated. "Sounds like that's where you want me to go."

Truth was, Bray feared going back. This place felt whole, complete, like there would never be any uncomfortable work to do ever again. She was tired and she was only seventeen. How was she supposed to live a long life in a harsh world like that and feel this content?

"It doesn't work like that, either," the apparition replied. Suddenly its form broke apart into millions of microscopic particles, changed colors from pink to white and black, and formed into a cow, into the cow Bray recognized as Rhea.

Rhea sat down on all fours and looked at Bray, her eyes full, her body free of injury.

Bray began to cry.

"You have to make the choice, Bray. I won't send you anywhere without your permission. You want to come with me, you can come with me. I only want you to consider what, and whom, you are leaving behind if you do."

Rhea quieted and kept her gaze on Bray, as if expecting Bray to sit and think.

And Bray did think. Her closest friend, Alice, was gone. She thought about Elliott, whom she certainly loved on some level, and appreciated for how he'd helped her again, but even that relationship wasn't what it used to be. She adored Ethan and got a lot from her time with Emily. If she'd met them sooner, she probably would have been much happier. Which led her to think about her dad. She always wanted more from him. It had taken him seventeen years to come around and finally do the right thing last month by helping her keep Alice and the sows safe from her mother and S-Corp after she'd rescued them.

Her mother. There would never be a relationship there again. And sitting in this open, beautiful, energetic space actually made her *feel* sad about that for once.

Beyond that, who else was back there? She observed Rhea's face, her eyes in particular. They had welled up and remained that way, as if

Rhea were in some perpetual space of emotion that never dissipated. The kind of emotion Bray only really experienced when connecting with animals. Animals were the only beings with whom she had shared deep vulnerability. Until she met Emily.

"Are there animals wherever you are going?" Bray asked, still contemplating her decision.

"Yes. They're not the ones that need help."

"Now I feel like you're being suggestive, like you want me to go back, but then you say it's my choice."

"Yes," Rhea replied, almost seeming to smile. "You nailed the whole purpose of humanity's design of God. I, as higher intelligence, am happy to give you insight, but what you fail to see is that you have that same insight already inside of you. I am only helping you see it. Would it be better if I came to you in the form of a mirror, or would that be too shocking?"

Bray raised her eyebrows in response. She suddenly remembered how she'd saved Alice, how she was capable of saving animals. A series of tears flooded her eyes. How was she supposed to really save them, though? She knew if her plan had worked she wouldn't be here.

Or had it?

Was it possible that maybe her efforts had caught on and people had felt the cows' experience, had heard her speech, and maybe things back home were changing as she sat here? As she sat here in this balance between her life and the chance to leave it all behind, her friends must've been awaiting her. *Worried* for her. And her dad. . .did he see? Did her mother see, not that it would've made any difference. Had enough people in the nation felt those slaughters that if Bray stepped out she might be stepping out—bowing out—prematurely?

Bray took a deep breath, closed her eyes. A soft breeze touched her shoulders and head. She felt hair falling around her and she reached up and touched it. Opening her eyes, she looked over at Rhea, wondered what it might be like to be with her and Alice and live like this forever.

But if she could live like this and animals back home could not, would it eventually eat away at her? Would it eventually turn into some kind of hell, to know her friends and billions of animals were suffering while she la-dee-dawed wherever here was? She realized it was probably unfair and she also realized it was all she ever wanted; peace in a natural space like this, even if it wasn't life anymore.

Chapter Thirty-Three

Cole

Cole had to find out where Dianna was. If he didn't keep her away from Bray, he might never see his daughter again. Especially after what had happened. If he could find Bray first, he could pull his resources and get her into hiding. Although what she had done, or the way she went about it, was wrong, he still needed to protect her.

He called Dianna. It went to voicemail.

"Dianna," he said. "Please call me. I'm sure you saw Bray. Can we please talk about this before you go doing anything. . .extreme?"

He hung up.

Sitting at his dining room table, he looked out the window at a bland, gray sky. He couldn't sit here and do nothing. He couldn't stand by and allow Dianna to take the lead, not like he used to. All those years he'd avoided confrontation with her by allowing her to make unilateral decisions about Bray's mental health.

So he texted her:

WHERE ARE YOU? WE NEED TO TALK.

After several minutes and no response, he grew angered. Dianna was as attached to her phone as she was her own arm, so she had to have seen his message, known that he'd called. He didn't know why he was surprised she hadn't responded.

He called her office. Her assistant answered.

"It's Cole Hoffman. Where's Dianna?" he asked.

"Hello, Mr. Hoffman. Seeing as you divorced her, I don't have to answer that anymore," the assistant replied quickly.

"It's an emergency. It's about our daughter."

He grimaced.

"If she wanted you to know where she was, she'd tell you. Why don't you call her directly? Now I've got more pressing issues to respond to."

The assistant hung up.

"Damn it!" Cole yelled, throwing his phone on the floor.

There was no one else he knew who would tell him where Dianna was. He suspected she was tracking down Bray. The longer he sat here and waited, the more at risk his daughter was.

Cole thought. Maybe if there was a way to contact Elliott, he could at least get a warning to them. Give them a head start so maybe they could escape before Dianna found them. But how?

His laptop lay closed beneath a stack of court documents detailing his divorce. He slid it out from beneath the papers and opened it. He did an internet search for animal rights activists, found close to nothing. He searched Bray's name, and a news story popped up about recent events. He ignored it. If he read today's news he'd get sucked in, lose time.

His memory caught him. The video of Bray. During the video, a website address had popped up on the screen. A website they wanted people to use to see the evidence against S-Corp.

Cole clicked on the video through a news link and watched it. Watched his daughter sitting outside, somewhere in the west, not Wyoming, but maybe somewhere not too far away. Talking about S-Corp with an air of disappointment in her voice that he hadn't noticed before.

The website address popped up.

He rushed to find paper and wrote it down.

Closing the video, he typed the website into the Quest address bar. A second later, a white screen appeared. There on the home page was a blog titled, *The Truth About S-Corp.*

His heart leapt. Finally, this had to be it.

No names were mentioned, but it detailed the evidence of the 2027 terrorist attack. The S-Corp

documents and emails showing the mistake they'd
made with Oxygen-11. Email correspondence with
the government where the government agreed to
keep it confidential. A cover-up.

It really was astonishing.

No wonder Bray was disappointed.

Cole took a few moments to read the blog about
the animal rights activists who had disappeared.
It listed actual names of people. . .when they'd
last been seen by family or friends. At some
point he'd need to have this fact-checked.

He searched the page for a contact form.
Scrolling all the way down the page, his heart
begging with hope as he got closer to the bottom,
he finally found, in the lower right corner, the
magic word: CONTACT.

He clicked on it. A square box popped up with
a space for his name and email address. His eyes
teared up.

"God, I hope they check this thing," he
whispered to himself.

Cole typed a clear message:

WHOEVER IS READING THIS:
YOU NEED TO GET OUT. FIND A PLACE TO HIDE.
DIANNA HOFFMAN WILL FIND YOU. MAYBE NOT TODAY.
MAYBE NOT TOMORROW. BUT DO NOT UNDERESTIMATE
HER RESOURCES.
PLEASE, KEEP MY DAUGHTER SAFE.
COLE HOFFMAN.

Cole hit *Send*.

He sat back and stared at the computer screen.
He couldn't believe it had come to this: that the
only way he could reach his daughter was by
sending a message to some website. It revealed
more clearly how he hadn't listened to her,
hadn't been a good enough father to show her he
could be trusted with her life and her plans.

He would have to keep working to change this.

Chapter Thirty-Four

Kage

Four hours passed. Kage had never felt so agitated in his entire life. He'd tried remaining in the front room as Bray lay in the bed upstairs, Virgil and Dennis doing their best to care for her while she remained unconscious. Emily and Trevor were up there as well.

Kage and Ethan sat waiting. Waiting for Bray to wake up. Any moment. . .any moment.

Another hour passed.

And another.

Kage fidgeted. He paced the floor.

"Try and remain calm, Kage," Ethan asked. He'd been sitting in the front room when they ran into the house, Kage carrying Bray in his arms. Now he was standing by the dining room table, watching Kage pace around as if there was no one else in his presence.

And it certainly felt that way. When things got this uncertain, Kage's tunnel vision narrowed into a deep, never-ending well of darkness where he could not see. There was nothing past this.

If Bray did not survive, he would never forgive himself.

Elliott was sitting at the dining room table. He had his laptop open. Lana sat beside him as he checked her phone to ensure it was encrypted. Maybe they could reach out to Ruben, find out where he and Bertan were.

Yeah. Kage thought. *Where the hell were you, Bertan?*

Kage shook off the uneasiness and went to stand behind Elliott and Lana. Ethan turned and looked down at them. He was not smiling.

Elliott held Lana's phone in his hand, scrolling through her call and text history.

"Wait a minute," he said.

"What?" Lana replied, glancing over at her phone.

"You were on a call with Ruben last week?"

"Of course. To make sure everything was in place, remember? Why?"

Elliott's body went stiff. Kage could not see his face, but by the tension in his shoulders Kage could tell he was concerned about something.

"Uh oh," he said, rubbing his forehead with his fingers.

"What?" Lana asked.

"Your phone was not as encrypted as you thought when you made that call."

"What?" Lana said, grabbing the phone from his hand and looking at the screen. "But we had all of our phones encrypted."

"I'm sure you did. But there are certain. . .*layers* to encryption. As far as tracking capabilities, whoever encrypted it did a decent job. But they missed some things."

"Like what?"

Kage felt the concern bear down on his own shoulders. Things were going from bad to worse.

"This is going to sound like the simplest thing on earth, which is why people so often miss it. Your bluetooth wasn't disabled. And. . .the longer you leave your battery in your phone after you've used it, the more likely it can be traced."

"So. . .you think someone tapped my phone?"

"Not your phone," Elliott replied, looking over at her. "His. The fact that you haven't heard from him yet tells me he and Bertan were both compromised, or at least Ruben was."

They both silently stared at one another.

Kage shook his head.

"Shit," he said aloud, thinking of Bertan and their plan to try to save Bray. No wonder it hadn't worked. And this entire time Kage had been more concerned about Bertan saving Bray than whether the man himself was actually okay.

"I can check my email, see if he tried to get in touch that way."

"Is it encrypted though?" Elliott asked.

"Yes," she replied, looking at his laptop. "My team encrypted everything. . ." her voice trailed off.

Kage felt for Lana, how she'd lost her whole team. How he was at fault for that.

Once again it dawned on him that he may have been the one who caused Bertan to get caught. Possibly Ruben, as well.

"Here," Elliott said, turning the laptop toward Lana.

Lana reached over and typed in some website. A white screen popped up. She scrolled down where, in the lower left corner, was a silhouette of a black chicken. She clicked on it. A login box popped up. She entered some information. Seconds later, an email account revealed itself, with an entire list of emails she'd previously read.

But there looked to be nothing new. No "Ruben" or anything highlighted to indicate a new email.

"Dang," she spoke under her breath. "Nothing."

"I have another idea," Elliott said, a faint twinge of hope sparking his voice.

Lana closed her email and pushed the laptop back over to Elliott.

"Kage," Elliott said, turning and glancing up at Kage.

Kage's eyes lit up. He was surprised to hear his name.

"Let's check that email we created for the S-Corp evidence website. Maybe he tried it."

"Okay," Kage said, feeling a smidgen of hope. He went over and sat in the chair across from Elliott and Lana. Ethan also sat down with them.

"Elliott," Ethan finally spoke. "I sure hope you're not implying that there's a chance they could have traced Lana's phone here."

Elliott shot a glance over to Kage before looking at Ethan.

"I hope not, either."

The room went quiet. It was as though an invisible weight had fallen in the room, crushing the space between them. The upstairs remained relatively quiet.

Elliott slid the laptop over to Kage. Kage took a deep breath. He was about to open the email account he'd created for his blog. He had no idea whether he'd see any emails at all.

When the email account opened, Kage's eyes lit up. His mouth dropped open a bit. There on the screen was an entire list of unread emails. He scrolled through them, and the list kept going.

There had to be hundreds.

"I don't believe it," Kage said.

"What is it?" Lana asked, looking over at Kage.

"Emails. . ." Kage said, still shocked. "Tons of them. All from today."

"Seriously?" Elliott asked.

Kage looked up at him and nodded.

"We'll have to look at those later. For now, can you check and see if Ruben emailed you?"

Kage's eyes scanned the subject headings. The hate mail he'd expected. But it was the overwhelming number of offers to help and support that caused his knees to shake. If only Bray could see this. . .

"This is. . .unbelievable," Kage said.

"Let me see," Ethan spoke, standing up and leaning over beside Kage.

They both sat and stared at the screen. Kage slowly scrolled down, his mind searching for anything with Ruben's name while also noticing the unexpected responses from everyday citizens.

"I think you started a revolution," Ethan said, the smile returning to his face.

They both sat and stared at the screen. Elliott got back to the matter at hand.

"See anything that might've come from Ruben?"

Kage's eyes scanned the screen for a few more moments.

"No," he replied. "Nothing."

Kage's eyes caught one email whose subject heading blared out at him in all capital letters: PROTECT BRAY! HIDE NOW! S-CORP COMING FOR YOU!

He saw that the email had come from Cole Hoffman.

"Bray's dad!" Kage said, opening the email.

Elliott and Lana got up from their seats and came over, standing behind Kage.

WHOEVER IS READING THIS:
YOU NEED TO GET OUT. FIND A PLACE TO HIDE.
DIANNA HOFFMAN WILL FIND YOU. MAYBE NOT TODAY.
MAYBE NOT TOMORROW. BUT DO NOT UNDERESTIMATE
HER RESOURCES.
PLEASE, KEEP MY DAUGHTER SAFE.
COLE HOFFMAN.

"Holy shit," Lana said. "You think he's telling the truth?"

Kage remembered what Bray's dad had done for her when she rescued Alice from getting slaughtered, how he sent those men to protect the sows Bray had saved.

"Yes. We gotta do something. We can't risk getting caught."

"Right. Better to be safe than sorry," Ethan replied.

"Ethan, go hide the cars away from the house," Kage said. "The keys to my bike and the Jeep are down in the kitchen, hanging by the back door."

"I'll help," Elliott replied, following Ethan into the kitchen.

Kage bolted upstairs. The door to Bray's room was slightly ajar. Kage gently knocked and entered.

Bray was lying unconscious in his bed. The window curtains were open. A blank sunlight was glaring in, but it brought with it no sense of warmth. The only warmth he noticed came from the room itself, where the scent of sage hung in the air.

Virgil and Emily were standing on either side

of the bed. Trevor sat alone in the corner of the room, watching. Dennis was next to the bed placing a wet towel over Bray's forehead.

"Everyone," Kage said. "We got a message from Bray's dad."

"What?" Trevor said, standing up from the chair.

"He seems to believe S-Corp is coming for us. . .that we should hide."

Trevor exchanged glances with Virgil and Emily.

"We knew this day would come eventually," Emily said, shrugging. She looked down at Bray.

Moments later, Kage had Bray in his arms, quickly yet carefully carrying her downstairs. He followed behind Emily, Virgil and Trevor, who shut and locked the front door and led them through the kitchen. The place was empty. Ethan and Elliott must've still been outside, moving the vehicles.

Kage followed everyone outside and into the garden. Behind him, Virgil closed the back door. Up ahead the steel cellar door hung open. Ethan's head was poking out, waving to Kage.

Kage ran for the cellar, Bray's body held close to his chest, as Trevor and Virgil disappeared down into the cellar. Emily climbed down inside next, leaving only Dennis behind him.

As Kage approached the cellar, he came down onto his knees. Trevor stepped up the ladder and reached out for Bray. Kage passed Bray's body down to Trevor, watched as her head dropped, wishing she'd wake up. This was no time to be unconscious.

Kage climbed down into the shelter and, shaking, went to sit beside Elliott. Ethan stood beside him. Trevor lay Bray down on the floor. Everyone else stood around her. Dennis came down the ladder and closed the door shut, sliding a metal rod across and into a steel casing to lock them all in.

Then came the worst waiting of Kage's life:

waiting for his new friend to wake—if she ever did, waiting for Cole to be proven right or wrong, awaiting a fate over which he had little control.

Chapter Thirty-Five

Dianna

Night came gradually, the sun lowering along the horizon without much notice. Two silver SUVs passed through the abandoned town of Meeteetse. Inside one of the cars, Dianna stared out the window at empty houses as they passed. Roads mostly emptied of vehicles. Small businesses with *CLOSED* signs posted in their windows. Others boarded up as if for an apocalypse.

A stark reminder for Dianna of how things would continue to go in the west if they didn't get into Wyoming and tap the fresh water sources here. Even if citizens were mostly secure in cities post Migration, they would always need water.

And there was never enough.

First, though, the issue at hand: S-Corp breathing down her neck after her daughter and whomever she was working with or for had sent the country into a panic.

The SUVs made a sudden turn onto a bumpy, dirt path. It was so dark the path was only visible within range of the SUVs' headlights. Dan had supplied both SUVs. . .one to detain the activists who had assisted Bray, or as Dianna liked to believe, the other way around. And the second truck was for Bray.

Dianna had somewhere else in mind for Bray.

They shifted and rolled through a dried-up field of corn.

"Corn?" the driver spoke. "How on earth? Is this *real* corn?"

Dianna did not reply. Of course it was real corn, but she wasn't going to admit it and implicate herself. At this point, most of the country was now exposed to the truth that the soil was safe enough to use. That yes, indeed, S-Corp had made a mistake.

When the mistake had occurred, Dianna was a director with S-Corp. She didn't know about the Oxygen-11 blunder at first. It wasn't until she became Regional President that Carl made her aware. He told her everything, kept no secrets from her.

She wished she hadn't known. At least she might've been able to prove that to her daughter. Now, the fact that she'd perpetuated the cover-up for years was going to pit Bray against her, even more than before.

How she would ever salvage a relationship with her daughter, she did not know.

The SUV pulled out of the corn stalks into a yard. There standing in the night like a stunning revelation was a two-story white farm house. Dianna's heart nearly stopped at the sight of it.

"Wow," the driver said, stopping the SUV.

The two of them stared at it for a moment.

"Let's stop wasting time," Dianna said, opening the car's back door.

She stepped out into the fresh grass. Her heels nearly stumbled on the uneven earth. The scent of fresh grass and soil enlivened her senses. She hadn't smelled this much "earth" since she was in her twenties.

Instantly she had a flashback to a time she and Cole had gone camping. She wasn't yet pregnant with Bray, but they were trying. The camping trip was set up to give them space and time to relax, away from work, so that maybe Cole could get it up. She hated thinking of it that way, but she was always secretly resentful of his erectile disfunction. It was why they'd only been able to have one child.

If it had been up to her, she'd have had three.

"What's the plan?" Dan asked, breaking into her memory and coming to stand beside her.

Two additional men in bulletproof vests, both

holding rifles, gathered behind them. "Place looks deserted, aside from the garden."

"It's definitely not deserted," Dianna replied, looking around. "They're here somewhere. Search the garden, then let's get inside."

"Without a search warrant we could get in trouble for this," one of the men replied.

Dianna and Dan both turned and looked at him. Even in the dark Dianna could see the youth in his face. The quarter moon brightened the smoothness of his skin. The moonlight caused Dianna to look up. She was temporarily awe-struck by the incredible audacity of the stars, how they seemed to climb on top of one another and clamber in the night sky for space, there were so many. Overcrowded yet so still and blinking they worked together to form this display of light, the likes of which Dianna had never seen, not even on her camping trips with Cole.

"You're about to learn the difference between S-Corp and Marshals," Dan said, glaring at the young security officer. "We don't need a warrant. These are *ecoterrorists* we're dealing with. They've already broken the law a hundred times over. The Marshals will thank us for this, trust me."

The officer shrugged. He nodded at the second officer beside him. The two of them scattered across the property, disappearing into the dark, guns raised, lights pointing, searching.

"You really think they're here?" Dan asked as he remained beside Dianna.

"Where else would they be?" Dianna said, but mostly to herself.

"Well, with everything that's happened, if they were smart enough to pull off that attack, then they're smart enough to go into hiding."

Dianna thought about Elliott and Bray. They were only kids. They knew nothing of the world, how it worked.

"They're not that smart."

The two officers jogged back to Dianna.

"No sign of anything," one of them said.

"Let's get inside," Dianna replied, glancing up at the front porch.

The officers disappeared into the trunk of the second SUV and came back with a pry bar.

"And you're sure they're not armed?" Dan asked her, whispering.

Dianna remembered back to that Marshal who was killed in Douglas after Bray had first escaped from the hospital. The Marshal was found mauled to death by a pair of dogs. She still believed Elliott had something to do with that.

"I think Elliott's the one we need to look out for. Who knows about the rest or how many are even here."

Dianna leaned against the side of the SUV as Dan and the two officers swiftly moved up the porch steps and forced open the front door. Once they disappeared inside, she continued observing the garden from afar.

When she was a child, her mother had a garden. It was narrow, as the only yard they had ran along the side of their house in a suburb of Denver. Her mother grew zucchini, carrots, watermelon. Dianna tried to remember what else, but couldn't. It felt like so long ago, because of how drastically the climate and their lifestyles had changed.

Dan came out onto the porch and waved at her. She walked over to the steps, careful not to slip in the grass. She stepped up onto the porch, peered inside the house as she entered.

The front room was uncomplicated. Some furniture. Curtains. Paintings of farm animals on the walls.

Not surprising.

In the dining room, a long, wood dining table graced the space with an almost overwhelming presence. Two windows looked in on it, where the moonlight touched the deep brown wood and the silence made her hairs stand on end.

But it was what she saw sitting on the table

that most intrigued and excited her.

Dianna stepped around the table and looked at the silver laptop that sat open.

"We checked the device for explosives," one of the officers said. "It's clean."

"Take it," Dianna said. "Evidence."

One of the officers approached with his gloved hands and lifted the laptop, closing it up and holding it under his arm.

Dianna continued into the kitchen. Pots sat on the stove, half full of some kind of stew. A bamboo cutting board sat on the counter, a head of cabbage cut in two and waiting there alone. It all looked so "normal," so akin to the days before the 2030 Migration. Days when life was a lot simpler, and that simpleness could be felt in the walls of this place. It gave Dianna mixed feelings. She found herself envying aspects of this life they had here. The fresh food. The large house. The freshness of Wyoming.

"Clearly they left out in a hurry," she said, eying the cabbage. "And not long ago. Did you search upstairs?"

The two officers shook their heads. Dianna glanced over at Dan.

"Take them back upstairs. See what evidence you can find."

"What about you?" he asked in reply.

"I'm going back outside."

Dianna exited the house. She returned to the front yard, facing the garden. Up on the second floor of the house, flashlights danced through open windows. Before her, the grass led back around the house to the garden and a shed. She couldn't believe the amount of food they grew here. It was impressive.

She took a deep breath and spoke as loudly as she could.

"Bray Hoffman, I know you're here. Come out, now!" she yelled. "I want Bray Hoffman and Elliott Bansfield. Anyone else will be spared. You have five minutes."

Dianna pulled out her phone and set a timer for five minutes, stood, and waited. She'd get what she wanted, soon enough. As each minute passed, she spoke again, asking only for Bray and Elliott. She would stand here and wait them out, even if it took days.

She wasn't leaving here without them.

Chapter Thirty-Six

Bray

"Bray Hoffman. . ."

The voice echoed through the sky, coming from somewhere beyond. Bray recognized the voice immediately. It was her mother. She was being summoned.

She had no choice.

She had to go back.

Rhea was right. Her work wasn't done. As much as it saddened her to return to such a complicated and heartbreaking world, she had to help her friends.

"Elliott Bansfield," the voice echoed through the landscape before her.

"No," Bray whispered back in defiance.

All at once, the sky and fields around her blew away as if dust particles blown off a table. Rhea had already gone. For a while there was darkness, and Bray felt herself traveling back, back, back, down, falling into her body.

Her eyes shot open. It was dark. Save one candlelight dancing inside a. . .cellar? The surface beneath her felt cold, hard. She was lying on a floor. Shelves of food and supplies came into view around her. It was the cellar beneath the garden in Meeteetse.

She was back.

As she sat up, an immense pain struck her temple. She groaned. Elliott, Kage and Trevor turned and looked down at her. Everyone had been standing around the shelving units. She sensed their tension immediately.

"Bray!" Elliott said. He knelt down and pulled her into his arms. "You're alive!"

Her mom called out again.

"I only want Bray Hoffman and Elliott

Bansfield. You have four more minutes."

Bray gently brought herself to stand as Elliott helped her up by her arm. Ethan moved up the ladder and unlocked the cellar door.

"Ethan, no!" Trevor whispered.

But Ethan moved so quickly he must not have heard. He slid out into the night, shut the door, and was gone.

"Two more minutes," Dianna's voice screamed. It sent tingles of warning down Bray's spine. If they remained in this cellar much longer, Dianna would eventually find them. If there was one thing Bray knew about her mother, it was her incredible sense of determination.

Something they both had in common.

That was when Bray realized the reason she'd returned.

She couldn't save Rhea or any of those cows, but she *could* save her friends.

In bare feet, she pulled away from Elliott. She ran for the ladder. Kage grabbed her.

"Stop! What are you—"

The sound of a pop, followed by a brief echo, permeated the air above the cellar. Everyone froze. Kage's arms slightly released Bray in response. They all seemed to understand what the sound was.

Ethan!

Bray took the chance to run up the ladder. The door was already unlocked, so she pushed it slightly ajar and glared out. She could not see her mother, which meant most likely her mother could not see her. If she was going to expose herself she'd only do it if it meant the rest of her friends could remain hidden.

Bray turned, quietly closed the cellar door, and ran around the side of the house. As she did, two silver SUVs in front came into view. Before them, her mother stood with three men. Two of the men she recognized as S-Corp security officers, same guns and gear as the ones who tried to stop her when she had gone after the transport truck to save Alice.

But this time, she was not afraid. She knew where she was headed if they killed her, and she was more than okay with it.

"Don't shoot!" Dianna screamed.

The men dropped their weapons.

There sprawled out on the grass was a body. Bray's heart sank as she neared it. She nearly fell backward at the sight of Ethan lying there like a stone. She dropped to her knees. She felt like crying. She crawled over to his body, looked into his face. His eyes were open. Blood rolled down from his lip. Her eyes met the gunshot wound in the center of his chest.

"Ethan?" she whispered.

No response. She knew he was dead. She sat there and stared at him. Her mother stood only feet away. The two security guards came toward Bray. She did not run. She was done running. This time she'd let them take her, distract them from the others.

Bray bent forward and whispered into Ethan's ear. "Maybe I'll be with you someday soon, my friend."

The two men stepped behind Bray. They bent down and grabbed her by each arm, lifting her to stand. Her thoughts remained on Ethan as an emotion of relief overcame her. At least she knew where he was headed, and it would be beautiful. She felt slightly envious, but at least she did not feel sad. This was a cruel, cruel world indeed. She'd come back to try to help it, but if that couldn't happen, at least she had somewhere better she could go.

The men walked her over to one of the SUVs, stopping before Dianna.

"I hope you know this was an accident. We had no intent to hurt—certainly not kill—anyone," Dianna said to Bray.

Bray only looked at her, barely recognized the woman beneath the silky moonlight. She'd killed plenty in her work for S-Corp.

"I need to know where Elliott is," Dianna said.

"Elliott's been gone for months," Bray replied, thinking about the time they'd separated back in Casper. "I haven't seen him since I left Casper, way before you tried to take me away."

Bray's voice remained composed, monotone. Calm. Stoic. Dianna's eyes searched her face.

"Put her in the back," Dianna said, looking over at the two men.

Bray was led to the back of the first SUV and pushed inside, door closed. She sat in the back seat and looked up at the driver. The windows were rolled up, but she could still hear her mother's voice.

"Keep some drones on the place," Dianna said. "I still think there are others here."

"Sure thing," one of the men replied.

The two guards disappeared. Bray heard two sets of car doors slam shut. Dianna got inside beside her and shut the door. The distance between them was far greater than a middle seat in the back of an SUV.

"We're going to find whoever helped you," Dianna said, her head kept forward.

"That was it," Bray replied. "Ethan. . .he did everything. I did the video and. . ." Bray paused. Her relationship with her mother had been strained for ages. "You're never going to believe anything I say. You never have. If I told you I was the one who connected with those cows, I was the one who linked them because I have a gift, you'll just roll your eyes."

Dianna turned and looked at her.

"Do the names Ruben Sanchez or Bertan Duarte ring a bell?" Dianna asked.

Bray shot a glance at Dianna. She tried her best not to show any sign of recognition on her face, but hearing their names caused her to shiver.

"Driver," Dianna called up to the man in the front seat. "You know where we're going?"

"Yes, ma'am," the man replied, starting the engine.

The SUV rolled through the field of corn. The house disappeared behind them. Bray could only hope that Kage and the others would not be found. Any chance that remained of stopping S-Corp was left to them. And that was when she grew sad about Ethan. He was really gone. The world really needed him, too.

Chapter Thirty-Seven

Kage

After Kage heard the gun go off and watched Bray disappear out into the night, it must've taken all of Trevor's strength to stop him from running after them.

"No, no, no!" Kage yelled, fighting against Trevor as Trevor had his arms wrapped tightly around Kage's torso.

"Shh, Kage!" Trevor whispered, bringing Kage down to his knees.

Virgil came over and joined them, helping Trevor to contain Kage.

"You know you can't go out there," Trevor said in a low voice.

Again, Trevor was right.

Kage settled down, his knees burrowing into the ground as his bottom rested on his boots. Virgil let go of his grasp, sitting down between Kage and the ladder. Trevor pulled back, rubbing Kage's shoulder.

"We have to wait them out. We can't help Bray right now," Trevor said calmly.

"But Ethan. . .that gunshot." Kage looked up at the cellar door.

"I know," Trevor replied, saying nothing else.

Kage remained in his place. He didn't feel like moving. He sat there and waited, staring at the cellar door as if at any moment Bray and Ethan might return.

When Trevor had first brought him here to Meeteetse, he remembered how it felt waiting for his parents to arrive. At first he'd sat in the front room and waited by the door. As days passed, he tried to go on creating a life here without them, but any time he came downstairs, he'd stop and watch the door, fantasize about them entering. But they never did.

On top of losing his parents, now he had lost Ethan and probably Bray. An emptiness grew in Kage's chest. There were no tears where there should have been. He was tired of crying.

#

They remained in the cellar another day, silent. Most everyone slept against the shelves or quietly sat in what Kage felt was a deep pit of uncertainty.

Elliott finally spoke up.

"What are we going to do? We can't stay here forever." He had picked up a glass jar of pickled vegetables and was squeezing it in his hand. If he squeezed any more, he'd run the risk of breaking the thing open. Clearly he was upset. His voice broke when he spoke.

"I know," Trevor replied. "I for one am still in shock, trying to piece together what just happened."

"We lost Ethan and Bray, and we've done nothing about it, that's what happened," Elliott replied, his voice more strained.

Kage was sitting beside Lana, watching the conversation go back and forth.

"I'm not sure there's anything we can do," Dennis chimed in. "At least not until we can get out of the line of danger."

"Chances are, even if they left, there'll be drones monitoring the place. We aren't safe here anymore," Virgil said, looking down at his feet. He was sitting up against the wall beside the ladder. He was frowning. There appeared to be more wrinkles on his face that Kage had never before noticed. Maybe it was the candlelight.

Kage's tired and wired eyes drifted up along the shelves across from him. Rows of dusty, canned vegetables sat with little hope of ever being consumed, as if they knew their purpose here in Meeteetse had come to an end.

Elliott walked to the back of the cellar, turned and buried his head in his hands. Down near his feet was the locked box Ethan had used when he encouraged Kage to hit the road last month in search of his parents. Kage had been in Meeteetse for twelve years after they'd disappeared and no one, not even Trevor, had made an attempt to go back to Salt Lake and find them. Kage hadn't been able to sit by any longer without finding out what had happened to them, so when Ethan told him to leave, he did.

Before the night he'd chosen to leave, everything here had been simple. It was an easy life. And to think Kage had hated it at one point when all he wanted was to have things go back to the way they had been. He was no closer to finding his parents, his new friend was gone, and the one man he'd come to know as a parent might be dead.

The home that once was could no longer be home again. Not without Ethan. Not without Bray.

It was safe to assume, with more than minutes having passed since Bray disappeared up into the world, that someone had her.

Cole must've been right.

Dianna had her. Somehow, they found their way here.

Which meant if he and the others tried to leave, they risked being followed.

Kage remembered back to the trailer in Idaho. They'd spent a couple days there and were never found. How did that happen?

"Wait," he spoke, coming to stand. "Elliott, didn't you set up some device that could keep drones away from that trailer?"

Elliott lifted his head and looked at Kage. His face was wet.

"You mean the RF repeater?" he asked softly.

"Yes," Kage replied, his heart lifting. "Did you bring it with you?"

"No…but there's one duct-taped to the

underside of my car, and I keep a couple extras in the trunk."

"Then hypothetically we could leave without being followed?"

"Yeah. . .I completely forgot." Elliott's eyes lit up.

"They could be out there now, waiting us out." Trevor chimed in.

"Yes, but we can leave," Kage said. He stepped back so that he was facing everyone. They all looked to him. "Dennis is right, we can't stay here anymore. The longer we do, the greater our risk of getting caught. Maybe our time here is done. We have to move on."

"And where do you suggest we go? They'll be looking for us," Trevor said.

"Not if we head north," Elliott replied. He came to stand beside Kage.

"What's up north?" Dennis asked.

"Red Lodge," Kage answered, looking at Elliott and smiling.

"We can hide there," Elliott agreed.

"And there's space for all of us?" Emily asked.

"Red Lodge is a mecca for outsiders. You'll fit right in."

Lana stood up and crossed her arms. She looked over at Kage. Their eyes met. Lana gave Kage a faint smile.

"We grab everything we can from in here—all we can fit into the Jeep and Elliott's car. We'll take the cars, head out at night," Kage said, feeling empowered.

"Trevor, thoughts?" Dennis turned to Trevor, who was standing beside the ladder. Kage was slightly annoyed that Dennis still seemed to need Trevor's approval, but Kage let it go.

"We don't have any choice. At this point, anything we do is going to be a risk. Might as well try to mitigate it," Trevor replied. He looked over at Kage. In their exchange Kage got the feeling that he was being given the lead.

Trevor turned and stepped slowly up the ladder. He cracked open the cellar door. Light seeped into the cellar. He closed it back.

"Looks like we have to wait a bit longer," Trevor said.

And so they waited.

#

Often times at night the Wyoming stars gazed down upon the land with a kind of dancing revelry that made one feel less alone. The moon—tonight showing only half its self to the world—cast a silver-white blanket down along the garden as Kage and the others slowly exited the cellar. Kage felt the connection of the stars, of how he and Trevor and their remaining crew had come to a decision on what needed to be done.

That all changed as he approached the body that lay a few yards from the front porch. He didn't notice Elliott disappear off to his car for the RF repeater. He didn't hear Emily's voice as the wind was pulled from her in a gasp. He didn't notice Trevor stop cold in his tracks behind him.

It registered in Kage's mind that Dianna Hoffman and whoever she'd brought with her had since departed, leaving death in her wake.

Kage's vision tunneled in on the body of Ethan Calter, the leader of the Animal Rights Movement, his family, his friend, his mentor. Kage approached the body already knowing Ethan was long gone.

His eyes caught the color of black blood in the night where it had pooled beneath Ethan's torso, soaking the grass. There was no rise or fall in Ethan's chest. The stillness is what always got Kage about seeing death. He'd seen plenty in wild animals over the years.

Kage didn't want to get any closer, but he had

to do right by his one true friend in life.

"Oh no," he whispered, coming down to his knees.

Kage pulled Ethan into his arms and cried. His body shook as the grief poured out, his tears landing on Ethan's head as it lay against Kage's chest. The blood covered Kage's hands and he did not pull away.

This was what S-Corp did to everyone, eventually. He needed to experience this reality, let it sink in, so he would never forget. So that this time, he wouldn't run away.

They killed his friend, took Bray, took so many others. As he rocked back and forth, holding Ethan tightly, he removed himself from the guilt of the past. He pulled away, laying Ethan back down in the grass. He took one deep, sobering breath.

This was S-Corp's doing, all right. . .and Kage would have to do something in response. Ethan deserved nothing less.

"I'm so sorry, Kage," Lana's voice carried down to him from where she stood near. Kage did not respond.

"Let's bury him down in the cellar," Trevor said, stepping up beside Kage. "He would've liked that, I think."

Trevor, Emily, Dennis and Virgil carried Ethan's body back over to the cellar. They laid him down outside the door. Kage swallowed a twinge of guilt, thinking how maybe none of this would have happened had he listened to Trevor and not gone about this plan. He felt drawn back to the cellar, not ready to see Ethan disappear. It felt so wrong not to have him here right now.

"Let's give him a proper goodbye," Emily said between tears.

Kage's eyes welled up again. He felt Lana's presence as she came and stood beside him. Elliott did the same.

Emily picked out a bunch of black-eyed Susans from the side garden, flowers Ethan had planted to attract the dying bee population. Rarely would they see any bees, but Ethan was one to never give up.

Emily placed the flowers in Ethan's lifeless hands and crossed one over the other to hide the gunshot wound in his chest.

Words were said. None of them did Ethan any justice. No words ever could. How many people were left in the world who would dedicate their entire lives to ensuring the freedom of others at the expense of their own? Who left on this planet had Ethan's wisdom, his deep, deep compassion for every thing and every situation?

Kage did not know.

After some time, everyone grew silent. Emily finished with a song she always sang whenever someone in the house was feeling low, her voice deep and shaken, haunting and equally healing:

Among the marsh. . .blazing star,
You find out who you are.
The wind whistles itself
Into your soul.
Guiding your way,
Guiding your way,
Guiding your way,
back home.

When you feel you are
alone,
Remember there is a star
Out there waiting on you
To come be part of the few
Who make this world one,
Who make this world. . .
One.

Ethan's body was laid down beside the cellar while everyone grabbed canned goods and bags of rice. They packed Elliott's car and Trevor's Jeep with the delicate food that they'd spent years planting, growing, nurturing.

Kage checked his bike to make sure it was fit for the two-hour ride up to Red Lodge. He heard someone come up behind him. He turned.

"RF repeater is attached to the Jeep. Here's one for the bike," said Elliott, handing him the square box that almost looked like a walkie-talkie. "We can use them to block signals while on the road."

"Genius," Kage replied, patting Elliott on the shoulder. He slid the repeater into the bike's compartment as Elliott walked back to his car.

Kage thought about Ethan again, how they had embraced before he left for Salt Lake to search for his parents. How Ethan was one of the few people who had understood him.

The sound of the Jeep's trunk slamming shut jolted Kage back to the present. Suddenly he realized most everyone was standing around him, save Trevor and Virgil, who were carefully carrying Ethan's body down into the cellar.

Kage stood and waited for them. Elliott got into the driver's seat of his car. Lana got in beside him.

Emily stepped up to Kage.

"How are you feeling?" she asked him.

"I don't know," he replied, trying to grin.

Emily nodded. She reached over and squeezed his shoulder.

"He would be very proud of you right now," she said.

He teared up. Behind her, Trevor closed the cellar door, turned and walked toward them, Virgil right behind. The sight of the cellar being closed on Ethan only intensified Kage's tears.

Emily pulled him into her arms and hugged him. He accepted the embrace. It felt good to allow someone to be there for him, for once.

As Trevor and Virgil came near, he pulled away. It was, after all, time to go.

Emily disappeared into the back of the Jeep where Dennis had been waiting. Trevor got into the driver's seat, shut the door. Virgil turned to Kage and looked at him.

"You ready?" he asked.

"I'd better be," Kage replied, shrugging.

Virgil grinned and crawled into the Jeep's passenger seat.

Kage walked over to his bike. As the other engines started, he felt the bike come to life beneath him. A sadness overcame him again. He turned and glanced back at the house, the garden. He had spent the past twelve years of his life in this place; how he wished now he didn't have to leave. How he wished Ethan were still here, sitting with him back in the garden. How simple it had been to plant seeds, watch them grow.

Elliott's car pulled off into the corn crops, followed by the Jeep. Kage would have to follow. He would have to take his feet off the ground, and he would have to move forward. He would miss this place, his home that had kept him safe and alive all these years. And Ethan had every bit to do with where Kage stood in this very moment, the fact that he was standing here at all.

He turned and faced the corn stalks. The other vehicles were gone. He pressed down on the gas, and he sped off and away, following behind the others toward some unknown future where, looming ever-closer, was the reality that Bray was missing like all the others.

And Kage, for one, would not stand for that.

Chapter Thirty-Eight

Bray

They arrived in Denver the next morning.

Bray did not speak to her mother the entire way.

She was handcuffed and then transferred into a helicopter, which looked exactly the same as the helicopter her mother had attempted to force her into back when she rescued Alice and the sows from that transport truck.

History repeating itself.

Except this was not the same, and Bray had to remind herself that this time, the plan had worked. But she did not feel any better. Not because she'd gotten caught, but because Rhea was dead. She knew it because, as with Alice, she no longer felt Rhea's presence.

Once again, she was alone.

This time, it was okay with her.

Bray rode in the back of the helicopter for hours. Her mother sat beside her. Neither of them spoke. Bray was too busy wondering about the others, how worried they must've been for her. How she worried for them. Finally she'd found a good group of friends, and they were gone. No thanks to her mother. And most likely her father had no idea what was happening. He wouldn't be coming to her aid this time. Calling out for animals to help her didn't feel like an option, either.

Deep down inside, Bray knew this was where she was supposed to be. She tried not to question it. Emily had taught her how to get in touch with her intuition, and she felt that sense of stillness. Nothing inside gave her any indication that she was to fight.

So she sat and she waited.

Out her window, they passed over miles and miles of dry, deserted land. The American west. Not what it used to be. Not from what she'd watched on old movies or read in books. It was a true desert. Rivers had run dry. No sight of animals, very few birds. How rare it was that she'd encountered those wild horses running north from Colorado. It was clear to her that the only place for them was in Wyoming, one of the last states still habitable in the west.

The country was dying, and would continue to. Neither Bray nor any of her friends, it seemed, would be able to stop the inevitable. That was how it seemed right now. A sad place to be.

More hours passed. Bray was starving and thirsty but she didn't dare speak. The air in the helicopter was both loud and thick, and it actually gave her some comfort, some sense of safety amidst this unpredictability.

As the helicopter pushed forward over the desert, Dianna finally spoke, breaking the tension between them.

"I guess now is a good time to tell you where you're headed."

"Where is that?" Bray asked, her eyes set out the window as they passed over a major city, deep canyons of layered sandstone and mudstone rock.

The Grand Canyon!

Like most places in this country, Bray only knew of it through images in magazines. It spanned a number of miles. Where the Colorado River once flowed was a meandering path of dirt.

Bray sat back. That was depressing enough to see. She didn't need to see anymore. Her mind shifted to the state of Arizona. Why there?

"It's a maximum facility prison," Dianna replied.

"Ha!" Bray let out an unexpected laugh. "You think *I* need to be in prison? You're the one who just murdered someone. In fact," Bray said, turning to her mother, nearly crying in anger. "You've allowed the murders of thousands of humans, billions of animals."

"Can't you see what your little plan did to people?" Dianna replied, turning to her. "You're lucky no one is dead, Bray. The hospitals are at full capacity because of what you did. You've put thousands of people into a panic."

Bray looked over at Dianna. Her face was tight, lacking smile or warmth. She was visibly upset.

"It wasn't my intent for anyone to be harmed," she replied sincerely, feeling a sudden edge of grief hit her throat. She tried not to cry. All she could think about was Ethan. Rhea. The hundreds of cows that were slaughtered each day, still, and no one noticed.

"You'll never understand why I did what I did," Bray finished. She looked away.

"Bray. . .there are so many things in this world that *you* don't understand. Like the enormous pressure we are under to keep enough water in the homes of our citizens. Like our climate crisis—"

"Which is only being worsened by your exploitation of animals," Bray interrupted.

"I'm not going to argue with you," Dianna replied, pausing. "At least now we can keep you somewhere safe where you won't hurt anyone. . .and we can get you back on your meds."

"If you're sending me to prison, then when do I get my fair trial?" Bray asked.

"You'll get one. First we get you stable."

"Stable?" Bray asked, anger rising into her head, turning her hot. "I've been sitting peacefully in this helicopter with you for hours. I'm coherent. I speak full sentences. I haven't tried to escape or harm you or anyone. What part of that isn't stable?"

"I'm not having this conversation with you," Dianna replied, crossing her arms and looking up toward the pilot.

The helicopter began to drop toward the earth. Bray felt it in her chest. It was a little nauseating. She grabbed on to her armrest and turned to look out the window.

They gradually descended outside a series of buildings surrounded by fences. The fences were shaped like a hexagon around the buildings. There were more than ten buildings. They reminded Bray of factory farms.

Her heart shrank the closer the helicopter dropped to the ground.

The helicopter landed. Stabilized. Its blades gradually slowed. Bray prepared herself to be forced into the prison. It was all incredibly surreal.

Dianna stepped out of the helicopter. Bray's door opened. A prison guard pulled her out by her arm. The desert heat smacked Bray right in the cheeks and nose. The sun was high in the sky, letting her know it was right around noon. And it was hot.

Two guards walked her up to the fences. They were ten feet high with barbed wire at the top. She gazed up at them as they passed through a gate. Approaching the nearest building, her mother right behind, Bray began to feel what it may have been like for all those cows to be corralled to their deaths. She'd experienced it enough times to suddenly realize she was not concerned.

Far worse things had happened to her, things that had brought her beyond death to places her mother knew nothing of. Places that made her who she was. She allowed the guards to guide her inside the building.

There, a tile floor led to a single elevator. They passed through a set of metal detectors. Another guard stood beside the elevator. He wore a black vest over a long-sleeved black shirt. A gun rested in a holster clipped to his thigh. His arms were crossed. He stared at Bray while pressing a button on the wall.

The elevator doors opened. Bray was led inside. Her mother came in and stood beside her.

She could almost feel her mother breathing down on her. The suffocation was only the beginning.

The elevator lowered.

The doors opened to a dim hallway. Concrete walls, fluorescent lights running along below a concrete ceiling. Long corridor with steel doors that they passed, one by one, as Bray's ears picked up tinkering sounds. A far-off whimpering. Scratching. The air was cold and it made her shiver. Her eyes darted all around in search of a way out.

"Don't I get some kind of due process?" Bray asked, her muscles tightening with resistance.

"You had that right taken away when you decided to terrorize half the country," Dianna replied from behind.

They walked deeper down the corridor, deeper into this maximum prison. Passing more closed doors, each one leading to whomever sat inside, where Bray was headed next. Unless her father found her here, this was where she'd probably be kept for ages. Especially if her mother had anything to do with it. And she didn't want to think about the medication. They'd probably put her on an injection like they'd discussed right before she escaped the psych ward. Hearing the psychiatrist proceed with an injection medication order because she would not *adhere* to taking pills had frightened her to no end. It was something she would not be able to purge out of her system, and that was just the first in a series of revelations that had led her to escape the hospital in Denver.

They approached an empty cell and stopped at its open door. Bray looked inside. It was narrow. She saw a twin-sized bed with a perfectly-fitted brown blanket and pillow. A metal toilet poked out of the wall near the foot of the bed. A small shelf jutted out of the wall beside the bed. She assumed it was supposed to be a desk.

One of the guards turned and faced her. He looked down into her eyes. A long tear rolled down her face. He watched the tear fall. He gave her a nod and removed her handcuffs.

"Can I have a moment alone with my mother, please?" Bray asked him.

The guard looked to Dianna.

"It's fine," Dianna replied.

The two guards stepped down the hall and waited a few feet away.

Bray turned and faced her mother. She could no longer recognize this person before her.

"When I was a child, my mom and I used to have fun. I remember how she always took me to the library so I could pick out books to read. I used to love reading with her. I'm not sure where she went, but she's not here anymore."

Dianna's eyes welled up.

"The worst of all of this is not that you're going to put me in here, not even that you're going to make sure I get back on meds I don't need," Bray continued. "It's that you chose your career over me, your daughter. If you decide to leave me in here, then you'd better say goodbye now because I am never speaking to you again."

Dianna looked at Bray for the longest time. The tears disappeared from her eyes. Bray watched as Dianna stiffened, turned, and started down the hall. She stopped for a moment, nearly stumbling, and pressed her hand to the wall to compose herself. Her shoulders visibly slumped. Bray thought for a moment that her mother might look back, but she didn't. She eventually proceeded down the hall, turned a corner, and was gone.

The two guards returned.

"Go on in," one of them said, nodding into the cell.

Bray took a deep breath. She turned and slowly entered the small room. The door slammed shut, locked.

Bray walked over and sat down on the firm bed, her back up against the wall. There was nothing else to do but sit and allow what was to come. If her job here on earth truly wasn't done yet, she would trust that. If, at the least, this gave her friends the chance to get away, it would have to be worth it.

That was the only hope she had left.

THE END.

ACKNOWLEDGEMENTS

First, to my Higher Power. Thanks for helping me tell the story. Thank you to my mom, my family and friends for your continued support of my author journey. To all my fans and patrons who follow me on social media, my newsletter, and come to my events: you are a significant part of what makes my author life so complete. Thank you.

Thank you to my writing mentor and coach, Robin G. White. Your guidance and support over the last three years has resulted in the physical product of books I can be proud of. Thank you dearly.

And thank you to my Editor, Susan Reu. Your meticulous, thorough dedication to the wellbeing of the story, the characters and the plot have saved me time and time again. My book would be a sad tale of self-publishing gone wrong without you.

Thank you to Jon Gann for your work on the cover art and book design.

Thank you to Kelly and Kerri Knox, and Molly Wavra for giving of your time and your brains for the research of this novel. Your knowledge has given *Sentient Rising* the reality-based edge it needed.

Lastly, I thank you, dear reader, for being you.

Blessings,

Jay.

Also by Jay VanLandingham:

Sentient (The Sentient Trilogy Book One)

The Animalist Code Mini Series

The Movement of Whales (Novelette)

AVAILABLE AT:

AMAZON
KOBO
www.jayvanlandingam.com

About the Author

Jay VanLandingham (he/him) is the author of The Animalist Code novellas and the dystopian novel Sentient.

As an avid animal rights activist and longtime vegan, Jay's writing focuses primarily on issues of climate change, animal agriculture, and the significance of nature as a place to call home.

Jay holds a Master's degree in Social Work as well as a Bachelor's degree in English.

When not writing, Jay can be found coaching clients on achieving writing goals and providing telehealth therapy.

Jay is based in Cincinnati, Ohio.

www.ingramcontent.com/pod-product-compliance
Lightning Source LLC
Chambersburg PA
CBHW060608300726
48975CB00005B/1488